"Korelitz pulls off a true page-turner with, yes, a killer plot."

—*AARP, The Magazine*

"[A] wickedly clever tale of stolen genius." —*Lit Hub*

"Fans of slow-burn, character-driven thrillers will enjoy this story of an author who has a secret he is desperately trying to keep. Recommended for fans of secret-fueled suspense writers like Jennifer Hillier, Clare Mackintosh, and Gilly Macmillan." —*Library Journal*

Also by Jean Hanff Korelitz

The Devil and Webster

You Should Have Known

Admission

The White Rose

The Sabbathday River

A Jury of Her Peers

Middle Grade Fiction

Interference Powder

Drama

The Dead, 1904 (with Paul Muldoon)

Poetry

The Properties of Breath

Praise for *The Plot*

"*The Plot* is one of the best novels I've ever read about writers and writing. It's also insanely readable and the suspense quotient is through the roof. It's remarkable." —Stephen King

"*The Plot* is so well-crafted and compelling it's nearly impossible to put down. Clever and chilling, this page-turner grabs you from the first chapter and doesn't let you go until its startling, breathtaking conclusion."
—Greer Hendricks and Sarah Pekkanen, *New York Times* bestselling authors of *The Wife Between Us*

"From its first pages, Jean Hanff Korelitz's *The Plot* ensnares you in a rich tangle of literary vanities, treachery, and fraud. Psychologically acute and breathtakingly suspenseful, you'll find yourself rushing toward a finale both astonishing and utterly earned." —Megan Abbott, bestselling author of *Give Me Your Hand*

"The plot of *The Plot*—the best thriller of the year (so far)—is too good to give away." —*The Washington Post*

"Korelitz's own plot is fiendishly clever, and here's the ultimate twist: that any novel about a writer's life (lonely, anxious drudgery) could be this wildly suspenseful and entertaining."
—*People* (Book of the Week)

"As a longtime fan of Korelitz's novels (including *You Should Have Known*, which was made into HBO's *The Undoing*), I will say that I think *The Plot* is her gutsiest, most consequential book yet. It keeps you guessing and wondering, and also keeps you thinking: about ambition, fame, and the nature of intellectual property (the analog kind)."
—*The New York Times Book Review*

"*The Plot* is wickedly funny and chillingly grim. . . . It deserves to garner all the brass rings." —*The Wall Street Journal*

"Gripping and thoroughly unsettling: this one will be flying off the shelves." —*Kirkus Reviews*

"Deep character development, an impressively thick tapestry of intertwining story lines, and a candid glimpse into the publishing business make this a page-turner of the highest order. Korelitz deserves acclaim for her own perfect plot." —*Publishers Weekly* (starred review)

"Readers may find themselves batting away sleep and setting an alarm for early the next day to continue Jean Hanff Korelitz's propulsive literary thriller *The Plot.* Korelitz is an audacious writer who delivers on her promises. Her next big-screen adaptation surely awaits." —*BookPage*

"[Korelitz] effortlessly deconstructs the campus novel and, much like Michael Chabon in *Wonder Boys* (1995), acerbically mocks the publishing industry. Fearless Korelitz presents a wry and unusual joyride of a thriller, full of gasp-inducing twists as it explores copyright, ownership, and the questionable morals of writers." —*Booklist*

"Stay tuned to this devilishly compelling tale of ambition run amok." —Oprah Daily

"This staggeringly good literary thriller is about a staggeringly good literary thriller written by a failed novelist who has stolen the book's plot from a deceased student." —*Shelf Awareness*

"The author behind suspense novel *You Should Have Known* turned HBO series *The Undoing* outdoes herself in this literary-centric thrill ride." —*Newsweek*

The Plot

Jean Hanff Korelitz

New York

This is a work of fiction. All of the characters, organizations, and events portrayed in this novel are either products of the author's imagination or are used fictitiously.

THE PLOT. Copyright © 2021 by Jean Hanff Korelitz. All rights reserved.
Printed in the United States of America. For information, address Celadon Books, a division of Macmillan Publishers, 120 Broadway, New York, NY 10271.

For seal on cover:
From *The New York Times*. © 2021 The New York Times Company. All rights reserved. Used under license.

www.celadonbooks.com

Designed by Michelle McMillan

The Library of Congress has cataloged the hardcover edition as follows:

Names: Korelitz, Jean Hanff, 1961– author.
Title: The plot / Jean Hanff Korelitz.
Description: First Edition. | New York, NY : Celadon Books, 2021.
Identifiers: LCCN 2020053267 | ISBN 9781250790767 (hardcover) | ISBN 9781250790743 (ebook)
Subjects: GSAFD: Mystery fiction. | Suspense fiction.
Classification: LCC PS3561.O6568 P56 2021 | DDC 813/.54—dc23
LC record available at https://lccn.loc.gov/2020053267

ISBN 978-1-250-79075-0 (trade paperback)

Our books may be purchased in bulk for promotional, educational, or business use. Please contact your local bookseller or the Macmillan Corporate and Premium Sales Department at 1-800-221-7945, extension 5442, or by email at MacmillanSpecialMarkets@macmillan.com.

First Celadon Books Paperback Edition: 2022

10 9 8 7 6 5 4 3 2 1

For Laurie Eustis

Good writers borrow, great writers steal.

—T. S. Eliot (but possibly stolen from Oscar Wilde)

PART ONE

CHAPTER ONE

Anybody Can Be a Writer

Jacob Finch Bonner, the once promising author of the "New & Noteworthy" *(The New York Times Book Review)* novel *The Invention of Wonder,* let himself into the office he'd been assigned on the second floor of Richard Peng Hall, set his beat-up leather satchel on the barren desk, and looked around in something akin to despair. The office, his fourth home in Richard Peng Hall in as many years, was no great improvement on the earlier three, but at least it overlooked a vaguely collegiate walkway under trees from the window behind the desk, rather than the parking lot of years two and three or the dumpster of year one (when, ironically, he'd been much closer to the height of his literary fame, such as it was, and might conceivably have hoped for something nicer). The only thing in the room that signaled anything of an actual literary nature, that signaled anything of any warmth at all, was the beat-up satchel Jake used to transport his laptop and, on this particular day, the writing samples of his soon-to-arrive students, and this Jake had been carrying around for years. He'd acquired it at a flea market shortly before his first novel's publication with a certain writerly self-consciousness: *acclaimed young novelist still carries the old leather bag he used throughout his years of struggle!* Any residual hope of becoming that person now was long gone. And even if it wasn't there was no way to justify the expense of a new bag. Not any longer.

Richard Peng Hall was a 1960s addition to the Ripley campus, an unlovely construction of white cinder block behind the gymnasium and beside some dormitories slapped together for "coeds" when Ripley College began admitting women in the year 1966 (which, to its credit, had been ahead of the curve). Richard Peng had been an engineering student from Hong Kong, and though he probably owed more of his eventual wealth to the school he'd attended *after* Ripley College (namely MIT), that institution had declined to construct a Richard Peng Hall, at least for the size of donation he'd had in mind. The Ripley building's original purpose had been to accommodate the engineering program, and it still bore the distinct tang of a science building with its windowed lobby nobody ever sat in, its long, barren corridors, and that soul-killing cinder block. But when Ripley got rid of engineering in 2005 (got rid of all its science programs, actually, and all of its social science programs) and dedicated itself, in the words of its frantic board of supervisors, "to the study and practice of the arts and humanities in a world that increasingly undervalues and needs them," Richard Peng Hall was reassigned to the low-residency Master of Fine Arts Program in Fiction, Poetry, and Personal Non-Fiction (Memoir).

Thus had the writers come to Richard Peng Hall, on the campus of Ripley College, in this strange corner of northern Vermont, close enough to the fabled "Northeast Kingdom" to bear some trace of its distinct oddness (the area had been home to a small but hardy Christian cult since the 1970s) but not so far from Burlington and Hanover as to be completely in the back of beyond. Of course creative writing had been taught at the college since the 1950s, but never in any serious, let alone enterprising way. Things got added to the curriculum of every educational institution concerned with survival as the culture changed around it and as the students began, in their eternally student-y way, to *make demands*: women's studies, African-American studies, a computer center that actually acknowledged computers were, you know, *a thing*. But when Ripley underwent its great crisis in the late 1980s, and when the college took a sober, and deeply trepidatious look at what might be required for actual institutional survival, it was—surprise!—the *creative writing* that signaled the most optimistic way forward. And so it had launched its first (and, still, only) graduate program, the Ripley Symposia in Creative Writing, and over the following years the Symposia basically ate up the rest of the college until all that was left was its low-residency program, so much more accommodating for students who couldn't drop everything for a two-year MFA course. And shouldn't be expected to! Writing, according to Ripley's own glossy prospectus and highly enticing website, was not some elitist activity out of bounds to all but the fortunate few. Every single person had a unique voice and a story nobody else could tell. And anybody—especially with the guidance and support of the Ripley Symposia—could be a writer.

All Jacob Finch Bonner had ever wanted to be was a writer. *Ever, ever, ever,* all the way back to suburban Long Island, which was the last place on earth a serious artist of any kind ought to come from but where he, nonetheless, had been cursed to grow up, the only child of a tax attorney and a high school guidance counselor. Why he'd affixed his star to the forlorn little shelf in his local library marked AUTHORS FROM LONG ISLAND! was anyone's guess, but it did not pass unnoticed in the young writer's home. His father (the tax attorney) had been forceful in his objections (Writers didn't make money! Except Sidney Sheldon. Was Jake claiming he was the next Sidney Sheldon?) and his mother (the guidance counselor) had seen fit to remind him, *constantly,* of his mediocre-at-best PSAT score on the verbal side. (It was greatly embarrassing to Jake that he'd managed to *do better on the math than the verbal.*) These had been grievous challenges to overcome, but what artist was without challenges to overcome? He'd read stubbornly (and, it should be noted, already competitively, and with envy) throughout his childhood, departing the mandatory curriculum, leapfrogging the usual adolescent dross to vet the emerging field of his future rivals. Then off he had gone to Wesleyan to study creative writing, falling in with a tight group of fellow proto-novelists and short story writers who were just as insanely competitive as he was.

Many were the dreams of young Jacob Finch Bonner when it came to the fiction he would one day write. (The "Bonner," in point of fact, wasn't entirely authentic—Jake's paternal great-grandfather had substituted Bonner for Bernstein a solid century before—but neither was the "Finch," which Jake himself had added in high school as an homage to the novel that awakened his love of fiction.) Sometimes, with books he especially loved, he imagined that he had actually written them himself, and was giving interviews about them to critics or reviewers (always humble in his deflection of the interviewer's praise) or reading from them to large, avid audiences in a bookstore or some hall full of occupied seats. He imagined his own photograph on the back jacket flap of a hardcover (taking as his templates the already outdated writer-leaning-over-manual-typewriter or writer-with-pipe) and thought far too often about sitting at a table, signing copies for a long, coiling line of readers. *Thank you,* he would intone graciously to each woman or man. *That's so kind of you to say. Yes, that's one of my favorites, too.*

It wasn't precisely true that Jake never thought about the actual writing of his future fictions. He understood that books did not write themselves, and that real work—work of imagination, work of tenacity, work of skill—would be required to bring his own eventual books into the world. He also understood that the field was not uncrowded: a lot of young people just like himself felt the way he did about books and wanted to write them one day, and it was even possible that some of these other young people might conceivably have *even more natural talent* than he did, or possibly a more robust imagination, or just a greater will to get the job done. These were not ideas that gave him much pleasure, but, in his favor, he did know his own mind. He knew that he would not be getting certified to teach English in public schools ("if the writing thing doesn't work out") or taking the LSATs ("why not?"). He knew that he had chosen his lane and begun swimming, and he would not stop swimming until he held his own book in his own hands, at which point the world would surely have learned the thing he himself had known for so many years:

He was a writer.

A great writer.

That had been the intention, anyway.

It was late June and it had been raining all over Vermont for the better part of a week when Jake opened the door to his new office in Richard Peng Hall. As he stepped inside he noticed that he had tracked mud along the corridor and into the room, and he looked down at his sorry running shoes—once white, now brown with damp and dirt, never in fact used for actual running—and felt the pointlessness of taking them off now. He'd spent the long day driving up from the city with two plastic Food Emporium bags of clothes and that elderly leather satchel containing the nearly as elderly laptop on which his current novel—the novel he was theoretically (as opposed to actually) working on—and the folders of submitted work by his assigned students, and it occurred to him that he had brought progressively less with him each time he'd made the trip north to Ripley. The first year? A big suitcase stuffed with most of his clothing (because who knew what might be considered appropriate attire for three weeks in northern Vermont, surrounded by surely fawning students and surely envious fellow teachers?) and every printed-out draft of his second novel, the deadline for which he'd had a tendency to whine about in public. This year? Only those two plastic bags of tossed-in jeans and shirts and the laptop he now mainly used for ordering dinner and watching YouTube.

If he was still doing this depressing job a year from now, he probably wouldn't even bother with the laptop.

No, Jake was not looking forward to the about-to-begin session of the Ripley Symposia. He was not looking forward to reconvening with his dreary and annoying colleagues, not one of them a writer he genuinely admired, and certainly he was not looking forward to feigning excitement for another battalion of eager students, each and every one of them likely convinced they would one day write—or perhaps had *already written*—the Great American Novel.

Most of all, he was not looking forward to pretending that he himself was still a writer, let alone a great one.

It went without saying that Jake had not done any preparation for the imminent term of the Ripley Symposia. He was utterly unfamiliar with any of the sample pages in those annoyingly thick folders. When he'd begun at Ripley he'd persuaded himself that "great teacher" was a laudable addition to "great writer," and he'd given the writing samples of these folks, who'd put down real money to study with him, some very focused attention. But the folders he was now pulling out of his satchel, folders he ought to have begun reading weeks earlier when they'd arrived from Ruth Steuben (the Symposia's highly acerbic office manager) had traveled from Priority Mail box to leather satchel without ever once suffering the indignity of being opened, let alone subjected to intimate examination. Jake looked at them balefully now, as if they themselves were responsible for his procrastination, and the appalling evening that lay ahead of him, as a result.

Because after all, what was there to know about the people whose inner lives these folders contained, who were even now converging on northern Vermont, and the sterile conference rooms of Richard Peng Hall, and this very office, once the one-on-one conferences began in a few days? These particular students, these ardent apprentices, would be utterly indistinguishable from their earlier Ripley counterparts: mid-career professionals convinced they could churn out Clive Cussler adventures, or moms who blogged about their kids and didn't see why that shouldn't entitle them to a regular gig on *Good Morning America*, or newly retired people "returning to fiction" (secure in the knowledge that fiction had been waiting for them?). Worst of all were the ones who reminded Jake most of himself: "literary novelists," utterly serious, burning with resentment toward anyone who'd gotten there first. The Clive Cusslers and mom bloggers might still be persuadable that Jake was a famous, or at least a "highly regarded" young (now "youngish") novelist, but the would-be David Foster Wallaces and Donna Tartts who were certainly present in the pile of folders? Not so much. This group would be all too aware that Jacob Finch Bonner had fumbled his early shot, failed to produce a good enough second novel or any trace of a third novel, and been sent to the special purgatory for formerly promising writers, from which so few of them ever emerged. (It happened to be untrue that Jake had not produced a third novel, but in this case the untruth was actually preferable to the truth. There had indeed been a third novel, and even a fourth, but those manuscripts, the making of which had together consumed nearly five years of his life, had been rejected by a spectacular array of publishers of declining prestige, from the "legacy" publisher of *The Invention of Wonder* to the respectable university press that had published his second book, *Reverberations,* to the many, many small press publication competitions listed in the back of *Poets & Writers*, which he had spent a small fortune entering, and, needless to say, had failed to win. Given these demoralizing facts, he actually preferred that his students believe he was still struggling to reel in that mythical and stupendous second novel.)

Even without reading the work of his new students, Jake felt he already knew them as intimately as he'd known their earlier counterparts, which was better than he wanted to know them. He knew, for example, that they were far less gifted than they believed they were, or possibly every bit as bad as they secretly feared they were. He knew they wanted things from him that he was utterly unequipped to deliver and had no business pretending he possessed in the first place. He also knew that every one of them was going to fail, and he knew that when he left them behind at the end of the current three-week session they would disappear from his life, never to be thought of again. Which was all he wanted from them, really.

But first, he had to deliver on that Ripley fantasy that they were all, "students" and "teachers" alike, colleagues-in-art, each with a unique voice and a singular story to tell with it, and each equally deserving of being called that magical thing: *a writer*.

It was just past seven and still raining. By the time he met his new students the following evening at the welcome cookout he would have to be all smiles, all personal encouragement, and full of such scintillating guidance that each new member of the Ripley Symposia Master of Fine Arts Program might believe the "gifted" (*Philadelphia Inquirer*) and "promising" (*Boston Globe*) author of *The Invention of Wonder* was personally prepared to usher them into the Shangri-La of Literary Fame.

Unfortunately, the only path from here to there led through those twelve folders.

He turned on the standard Richard Peng desk lamp and sat down in the standard Richard Peng office chair, which gave a loud squeak as he did, then he spent a long moment tracing a line of grime along the ridges of the cinder blocks on the wall beside his office door, delaying till the last possible moment the long and deeply unpleasant evening that was about to commence.

How many times, looking back at this night, the very last night of a time he would always afterward think of as "before," would he wish that he hadn't been so utterly, fatally wrong? How many times, in spite of the astonishing good fortune set in motion by one of those folders, would he wish he'd backed his way out of that sterile office, retraced his own muddy footprints down the corridor, returned to his car, and driven those many hours back to New York and his ordinary, personal failure? Too many, but no matter. It was already too late for that.

CHAPTER TWO

The Hero's Welcome

By the time the welcome cookout commenced the following afternoon Jake was running on fumes, having dragged himself into that morning's faculty meeting after a scant three hours' sleep. It had been a small victory this year that Ruth Steuben was finally shifting the students who self-identified as poets away from him and to other teachers who also self-identified as poets (Jake had nothing of value to teach aspiring poets. In his experience, poets often read fiction, but fiction writers who said they read poetry with any regularity were *liars*), so it could at least be said that the dozen students he'd been assigned were prose writers. But what prose it was! In his through-the-night and fueled-by-Red-Bull read-through, narrative perspective hopped about as if the true narrator was a flea, traipsing from character to character, and the stories (or . . . chapters?) were so simultaneously flaccid and frenetic that they signified—at worst, nothing, and at best, not enough. Tenses rolled around within the paragraphs (sometimes within the sentences!) and words were occasionally used in ways that definitely implied the writer was not overly clear on their meanings. Grammatically, the worst of them made Donald Trump look like Stephen Fry and most of the rest were makers of sentences that could only be described as . . . utterly ordinary.

Encompassed in those folders had been the shocking discovery of a decaying corpse on a beach (the corpse's breasts had been, incomprehensibly, described as "ripe honeymelons"), a writer's histrionic account of discovering, via DNA test, that he was "part African," an inert character study of a mother and daughter living together in an old house, and the opening of a novel set in a beaver dam ("deep in the forest"). Some of these samples had no particular pretensions to literature, and would be easy enough to deal with—nailing down the plot and red-penciling the prose into basic subservience would be enough to justify his paycheck and honor his professional responsibilities—but the more self-consciously "literary" writing samples (some of them, ironically, among the worst written) were going to suck his soul. He knew it. It was already happening.

Fortunately, the faculty meeting wasn't terribly taxing. (It was possible Jake had even dozed, briefly, during Ruth Steuben's ritual intoning of Ripley's sexual harassment guidelines.) The returning professors of the Ripley Symposia got on reasonably well, and while Jake couldn't have said he'd become actual *friends* with any of them, he did have a well-established tradition of a once-per-session beer at The Ripley Inn with Bruce O'Reilly, retired from Colby's English Department and the author of half a dozen novels published by an independent press in his native Maine. This year there were two newcomers in the Richard Peng lobby-level conference room, a nervous poet called Alice who looked to be about his own age and a man who introduced himself as a "multigenric" writer, who intoned his name, Frank Ricardo, in a way that definitely implied the rest of them recognized it—or at any rate *ought to* recognize it. (Frank Ricardo? It was true that Jake had stopped paying close attention to other writers around the time his own fourth novel began to collect rejections—it had simply been too painful to continue—but he didn't think he was supposed to have heard of a Frank Ricardo. Had a Frank

Ricardo won a National Book Award or a Pulitzer? Had a Frank Ricardo lobbed an out-of-nowhere first novel onto the top of the *New York Times* bestseller list via viral word of mouth?) After Ruth Steuben finished her recitation and went over the schedule (daily and weekly, evening readings, due dates for written evaluations, and deadlines for judging the Symposia's end-of-session writing awards) she dismissed them with a smiling but steely reminder that the welcome cookout was not optional for faculty. Jake leapt for the exit before any of his colleagues—familiar or new—could talk to him.

The apartment he rented was a few miles east of Ripley, on a road actually named Poverty Lane. It belonged to a local farmer—more accurately his widow—and featured a view over the road to a falling-down barn that had once housed a dairy herd. Now the widow leased the land to one of Ruth Steuben's brothers and ran a daycare in the farmhouse. She professed herself to be mystified about the thing Jake did that got made into books, or how it was getting taught over at Ripley, or who might actually pay to learn such a thing, but she had held the apartment for him since his first year at Ripley—quiet, polite, and responsible with rent were apparently too rare a combination not to. He had made it to bed at about four that morning and slept until ten minutes before the faculty meeting began. It wasn't enough. Now he pulled the curtains and passed out again, waking at five to begin assembling his game face for the official start of the Ripley term.

The barbeque was held on the college green, surrounded by the Ripley's earliest buildings, which—unlike Richard Peng Hall—were reassuringly collegiate and actually very pretty. Jake loaded up a paper plate with chicken and cornbread and reached into one of the coolers to extract a bottle of Heineken, but even as he did a body leaned against him, and a long forearm, thickly covered with blond hair, tipped his own forearm out of its trajectory.

"Sorry, man," said this unseen person, even as his fingers closed around Jake's intended beer bottle and pulled it from the water.

"Okay," Jake said automatically.

Such a pathetically small moment. It made him think of those bodybuilding cartoons in the back of old comic books: bully kicks sand in the face of ninety-eight-pound weakling. What's he going to do about it? Become a bulked-up bully himself, of course. The guy—he was middling tall, middling blond, thick through the shoulders—had already turned away, and was popping the bottle cap and lifting it to his mouth. Jake couldn't see the asshole's face.

"Mr. Bonner."

Jake straightened up. A woman was standing beside him. It was the newcomer, from the faculty meeting that morning. Alice something. The nervous one.

"Hi. Alice, right?"

"Alice Logan. Yeah. I just wanted to say how much I like your work."

Jake felt, and noted, the physical sensation that generally accompanied this sentence, which he still did hear from time to time. In this context "work" could only mean *The Invention of Wonder,* a quiet novel set in his own native Long Island and featuring a young man named Arthur. Arthur, whose fascination with the life and ideas of Isaac Newton provides a through line for the novel and a stay against chaos when his brother dies suddenly, was not, emphatically *not*, a stand-in for Jake's own younger self. (Jake had no siblings at all, and he'd had to do extensive research to create a character knowledgeable about the life and ideas of Isaac Newton!) *The Invention of Wonder* had indeed been read at the time of its publication, and, he supposed, was still read on occasion, by people who cared about fiction and where it might be heading. Never once had anyone used the phrase "I like your work" to refer to *Reverberations* (a collection of short stories which his first publisher had rejected, and which the Diadem Press of the State University of New York—a *highly respected* university press!—had recast as "a novel in linked short stories"), despite the fact that innumerable copies had been dutifully sent out for review (resulting in *not a single one*).

It ought to be nice when it still happened, but somehow it wasn't. Somehow it made him feel awful. But really, didn't everything?

They went to one of the picnic tables and sat. Jake had neglected, in the aftermath of that Heineken theft, to grab another drink.

"It was so powerful," she said, picking up from where she'd left off. "And you were . . . what, twenty-five when you wrote that?"

"About that, yes."

"Well, I was blown away."

"Thank you, that's so nice of you to say."

"I was in my MFA program when I read it. I think we were in the same program, actually. Not at the same time."

"Oh?"

Jake's program—and, apparently, Alice's—had not been this newer "low residency" type but the more classic drop-your-life-and-devote-yourself-to-your-art-for-two-straight-years variety, and frankly it was also a far more prestigious program than Ripley's. Attached to a Midwestern university, the program had long produced poets and novelists of *great importance* to American letters, and was so hard to get into that it had taken Jake three years to manage it (during which time he had watched certain less talented friends and acquaintances get accepted). He'd spent those years living in a microscopic apartment in Queens and working for a literary agency with a special interest in science fiction and fantasy. Science fiction and fantasy, never genres to which he had personally been drawn, seemed to attract a high quotient of—well, why not be blunt?—*crazy* in its aspiring author pool, not that Jake had anything to compare that to since every one of the very distinguished literary agencies he'd applied to after graduating from college had declined to make use of his talents. Fantastic Fictions, LLC, a two-man shop in Hell's Kitchen (actually in the tiny back room of the owners' railroad flat in Hell's Kitchen) had a client list of about forty writers, most of whom left for larger agencies the moment they experienced any professional success. Jake's job had been to sic the attorney on these ungrateful writers, to discourage over-the-transom authors intent on describing their ten-novel series (written or unwritten) with the agents over the phone, and above all to read manuscript after manuscript about dystopian alternate realities on distant planets, dark penal systems far below the surface of the earth, and leagues of post-apocalyptic rebels bent on the overthrow of sadistic warlords.

Once he actually *had* ferreted out an exciting prospect for his bosses, a novel about a spunky young woman who escapes from a penal colony planet aboard some kind of intergalactic junk ship, and discovers a mutant population among the garbage which she transforms into a vengeful army and ultimately leads into battle. It had definite potential, but the two losers who'd hired him let the manuscript languish on their desk for months, waving off his reminders. Eventually, Jake had given up, and a year later, when he read in *Variety* about ICM's sale of the book to Miramax (with Sandra Bullock attached), he'd carefully clipped the story. Six months later, when his golden ticket to the MFA party arrived and he quit his job—*O Happy Day!*—he'd placed the clipping squarely on his boss's desk atop the dusty manuscript itself. He'd done what he'd been hired to do. He'd always known a good plot when he saw one.

Unlike many of his fellow MFA students (some of whom entered the program with actual publications, mostly in literary journals but in one case—thankfully that of a poet and not a fiction writer—the effing *New Yorker*!), Jake had not wasted a moment of those two precious years. He dutifully attended every seminar, lecture, reading, workshop, and informal gathering with visiting editors and agents from New York, and declined in the main to wallow in that (itself fictional) malady, "Writer's Block." When he wasn't in class or auditing lectures at the university he was writing, and in two years he'd banged out an early draft of what would become *The Invention of Wonder*. This he submitted as his thesis and for every eligible award the program offered. It won one of them. Even more consequentially, it got him an agent.

Alice, it turned out, had arrived at the Midwestern campus only weeks after his own departure. She'd been there the following year when his novel was published, and a copy of its cover pinned to the bulletin board marked ALUMNI PUBLICATIONS.

"I mean, so exciting! Only a year out of the program."

"Yeah. Heady stuff."

That sat between them like something dull and unpleasant. Finally he said: "So, you write poetry."

"Yes. I had my first collection out last fall. University of Alabama."

"Congratulations. I wish I read more poetry."

He didn't, actually, but he *wished* he wished he read more poetry, which ought to count for something.

"I wish I could write a novel."

"Well, maybe you can."

She shook her head. She seemed . . . it was ridiculous, but was this wan poet actually flirting with him? What on earth for?

"I wouldn't know how. I mean, I love reading novels, but I'm exhausted just writing a line. I can't imagine, pages and pages of writing, not to mention characters that have to feel real and a story that needs to surprise you. It's absurd, that people can actually do that. And more than once! I mean, you wrote a second one, didn't you?"

And a third and a fourth, he thought. A fifth if you counted the one currently on his laptop, which he'd been too disheartened to even look at for nearly a year. He nodded.

"Well, when I got this job you were the only person on faculty I knew. I mean, whose work I knew. I figured it was probably okay if you were here."

Jake took a careful bite of his cornbread: predictably dry. He hadn't encountered this degree of writerly approbation for a couple of years, and it was incredible how quickly all of the narcotically warm feelings came rushing back. This was what it was to be admired, and thoughtfully admired at that, by someone who knew exactly how hard it was to write a good and transcendent sentence of prose! He had once thought his life would be crowded with encounters just like this, not just with fellow writers and devoted readers (of his ever-growing, ever-deepening *oeuvre*) but with students (perhaps, ultimately, at much better programs) thrilled to have been assigned Jacob Finch Bonner, the rising young novelist, as their supervising writer/instructor. The kind of teacher you could grab a beer with after the workshop ended!

Not that Jake had ever grabbed a beer with one of his students.

"Well, that's kind of you to say," he told Alice with studied modesty.

"I'm starting as an adjunct at Hopkins this fall, but I've never taught. I might be in pretty far over my head."

He looked at her, his reserve of goodwill, already small, now swiftly draining away. Adjunct at Johns Hopkins was nothing to sneeze at. It probably meant a fellowship for which she'd had to beat a few hundred other poets. The university press publication was likely also the result of a prize, it occurred to him now, and just about everyone coming out of an MFA program with a manuscript went in for every one of those. This girl, Alice, was quite possibly some version of a big deal, or at least what passed for a big deal in the poetry world. The thought of that deflated him utterly.

"I'm sure you'll do fine," he said. "When in doubt just encourage them. That's why they pay us the big bucks." He went for a grin. It felt horribly awkward.

Alice, after a moment, produced her own grin, and looked just as uncomfortable as he was.

"Hey, you using that?" said a voice.

Jake looked up. He might not have recognized the face—long and narrow, blond hair flopping forward into hooded eyes—but he recognized that arm. He followed it to its point of termination: a rather sharp fingernail on an extended index finger. There was a bottle opener on the picnic table's red check plastic table covering.

"What?" said Jake. "Oh, no."

"Because people are looking for it. It's supposed to be over by the beers."

The accusation was plain: Jake and Alice, two obviously unimportant people, had deprived this throbbing talent at the heart of the Ripley Symposia, and his friends, of access to the crucial bottle-opening tool, which in turn deprived these obviously talented students access to their beverage of choice.

Neither Alice nor Jake responded.

"So I'll be taking it back," the blond guy said, doing just that. The two faculty members watched in silence: again, that back turned, middling height, middling blond, broad shouldered, stalking away, bottle opener brandished in triumph.

"Well, there's a charmer." Alice spoke first.

The guy stalked off to one of the other tables, which was packed to capacity, people sidesaddle at the ends of the benches and seated in dragged-over lawn chairs. The very first night of the session and this group of brand-new students had clearly established itself as an alpha-clique, and judging from the hero's welcome the blond guy with the bottle opener was receiving from his table-mates, their censorious friend was its obvious epicenter.

"Hope he doesn't turn out to be a poet," Alice said with a sigh.

Not much chance of that, Jake thought. Everything about the guy screamed FICTION WRITER, though the species itself broke down more or less evenly into the subcategories:

1. Great American Novelist

2. *New York Times* Bestselling Author

Or that highly rare hybrid . . .

3. *New York Times* Bestselling Great American Novelist

The triumphant savior of the abducted bottle opener might want to be Jonathan Franzen, in other words, or he might want to be James

Patterson, but from a practical standpoint it made no difference. Ripley did not divide the literary pretentious from the journeyman storyteller, which meant that one way or another this legend in his own mind was very likely going to walk into Jake's own seminar the following morning. And there wasn't a damn thing he could do about it.

CHAPTER THREE

Evan Parker/Parker Evan

And lo: there he was, swaggering into Peng-101 (the lobby-level conference room) with the others the following morning at ten, glancing idly at the end of the seminar table where Jake was sitting, showing not the slightest recognition of the person (Jacob Finch Bonner!) who was the obvious authority figure in the room, and taking a seat. He reached for the stack of photocopies at the center of the table and Jake watched him impassively flip through the pages, give them a preemptive sneer, and set them down beside his own notebook and pen and water bottle. (The Ripley Symposia gave the bottles out at registration, the program's first and final freebie.) Then he fell into loud conversation with his neighbor, a rotund gentleman from the Cape who'd at least introduced himself to Jake the night before.

At five past the appointed time, the class commenced.

It had been another moist morning and the students—nine of them in all—began to shed layers of outerwear as the workshop got underway. Jake did much of this on autopilot: introducing himself, sketching his own autobiography (he didn't dwell on his publications; if they didn't care, or if they declined to hold his accomplishments in high esteem, he preferred not to see it on their faces), and talking a bit about what could and could not be accomplished in a creative writing workshop. He set some optimistic parameters for best practices (Positivity was the rule! Personal comments and political ideologies were to be avoided!) and then invited them each to say a bit about themselves: who they were, what they wrote, and how they hoped the Ripley Symposia might help them to grow as writers. (This had always been a reliable way to use up most of the inaugural class. If it didn't, they would move on to the three writing samples he'd had photocopied for their first meeting.)

Ripley cast a big net when it came to attracting students—in recent years the glossy brochure and website had been joined by targeted Facebook ads—but though the applicant pool had certainly swelled, there hadn't yet been a session for which the number of applicants had been greater than the number of spots. In short, anyone who wanted to attend Ripley, and could afford to attend Ripley, was welcome at Ripley. (On the other hand, it wasn't impossible to get thrown out once you were in; this distinction had been achieved by more than a few students since the Symposia began, most commonly due to extreme obnoxiousness in class, carrying a firearm, or just generally acting batshit crazy.) As predicted, the group broke down more or less evenly between students who dreamed of winning National Book Awards and students who dreamed of seeing their books in a spinning rack of paperbacks at the airport, and as neither of these were goals Jake himself had accomplished he knew he had certain challenges to overcome as their teacher. His workshop contained not one but two women who cited Elizabeth Gilbert as their inspiration, another who hoped to write a series of mysteries organized around "numerological principles," a man who already had six hundred pages of a novel based on his own life (he was only up to his adolescence) and a gentleman from Montana who seemed to be writing a new version of *Les Misérables,* albeit with Victor Hugo's "mistakes" corrected. By the time they reached the savior of the bottle opener, Jake was fairly sure the group had coalesced around the absurdity of the numerologist and the post–Victor Hugo guy, mainly because of the blond dude's barely hidden smirking, but he wasn't sure. Much would depend on what happened next.

The guy crossed his arms. He was leaning back in his chair, and somehow made that position look comfortable. "Evan Parker," the guy said without preamble. "But I'm thinking about reversing it, professionally."

Jake frowned. "You mean, as a pen name?"

"For privacy, yeah. Parker Evan."

It was all he could do not to laugh, the lives of the vast majority of authors being far more private than they likely wished. Maybe Stephen King or John Grisham got approached in the supermarket by a quavering person extending pen and paper, but for most writers, even reliably published and actually self-supporting writers, the privacy was thunderous.

"And what kind of fiction?"

"I'm not so much about the labels," said Evan Parker/Parker Evan, sweeping that lock of thick hair off his forehead and back. It fell immediately over his face again, but perhaps that was the point. "I just care about the story. Either it's a good plot or it isn't. And if it's not a good plot, the best writing isn't going to help. And if it is, the worst writing isn't going to hurt it."

This rather remarkable sentence was met with silence.

"Are you writing short stories? Or are you planning on a novel?"

"Novel," he said curtly, as if Jake doubted him somehow. Which, to be fair, Jake absolutely did.

"It's a big undertaking."

"I'm aware of that," Evan Parker said caustically.

"Well, can you tell us something about the novel you'd like to write?"

He looked instantly suspicious. "What kind of 'something'?"

"Well, the setting, for instance. The characters? Or a general sense of the plot. Do you have a plot in mind?"

"I do," said Parker, with now overflowing hostility. "I prefer not to discuss it." He looked around. "In this setting."

Even without looking at any of them directly, Jake could feel the reaction. Everyone seemed to be at the same impasse, but only he was expected to respond to it.

"I suppose," Jake said, "that what we'd need to know, then, is how I—how this class—can best help you improve as a writer."

"Oh," said Evan Parker/Parker Evan, "I'm not really looking to improve. I'm a very good writer, and my novel is well on track. And actually, if I'm being honest about it, I'm not even sure writing can even be taught. I mean, even by the best teacher."

Jake noted the wave of dismay circling the seminar table. More than one of his new students, more likely than not, were considering his wasted tuition money.

"Well, I'd obviously disagree with that," he said, trying for a laugh.

"I certainly hope so!" said the man from Cape Cod.

"I'm curious," said the woman to Jake's right, who was writing a "fictionalized memoir" about her childhood in suburban Cleveland, "why would you come to an MFA program if you don't think writing can be taught? Like, why not just go and write your book on your own?"

"Well"—Evan Parker/Parker Evan shrugged—"I'm not *against* this kind of thing, obviously. The jury's out on whether it works, that's all. I'm already writing my book, and I know how good it is. But I figured, even if the program itself doesn't actually help me, I wouldn't say no to the degree. More letters after your name, that never hurts, right? And there's a chance I could get an agent out of it."

For a long moment, no one spoke. More than a few of the students seemed newly distracted by the stapled writing samples before them. Finally, Jake said: "I'm glad to hear you're well along on your project, and I hope we can be a resource for you, and a support system. One thing we do know is that writers have always helped other writers, whether or not they're in a formal program together. We all understand that writing is a solitary activity. We do our work in private—no conference calls or brainstorming meetings, no team-building exercises, just us in a room, alone. Maybe that's why our tradition of sharing our work with fellow writers has evolved the way it has. There've always been groups of us coming together, reading work aloud or sharing manuscripts. And not even just for the company or the sense of community, but because we actually need other eyes on our writing. We need to know what's working and, even more important, what's not working, and most of the time we can't trust ourselves to know. No matter how successful an author is, by whatever metric you measure success, I'm willing to bet they have a reader they trust who sees the work before the agent or publisher does. And just to add a layer of practicality to this, we now have a publishing industry in which the traditional role of 'editor' is diminished. Today, editors want a book that can go straight into production, or as close to that as possible, so if you think Maxwell Perkins is waiting for your manuscript-in-progress to arrive on his desk, so he can roll up his sleeves and transform it into *The Great Gatsby,* that hasn't been true for a long time."

He saw, to his sadness but not his surprise, that the name "Maxwell Perkins" was not familiar to them.

"So in other words, if we're wise we'll seek out those readers and invite them into our process, which is what we're all doing here at Ripley. You can make that as formal or informal as you like, but I think our role in this group is to add what we can to the work of our fellow writers, and open ourselves to their guidance as much as possible. And that includes me, by the way. I don't plan on taking up the class's time with my own work, but I do expect to learn a great deal from the writers in this room, both from the work you're doing on your own projects and from the eyes and ears and insights you bring to your classmates' work."

Evan Parker/Parker Evan had not stopped grinning once during this semi-impassioned speech. Now he added a head shake to underscore his great amusement. "I'm happy to give my opinion on everyone's writing," he said. "But don't expect me to change what I'm doing for anyone else's eyes or ears or noses, for that matter. I know what I've got here. I don't think there's a person on the planet, no matter how lousy a writer he is, who could mess up a plot like mine. And that's about all I'm going to say."

And with that he folded his arms and shut tight his mouth, as if to ensure that no further morsel of his wisdom might slip past his lips. The great novel underway from Evan Parker/Parker Evan was safe from the lesser eyes, ears, and noses of the Ripley Symposia's first-year prose fiction workshop.

CHAPTER FOUR

A Sure Thing

The mother and the daughter in the old house: that was his writing sample. And if ever a work of prose pointed less to a stupendous, surefire, can't-douse-its-fire plot it could only be something along the lines of an exposé on the drying of paint. Jake took extra time with the piece before his first one-on-one meeting with its author, just to make sure he wasn't missing a buried *Raiders of the Lost Ark* springboard or the seeds of some epic *Lord of the Rings* quest, but if they were there, in the quotidian descriptions of the daughter's homework practices, or the mother's way of cooking creamed corn from a can, or the descriptions of the house itself, Jake couldn't see it.

At the same time, it sort of annoyed him to note that the writing itself wasn't terrible. Evan Parker—and Evan Parker he would be, unless and until he actually succeeded in publishing his threatened masterwork and requiring a privacy-saving pen name—might have dwelt upon his supposedly spectacular plot in the workshop but Jake's obnoxious student had produced eight pages of entirely inoffensive sentences without obvious defects or even the usual writerly indulgences. The bald fact of it was: this asshole appeared to be a natural writer with the kind of relaxed and appreciative relationship with language even those writing programs far higher up the prestige scale than Ripley's were incapable of teaching, and which Jake himself had never once imparted to a student (as he, himself, had never once received it from a teacher). Parker wrote with an eye for detail and an ear for the way the words wove into sequence. He conjured his two apparent protagonists (a mother named Diandra and her teenage daughter, Ruby) and their home, a very old house in some unnamed part of the country where snow was general in winter, with an economy of description that somehow conveyed these people in their setting, as well as the obvious and even alarming level of tension between them. Ruby, the daughter, was studious and sullen, and she came up out of the page as a closely observed and even textured character. Diandra, the mother, was a less defined but heavy presence at the edges of the daughter's perspective, as Jake supposed one might expect in a capacious old house with only two people in it. But even at opposite ends of the home they shared, their mutual loathing was radiant.

He had been through the piece twice, already; once a few nights earlier in the course of his all-nighter, and again the night after his first class, when sheer curiosity had driven him back to the folders, hoping to learn a bit more about this jerk. When Parker made such sensational claims for his plot Jake had thought inevitably of that body discovered in the sand, aggressively decaying while still illogically in possession of "honeymelon" breasts, and he'd been more than a little surprised to discover that this memorable incongruity had sprung from the fertile mind of his student Chris, a hospital administrator from Roanoke and the mother of three daughters. A few moments later, when he realized that Evan Parker was the author of these particular pages—well written, to be sure, but utterly devoid of any plot, let alone a plot so scintillating even a "lousy writer" couldn't mess it up—Jake had wanted to laugh.

Now, with the author himself about to arrive for his first student-teacher conference, he sat down with the excerpt for a third and hopefully final time.

Ruby could hear her mother, all the way upstairs in her bedroom and on the phone. She couldn't hear the actual words, but she knew when Diandra was on one of her Psychic Hotline calls because the voice went up and got billowy, as if Diandra (or at least her psychic alias, Sister Dee Dee) were floating overhead, looking down at everything in the poor caller's life and seeing all. When her mother's voice was mid-range and her tone flat, Ruby could tell that Diandra was working for one of the off-site customer service lines she logged in to. And when it got low and breathy, it was the porn chat line that had been the soundtrack of most of the last couple of years of Ruby's life.

Ruby was downstairs in the kitchen, retaking an at-home history test by her own special request to her teacher. The test had been on the Civil War up through the postwar reconstruction, and she'd gotten an answer wrong about what a carpetbagger was, and where the word came from. It was only a little thing, but it had been enough to kick her out of her usual spot at the top of the class. Naturally she'd asked for another fifteen questions.

Mr. Brown had tried to tell her the 94 on her original test wasn't going to hurt her grade, but she refused to let it go.

"Ruby, you missed a question. It's not the end of the world. Besides, for the rest of your life you're going to remember what a carpetbagger is. That's the whole point."

It wasn't the whole point. It wasn't any part of the point. The point was to get an A in the class so she could argue her way out of the so-called Advanced American History junior spring class and take history at the community college instead, because that would help her get out of here and into college—hopefully with a scholarship, hopefully far, far away from this house. Not that she felt the least inclination to explain any of this to Mr. Brown. But she pleaded, and eventually he gave in.

"Okay. But a take-home test. Do it on your own time. Look stuff up."

"I'll do it tonight. And I promise, I absolutely will not look stuff up."

He sighed and sat down to write another fifteen questions, just for her.

She was writing a longer than necessary response about the Ku Klux Klan when her mother came down the stairs and padded into the kitchen, phone wedged between her ear and her shoulder, already reaching for the refrigerator door.

"Honey, she's close by. Right now. I can feel her."

There was a pause. Her mother, apparently, was gathering information. Ruby tried to return to the Ku Klux Klan.

"Yes, she misses you, too. She's watching over you. She wanted me to say something about . . . what is it, honey?"

Diandra was now standing before the open refrigerator. After a moment, she reached for a can of Diet Dr Pepper.

"A cat? Does a cat mean anything to you?"

Silence. Ruby looked down at her test sheet. She still had nine answers to go, but not with the psychic world filling the little kitchen.

"Yes, she said it was a tabby cat. She used the word 'tabby.' How's the cat doing, honey?"

Ruby sat up straight against the little banquette. She was hungry, but she'd promised herself not to make any dinner until she'd done what she needed to do, and finished proving to him what she needed to prove. It was the tail end of their grocery week, and not a whole lot in the fridge, she'd checked, but there was a frozen pizza, and some green beans.

"Oh, that's good to know. She's so happy about that. Now honey, we're almost at half an hour. Do you have more questions for me? Do you want me to stay on the line with you?"

Now Diandra was walking back to the staircase and Ruby watched her go. The house was so old. It had belonged to her grandparents, and her grandfather's parents even farther back, and though there'd been changes, wallpaper and paint and a wall-to-wall carpet in the living room that was supposed to be beige, there was still old stenciling on the walls in some of the rooms. Around the inside of the front door, for example: a row of misshapen pineapples. Those pineapples had never made sense to Ruby, at least not until her class had gone on a day trip to some early American museum and she'd seen the exact same thing in one of the buildings there. Apparently, the pineapple symbolized hospitality, which made it about the last thing that belonged on the wall of their home, because Diandra's entire life was the opposite of hospitality. She couldn't even remember the last time somebody had stopped by with a misdelivered piece of mail, let alone for a cup of her mother's terrible coffee.

Ruby returned to her test. The tabletop was sticky from that morning's breakfast syrup, or maybe the mac and cheese of last night's dinner, or maybe something her mother had eaten or done at the table while she'd been at school. The two of them never ate at the table together. Ruby declined, as much as was possible, to place her nutritional well-being in the hands of her mother, who evidently maintained her girlish physique—literally girlish: from the back, mother and daughter looked absurdly alike—through an apparent diet of celery sticks and Diet Dr Pepper. Diandra had stopped feeding her daughter around the time Ruby turned nine, which was also around the time Ruby had learned how to open a can of spaghetti for her own damn self.

Ironically, as the two of them grew ever more physically similar they had less and less to say to each other. Not that they'd ever enjoyed what you might call a loving mother-and-daughter relationship; Ruby could remember no bedtime cuddles or pretend tea parties, no indulgent birthdays or tinsel-strewn Christmas mornings, and never anything in the way of maternal advice or unsolicited affection, the kind she sometimes encountered in novels or Disney movies (usually right before the mother died or disappeared). Diandra seemed to skate by with the barest minimum of maternal duties, mainly those related to keeping Ruby alive and vaccinated, sheltered (if you could call this freezing house a source of shelter), and educated (if you could call her unambitious rural school a source of education). She seemed to want it all to be over every bit as fervently as Ruby herself did.

But she couldn't want it as fervently as Ruby herself did. She couldn't even come close.

The previous summer Ruby had gone to work for the bakery in town, off the books, of course. And then, that fall, she picked up a Sunday job for a neighbor, watching a couple of the younger kids while the rest of the family went to church. Half of whatever she made went into the house account for food and the occasional repair, but the other half Ruby wedged into an AP Chemistry textbook, which had to be the last place her mother would ever think to look for it. The chemistry had been a necessary slog the year before, a deal she'd made with her advisor to let her move ahead in her school's bare-bones science track, and it hadn't been easy to manage alongside her humanities classes at the community college, the independent French project, and of course her two jobs, but it was all part of the plan she had formed around the time she'd opened that first can of spaghetti. That plan was called Get-The-Fuck-Away-

From-Here, and she'd never deviated from it for a single second. She was fifteen now and an eleventh grader, having already skipped her kindergarten year. In a couple of months she'd be able to apply to college. A year from now, she'd be gone for good.

She hadn't always been this way. She could recall, without too much mental heavy lifting, a time when she'd felt at least neutral about living in this house and in the orbit of her mother, who was pretty much her only extant family member (certainly the only family member she ever saw). She could recall doing the things she supposed most other children did—playing in dirt, looking at pictures—without any accompanying grief or anger, and she knew enough by now to recognize that as unpleasant as her home life and "family" might be, there were endless versions of worse out there in what she had come to understand as the wider world. So what had brought her to this bitter precipice? What had made her normal child-self into the Ruby huddled over her at-home history test on which so much—in her mind, at least—depended, who (literally) counted the days until her departure? The answer was inaccessible. The answer had never been shared with her. The answer was no longer of any concern, only its attendant truth, which she'd figured out years ago and had never once questioned: her mother loathed her, and probably always had.

What was she supposed to do with such information?

Exactly.

Pass her test. Ask Mr. Brown to write a teacher recommendation (for which, with luck, he'd regurgitate this very anecdote about the girl who insisted on being assigned *extra work*). And then, take her clearly superior brain out from under that canopy of old pineapples and into a world that would at least appreciate her. She had learned not to expect love, and wasn't even sure she wanted it. This was the most profound wisdom she'd managed to glean from the fifteen years she had spent in her mother's presence. Fifteen down. One—please, God, only one—to go.

Jake set the pages down. Mother and daughter, closely confined, somewhat isolated but hardly hermits (mother shops at supermarket, daughter attends high school and has a teacher interested in her welfare), with obvious and extreme tension between them. Okay. Mother is gainfully (if dubiously) employed and keeping a roof over their head and subprime food on the table. Okay. Daughter is ambitious and aiming to leave home and Mom for college. Okay, okay.

As his own writing teacher in his own MFA program had once said to one of the more self-indulgent prose writers in their workshop: "And . . . so what?"

A plot like mine, Evan Parker had called it. But in fact, was there even such a thing as "a plot like mine"? Greater minds than Jake's (and even, he was willing to bet, than Evan Parker's) had identified the few essential plots along which pretty much every story unfurled itself: The Quest, The Voyage and Return, Coming of Age, Overcoming the Monster, et al. The mother and the daughter in the old clapboard house—well, specifically the daughter in the old clapboard house—looked pretty likely to be a Coming of Age story, or Bildungsroman, or maybe a Rags to Riches story—but compelling as these stories could be, they hardly acted as stunning, surprising, twisting and hurtling stories, so compelling in themselves that they could be immune to bad writing.

Over the years of his teaching career, Jake had sat down with plenty of students who'd possessed an imperfect grasp of their own talent, though the disconnect tended to center on basic writing ability. Many fledgling writers labored under the misperception that if they themselves knew what a character looked like, that was sufficient to magically communicate it to the reader. Others believed a single detail was enough to render a character memorable, but the detail they chose was always so pedestrian: female characters merely described as "blond," while for a man "six-pack abs"—He had them! Or he didn't have them!—were all any reader apparently needed to know. Sometimes a writer set out sentence after sentence as an unvarying chain—*noun, verb, prepositional phrase, noun, verb, prepositional phrase*—without understanding the teeth-grinding irritation of all that monotony. Sometimes a student got bogged down in their own specific interest or hobby and upchucked his or her personal passion all over the page, either with an overload of less than scintillating detail or some kind of shorthand he or she thought must be sufficient to carry the story: man walks into a NASCAR meet, or woman attends reunion of college sorority friends on exotic isle (which, indeed, was how one particular honeymelon-endowed corpse had ended up on a beach). Sometimes they got lost in their pronouns, and you had to go back, over and over, to figure out who was doing what to whom. Sometimes, amid pages of perfectly serviceable or even better-than-all-right writing . . . absolutely nothing happened.

But they were student writers; that's why, presumably, they were here at Ripley and why they were in Jake's office in Richard Peng Hall. They wanted to learn and get better, and they were on the whole open to his insights and suggestions, so when he told them he couldn't tell from their actual words on the page what a character looked like or what they cared about, or that he didn't feel compelled to go along with them on their personal journeys because he hadn't been sufficiently engaged in their lives, or that there wasn't enough information about NASCAR or the college sorority reunion for him to understand the significance of what was being described (or not described), or that the prose felt heavy or the dialogue meandered or the story itself just made him think *so what?* . . . they tended to nod, take notes, perhaps wipe away a tear or two, and then get down to work. The next time he saw them they'd be clutching fresh pages and thanking him for making their work in progress better.

Somehow he didn't think that was going to be the case here.

Evan Parker could be heard making his leisurely way down the corridor, despite the fact that he was nearly ten minutes late for their appointment. The door was ajar and he entered without knocking, setting his Ripley water bottle down on Jake's desk before taking the extra chair and angling it, as if the two of them were gathered around a coffee table for a comradely discussion rather than facing each other across a desk with any degree of formality or disparity in (nominal) authority. Jake watched him take from his canvas bag a legal pad, its topmost pages torn raggedly away. This he put on his own lap, and then—just as he had in the conference room—he crossed his arms tightly against his chest and gave his teacher an expression of not entirely benevolent amusement. "Well," he said, "I'm here."

Jake nodded. "I've been looking again at the excerpt you sent in. You're quite a good writer."

He had made up his mind to open with this. The use of the words "quite" and "good" had been thoroughly interrogated, but in the end this he had felt to be the best way forward, and indeed his student seemed ever so slightly disarmed.

"Well, glad to hear that. Especially since, as I said, I'm not at all sure writing can be taught."

"And yet here you are." Jake shrugged. "So how can I help?"

Evan Parker laughed. "Well, I could use an agent."

Jake no longer had an agent, but he did not share this fact.

"There's an industry day at the end of the session. I'm not sure who's coming, but we usually have two or three agents and editors."

"A personal recommendation would probably go even farther. You probably know how hard it is for an outsider to get his work in front of the right people."

"Well, I'd never tell you connections don't help, but just remember, no one has ever published a book as a favor. There's too much at stake, too much money and too much professional liability if things don't go well. Maybe a personal relationship can get your manuscript into somebody's hands, but the work has to take it from there. And here's something else: agents and editors really are looking for good books, and it's not like the doors are shut to first-time authors. Far from it. For one thing, a first-time author isn't dragging around disappointing sales numbers from previous books, and readers always want to discover someone new. A new writer's interesting to agents because he might turn out to be Gillian Flynn or Michael Chabon, and the agent might get to be his agent for all the books he's going to write, not just this one, so it's not just income now, it's income in the future. Believe it or not, you're actually much better off than somebody who's connected, if they've published a couple of books that weren't wildly successful."

Somebody like me, in other words, thought Jake.

"Well, that's easy for you to say. You were actually once a big deal."

Jake stared at him. So many directions to go. All of them dead ends.

"We're all only as good as the work we're doing now. Which is why I'd like to focus on what you're writing. And where it might be going."

To his surprise, Evan threw back his head and laughed. Jake looked up at the clock over the doorway. Four thirty. The meeting was half over.

"You want the plot, don't you?"

"What?"

"Oh, please. I told you I had something great I was working on. You want to know what it is. You're a writer, aren't you?"

"Yes, I'm a writer," Jake told him. He was doing everything he could to remove the offense from his voice. "But right now I'm a teacher, and as a teacher I'm trying to help you write the book you want to write. If you don't want to say more about the story, we can still do some work on the excerpt you submitted, but without knowing how that's going to connect, ultimately, within the context of a larger story, I'm going to be at a disadvantage."

Not that it makes any difference to me, he added silently. *It's not as if I give a fuck.*

The blond asshole in his office said nothing.

"The excerpt," Jake tried. "It's part of the novel you mentioned?"

Evan Parker seemed to sit with this very innocuous question for far longer than it warranted. Then he nodded. His thick blond wedge of hair nearly obscured one eye. "From an early chapter."

"Well, I like the detail. The frozen pizza and the history teacher and the psychic help line. I get a stronger sense of who the daughter is than the mother from these pages, but that's not a problem, necessarily. And of course I don't know what decisions you're making about narrative perspective. Right now it's the daughter, obviously. Ruby. Are we going to stay with Ruby all through the novel?"

Again, that hardly warranted pause. "No. And yes."

Jake nodded, as if that made sense.

Parker said: "It's just . . . I didn't want to, you know, give it all away in that room. This story I'm writing, it's like, a sure thing. You understand?"

Jake stared at him. He wanted desperately to laugh. "I don't think I do, actually. A sure thing for what?"

Evan sat forward. He took his Ripley water bottle and unscrewed the top, and he tipped it back into his mouth. Then he folded his arms again and said, almost with regret: "This story will be read by everybody. It will make a fortune. It will be made into a movie, probably by somebody really important, like an A-list director. It will get all the brass rings, you know what I mean?"

Jake, now truly lost for words, feared that he did.

"Like, Oprah will pick it for her book thing. It will be talked about on TV shows. TV shows where they don't usually talk about books. Every book club. Every blogger. Every everything I don't even know about. This book, there's no way it can fail."

That was too much. That broke the spell.

"Anything can fail. In the book world? Anything."

"Not this."

"Look," said Jake. "Evan? Is it okay if I call you that?"

Evan shrugged. He seemed suddenly tired, as if this declaration of his greatness had exhausted him.

"Evan, I love that you believe in what you're doing. It's how I hope all of your classmates feel, or will eventually feel, about their work. And even if a lot of the . . . the brass rings you've mentioned just now are very, very unlikely to happen, because there are a lot of great stories out there and they're being published all the time, and there's a lot of competition. But there are so many other ways to measure the success of a work of art, ways that aren't connected to Oprah or movie directors. I'd like to see lots of good things happen to your novel, but before any of that you need to write the best possible version of it. I do have some thoughts about that, based on the little you've submitted, but I have to be honest: what I'm seeing in the actual pages I've read is a quieter kind of book, I mean, not one that screams *A-list directors* and *bestseller,* necessarily, but a potentially very good novel! The mother and the daughter, living together, maybe not getting along so well. I'm rooting for the daughter already. I want her to succeed. I want her to get away if that's what she wants. I want to find out what's at the root of it all, why her mother seems to hate her, if in fact her mother does hate her—teenagers are maybe not the most reliable guides on the subject of their parents. But these are all very exciting foundations for a novel, and I guess what I don't understand is why you're holding out for such extreme benchmarks of validation. Won't it be enough to write a good first novel, and—I mean, let's throw in a couple of goals we have less control over—find an agent who believes in you and your future, and even a publisher willing to take a chance on your work? That's going to be a lot! Why put yourself in a position where, I don't know, it will have failed if the director for the movie is B-list instead of A-list."

For another long moment, maddeningly long, Evan did not respond. Jake was on the point of saying something else, just to cut the sheer discomfort, even if it meant ending the conference early, because what progress were they actually making, the two of them? They hadn't even begun to look at the actual writing, let alone to talk about some of the more macro issues going forward. And also the dude was a narcissistic jerkoff of the first degree, this was now undeniable. Probably, even if he did manage to finish his tale of a smart girl growing up in an old house with her mother, the best it could likely aspire to was the same degree of literary notice Jake himself had too briefly enjoyed, and he was completely available to describe, if asked to do so, how profoundly painful that experience, or at least its aftermath, had been. So if Evan Parker/Parker Evan wanted to be the author of the next *The Invention of Wonder,* he was welcome to it. Jake himself would fashion a garland of laurels for him and throw him a party, and pass along the sad, sad advice his own MFA advisor had once tried to give him: *You're only as successful as the last book you published, and you're only as good as the next book you're writing. So shut up and write.*

"It's not going to fail," Jake heard Evan say. Then he said: "Listen."

And then he spoke. He spoke and spoke, or more precisely, he told and told. And as he told it Jake felt both of those indelible women enter the room and stand bleakly on either side of the doorway, as if daring the two men to try to escape them. Jake had no thought of escape. He had no thought of anything but this story, which was none of the great plots—Rags to Riches, Quest, Voyage and Return, Rebirth (not *really* Rebirth), Overcoming the Monster (not *really* Overcoming the Monster). It was something new to him, as it would be new to every single person who read it, and that was going to be a lot of people. That was going to be, as his terrible student had so recently said, every book group, every blogger, every person out there in the vast archipelago of publishing and book reviewing, every celebrity with a bespoke book club of her own, every reader, everywhere. The breadth of it, the wallop of it, this out-of-nowhere and outrageous story. When his student finished talking, Jake wanted to hang his head, but he couldn't show what he felt, the horror of what he felt, to the justly arrogant asshole who would one day, he now felt certain, become Parker Evan, the pseudonymous author of this *stunning first novel, catapulted onto the top of the* New York Times *bestseller list via viral word of mouth.* He couldn't. So he nodded and made some suggestions about how to gradually bring the mother's character into the foreground, and a couple of ways to consider developing and adapting the narrative perspective and the voice—all pointless, all thoroughly irrelevant. Evan Parker had been entirely correct: the worst writer on the planet could not mess up a plot like this. And Evan Parker could write.

After he'd gone, Jake went to the window and watched his student walk away in the direction of the dining hall, which was on the far side of a small grove of pine trees. Those trees, he'd never noticed, formed a kind of opaque obstacle through which the lights of the campus buildings on the far side could barely be seen, and yet everyone went through them instead of around, every single time. *Midway upon the journey of our life,* he heard himself think, *I found myself within a forest dark, for the straightforward pathway had been lost.* Words he had known forever, but never, until this moment, truly understood.

His own pathway had been lost a long time ago, and there was no chance, no chance at all, of finding it again. The novel-in-progress on his laptop was not a novel, and it was hardly in progress. And any ideas he might have had for another story would, from this afternoon on, suffer the fatal impact of not being the story he had just been told, in his temporary cinder-block office in a third-rate MFA program that nobody—not even its own faculty—took seriously. The story he had just been told, that was the only story. And Jake knew that everything the future Parker Evan had bragged about his novel's future was absolutely going to happen. Absolutely. There would be a battle to publish it, and then more battles to publish it all around the world, and another battle to option it for film. Oprah Winfrey would hold it up to the cameras, and you would see it on the table closest to the front door of every bookstore you walked into, likely for years to come. Everyone he knew was going to read it. Every writer he'd competed with in college and envied in graduate school, every woman he'd slept with (admittedly not many), every student he'd ever taught, every Ripley colleague and every one of his former teachers, and his own mother and father who never even read books, who'd had to force themselves to read *The Invention of Wonder* (if, indeed, they actually had read it—he'd never made them prove it), not to mention those two jokers at Fantastic Fictions who had missed a chance to represent a novel that became a Sandra Bullock movie. Not to mention Sandra Bullock herself. Every last one of them would buy it and borrow it and download it and lend it and listen to it and gift it and receive it, the book this arrogant, piece of shit, undeserving, son of a bitch Parker Evan was writing. *That fucking asshole,* Jake thought, and immediately he was assailed by the fact that "fucking asshole" was a pathetic choice for someone of his supposed ability when it came to wielding words. But it was all he could come up with at that particular moment.

PART TWO

CHAPTER FIVE

Exile

Two and a half years later, Jacob Finch Bonner—author of *The Invention of Wonder* and former faculty member at the at least respectable low-residency Ripley Symposia—edged his elderly Prius into the icy lot behind the Adlon Center for the Creative Arts in Sharon Springs, New York. The Prius, never particularly robust, was trudging through its third January in this area west of Albany (known, somewhat whimsically, as "The Leatherstocking Region") and its ability to climb even gentle inclines in snow—the hill leading to the Adlon was anything but gentle—had diminished with each passing year. Jake was not optimistic about its survival, or frankly his own while continuing to drive it in winter, but he was even less optimistic about his ability to afford another car.

The Ripley Symposia had laid off its teaching staff in 2013, abruptly and by means of a tersely worded email. Then, less than a month after that, the program had managed to reconstitute itself as an even *lower*-residency, in fact an entirely-online-*no-residency-at-all* program, swapping video conferencing for the now nostalgic charms of Richard Peng Hall. Jake, along with most of his colleagues, had been rehired, which was a definite salve to his sense of self-worth, but the new contract Ripley offered him fell well short of sustaining even his modest New York City existence.

And so, in the absence of other options, he had been forced to consider the dreadful prospect of leaving the center of the literary world.

What was out there, in 2013, for a writer whose two tiny patches of real estate on the great cumulative shelf of American fiction were being left farther and farther behind with each passing year? Jake had sent out fifty résumés, signed up for all of the online services promising to spread the good news of his talents to prospective employers everywhere, and gotten back in touch with every single person he could bear to see, letting them know he was available. He went in for an interview at Baruch, but the program administrator couldn't stop himself from mentioning that one of their own recent graduates, whose first novel was about to come out from FSG, had also applied for the position. He'd chased down a former girlfriend who now worked for a wildly successful subsidy publisher based in Houston, but after twenty minutes of forced reminiscences and cute stories about her twin toddlers, he just couldn't bring himself to ask about a job. He even went back to Fantastic Fictions, but the agency had been sold and was now a tiny part of a new entity called Sci/Spec, and neither of his two original bosses seemed to have survived the transition.

Finally, and with a sense of utter defeat, he did what he knew others had done, and created a website touting his own editorial skills as the author of two well-received literary novels and a longtime faculty member at one of the country's best low-residency MFA programs. And then he waited.

Slowly, came the nibbles. What was Jake's "success rate"? (Jake responded with a lengthy exploration of what the term "success" might mean to an artist. He never heard back from that particular correspondent.) Did Mr. Bonner work with Indie Authors? (He immediately wrote: Yes! After which that correspondent also disappeared.) What were his feelings on anthropomorphism in YA fiction? (They were positive! Jake emailed back. What else was he going to say?) Would he be willing to do a "sample edit" of fifty pages of a work-in-progress, so the writer could judge whether there was value in continuing? (Jake took a deep breath and wrote: No. But he would agree to a special fee discount of fifty percent for the first two hours, which ought to be enough *for each of them* to make a decision on whether or not to work together.)

Naturally, this person became his first client.

The writing he encountered in his new role of online editor, coach, and consultant (that marvelously malleable word) made the least of his Ripley students seem like Hemingway. Again and again he urged his new correspondents to check their spelling, keep track of their characters' names, and give at least a tiny bit of thought to what basic ideas their work should convey, *before* they typed those thrilling words: THE END. Some of them listened. Others seemed somehow to believe that the act of hiring a professional writer magically rendered their own writing "professional." What surprised him most, however, was that his new clients, far more than even the least gifted of his Ripley students, seemed to regard publication not as the magical portal it had always represented to him and to every other writer he admired (and envied), but as a purely transactional act. Once, in an early email exchange with an elderly woman in Florida who hoped to complete a second tranche of her memoir, he had politely complimented her on the recent publication of part one (*The Windy River: My Childhood in Pennsylvania*). That author, to her credit, had bluntly declined his flattery. "Oh please," she'd responded, "anybody can publish a book. You just write a check."

It was, he had to admit, a version of *anybody can be a writer* that even he could get behind.

In some ways, things were actually a whole lot nicer on this side of the divide. There were still astounding egos to contend with, of course, and there were still huge distances between the perceived and actual qualities of the stories and novels and memoirs (and, even though he certainly didn't seek it out, poetry) his clients emailed him. But the honest, direct exchange of filthy lucre for services, and the clarity of the relationships between Jake and the people who came to his website (some of them even referred by clients he'd already "helped") was, after so many years of false camaraderie . . . downright refreshing.

Even with semi-regular consulting work alongside his new Ripley responsibilities, however, Jake couldn't make things work in New York anymore. When one client, a Buffalo-based writer of short stories, mentioned that she'd recently returned from a "residency" at the Adlon Center for the Creative Arts, Jake jotted down the unfamiliar name, and after the video call ended he found the website and read up on what had to be a fairly new idea: a subsidy artists' colony doing apparently good business in a place he'd never heard of, an upstate village called Sharon Springs.

He himself, of course, was a veteran of the traditional artists' colonies, which existed to offer succor and respite to serious artists. Back in his own halcyon period just after *The Invention of Wonder* was published he'd received a named fellowship to Yaddo, and flown out to Wyoming to spend a couple of productive weeks at the Ucross Center. He'd done Virginia Center for the Creative Arts, too, and also Ragdale, and if Ragdale had marked the end of his lucky streak a year after *Reverberations* was published, then at least he could (and did!) list those august institutions on his résumé and on his website for their sheer writerly luster. At none of these places had Jake ever been asked for a dime of his own money, however, so he had to read deep into the Adlon website before he understood what new entity this place represented: a self-sponsored artists' retreat, at which the celebrated environment of a Yaddo or a MacDowell was made available, not just to the elite or *traditionally advantaged* person of letters, but to anyone in need of it. Or at least, anyone in need of it with a thousand dollars per week to spend.

Jake examined the photographs of the old place: a great white hulk of hotel, listing slightly (or was that merely the angle of the photograph?), and dating to the 1890s. The Adlon was one of several large hotels still standing in Sharon Springs, a former vacation town arrayed around sulfur springs and once dotted by Victorian spa buildings. Sharon Springs was located an hour southwest of its more celebrated counterpart, Saratoga Springs, but had been rather less prosperous even back then and certainly was today. The town had entered its decline at the turn of the last century, and by the 1950s its half-dozen hotels were variously collapsed, torn down, shut up, or withering away as their guests abandoned longstanding summer routines or simply died. Then, somebody in the family that owned the Adlon had come up with this novel idea to avert or at least temporarily delay the inevitable, and so far it was working. Writers had apparently been gathering at the hotel since 2012, paying for the peace and quiet, the clean rooms and studios, and the communally served breakfasts and dinners (plus lunch in a folksy wicker basket, discreetly left at the door so as not to interrupt the writing of Kubla Khan). They came when they wished, spent their time as they wished, and socialized with their fellow artists if and when they wished, and left when they wished.

Actually, the place kind of sounded like . . . a hotel.

At the top of the web page, he had idly clicked on Opportunities and found himself reading the job description for a program coordinator, on site, to begin just after the New Year. It didn't mention a salary. He looked up the town to see if it was commutable from the city. It wasn't. Still, it was a job.

He really had needed a job.

A week later he was on a train to Hudson to meet the young entrepreneur—"young" meaning, in this case, a full six years his junior—whose family had run the Adlon for three generations and who'd managed to pull this particular rabbit out of the hat. By the time they finished their meeting at a coffee shop on Warren Street, and despite Jake's obvious lack of program-directing experience, he was hired.

"I like the idea of a successful writer greeting the guests when they arrive. Gives them something real to aspire to."

Jake opted not to correct this remarkable statement in any of the ways he might have done.

It was a temporary solution, anyway. Nobody left New York for a tiny town in the exact middle of nowhere on purpose, or at least not without a plan to return. His own plan had a lot to do with the relative rent he was paying in newly fabulous Brooklyn and the one he expected to pay in Cobleskill, a few miles south of Sharon Springs, and the fact that he would be retaining his private writing clients and his gig work for the reconstituted Ripley Symposia even as he received a paycheck from the Adlon Center for the Creative Arts. All of it added up to an exile of a couple of years, three at the most, which was also ample time to begin and even complete another novel after the one he was writing now!

Not that he was really writing one now, or had the tiniest idea for another.

The job itself was a kind of hybrid of admissions officer, cruise director, and plant supervisor, but even cumulatively these were not particularly taxing. More onerous, of course, was the fact that he was required to be physically present at the Adlon during the daytime (and technically on call at night and on the weekends), but given the actual labor associated with most jobs, Jake tended to feel pretty fortunate. He was living frugally and saving money. He was still in the world of writing and writers (albeit farther than he had ever been from his own writerly ambitions). He was still able to work on his novel in progress (or he would be, if he had one), and in the meantime he could continue to nurture and mentor other writers, beginning writers, struggling writers, even writers like himself undergoing what might be called a mid-career retrenchment. As he had once long ago opined, in a cinder-block conference room on the old Ripley campus (which, last he'd heard, had been purchased by a company that did corporate retreats and conferences), this was merely what writers had always done for one another.

The Adlon, on this particular day, had six guest-writers, which meant that the center was only at about 20 percent capacity (though that was six people more than Jake imagined would choose to spend January in a snowbound latter-day spa town that hadn't even had the good sense to turn into Saratoga Springs). Three of the guests were sisters in their sixties who were collaborating on a multigenerational family story, unsurprisingly based on their own family. Another was a vaguely menacing man who actually lived just south of Cooperstown, but drove to the hotel every morning, wrote all day, and left after dinner. There was a poet from Montreal—she didn't say much, even when she was down for meals—and a guy who'd arrived a couple of days earlier from Southern California. (Why would any sane person leave Southern California in January to travel to upstate New York?) So far they were a quietly cooperative and nondramatic group, a far cry from some of the intramural insanity he'd personally witnessed at Ragdale and VCCA! The hotel itself was running as smoothly as a hundred-and-thirty-year-old building could be expected to run, and the Adlon's pair of cooks, a mother and daughter from Cobleskill, were turning out very tasty meals, remarkable given the remoteness of the region in winter. And that morning, as far as Jake knew, the hours ahead promised nothing more than an opportunity to sit in his office behind the hotel's former check-in desk and begin editing the fourth revision of a profoundly unthrilling thriller from a client in Milwaukee.

An ordinary day, in other words, in a life that was about to become a whole lot less ordinary.

CHAPTER SIX

What Terrible Thing

The guy from California made an appearance shortly after lunch, or at least after the lunch baskets had been taken upstairs and left by the doors of the writers' rooms. He was a burly man in his late twenties with tattooed forearms and a kind of swept-aside chunk of hair that always fell back right away. He came storming into Jake's little office behind the former check-in desk and set his basket down on Jake's table.

"Well, this is crap."

Jake looked up at him. He'd been deep in his client's terrible thriller, a narrative so formulaic that he could have told you exactly what was going to happen, and in what order, even if this were the first time he was clawing his way through it, rather than the fourth.

"Lunch?"

"Crap. Some kind of brown meat. What is it, something you hit on the drive over here?"

Jake actually smiled. The roadkill of Schoharie County was indeed broad in its range.

"Do you not eat meat?"

"Oh, I eat meat. I don't eat crap, though."

Jake sat back in his chair. "I'm so sorry. Why don't we go into the kitchen and we can talk to Patty and Nancy about what you like and don't like. We can't always guarantee a separate meal, but we want you to be happy. With only six of you in residence now, we should be able to tweak the menus."

"This town is, like, pathetic. There's nothing here."

Well, now. In *that,* Jake's Californian friend was rather decisively wrong. Sharon Springs's glory days might have been in the late nineteenth century (Oscar Wilde himself had once lectured at the Pavilion Hotel), but recent years had brought a promising revival. The town's flagship American Hotel had been restored to a certain degree of elegance, and a couple of surprisingly good restaurants had taken root on the tiny main street. Most important of all, a couple of men from Manhattan, involuntarily separated from their media jobs in the 2008 downturn, had bought a local farm, acquired a herd of goats, and commenced making cheese, soap, and, more importantly, a great big stir in the world well beyond Sharon Springs, New York. They'd written books, starred in their own reality television show, and opened a shop that would have been right at home on the main streets of East Hampton or Aspen, directly across from the American Hotel. That place was getting to be a bona fide tourist attraction. Though maybe not in January.

"Have you been out to explore? A lot of the writers go over to the Black Cat Café in the morning. The coffee there is great. And the food at the Bistro is excellent."

"I'm paying you enough to be *here,* and to work on my book *here.* The coffee *here* should be great. And the food *here* shouldn't be shit. I mean, would it kill you to do an avocado toast?"

Jake looked at him. In California, avocados might grow on trees—literally—in January, but he doubted this dude would approve of the rock-hard specimens down at the Cobleskill Price Chopper.

"Milk and cheese are kind of the main thing around here. Maybe you've noticed all the dairy farms?"

"I'm lactose intolerant."

"Oh." Jake frowned. "Did we know that? Is it on your forms?"

"I don't know. I didn't fill out any forms."

The guy flipped back his thick hair. Again. And it fell forward into his eyes. Again. It made Jake think of something.

"Well, I hope you'll write down some of the foods you'd be happy to see at meals. I wouldn't count on good avocados up here, not at this time of year, but if there are dishes you like I'll talk to Patty and Nancy. Unless you want to do that."

"I want to write my book," the guy said, so fiercely he might have been uttering a tagline in an adventure movie, something along the lines of *You haven't seen the last of me* or *Don't underestimate what I'm capable of.* "I came here to get this done, and I don't want to be thinking about anything else. I don't want to be listening to those three witches, cackling away all the time on the other side of my wall. I don't want to have a bathroom with pipes that wake me up in the morning. And what's with the fireplace in my bedroom I'm not allowed to have a fire in. I distinctly remember a fire in one of the rooms when I looked at your website. What the fuck is that?"

"That was the parlor fire," Jake said. "We haven't been cleared for fires in the rooms, unfortunately. But we light the parlor fire every afternoon, and I'd be happy to do it earlier if you'd like to work down there, or read. Everything we do here is to try and support our guest-writers, and see they have what they need to do their work. And of course to support one another, as writers."

Jake thought, even as he said this, of all the times he had said it in the past, or said something like it, and when he'd said it the people he'd said it to always nodded in agreement, because they, too, were writers, and writers understood the power of their commonalities. That had always been true. Except for right this minute. And, now it dawned on him, one other time.

Then the guy folded his arms tightly across his chest and glared at Jake, and the final part of the connection snapped into place.

Evan Parker. From Ripley. The one with the story.

Now he understood why, throughout this encounter, his brain had felt like it was circling back on itself, why his thoughts had been looping around and around an as yet unspecified thing. No, he had never met this particular asshole until a couple of days ago, but did that mean he wasn't familiar to Jake? He was familiar. *Hugely* familiar.

Not that he'd spent the past couple of years ruminating on that asshole, because what writer of *any* degree of professional success, not just Jake's own—would want to dwell on a *first-time writer* who'd somehow managed to pull the lever on the slot machine of spectacular stories at exactly the right moment, with his very first dime, no less, sending an utterly unearned jackpot of success shuddering into his lap? Always, when Evan Parker came drifting through Jake's thoughts, it was with the usual surge of envy, the usual bitterness at the unfairness of it all, and then the brief observation that the book itself had not yet—to his knowledge, and it would obviously have been to his knowledge—reached actual publication, which might have meant that Jake's former student had overestimated his own ability to get the thing finished, but he took no great comfort in that. The story, as its author himself had pointed out, was a silver bullet, and whenever the book did emerge it would be successful, and its author also successful beyond his (or, more painfully, Jake's) wildest dreams.

Now, in his little office at the Adlon Center for the Creative Arts, that person, Evan Parker, once again returned to him, and so sharply it was as if he too had entered the little room and was standing just behind his Californian counterpart.

The guy was still talking—no, raging. He had moved on from his fellow guest-writers, on from the Adlon and the food and the town of Sharon Springs. Now Jake was hearing about an "East Coast agent" who'd actually suggested he *pay* somebody, *out of his own money,* to guide additional work on his novel before resubmitting it (*Wasn't that what editors were for? Or agents for that matter?*) and the film scout he'd met at a party who'd told him to think about adding a female character to his story (*Because men didn't read books or go to movies?*) or the assholes at MacDowell and Yaddo who'd rejected him for residencies (*Obviously they favored "artistes" who were hoping to sell ten copies of their book-length poems!*) and the losers typing away at every single table in every single coffee shop in Southern California, who thought they were God's gift, and the world was obviously waiting for their short story collection or their screenplay or their novel . . .

"Actually," Jake heard himself say, "I'm the author of two novels myself."

"Of course you are." The guy shook his head. *"Anybody can be a writer."*

He turned and stalked out of the room, leaving his folksy wicker basket behind him.

Jake listened to the guest (guest-*writer*!) as he clomped up the stairs, and then to the silence filling the wake of that, and again he wondered what he had done, what terrible thing, to merit the company of people like this, let alone their scorn. All he had ever wanted was to tell—in the best possible words, arranged in the best possible order—the stories inside him. He had been more than willing to do the apprenticeship and the work. He had been humble with his teachers and respectful of his peers. He had acceded to the editorial notes of his agent (when he'd had one) and bowed to the red pencil of his editor (when he'd had one) without complaint. He had supported the other writers he'd known and admired (even the ones he hadn't particularly admired) by attending their readings and actually purchasing their books (in hardcover! at independent bookstores!) and he had acquitted himself as the best teacher, mentor, cheerleader, and editor that he'd known how to be, despite the (to be frank) utter hopelessness of most of the writing he was given to work with. And where had he arrived, for all of that? He was a deck attendant on the *Titanic,* moving the chairs around with fifteen ungifted prose writers while somehow persuading them that additional work would help them improve. He was a majordomo at an old hotel in upstate New York, pretending that the "guest-writers" upstairs were no different than the Yaddo fellows an hour to the north. *I like the idea of a successful writer greeting the guests. Gives them something real to aspire to.*

But no guest-writer had ever acknowledged Jake's professional achievements, let alone drawn inspiration from his success in the field they supposedly hoped to enter. Not once in three years. He was as invisible to them as he had become to everyone else.

Because he was a failed writer.

Jake gasped when the words came to him. It was, unbelievably, the very first time this truth had ever broken through.

But . . . but . . . the words came spinning through his head, unstoppable and absurd: *The New York Times* New & Noteworthy! "A writer to watch" according to *Poets & Writers*! The best MFA program in the country! That time he had walked into a Barnes & Noble in Stamford, Connecticut, and seen *The Invention of Wonder* on the Staff Picks shelf, complete with a little index card handwritten by someone named Daria: *One of the most interesting books I've read this year! The writing is lyrical and deep.*

Lyrical! And deep!

All of it years ago, now.

Anybody could be a writer. Anybody except, apparently, him.

CHAPTER SEVEN

Tap, Tap

Late that night, in his apartment in Cobleskill, he did something he had never done, not once since he'd watched his fortunate student walk into a grove of trees on the Ripley campus.

At his computer, Jake typed in the name "Parker Evan," and clicked Return.

Parker Evan wasn't there. Which meant not much: Parker Evan had been his former student's *intended* pen name *at one point,* but that point had been three years earlier. Maybe he'd decided on another name, either because switching his own actual name around was a dumb idea or because he'd opted for even more privacy from the infinity of other possibilities.

Jake went back to the search field and typed: "Parker, novel, thriller."

Parker, novel, thriller returned pages of references to Donald Westlake's "Parker" novels, and also another series of mysteries by Robert B. Parker.

So even if Evan Parker had gotten his book all the way to a publisher, the first thing they'd probably have done was instruct him to drop Parker as a pen name.

Jake removed the name from his search field and tried: "thriller, mother, daughter."

It was an onslaught. Pages and pages of books, by pages and pages of writers, most of whom he'd never heard of. Jake ran his eye down the entries, reading the brief descriptions, but there was nothing that fit the very specific elements of the story his student had told him back in Richard Peng Hall. He clicked on some random author names, not really expecting to find an image of Evan Parker's only half-remembered face, but there was nothing even remotely like it: old men, fat men, bald men, and plenty of women. He wasn't here. His book wasn't here.

Could Evan Parker have been wrong? Could he, Jake, have also been wrong, all this time? Could *that* plot possibly have disappeared into the sea of stories, novels, thrillers, and mysteries published each year, and sunk into silence? Jake thought not. It seemed more likely that, despite his boundless faith in himself, Parker had somehow not managed to finish his book at all. Maybe the book wasn't here on his computer, comfortably ensconced in the first page of each and every one of his search results, because it wasn't anywhere. It wasn't in the world at all. But why?

Jake typed the name, the real name, "Evan Parker" into the search field.

More than a few Facebook Evan Parkers appeared in the search results. Jake clicked over to Facebook and ran his eye down the list. He saw more men—bigger, slighter, balder, darker—and even a few women, but no one remotely like his former student. Maybe Evan wasn't on Facebook. (Jake himself wasn't on Facebook; he'd quit when it became too demoralizing to see his "friends" posting news about their forthcoming books.) He returned to the search results and clicked the "Images" tab, and scanned the page and then the next page. So many Evan Parkers, none of them his. He clicked back to the "All Results" page. There were Evan Parkers who were high school soccer players, ballet dancers, career diplomats currently stationed in Chad, racehorses, and engaged couples ("The future Evan-Parkers welcome you to our wedding site!"). There was no male human even vaguely his former student's age who looked anything like the Evan Parker Jake had known at Ripley.

Then he saw, at the bottom of the page: "Searches related to 'evan parker.'"

And below that the words: "evan parker obituary."

Even before his cursor found the link he knew what he would see.

Evan Luke Parker of West Rutland, VT (38) had died unexpectedly on the evening of October 4, 2013. Evan Luke Parker had been a 1995 graduate of West Rutland High School and had attended classes at Rutland Community College and was a lifelong resident of central Vermont. Predeceased by both parents and a sister, he was survived by a niece. Memorial services were to be announced at a future time. Burial would be private.

Jake read it through twice. There wasn't much to it, really, but it refused to punch its way through, even so.

He was dead? *He was dead.* And . . . Jake looked now at the date. This had not happened recently, either. This had happened . . . incredibly, it had happened only a couple of months after their own doomed attempt at a teacher-student relationship. Jake hadn't even realized that Evan was a Vermonter, or that his parents and sister were already dead, which was very tragic in light of the fact that he was fairly young, himself. Not one of these things had ever come up in conversation between them, of course. They'd had no conversation, really, about anything else but Evan Parker's remarkable novel in progress. And even that, not much. For the rest of the Ripley session, in fact, his student had been downright reticent in workshop, and he had declined or not turned up for the remaining one-on-one conferences. Jake had even wondered if Parker regretted sharing his extraordinary novel idea with his teacher, or if he'd at least thought better of sharing it with his peers in the workshop, but he himself never let on that he had been told anything about what Parker was working on, or that he thought it was at all out of the ordinary. When the session ended, this pompous, withholding, and profoundly irritating person had simply gone away, presumably to do what he needed to do in order to bring his book to the light. But actually, just to die. Now he was gone and his book, in all likelihood, unwritten.

Later, of course, Jake would go back to this moment. Later, he would recognize it for the crossroads it was, but already he was wrapping this stark, years-after-the-fact set of circumstances in the first of what would be many layers of rationalization. Those layers had not much at all to do with the fact that Jake was a moral human being with, presumably, a code of ethical conduct. Mainly they had to do with the fact that he was a writer, and being a writer meant another allegiance, to something of even higher value.

Which was the story itself.

Jake didn't believe in much. He didn't believe that any god had made the universe, let alone that said god was still watching the goings-on and keeping track of every human act, all for the purpose of assigning a few millennia of Homo sapiens to a pleasant or an unpleasant afterlife. He didn't believe in an afterlife. He didn't believe in destiny, fate, luck, or the power of positive thinking. He didn't believe that we get what we deserve, or that everything happens for a reason (what reason would that be?), or that supernatural forces impacted anything in a human life. What was left after all of that nonsense? The sheer randomness of the circumstances we are born into, the genes we've been dealt, our varying degrees of willingness to work our asses off, and the wit we may or may not possess to recognize an opportunity. Should it arise.

But there was one thing he actually did believe in that bordered on the magical, or at least the beyond-pedestrian, and that was the duty a writer owed to a story.

Stories, of course, are common as dirt. Everyone has one, if not an infinity of them, and they surround us at all times whether we acknowledge them or not. Stories are the wells we dip into to be reminded of who we are, and the ways we reassure ourselves that, however obscure we may appear to others, we are actually important, even crucial, to the ongoing drama of survival: personal, societal, and even as a species.

But stories, despite all that, are also maddeningly elusive. There is no deep mine of them to blast around in, or big-box store with wide aisles of unused, undreamed-of, and thrillingly new narratives for a writer to push a big, empty shopping cart through, waiting for something to catch their eye. Those seven story lines Jake had once measured against Evan Parker's not very exciting mother and daughter in an old house—*Overcoming the Monster? Rags to Riches? Journey and Return?*—they were the same seven story lines writers and other storytellers had been rummaging around in forever. And yet . . .

And yet.

Every now and then, some magical little spark flew up out of nowhere and landed (yes, *landed*) in the consciousness of a person capable of bringing it to life. This was occasionally called "inspiration," though "inspiration" was not a word writers themselves often used.

Those magical little sparks tended not to waste time in declaring themselves. They woke you up in the mornings with an annoying *tap, tap* and a sense of unfolding urgency, and they hounded you through the days that followed: the idea, the characters, the problem, the setting, lines of dialogue, descriptive phrases, an opening sentence.

To Jake, the word that comprised the relationship between a writer and their spark was "responsibility." Once you were in possession of an actual idea, you owed it a debt for having chosen *you*, and not *some other writer*, and you paid that debt by getting down to work, not just as a journeyman fabricator of sentences but as an unshrinking artist ready to make painful, time-consuming, even self-flagellating mistakes. Rising to this responsibility was a matter of facing your blank page (or screen) and muzzling the critics inside your head, at least long enough for you to get some work done, all of which was profoundly difficult and none of which was optional. What's more, you stepped away from it at your peril, because if you failed in this grave responsibility you might well find, after some period of distraction, or even less than fully committed work, that your precious spark had . . . left you.

Gone, in other words, as suddenly and unexpectedly as it had appeared, and your novel along with it, though you might spin your wheels for a few months or a few years or the rest of your life, hopelessly throwing words onto the page (or screen) in a stubborn refusal to face what had happened.

And there was something else: an extra, dark superstition for any writer hubristic enough to ignore the spark of a great idea, even if that writer was not of a religious bent, even if he did not believe that "everything happens for a reason," even if, indeed, he resisted magical thinking of every other conceivable kind. The superstition held that if you did not do right by the magnificent idea that had chosen *you, among all possible writers,* to bring it to life, that great idea didn't just leave you to spin your stupid and ineffectual wheels. It actually *went to somebody else.* A great story, in other words, wanted to be told. And if you weren't going to tell it, it was *out of here*, it was going to find *another writer who would,* and you would be reduced to watching *somebody else* write and publish *your book.*

Intolerable.

Jake remembered the day a certain key moment in *The Invention of Wonder* had suddenly been *there* with him, in the world—no preamble, no warning—and despite the fact that this had never happened to him before, his very first thought in the instant that followed its appearance had been:

Grab it.

And he had. And he had done right by that spark, and written the best novel he could around it, the New & Noteworthy first book that had turned—so fleetingly—the attention of the literary world in his direction.

He'd lacked even a pallid little frisson of an idea with *Reverberations* (his "novel in linked short stories," which had really only ever been . . . short stories), though obviously he had finished that book, limping along to some point at which he was permitted to type the words "The End." It had been the end, all right, to his period of "promise" as "a young writer to watch," and it might have been wiser not to publish it at all, but Jake had been terrified to lose the validation of *The Invention of Wonder.* After each and every one of the legacy publishers, and then an entire tranche of the university presses, had rejected the manuscript, the importance of publishing his second book had swelled until his entire being seemed to be on the line. If he could only get this one out of his way, he'd told himself at the time, maybe the next idea, the next spark, would come.

Only it hadn't. And while he'd continued to have the occasional crusty and serviceable *idea* in the years since—*boy grows up in family obsessed with dog breeding, man discovers older sibling has been institutionalized since birth*—there'd been nothing *tap, tapping* away at him, compelling him to write. The work he'd done since then, on these and a couple of even worse ideas, had petered, excruciatingly, out.

Until, if he was being completely honest with himself, and just now he *was* being completely honest with himself, he'd stopped even trying. It had been more than two years since he had written a word of fiction.

Once, long ago, Jake had done his best to honor what he'd been given. He had recognized his spark and done right by it, never shirking the hard thinking and the careful writing, pushing himself to do well and then to do better. He had taken no short cuts and evaded no effort. He had taken his chance against the world, submitting himself to the opinions of publishers, reviewers and ordinary readers . . . but favor had passed over him and moved on to others, What was he to do, who was he to be, if no other spark ever came to him again?

It was unbearable to contemplate.

Good writers borrow, great writers steal, Jake was thinking. That ubiquitous phrase was attributed to T. S. Eliot (which didn't mean Eliot hadn't, himself, stolen it!), but Eliot had been talking, perhaps less than seriously, about the theft of actual language—phrases and sentences and paragraphs—not of a story, itself. Besides, Jake knew, as Eliot had known, as all artists ought to know, that every story, like every single work of art—from the cave paintings to whatever was playing at the Park Theater in Cobleskill to his own puny books—was *in conversation with* every other work of art: bouncing against its predecessors, drawing from its contemporaries, harmonizing with the patterns. All of it, paintings and choreography and poetry and photography and performance art and the ever-fluctuating novel, was whirling away in an unstoppable spin art machine of its own. And that was a beautiful, thrilling thing.

He would hardly be the first to take some tale from a play or a book—in this case, a book that had never been written!—and create something entirely new from it. *Miss Saigon* from *Madam Butterfly*. *The Hours* from *Mrs. Dalloway*. *The Lion King* from *Hamlet*, for goodness' sake! It wasn't even taboo, and obviously it wasn't theft; even if Parker's manuscript actually *existed* at the time of his death, Jake had never seen more than a couple of pages of the thing, and he remembered little of what he had seen: the mother on the psychic hotline, the daughter writing about carpetbaggers, the ring of pineapples around the door of the old house. Surely what he, himself, might make from so little would belong to him and only to him.

These, then, were the circumstances in which Jake found himself that January evening at his computer in his cruddy Cobleskill apartment in the Leatherstocking Region of upstate New York, out of pride, hope, time and—he could finally admit—ideas of his own.

He hadn't gone looking for this. He had upheld the honor of writers who listened to the ideas of other writers and then turned responsibly back to their own. He had absolutely not invited the brilliant spark his student had abandoned (okay, *involuntarily* abandoned) to come to *him*, but come it had and here it was: this urgent, shimmering thing, already *tap, tapping* in his head, already hounding him: *the idea, the characters, the problem*.

So what was Jake going to do about that?

A rhetorical question, obviously. He knew exactly what he was going to do about that.

PART THREE

CHAPTER EIGHT

Crib Syndrome

Three years later, Jacob Finch Bonner, author of *The Invention of Wonder* and of the decidedly less obscure novel *Crib* (over two million copies in print and the current occupant of the number two spot on the *New York Times* hardcover list—after a solid nine months at number one), found himself on the stage of the S. Mark Taper Foundation Auditorium of the Seattle Symphony. The woman seated opposite him was a type he'd come to know well during his interminable book tour: a breathless, hand-flapping enthusiast who might never have read a novel before, she was so enraptured at encountering this particular one. She made Jake's own job easier by virtue of the fact that she gushed incessantly and seldom formed a cogent question. Mainly all he was called upon to do was nod, thank her, and look out over the audience with a grateful, self-effacing smile.

This wasn't his first trip to Seattle to promote the book, but the earlier visit had taken place during the first weeks of the tour as the country was just becoming aware of *Crib,* and the venues had been the usual ones for a not-yet-famous author: The Elliot Bay Book Company, a

Barnes & Noble branch in Bellevue. To Jake, those were exciting enough. (There had been no book tour at all for *The Invention of Wonder,* and the personal request he'd made to read at the Barnes & Noble near his hometown on Long Island had yielded an audience of six, including his parents, his old English teacher, and the mother of his high school girlfriend, who must have spent the reading wondering what her daughter had ever seen in Jake.) What had been even more exciting about those first-round Seattle readings, and the hundreds like them all over the country, was that people actually came to them, people who were not his parents or high school teachers or otherwise somehow obligated to attend. The forty who'd shown up for that Elliott Bay reading, for example, or the twenty-five at the Bellevue Barnes & Noble, were complete strangers, and that was just astonishing. So astonishing, in fact, that it had taken a couple of months for the thrill to wear off.

It had worn off now.

That tour—technically the hardcover tour—had never really ended. As the book took off, more and more dates were added, increasingly for series where purchase of the book was part of the price of admission, and then the festivals started getting appended to the schedule: Miami, Texas, AWP, Bouchercon, Left Coast Crime (these last two, like so much else about the thriller genre he'd inadvertently entered, had heretofore been unfamiliar to him). In all, he'd barely stopped traveling since the book was first published, accompanied by a worshipful off-the-book-page profile in *The New York Times,* the kind that had once made him weak-kneed with envy. Then, after a few months of that, the novel's paperback had been rushed into print when Oprah named it her October selection, and now Jake was returning to some of his earlier stops, but in venues even he had never conceived of.

The S. Mark Taper Foundation Auditorium, for example, had over 2,400 seats—Jake had looked that up in advance. *Two thousand four hundred seats!* And as far as he could tell from where he was sitting, every single one of them was occupied. Out there he could make out the bright kelly green of the new paperback's cover on people's laps and in their arms. Most of these people had brought their own copies, which he supposed did not bode well for the four thousand copies Elliot Bay was now unpacking at the signing tables out in the lobby, but man it was gratifying to him. When *The Invention of Wonder* was published nearly fifteen years earlier, he had settled on the I'll-know-I've-made-it fantasy of seeing a stranger reading his book in public, and needless to say, this had never happened. Once, on the subway, he had seen a guy reading a book that looked tantalizingly like his, but when he edged closer, took a seat opposite, and checked it out, he'd discovered it was actually the new Scott Turow, and that had been only the first of several such crushing false alarms. Neither, obviously, had it happened with *Reverberations,* of which fewer than eight hundred copies had even been sold (and he'd purchased two hundred of them himself as cheap remaindered copies). Now this auditorium was full of living, breathing readers who had paid actual money for their tickets and were here in the enormous space, clutching his book as they leaned forward in their seats and laughing uproariously at everything he said, even the banal stuff about what his "process" was and how he still carried his laptop around in the same leather satchel he'd owned for years.

"Oh my god," said the woman in the other chair, "I have to tell you, I was on a plane and I was reading the book, and I came to the part—I think you all probably know the part I'm speaking of—and I just, like, gasped! Like, I made a noise! And the flight attendant came over and she said, 'Are you okay?' and I said, 'Oh my god, this book!' And she asked me what book I was reading, so I showed her, and she started to laugh. She said this has been happening for months, people yelping and gasping in the middle of a flight. It's like a syndrome. Like: *Crib* syndrome!"

"Oh, that's so funny," said Jake. "I always used to look at what people were reading on planes. It never used to be by me, I can tell you that!"

"But your first novel was a New & Noteworthy in *The New York Times.*"

"Yes, it was. That was a very great honor. Unfortunately it didn't translate to people actually going into bookstores and buying it. In fact, I don't think the book was even *in* bookstores. I remember my mother telling me they didn't have it at her local chain store on Long Island. She had to special order it. That's pretty rough on a Jewish mother whose kid isn't even a doctor."

Explosive laughter. The interviewer—her name was Candy and she was some sort of local public figure—doubled over. When she got control of herself, she asked Jake the thoroughly predictable one about how he'd first gotten the idea.

"I don't think ideas, even great ideas, are all that hard to come by. When people ask me where I get my ideas, my answer is that there are a hundred novels in every day's issue of *The New York Times,* and we recycle the paper or use it to line the birdcage. If you are trapped in your own experience you may find it hard to see beyond things that have actually happened to you, and unless you've had a life of *National Geographic*–worthy adventures you're probably going to think you have nothing to write a novel about. But if you spend even a few minutes with other people's stories and learn to ask yourself: *What if this had happened to me?* Or *What if this happened to a person completely unlike me?* Or *In a world that's different from the world I'm living in?* Or *What if it happened a little bit differently, under different circumstances?* The possibilities are endless. The directions you can go, the characters you can meet along the way, the things you can learn, also endless. I've taught in MFA programs, and I can tell you, that's maybe the most important thing anyone can teach you. Get out of your own head and look around. There are stories growing from trees."

"Well, okay," said Candy, "but which tree did you pick this one off of? 'Cause I'm telling you, I read all the time. Seventy-five novels last year, I counted! Well, Goodreads counted." She smirked at the audience, and the audience obligingly laughed. "And I can't think of another novel that would have had me making an actual noise on a plane. So how'd you come up with it?"

And here it was: that cold wave of terror descending inside Jake, from the crown of his head, past his grinning mouth and along each limb, down to the end of every finger or toe. Incredibly, he wasn't yet used to this, although it had been with him, every moment of every day, back through this tour and the tour preceding it, back through the heady months before publication, as his new publisher ramped up the temperature and the book world began to take notice. Back through the writing of the thing itself, which had taken six months of winter and spring in his apartment in Cobleskill, New York, and in his office behind the old front desk at the Adlon Center for the Creative Arts, hoping none of the guest-writers upstairs would bother him with complaints about the rooms or questions about how to get an agent at William Morris Endeavor, all the way back to that January night when he'd read the obituary of his most memorable student, Evan Parker. He had carried this around with him, *every moment of every day*, a perpetual threat of permanent harm.

Jake, needless to say, had taken *not one single word* from those pages he'd read back at Ripley. He hadn't had them to steal from, for one thing, and if he had he would have thrown them away in order not to look. Even the late Evan Parker, were he capable of reading *Crib,* would have found it impossible to locate his own language in Jake's novel, and yet, ever since the moment he'd typed the words "CHAPTER ONE" into his laptop back in Cobleskill he'd been waiting, horribly waiting, for someone who knew the answer to this very question—*How'd you come up with it?*—to rise to their feet and point their finger in accusation.

Candy wasn't that person, obviously. Candy didn't know much about much, and nothing, it was abundantly clear, even to him, about this particular thing. What Candy brought to their conversation was an admirable sense of ease while being stared at by upward of twenty-four hundred human beings, and this was not a quality Jake himself devalued, by any means. Behind her question, though, was clear vapidity. It was just a question. Sometimes a question was just a question.

"Oh, you know," he finally said, "it's not actually that interesting a story. It's actually a little bit embarrassing. I mean, think of the most banal activity you can imagine—I was taking my garbage out to the curb, and this mom from my block happened to drive by with her teenage daughter. The two of them were screaming at each other in their car. Obviously, you know, having a moment, like no other mother and teenage daughter has ever had."

Here Jake knew to pause for laughter. He had contrived the taking-the-garbage-out story for precisely these occasions, and he'd told it many times by now. People always laughed.

"And the idea of it just popped into my head. I mean, let's be honest. Can she who has never thought *I could kill my mother* or *This kid is going to drive me to murder* please raise her hand?"

The huge audience was still. Candy was still. Then there was another wave of laughter, this one far less exuberant. It was always like that.

"And I just started thinking, you know, how bad could that argument be? How bad could it get? Could it ever get, you know, *that bad*? And then what would happen if it did?"

After a moment Candy said: "Well, I guess we all know the answer to that, now."

More laughter then, and then applause. So much applause. He and Candy shook hands and got to their feet, and waved, and exited the stage, and parted, she to the greenroom and he to the signing table in the lobby, where the long and coiling line he had once fantasized about had already begun to form. Six young women were arrayed along the table to his left. One sold the copies of *Crib,* another wrote the name of any dedicatee on a Post-it and affixed that to the cover, and a third opened the books to the right page. All he had to do was smile and write his name, which he did, over and over, until his jaw ached and his left hand ached and every face began to look like the face before it, or the face after it, or both faces at once.

Hi, thanks for coming!

Oh, that's so nice!

Really? That's amazing!

Good luck with your writing!

It was his fifteenth evening event in as many days, except for the previous Monday night, which he'd spent in a hotel in Milwaukee, eating a terrible burger and answering emails before passing out during *Rachel Maddow*. He had not been home to his apartment—a new apartment, bought with the astonishing advance he'd received for *Crib,* and still barely furnished—since late August and it was now the end of September. He was living on hotel burgers, late-night whiskey sours, minibar jelly beans, and sheer strain, trying constantly to conjure up new or at least variant answers to the same questions he'd now been asked hundreds of times, and down—despite all those jelly beans—at least five pounds on a frame that couldn't afford to lose much more. His agent Matilda (who was *not* the agent who'd bungled Jake's first novel and resolutely detached herself from his second!) called every few days to casually ask how far into the next novel he was (answer: not far enough), and a chorus of writers he'd known in graduate school and college and during those New York years were following him like Furies, bombarding him with requests—everything from blurbs for their manuscripts to recommendations for artists' colonies to requests to be put in touch with Matilda. In short, he could look no farther ahead than a day or two. Farther than that he left to Otis, the liaison Macmillan had sent out on the road with him. It was a strange, almost disembodied way to live.

But also: his exact dream. Back when he'd dreamed, so long ago (not even a year ago!) of being a "successful writer," had he not pictured these very things? Audiences, stacks of books, that magical "1" beside his name on the fabled list at the back of *The New York Times Book Review*? He had, of course, but also hoped for the small, human connections that must come to a writer whose work was actually read: opening one's own book, writing one's own name, holding it out to a single reader intent on reading it. Was it wrong to want these simple, humble rewards? Hand to hand and brain to brain in the marvelous connection that was written language meeting the power of storytelling? He had these things now. And to think: he had acquired them with only his hard work and his pure imagination.

Plus a story that might not have been entirely his to tell.

Which somebody, somewhere out there, might conceivably know.

All of it, at any time, might be ripped away from him—*rip, rip, rip*—and so quickly that Jake would find himself helpless and annihilated even before he knew what was happening. Then he would be relegated to the circle of shamed writers forever and without hope of appeal: James Frey, Stephen Glass, Clifford Irving, Greg Mortenson, Jerzy Kosinski . . .

Jacob Finch Bonner?

"Thank you," Jake heard himself say as a young man mentioned some nice thing about *The Invention of Wonder*. "That's one of my favorites, too."

The words struck him as somehow familiar, and then he remembered that this exact phrase had been another fancy of his, and for the briefest moment this made him feel so utterly happy. But only the briefest moment. After that, he went back to being terrified again.

CHAPTER NINE

Not the Worst

On Jake's own printed schedule he had the following morning off, but on the ride back to the hotel after the last book was signed Otis let him know of a new event, a morning interview for a radio show called *Sunrise Seattle*.

"Remote?" Jake had asked hopefully.

"No. In studio. It was last minute, but the program director really wants to make this work. She moved the host's other stuff around to get you. Big fan."

"Oh. Nice," Jake said, though it wasn't, really. He had a midday flight to San Francisco in the afternoon and an appearance at the Castro Theatre that night, then he had to be in Los Angeles the following morning for nearly a week of meetings related to the film adaptation. One of these was a lunch with the director. An A-list director, by anyone's standard.

KBIK wasn't far from their hotel and only a few blocks north of the Pike Place Market. Early the next morning, Jake left Otis to retrieve their bags from the taxi and entered the station's lobby, where their obvious contact was waiting: a woman with gleaming gray hair held back off her face with a frankly girlish headband. He approached her with his hand outstretched and an entirely unnecessary: "I'm Jake Bonner."

"Jake! Hi!"

They shook. Her hand was long and narrow, like the rest of her. She had bright blue eyes and he noticed that she wore not a lick of makeup. He liked that. Then he noticed that he liked that.

"And you are?"

"Oh! Sorry, I'm Anna Williams. Anna. I mean, please call me Anna. I'm the director of programming. This is so fantastic that we got you to come in. I love your book so much."

"Well, thanks, that's so nice of you to say."

"Really, I couldn't get it out of my head, the first time I read it."

"First time!"

"Oh, I've read it a bunch of times. It's just amazing to meet you."

Otis arrived, dragging both their suitcases. He and Anna shook hands.

"So it's a straight interview?" Otis asked. "Do you need Jake to read anything?"

"No. Not unless you want to?" She looked at Jake. She looked almost stricken, as if she'd failed to make this important inquiry.

"Not at all." He smiled. He was trying to figure out how old she was. His own age? Or maybe a little bit younger. It was hard to tell. She was slender and wore black leggings and a kind of homespun tunic. Very Seattle. "Really, I'm pretty easygoing. Will people be calling in?"

"Oh, we never know. Randy's a bit difficult to predict, he does everything on the fly. Sometimes he'll take callers and sometimes he won't."

"Randy Johnson's a Seattle institution," Otis said helpfully. "What is it, like twenty years?"

"Twenty-two. Not all of it at this station. I don't think he's been off the air longer than a few days since he started." She was holding her clipboard tightly against her chest. Those long hands gripped the edges.

"Well, I was delighted when I heard he wanted a novelist on!" Otis said. "Usually if we're lucky enough to do Randy Johnson's show it's a sports biography, or sometimes politics. I can't remember ever bringing a fiction writer in before today. You should be proud," he said to Jake. "You got Randy Johnson to read a novel!"

"Ah," said the woman, Anna Williams. "You know, I wish I could promise you that he's read the whole novel. He's been briefed, obviously, but you're right, Randy's not what you'd call a natural reader of fiction. He gets what a huge thing *Crib* has become, though. He likes to be on top of a cultural phenomenon whether it's a novel or a pet rock."

Jake sighed. In the early weeks of the book's publication he'd endured more than a few interviews with people who hadn't read the book, and answering their basic questions—*So what's your book about?*—presented the significant challenges of describing *Crib* without giving away the plot's now infamous twist. By now, everyone seemed to know what his book was about, which had been a relief in more ways than one. Also, it wasn't fun covering for somebody's total unfamiliarity with your work while trying to sound pleasant and engaged yourself.

They went upstairs to the studio and found the host, Randy Johnson, in mid-interview with a state senator and her constituent, both highly exercised by a new regulation related to dogs and their waste. Jake watched Johnson, a large and hirsute man with a definite tendency to spit, expertly play these two antagonists against each other until the constituent, at least, was red in the face and the senator was threatening to get up and leave the room.

"Oh, now, you don't want to do that," said Johnson, who was definitely suppressing his own laughter. "Look, let's take a call."

The producer, Anna Williams, brought Jake a bottle of water. Her fingers, slipping past his, were warm, but the water was cool. He looked at her. She was pretty; very, undeniably pretty. He had not paused to consider the prettiness of a woman for a very long time. There had been a woman he'd met on Bumble the previous summer and gone out to dinner with a couple of times. Before that, a woman who taught statistics at SUNY Cobleskill. Before that, Alice Logan, the poet he'd met at Ripley, though that petered out when she headed south to Johns Hopkins at the end of the summer. She was tenured there now, Jake knew. She'd sent him a brief, congratulatory email when *Crib* made the *New York Times* bestseller list.

"He's about finished with those two," she said quietly.

When the commercial break began she led him to the seat the angry constituent had just vacated and held the earphones open for him. Randy Johnson was studying some papers and drinking from a KBIK mug. "Hang on," he said, without looking up. "Hang on a minute."

"Sure," said Jake. He looked around for Otis, but Otis wasn't nearby. Anna Williams took the other chair and put on her own headset. She gave him an encouraging smile.

"He has some good questions," she said, sounding less than certain. Obviously, she had written the questions herself. The uncertainty, Jake supposed, was whether the host would stick to them.

Just before they went back on air, Johnson looked up and grinned. "How you doing. Jack, right?"

"Jake," said Jake. He reached across to shake the host's hand. "Thanks for having me on."

Randy Johnson grinned. "This one"—he pointed at Anna—"gave me no choice."

"Well," Jake said, turning to her. Anna was looking down at her clipboard, pretending not to listen.

"Looks like a featherweight, but she's a heavyweight when it comes to getting her way."

"That's probably what makes her a great producer," Jake said, as if this complete stranger needed him to defend her.

"Five seconds," said a voice in Jake's ears.

"Okay!" Randy Johnson said. "Ready, all?"

Jake was, he supposed. By now he'd sat in any number of chairs just like this one, and smiled genially at any number of local blowhards. He listened to Randy Johnson opine about unleashed dogs on the streets of Seattle for a while, and then heard what he understood to be his own introduction. "Okay, so our next guest is probably the hottest writer in America at the moment. Am I talking about Dan Brown or John Grisham? You're probably getting pretty excited out there, am I right?"

He glanced at the woman beside him. Her sharp jaw was set and her eyes down on the clipboard.

"Well, too bad. But let me ask you something. Who out there's read a new book called *The Crib*? Sounds like it's about a baby. Is it about a baby?"

The host was silent then. After a horrified moment, Jake realized he was expected to actually answer this question.

"Uh, it's *Crib,* not *The Crib.* And nothing really to do with a baby. To 'crib' something means to steal it, or purloin it. And . . . thanks for having me on, Randy. We had a great event in Seattle last night."

"Oh yeah? Where?"

He couldn't remember the name of the actual hall. "Seattle Arts and Lectures. It was at the symphony. Gorgeous place."

"Yeah? That's big. How big is that place?"

Really? Jake thought. Now he was expected to answer trivia questions about the host's own city? But in fact he knew the answer.

"About twenty-four hundred, I think. I met some amazing people."

Beside him, Anna held up a piece of paper, but to the host, not to Jake. *FULL NAME: JACOB FINCH BONNER* it read.

Randy made a face. "Jacob Finch Bonner. What kind of name is that?"

The kind I got at birth, Jake thought. Except for the Finch, of course.

"Well, everyone calls me Jake. I have to admit to adding the 'Finch' myself. After Scout, Jem, and Atticus."

"After who?"

It was so hard not to shake his head. He had to fight against it.

"Characters in *To Kill a Mockingbird.* It was my favorite novel when I was a child."

"Oh. Yeah, I think I got out of reading that by watching the movie."

Here he interrupted himself with his own approving laughter. "So you got this hot first novel, everybody's reading it. Tell us what it's about, Jake Finch."

Jake tried for a laugh of his own. It came out sounding far less natural. "Just Jake! Well, there are things in this book I don't want to spoil for people who haven't read it, so let's just say it's about a woman named Samantha who becomes a mother at a young age. Very young. Too young."

"She was a naughty girl," Randy commented.

Jake looked at him in some disbelief. "Well, not necessarily. But she sort of gives up her own life to have her child, and the two of them live together in a kind of isolated way, in the house Samantha herself grew up in. But they're not close. And it gets worse between them as the daughter, Maria, becomes a teenager."

"Oh, you mean it's like my house," he said delightedly.

Anna held up another sign. *MORE THAN 2 MILL SOLD,* it said. And under that: *SPIELBERG DIRECTING MOVIE.*

"So, Jake! I hear Steven Spielberg is making it into a movie. How'd you hook the big one?"

It was a relief, at least, to move the subject away from himself and even his book. Jake talked a bit about the film, and what a fan of Spielberg he'd always been. "It's amazing to me that he connected so powerfully with this story."

"Yeah, but why? I mean, the guy probably has his pick of every film project that's out there. He picked *The Crib.* Why, do you think?"

Jake closed his eyes. "Well, I guess there was something in the characters that must have spoken to him. Or—"

"Oh, so like my daughter, who's sixteen, and my wife, who start screaming at each other when they get up in the morning and don't stop till midnight, I could get Steven Spielberg to make a movie about them? Because I'm down with that. My producer's right here. Anna? Can we get Steven Spielberg on the phone? I'll tell him whatever he's paying Jake, I'll sell him my wife and daughter for half."

Jake stared at him in horror. He turned to look for Otis. No Otis. Not that Otis could have done anything.

"Okay!" Randy said with a flourish. "Let's take some calls."

He stabbed his console with a forefinger, and a woman with a low voice asked if she could ask Jake a question.

"Sure!" said Jake, far more enthusiastically than he felt. "Hi!"

"Hi. I love the book so much. I gave it to everyone in my office."

"Oh, that's so nice," Jake said. "Do you have a question?"

"Yeah. I just wanted to know how you thought of that story. 'Cause I mean, I was really surprised."

He searched in his cerebral file for the most appropriate of his prepared answers.

"I think when you're writing a long story, like a novel, you don't think of every part of the story at once. You think of one part, and then the next, and the next. So it sort of evolves—"

"Thanks," Randy said, cutting off both the caller and Jake. "So you kind of make it up as you go along. You don't write an outline beforehand?"

"I never have. That's not to say I never will."

"Hi there, you're on with Randy."

"Hi, Randy. Do you know if the city is planning to do anything about all the people doing drugs around Occidental Square? I was down there last weekend with my in-laws, and it was just ridiculous, you know?"

"Oh, hell yeah," Randy concurred. "It's never been this bad, and the city, it's like: see no evil, hear no evil. You know what I think they ought to be doing about it?"

And he was off: the mayor, the council, the do-gooders handing out food and coupons, what was that supposed to accomplish? Jake looked at Anna, who was watching the host, her face ashen. There were no more scribbled signs. She seemed to have given up on that. And the time ran out.

"Okay, appreciate you coming in," said Randy Johnson as soon as a car insurance ad began. "It was fun. I'll look out for the film."

I'm sure you will, Jake thought. He got to his feet. "Thanks for having me."

"Thank Anna," Randy said. "Her idea."

"Well . . ." he started to say.

"Thanks, Anna." It was Otis, finally in the doorway. "This was great."

"I'll walk you out," said Anna. She went in front of him. He was suddenly far more nervous than he'd been while waiting for the interview to begin, or even after it had begun falling off the cliff that was Seattle institution Randy Johnson. Behind her, his eyes on her narrow back, the long gray hair between her shoulder blades, he descended the stairs to the ground floor. Then they were back in the lobby and Otis was retrieving their bags from behind the security guard's desk.

"I am so sorry," Anna said.

"Well, he's not the worst."

"No?"

He'd been pretty near the worst, actually. Anyone could be an idiot or a jerk, separately, but the combination of ignorance and mean-spiritedness—that was special.

"I've been asked if I paid somebody else to write my book for me. I've been asked to look at the interviewer's child's fiction. On the air. One woman on a TV show, just before it started, she said to me: 'I've read the beginning and the end of your book and I thought it was just great.'"

"Shut *up*." Anna grinned.

"Absolutely true. Of course it's a ridiculous format: a few minutes on a radio show or a television show, to say anything substantive about a novel."

"But he was . . . I just thought, y'know, he might rise to the occasion. He may not be a fiction guy, but he's interested in people. If he'd read it he'd have been a completely different person. But obviously . . ."

Otis was on his phone, and frowning. He was probably ordering an Uber to SeaTac.

"Please, it's fine."

"No, I just, I wish I could make it up to you. Would you . . . do you have time for coffee? I mean, I'm sure you don't. But there's a good place at the Market . . ."

It seemed to have surprised her as much as it surprised him, and immediately she tried to walk it back. "Oh never mind! You probably need to get going. Please forget I asked."

"I'd love to," said Jake.

CHAPTER TEN

Utica

She took him to a place on the top floor of a building opposite the market, and insisted on getting the coffee. It was a local chain called Storyville, and the place was warm with a fire going and a window overlooking the Public Market sign. She had recovered her cool at some point on the walk over and seemed almost serene. She was also exponentially more beautiful with every passing moment.

Anna Williams was not a Seattle native. She'd grown up in northern Idaho and moved the rest of the way west for college at the University of Washington—"famous for being Ted Bundy's first playground"—after which she'd spent a decade out on Whidbey Island working for a small radio station.

"What was that like?" said Jake.

"Oldies and talk. An unusual combination."

"No, I meant living on an island."

"Oh. You know. Quiet. I was in a little town called Coupeville, where the station was. Lots of weekenders from the city, so it never felt that remote. And you know, we're all used to the ferries up here. I don't think 'island' really means to Seattle people what it means to other people."

"Do you get back to Idaho?" he asked.

"Not since my adoptive mom died."

"Oh. I'm sorry." A moment later, he said: "So, you were adopted?"

"Never formally. My mom—my adoptive mom—was actually my teacher. I had a really bad situation at home, and Miss Royce just sort of took me in. I think everyone in our town understood my circumstances. There was kind of a silent agreement that no one would look too close or involve the authorities. I got more stability from her in a couple of years than I'd had my whole life before that."

Clearly they were poised at the edge of a fathomless lake. There were many things he wanted to know, but it was hardly the right moment.

"It's wonderful when the right person comes into your life at the right time."

"Well." Anna shrugged. "Right time, I don't know. A few years earlier would have been even better. But I certainly was able to appreciate what I had, while I had it. And I was extremely fond of her. I was a junior at the university when she got ill. I went home to take care of her. That's when my hair turned gray."

Jake looked at her. "Really? I've heard of that. Overnight, right?"

"No, it wasn't like that. The way people talk about it, it sounds like you wake up in the morning and BAM—every strand's been replaced. For me it just started to grow out and everything new was this color. That was kind of a shock of its own, but after a while I decided it was kind of an opportunity. I could go any direction I wanted with it. I did color it for the first couple of years, but eventually I decided I liked it like this. I liked that it was a little bit confusing. Not for myself, but for other people."

"What do you mean?"

"Oh . . . just that the combination of hair that signifies 'old' with a face that isn't old is confusing to a lot of people. I've noticed it can make some people think I'm older than my real age, and others think I'm younger."

"How old are you?" Jake asked. "Maybe I shouldn't ask."

"No, it's okay. I'll tell you, but only after you tell me how old you think I am. It's not a vanity thing. I'm just curious."

She smiled at Jake, and he took the opportunity to see it all again: the pale oval face, the streaked silver hair down her back, and that girlish hairband with the linen shirt and leggings he'd seen around town, and on her feet tan boots that looked ready to hike off home along a rugged wooded path. She was right, he realized, about her age. Not that he'd never been especially adept at assessing age, but with Anna he couldn't have said any number between, say, twenty-eight and forty, with any certainty at all. Because he had to say a number, he approximated his own.

"Are you . . . in your mid-thirties?"

"I am." She smiled. "Want to try for the bonus round?"

"Well, I'm thirty-seven, myself."

"Nice. A nice age."

"And you are . . . ?"

"Thirty-five. An even nicer age."

"It is," Jake said. Outside it had started to rain. "So. Why radio?"

"Oh I know, it's ridiculous. Radio broadcasting is an insane industry to want to go into in the twenty-first century, but I like my job. Well, not this morning, but most of the time. And I'm going to keep trying to get fiction on the air. Though I doubt many other novelists are going to be as mild-mannered about it as you were."

Inwardly, Jake winced. "Mild-mannered" had made him think, immediately, of that other version of himself, the Jake who'd once silently endured the diatribe of a narcissistic guest-writer from California: *noisy pipes! bad sandwiches! non-working fireplaces!* And the never to be forgotten: *Anybody can be a writer.*

On the other hand, that same diatribe had ultimately brought him here. And here was good. Despite the incandescent events of the past several months—Oprah! Spielberg!—and the ongoing astonishment of his book's ever-growing readership, he was actually happier right at this moment—with the silver-haired girl in the wood-lined coffee shop—than he'd been in months.

"Most of us," said Jake, "most fiction writers, I mean, we're not all that hung up about the sales and the rankings and the Amazon number. I mean, we care, we need to eat like everyone else, but we're just so glad people are reading our work. Like, *anyone*'s reading our work. And despite what your boss said on the air this morning, *Crib* wasn't my first book. Or even my second. Maybe a couple thousand people read my first novel, even though it had a good publisher and some nice reviews. But even that's way more than the number of people who read my second book. So you see, it's never a forgone conclusion that anyone is actually going to see your work, no matter how good it is. And if nobody reads it, it doesn't exist."

"Tree falls in the forest," Anna said.

"A suitable northwest interpretation. But if they do read it, you never get over the thrill of that: a person you don't even know, paying their hard-earned money so they can read what you wrote? It's amazing. It's unbelievable. When I meet people at these events and they bring in some grubby copy they've dropped in the bath or spilled coffee on, or folded down the corners of the pages, that's the best feeling. Even better than someone buying a brand-new copy right in front of me." He paused. "You know, I have an idea you're a secret writer, yourself."

"Oh?" She looked at him. "Why secret?"

"Well, you haven't mentioned it yet."

"Maybe it hasn't come up yet."

"Okay. So what is it? Fiction? A memoir? Poetry?"

Anna picked up her mug and gazed into it, as if the answer resided within. "Not a poetry person," she said. "Love reading memoirs, but not interested in digging around in my own dirt so I can share it with the rest of the world. I've always liked novels, though." She looked up at him, suddenly shy.

"Oh? Tell me a few of your favorites." It occurred to him that she might think he was asking for praise. "Present company excepted," he added, trying to make a joke of it.

"Well . . . Dickens, of course. Willa Cather. Fitzgerald. I love Marilynne Robinson. I mean, it would be a dream to write one, but there's absolutely nothing in my life that suggests I could do it. Where would I get an idea? Where do you get yours?"

He nearly groaned. Back in the cerebral file of acceptable answers he found the most obvious one, the one Stephen King had given them all. "Utica."

Anna stared. "I'm sorry?"

"Utica. It's in upstate New York. Someone asked Stephen King where he gets his ideas, and he said Utica. If it's good enough for Stephen King, it's certainly good enough for me."

"Right. That's funny," she said, looking as if she thought it was anything but. "Why didn't you use that line last night?"

For a moment he didn't reply. "You were there last night."

She shrugged. "Of course I was there. I'm a fan, obviously."

And he thought how astonishing it was that this very pretty woman was calling herself his *fan.* After a moment he heard her ask if he wanted another coffee.

"No, thanks. I'll need to go soon. Otis was giving me the side eye, back at the radio station. You probably noticed."

"He doesn't want you to miss your next gig. Totally understandable."

"Yes, though I'd love to have a little more time. I wonder . . . do you ever come east?"

She smiled. She had an odd smile: lips pressed together so hard it looked almost uncomfortable for her to hold the expression.

"I haven't yet," she said.

When they went outside he considered, thought better of, then reconsidered a kiss, and while he vacillated she actually reached out for him. Her silver hair was soft against his cheek. Her body was surprisingly warm, or was that his own? He had, in that moment, such a powerful idea of what could come next.

But then, a few minutes later in the car, he found the first of the messages. It had been forwarded from the contact form on his own author website (*Thanks for visiting my page! Have a question or a comment about my work? Please use the form!*) just around the time as he was about to go on the air with local Seattle institution Randy Johnson, and it had already been sitting there in his own email in-box for about ninety radioactive minutes. Reading it now made every good thing of that morning, not to speak of the last year of Jake's life, instantly fall from him and land with a brutal, reverberating crack. Its horrifying email address was TalentedTom@gmail .com, and though the message was brevity itself at a mere four words, it still managed to get its point across.

You are a thief.

CRIB

BY JACOB FINCH BONNER

Macmillan, New York, 2017, pages 3–4

She found out she was pregnant by throwing up on her desk in calculus. Samantha had been finishing up some notes on the problem set, making sure she had the right assignment as everyone left. (She had a theory that Mr. Fortis, who was generally a moron, didn't actually look through the equations themselves; he just checked to make sure the problems were the ones he'd actually given out.) Then she'd gotten to her feet, swooned like somebody in a soap opera, put out her arms to brace herself above the desk, and hurled all over her own notebook. Her very next cogent thought was: Fuck.

She was fifteen years old and not an idiot, thanks very much. Or maybe she was, but this wasn't happening because she'd been ignorant or naïve, or because she'd thought nothing bad (this was bad) could ever happen to *her*. It was because a true bastard had told her an outright lie. And probably more than one.

The vomit was slimy and kind of yellow and the sight of it made her want to throw up again. Her head was aching because that's what happened when you threw up, but the main thing concerning her now was the way her skin had kind of jumped to life all over her body in a really unpleasant way. That was probably also a sign of pregnancy, it occurred to her. Or just rage. It was clear to her that she had both.

She picked up her notebook, carried it to the metal trash bin in the corner of the room, and shook the thing over it; a gob of slime slid off, then she dried it the rest of the way with her shirtsleeve, because honestly she was past caring. In the last thirty seconds of her life, years of goals had simply disappeared. She was pregnant. She was pregnant. That complete fuck.

Samantha was not an especially lucky girl, she was well aware. *Clueless* had played at the movie theater in Norwich the previous summer; she knew there were girls her own age who drove cars around Beverly Hills and put together their outfits on a computer, and that obviously wasn't her, but at the same time she wasn't contending with violent child abuse or abject poverty, either. There was food in the house. There was school, which meant books, and they had cable, and her parents had even taken her down to New York City twice, but on both occasions they'd seemed mystified by what they should do once they actually got there: meals in the hotel, a bus that drove around with a guide making jokes she didn't understand, the Empire State Building (it made sense the first time, but the second time also?) and Rockefeller Center (also twice, and neither trip was around the holidays, so . . . why?). Not that she was all that knowledgeable, herself, about what the greatest city in the world might have to offer three yokels from the middle of New York state (which might as well have been the middle of Indiana) but she'd only been nine the first time and then twelve the second so it really shouldn't have been up to her.

The main thing she did have, which most people didn't, was a future.

Her parents had jobs and her father's was for the college in Hamilton, where his title was something important-sounding like "plant engineer" but it really meant he was the one who got called when some girl tried to flush a Kotex. Her mother cleaned too, but at the College Inn: her title was the far more honest "housekeeper." But what her father's job in particular really signified was something she'd had to explain to him, rather than the other way around: his fourteen years of service to the institution was a leg up when it came time for her to go to college herself, and a significant chunk of change to pay her way. According to her father's own employment handbook, which he himself had never read but which Samantha had been on intimate terms with for a couple of years, the college gave every consideration to the children of its faculty and staff when it came to admissions, and when it came to financial aid, that was actually spelled out in black and white: 80 percent scholarship, 10 percent student loan, 10 percent on-campus employment. In other words, for a person like Samantha, something along the lines of a golden ticket in a chocolate bar.

Or at least that had been true until today.

Her shitstorm was not to be blamed on substandard sex education at Earlville Middle School, let alone Chenango County (where the locals had done everything possible to prevent its young people from learning how babies were made); Samantha had been fully cognizant of the details since the fifth grade, when her father said something about an especially eventful weekend at one of the fraternities (an incident which had necessitated the presence of the police and resulted in a girl dropping out). She was used to finding things out for herself, especially when those things were cloaked in the distinctive parental silence of stuff-you-weren't-supposed-to-know-about. Over the following years, her peers caught up to her in basic knowledge (again, no thanks to the official policies of the school district and the state, which had actually declined to mandate sex education) but the knowledge was just that: basic. Two girls in her class of sixty had already moved to "homeschooling" and one had gone to live with a relative in Utica. But those girls were stupid. This was the kind of thing that was *supposed* to happen to stupid people.

She gathered up the rest of her stuff and left the classroom as a pregnant person. Then she went to her locker as a pregnant person and she joined the others outside and got on her bus, taking her customary seat at the back, but now as a pregnant person, meaning a person who, if she did nothing, was going to eventually produce another person and therefore let go of the reins of her own life, probably forever.

But obviously she wasn't going to do nothing.

CHAPTER ELEVEN

Talented Tom

He told no one. Of course.

He went to San Francisco and the Castro Theatre, and then, the following day, on to Los Angeles where the meetings went about as well as he could have hoped (and the thrill of being in a room with Steven Spielberg numbed his distress for days), but in time he had to return to New York, to the work on his next novel and to the new and sparsely furnished apartment in the West Village. By then, he'd nearly managed to persuade himself that the email had been a kind of phantasm, conjured by his own paranoia, propelled by some random bot under the control of an intentionless algorithm. That didn't last. Waking up on his unadorned box spring and mattress combo the day after his flight, he reached for his phone and found that a second message had landed in his in-box, again forwarded from the JacobFinchBonner website contact form and featuring the same You are a thief. This time, though, it also said: We both know it.

The website had been converted from his old writing coach site, and now looked like the sites of most successful writers: an About Me page, media and review attention for his individual books, a list of upcoming events, and a contact form that had been in heavy usage since *Crib*'s publication the previous year. Who was getting in touch? Readers who wanted him to know what was wrong with his book, or that *Crib* had kept them up all night (in a good way). Librarians hoping he'd come to speak and actors sure they were right for the parts of Samantha or Maria, plus pretty much every single person Jake had ever known and lost touch with: Long Island, Wesleyan, his MFA program, even those fools he'd worked for in Hell's Kitchen. Every time he saw one of these in his own in-box, with its tantalizing half-line of content (Hi, I don't know if you remember me but— Jake! I just finished your— Hello, I was at your reading at—) his chest tightened, and it stayed that way until the message turned out to be from a former classmate or a friend of his mother or a person whose book he'd signed at some bookstore in Michigan, or even a random crazy guy who believed an entity from Alpha Centauri had dictated *Crib* through an orange peel in Jake's fruit bowl.

And then there were the *writers*. Writers requesting mentorship. Writers requesting blurbs. Writers requesting an introduction (with endorsement, obviously) to Matilda, his agent, or Wendy, his editor. Writers wanting to know if he'd read their manuscripts and give an opinion as to whether they should let go of their lifelong dream or "hold on." Writers wanting him to confirm their theories about discrimination in the publishing world—Anti-Semitism! Sexism! Racism! Ageism!—as the sole and true reason their 800-page experimental non-linear punctuation-free neo-novel had been turned down by every publisher in the country.

In the months after his book was sold, Jake had formally (and gratefully) left behind both his MFA and private coaching work, but he fully understood that he now had a special responsibility to not be an asshole to other writers. Writers who were assholes to other writers were asking for it: social media had seen to that, and social media now claimed a significant portion of his mental bandwidth. He'd been a relatively early adopter on Twitter, that playground of word people, though he seldom posted anything, himself. (What was he supposed to tell his 74 "followers"? *Hello from upstate New York, where I didn't write today!*) Facebook had seemed harmless until the 2016 election, when it bombarded him with dubious ads and "push" polls about Hillary Clinton's supposedly nefarious deeds. Instagram mainly seemed to want him to prepare photogenic meals and frolic with adorable pets, neither of which were a part of his Cobleskill existence. But after *Crib* was purchased and he'd begun sitting down with Macmillan's publicity and marketing teams, Jake had been prevailed upon to maintain a vigorous presence on these three platforms at least, and given the option of stepping up his activity or handing the task over to a staff member to operate on his behalf. That had been a harder decision than it should have been. He'd certainly seen the appeal of offloading the chore of being tweeted at and DM'd and poked and contacted by every other avenue of connection the internet had dreamed up, but he'd still, in the end, opted to be the one in control, and since the day his book was published he'd been starting his days with a sweep of his social media accounts and a review of the Google alerts he'd set up to trawl the internet—Jacob+Finch+Bonner, Jake+Bonner, Bonner+Crib, Bonner+Writer, etc. It was time-consuming and irritating drudgery, and crammed with rabbit holes, most of which drilled straight into his personal labyrinth of unhappiness. So why hadn't he accepted the offer of some Macmillan intern or marketing assistant to do it?

Because of this. Obviously.

You are a thief. We both know it.

And yet, the messenger that was "TalentedTom@gmail.com" had not made his move on the open battlefields of Twitter, Facebook, or Instagram, or been netted by a Google alert. This guy hadn't gone public at all; instead, he'd opted for the more private transom provided on Jake's website. Was there some implicit negotiation here: *Deal with me now, by this single vector, or deal with me later, everywhere?* Or was it a shot across his private bow, a warning to brace for some imminent Battle of Trafalgar?

Jake had known, from that first moment in the back of the car to the Seattle airport, that this was no random message, and TalentedTom was no jealous novelist or disappointed reader or even troubled advocate of the Alpha Centaura/orange peel (or comparable!) origin story of his famous novel. Many years earlier, the adjective "talented" had been bound in eternal, indelible symbiosis to the name "Tom" by one Patricia Highsmith, forever augmenting its meaning to include a certain form of self-preservation and extreme lack of regard for others. That particular talented Tom had also happened to be a murderer. And what was his surname?

Ripley.

As in: Ripley. Where he and Evan Parker had so fatefully crossed paths.

The message was violently clear: whoever TalentedTom was, he knew. And he wanted Jake to know that he knew. And he wanted Jake to know that he meant business.

The person was a single click of the Return button away, but the notion of opening that aperture between the two of them was fraught with danger. Responding meant that Jake was afraid, that he took the accusation seriously, that TalentedTom, whoever he was, deserved the dignity of recognition. And showing even a tiny portion of himself to this malevolent stranger frightened Jake more than the diffuse and horrible notion of what might come next.

So, once again, he did not respond. Instead, he shakily consigned this second communiqué to the same place its predecessor was languishing, a folder on his laptop he'd labeled "Trolls." (This had in fact been established fully six months earlier, and already housed a few dozen illiterate attacks on *Crib,* no fewer than three of which accused him of being a member of the "Deep State," and a handful of emails from someone in Texas that referenced the "blood-brain barrier," which Jake had evidently crossed, or which had been crossed within him—the messages were, by their very nature, confounding.) But even as he did this he knew it was its own pointless gesture; the TalentedTom communications were different. Whoever he was, this person had managed to become, in the blink of an eye, among the most significant in Jake's life. And certainly the most terrifying.

Within minutes of receiving this second message Jake had powered off his phone, unplugged his router, and assumed a fetal position on the grubby couch he'd been hauling around since college, and there he remained for the following four days, working his way through a dozen cupcakes from Magnolia on Bleecker Street (some of them, at least, had healthy green icing) and the congratulatory bottle of Jameson that Matilda had sent after the film sale. There were, in these blurry hours, interludes of blissful numbness in which he actually forgot what was happening, but many more of sheer anguish during which he parsed and projected the many ways in which it could all be about to unfold: the various humiliations awaiting him, the revulsion of every single person he'd ever known, envied, felt superior to, had a crush on, or—lately—been in business with. At certain moments, and as if to usher in the inevitable and at least get it over with, he composed his own media campaign of punishing self-accusations, declaiming his crimes to the world. At other points he wrote himself long and rambling speeches of justification, and even longer and more rambling apologies. None of it even made a dent in his whirling, howling terror.

When Jake did, finally, surface, it wasn't because he'd managed to achieve some perspective or make anything resembling a plan; it was because he'd finished the whiskey and the cupcakes and developed a strong suspicion that the bad new smell he'd lately become aware of was coming from *inside the apartment*. After he'd opened a window, cleared the dishes away, and hauled himself through the shower, he reconnected his phone and laptop to the world and found a dozen increasingly concerned texts from his parents, a faux-cheerful email from Matilda, inquiring (again!) about the new book, and over two hundred additional messages requiring serious attention, including a third from TalentedTom@gmail.com:

I know you stole your "novel" and I know who you stole it from.

For some reason, that "novel" just put him over the edge.

He added it to the Trolls folder. Then, bowing to the inevitable, he made a new folder, just for the three TalentedTom messages. After a moment, he named it Ripley.

With great effort, he returned to the world beyond his own computer and phone and head, and forced himself to acknowledge some of the other things—some of them very nice things—that were also happening, more or less concurrently. *Crib* had recaptured the number one slot on the paperback bestseller list, thanks to the broadcast of his book club interview with Oprah Winfrey, and Jake had appeared on the cover of the October *Poets & Writers* (not exactly a periodical on the order of *People* or *Vanity Fair*, okay, but this had been a pipe dream of his all the way back to his Wesleyan days). He'd also received an invitation from Bouchercon to do a keynote speech, and he was being updated about an entire English tour organized around the Hay-on-Wye festival.

All good. All good.

And then there was Anna Williams of Seattle, and that was more than good.

Within days of their meeting, he and Anna had settled into what even Jake could not deny was a *warm* way of communicating with each other, and with the exception of that four-day sojourn on the couch with the cupcakes and the Jameson they'd been in at least daily contact via text. Jake now knew much more about Anna's daily life in West Seattle, her challenges (small and not-small) at KBIK, the avocado plant she struggled to keep alive in her kitchen window, her nickname for her boss, Randy Johnson, and the personal mantra she'd received from her favorite communications professor at the University of Washington: *Nobody else gets to live your life.* He knew that she really wanted to get a cat, but her landlord wouldn't permit it, and that she ate salmon at least four times a week, and that she secretly preferred what came out of her ancient Mr.

Coffee machine to anything she could get in Seattle's rarefied temples to java. He knew that she seemed to care as much about the Jake Bonner who predated the advent of *Crib* as she did about his current, weirdly bold-faced existence. That meant everything. That was the game changer.

He cleaned up his apartment. He began rewarding himself with a daily Skype call to Seattle: Anna on her front porch, himself at his living room window overlooking Abingdon Square. She started to read the novels he recommended. He started to try the wines she liked. He went back to work on his new novel and put in a solid month of focused effort, which brought him tantalizingly close to a finished first draft. Good things upon good things.

And then, toward the end of October, another message came through the JacobFinchBonner website:

> What will Oprah say when she finds out about you? At least James Frey had the decency to steal from himself.

He opened the new folder on his laptop and added this to the others. A few days later, there was a fifth:

> I'm on Twitter now. Thought you'd like to know. @TalentedTom

He went to look, and indeed there was a new account, but no actual tweets yet. It had the generic egg for a profile picture and a grand total of zero followers. Its profile bio consisted of one word: *Writer*.

He had been letting the clock run out without even attempting to identify his opponent. That had not been a good decision. TalentedTom, he suspected, was preparing to enter a new phase, and Jake had no time left to waste.

CHAPTER TWELVE

I'm Nobody. Who Are You?

Evan Parker was dead: to begin with. There was no doubt whatever about that. Jake had seen the death notice three years earlier. He had even perused an online memorial page, which, though not terribly well populated, did contain the reminiscences of a dozen people who'd known Parker, and they, certainly, seemed to be under the impression that he was dead. It was a simple matter to find that page again, and he wasn't at all surprised to see that there had been no additional entries to the memorial since his last visit:

> Evan and I grew up together in Rutland. We did baseball and wrestling together. He was a real natural leader and always kept the teams spirits up. Knew he'd had his struggles in the past, but thought he was doing really well. So sorry to hear about what happened.
>
> Took classes with Evan at RCC. Such a cool dude. Can't believe this. RIP man.

I grew up in the same town as Evan's family. These poor people had the worst luck.

I remember Evan when he played baseball for West Rutland. Never knew him personally but a great first baseman. Really sorry he had such demons.

Bye Evan, I'll miss you. RIP.

Met Evan in our MFA program up in Ripley. Super talented writer, great guy. Shocked that this happened to him.

Please accept my condolences for your loss, all family and friends of the deceased. May his memory be a blessing.

But there seemed not to be any *close* friends, and no reference to any spouse or significant other. What could Jake learn from this that he hadn't already known?

That Evan Parker had played sports in high school. That he'd had "struggles" and "demons"—perhaps they were the same?—at least at one point and then, apparently, again. That something suggestive of "worst luck" attached to him and his family. That at least one Ripley student remembered Evan from the program. How well had this student known him? Well enough to have been told the same extraordinary plot Evan had told Jake? Well enough to now be concerning himself with the "theft" of his classmate's unwritten novel?

The Ripley student who'd left the tribute had signed his first name only: Martin. That wasn't particularly helpful as far as Jake's memory went, but fortunately the 2013 Ripley MFA student roster was still on his computer, and he opened up the old spreadsheet. Ruth Steuben had likely never read a story or a poem in her life, but she'd been a great believer in orderly record keeping, and alongside each student's address, phone number, and email address a column had been given over to their genre of concentration: either an *F* for fiction or a *P* for poetry.

The only Martin was a Martin Purcell of South Burlington, Vermont, and he had an *F* next to his name. Even after looking up Purcell's Facebook profile and seeing multiple shots of his smiling face, however, Jake didn't recognize the guy, which might have meant he'd been assigned to one of the other fiction writers on the faculty, but it might also mean he'd simply been unmemorable, perhaps even to a teacher genuinely interested in knowing his students (which had never been Jake, as he'd recognized about himself even then). Apart from Evan Parker, the only people he remembered from that particular group were the guy who'd wanted to correct Victor Hugo's "mistakes" in a new version of *Les Misérables* and the woman who'd conjured the indelible non-word "honeymelons." The rest, like the faces and names of fiction writers from his third teaching year, and his second, and his first, were gone.

He commenced a deep dive on Martin Purcell, during which he paused only to order and eat some chicken from RedFarm and exchange at least twenty text messages with Anna (mainly about Randy Johnson's latest antics and a weekend trip she was planning to Port Townsend), and he learned that the guy was a high school teacher who brewed his own beer, supported the Red Sox, and had a pronounced interest in the classic California group, the Eagles. Purcell taught history and was married to a woman named Susie who seemed to be very engaged in local politics. He was a ridiculous over-sharer on Facebook, mostly about his beagle, Josephine, and his kids, but he posted nothing at all about any writing he might currently be doing, and he mentioned no writer friends nor any writers he was reading or had admired in the past. In fact, if it weren't for the Ripley College reference in his educational background you'd never know from Facebook that Martin Purcell even read fiction, let alone aspired to write it.

Purcell had a heart-sinking 438 Facebook friends. Who among them might be people he'd crossed paths with at the Ripley Symposia's low-residency Master of Fine Arts Program in 2012 or 2013? Jake went back to Ruth Steuben's spreadsheet and cross-referenced half a dozen names, then he started down those Ripley rabbit holes. But he had no idea what he was looking for, really.

Julian Zigler, attorney in West Hartford, who mainly did real estate and worked at a firm with sixty grinning attorneys, overwhelmingly male, overwhelmingly white. Completely unfamiliar face.

Eric Jin-Jay Chang, resident in hematology at Brigham and Women's Hospital.

Paul Brubacker, "scribbler" of Billings, Montana. (The Victor Hugo guy!)

Pat d'Arcy, artist from Baltimore, another face Jake could have sworn he'd never seen before. Six weeks ago, Pat d'Arcy had published a very short story on a flash fiction website called Partitions. One of the many conveyances of congratulations was from Martin Purcell:

> Pat! Awesome story! I'm so proud of you! Have you posted on the Symposia page?

The Symposia page.

It turned out to be an unofficial alumni page, through which half a dozen years' worth of low-residency graduates had been sharing work and information and gossip since 2010. Jake flew back and back through the posts: poetry contests, news of an encouraging rejection from the *West Texas Literary Review,* an announcement of a first novel's acceptance by a hybrid publisher in Boston, wedding photos, a reunion of 2011 poets in Brattleboro, a reading at an art gallery in Lewiston, Maine. Then, in October of 2013, the name "Evan" began to pop up in the messages.

Only "Evan." Of course. Jake supposed this was why the alumni page hadn't appeared in his initial "Evan Parker" searches. Naturally, the Evan in question would only require his first name, at least to anyone and everyone who'd known him. *Evan,* the triumphant rescuer of the kidnapped bottle opener. *Evan,* the guy who sat at the seminar table with his arms tightly folded across his chest. Everyone would know an asshole like that.

> Guys, I can't believe this. Evan died last Monday. Really sorry to have to share.

(This, it was hardly surprising, had been posted by Martin Purcell, Ripley 2011–2012.)

> Oh my god! What?

> Fuck!

> Holy shit that's so awful. What do you know Martin?

> We were supposed to meet up at his tavern last Sunday, I was coming down from Burlington. Then he didn't text me back. I figured he blew me off or forgot or something. Few days later I called him and I got a disconnect notice. I just had a bad feeling. So I Googled and it came right up. I knew he'd had some problems in the past, but Evan had been sober for a while.

> Oh man, that poor guy.

> That's my third friend to overdose! I mean, when are they going to call it what it is? AN EPIDEMIC.

Well, thought Jake. This certainly confirmed his assumption about what "unexpectedly," "struggles," and "demons" signified.

Jake's phone buzzed.

Crab Pot Seattle, Anna had written. There was a photo of a tangle of crab legs and cut-up ears of corn. Beyond that: a window, a harbor.

Jake went back to his laptop and googled the words "Evan+Parker+tavern," and a story from the *Rutland Herald* came up: Parker Tavern, a not-too-classy-looking spot on State Street in Rutland, was under new ownership following the death of its longtime owner, Evan Parker of West Rutland. Jake stared at the building, a run-down Victorian, the kind you'd find on most major streets in most New England towns. It had once probably been someone's lovely home, but now it had a green neon PARKER TAVERN FOOD AND LIQUOR over the front door, and what looked like a hand-painted sign announcing *Happy Hour 3–6*.

On his phone, the single word: Hello?

Jake wrote back: Yum.

Enough for two, she wrote immediately.

In the *Rutland Herald* story the new owners, Jerry and Donna Hastings of West Rutland, hoped to preserve the bar's traditional interior, eclectic draft selection, and, above all, warm and welcoming ambiance as a meeting place for the community and visitors alike. When asked about their decision to retain "Parker Tavern" as the bar's name, Jerry Hastings answered that it was out of respect: the late owner's family went back five generations in central Vermont, and before his tragic and untimely death Evan Parker had worked for years to make the tavern the success it was.

Okay then! Anna texted. Obviously not feeling chatty at the moment. No worries! Or maybe you're communing with your muse.

He picked up his phone again. No such thing as the muse. No such thing as "inspiration." It's all deeply unspiritual.

Oh? What happened to "everybody has a unique voice and a story only they can tell"?

It's gone to live with the Yeti and the Sasquatch and the Loch Ness Monster in Atlantis. But I actually am working right now. Can we talk later? I'll bring the Merlot.

How will you know which one?

I'll ask you. Of course.

He went back to Ruth Steuben's spreadsheet for Martin Purcell's email address, opened up Gmail, and wrote:

Hi Martin, this is Jake Bonner, from the Ripley program. Sorry to email you out of the blue, but wondered if I could give you a call about something? Let me know when might be a good time to chat, or feel free to phone me whenever you like. Very best to you, Jake.

And he added his phone number.

The dude called immediately.

"Oh wow," he said as soon as Jake answered. "I can't believe you emailed me. This isn't some kind of Ripley fundraising thing, is it? Because I can't right now."

"No, no," Jake said. "Nothing like that. Look, we've probably met, but I don't have my Ripley files with me so I'm not sure if you were in my class or not."

"I wish I was in your class. That guy I got assigned to, all he wanted us to do was write about place. *Place, place, place*. Like, every blade of grass had to have its own backstory. That was his thing."

He had to be talking about Bruce O'Reilly, the retired Colby professor and profoundly Maine-centric novelist with whom Jake had had an annual beer at The Ripley Inn. Jake hadn't thought about Bruce O'Reilly in years.

"That's too bad. It's better if they move students around. Then everyone gets to work with everyone."

It had also been years since he'd given any thought at all to the institutionalized teaching of creative writing. He hadn't missed it.

"I have to tell you, I loved your book. Man, that twist, I was like, holy crap."

No special significance to "that twist," Jake noted with intense relief. Certainly no: *And I've got a pretty good idea where that came from.*

"Well, that's kind of you to say. But the reason I got in touch, I just heard that a student of mine passed away. And I saw your post on that Ripley Facebook page. So I thought—"

"Evan, you're talking about. Right?" said Martin Purcell.

"Yes. Evan Parker. He was my student."

"Oh, I know." All the way up in northern Vermont Jake could hear Martin Purcell chuckle. "I'm sorry to say, not your fan, though. But I wouldn't take that too personally. Evan didn't think anyone at Ripley was good enough to be his teacher."

Jake took a moment to run through this sentence slowly. "I see," he said.

"I could tell within an hour or two, just that first night of the residency, Evan wasn't going to get much out of the program. If you're going to learn something, you need to have curiosity about it. He didn't have that. But he was still a cool guy to hang around with. Lot of charm. Lot of fun."

"And you kept in touch with him, obviously."

"Oh yeah. Sometimes he came up to Burlington, for a concert or something. We went to the Eagles together. I think he came up for Foo Fighters, too. And sometimes I drove down. He had a tavern down in Rutland, you know."

"Well, I don't really know. Would you mind telling me a little bit more? I just feel so badly I'm only hearing about this now. I would have written to his family when it happened."

“Hey, would you give me a second?” said Martin Purcell. “Let me just tell my wife I’m on a call. I’ll be right back.”

Jake waited. “I hope I’m not taking you away from anything important,” he said, when Purcell returned.

“Not at all. I said I’ve got a famous novelist on the phone. That kind of trumps talking to our fifteen-year-old about the party we don’t want her going to.” He stopped to laugh at his own wit. Jake forced himself to join in.

“So, do you know anything about Evan’s family? I suppose it’s too late for a condolence note.”

“Well, even if it’s not, I don’t know who you’d send it to. His parents died a long time ago. He had a sister who also passed, before he did.” He paused. “Hey, I’m sorry if this sounds rude, but I never got the impression you two had much of a . . . rapport. I’m a teacher, myself, so I’m sympathetic to anyone who has to deal with a difficult student. I wouldn’t have wanted to be Evan’s teacher. Every class has that person who slouches in his chair and just glares at you, like, *Who the fuck do you think you are?*”

“And *What makes you think you have a damn thing you can teach me?*”

“Exactly.”

Jake had been jotting down notes: *parents, sister—deceased.*

He knew all that from the obituary.

“Yeah, that was definitely Evan in that particular class. But I was used to having an Evan. My first year of teaching, my answer to ‘Who the fuck do you think you are?’ would have been ‘I’m nobody. Who are you?’”

He could hear Martin laugh. “Dickinson.”

“Yeah. And I’d have been out of the room.”

“Crying in the bathroom.”

“Well.” Jake frowned.

“I meant me. Crying in the bathroom. First year as a student teacher. You have to toughen up. But most of those kids, they’re just marshmallows, really. And seriously miserable, in their own lives. Sometimes they're the ones you worry about most of all, because they have no sense of themselves, no confidence at all. But that wasn't Evan. I've seen plenty of false bravado—that wasn't Evan either. He had absolute faith in his ability to write a great book. Or maybe it's more accurate to say he thought writing a great book wasn't all that hard, and why shouldn't he be able to do it? Most of us weren't like that."

Here Jake noted a cue—endemic among writers—to ask about Martin's own work.

"I haven't made much progress since finishing the program, to be honest."

"Yes. Every day's a challenge."

"You seem to be doing okay," Martin said. There was an edge to that.

"Not with my book in progress."

He was surprised to hear himself say it. He was surprised that he'd given Martin Purcell of Burlington, Vermont, a complete stranger, more of a suggestion of his vulnerability than he'd given his own editor or agent.

"Well, sorry to hear that."

"No it's okay, just need to push through. Hey, do you know where Evan was with his own book? Did he get much done after the residency? He was just at the start, I think. At least the pages I saw."

Martin said nothing, for the longest seconds of Jake's life. Finally, he apologized. "I'm just trying to remember if he ever talked about that. I don't think he ever told me how it was going. But if he was using again, and it looks like he was, I really doubt he was sitting down at his desk and turning out pages."

"Well, how many pages do you think he had?"

Again, that uncomfortable pause.

"Were you thinking of doing something for him? I mean, for his work? Because that's incredibly kind of you. Especially since he wasn't exactly a fawning acolyte, if you know what I mean."

Jake took a breath. He was not, of course, entitled to the approbation, but he supposed he'd better go with it.

"I just thought, you know, maybe there's a completed story I could send somewhere. You don't have any pages, yourself, I suppose."

"No. But you know, I wouldn't say we're talking about Nabokov, here, leaving behind an unfinished novel. I think you can consign the unwritten fiction of Evan Parker to history without too much guilt."

"I'm sorry?" Jake gasped.

"As his teacher."

"Oh. Yeah."

"Because I remember thinking—and I liked the guy—that he had to be pretty far off base the way he talked about this book. Like it was *The Shining* and *The Grapes Of Wrath* and *Moby-Dick,* all rolled into one, and what a huge success it was going to be. He did show me a couple of pages about this girl who hated her mother, or maybe it was the mother who hated her, and they were okay, but, you know, it wasn't exactly *Gone Girl.* I just kind of looked at him, like, *Yeah, dude, whatever*. I don't know, I just thought he was kind of ridiculously full of himself. But you've probably come across a lot of people like that. Man," said Martin Purcell, "I sound like an asshole. And I liked the guy. It's really decent of you to want to help him."

"I just wanted to do something good," Jake said, deflecting as best he could. "And since there isn't any family . . ."

"Well, maybe a niece. I think I read about her in the obituary."

Me, too, Jake didn't say. In fact, he hadn't learned a single thing from Martin Purcell that hadn't been in that bare-bones obituary.

"Okay," Jake said. "Look, thanks for talking to me."

"Hey! Thanks for calling. And . . ."

"What?" said Jake.

"Well, I'm going to kick myself in exactly five minutes if I don't ask you this, but . . ."

"What is it?" said Jake, who knew perfectly well.

"I was wondering, I know you're busy. But would you be willing to look at some of my stuff? I'd love to have your honest opinion. It would mean so much to me."

Jake closed his eyes. "Of course," he said.

CRIB

BY JACOB FINCH BONNER

Macmillan, New York, 2017, pages 23–25

They wanted to know *Who was it?* of course. Apparently even more than *What the fuck did she think she was doing?* and obviously far more than *How had they failed her as parents?* Whatever the details, this clearly was not *their fault,* and it wasn't going to be *their problem*. But *who it was* wasn't information Samantha felt like parting with, so her choices were, one, to withhold or, two, to lie outright. Lying, as a general principle, didn't matter to her one way or the other, but the issue with lying, at least about this particular thing, was that there were *tests*—you'd have to never have watched Jerry Springer not to know about the *tests*—and anyone she named (that is, anyone *else* she named) could eventually be shown not to be the person, which would in turn have revealed the lie and initiated the whole sequence again: *Who was it?*

So she went with the withholding.

"Look, it's not important."

"Our fifteen-year-old daughter's pregnant and it's not important who got her that way."

Pretty much, Samantha thought.

"Like you said, it's my problem."

"Yeah, it is," said her father. He didn't seem as angry as her mother. He was more his customary shut down.

"So what's the plan?" said her mother. "They been telling us for years how smart you are. And you go and do this."

She couldn't look at their blasted faces, so she went upstairs and slammed her bedroom door behind her, throwing her book bag on the floor next to the old desk. Her room was in the back, overlooking the slope down to Porter Creek, which was narrow and rocky through this patch of the woods and wide and rocky to the north and the south. The house was old, more than a hundred years. It had been the house of her father and his parents, and before that, the house of her great-grandparents. She guessed that meant it was supposed to be hers one day, but that had never mattered to her before and it didn't matter now, since she wasn't going to live here a minute longer than necessary. That—in point of fact—had always been the plan and it was still the plan. Just as soon as she sorted out her problem, finished up her credits, and got her scholarship to college.

Who it was was a person named Daniel Weybridge, who was also none other than her mother's boss at the College Inn and in fact the *proprietor* of the College Inn, like his father before him, because the place was *Family run for three generations!*—it said so on the inn's sign, its stationery, even on the paper coasters left in every room. Daniel Weybridge was married and the father of three bouncing boys, who would certainly be the next proprietors of the College Inn. He'd also had a vasectomy, or so he'd promised, the lying shit. No, she hadn't told him she was pregnant, and she wasn't going to. He didn't deserve to know.

The story with Daniel Weybridge was that he'd been after her for at least a year to her knowledge, and probably longer than that, since before she'd been paying attention. Any number of times she'd skittered past him in a corridor of the inn, or in one of the hallways at the high school when he turned up to watch one of the three precious sons play whatever sport they were playing, and she'd felt the heat of him as they passed each other, and sensed the fixing of his attention on her fifteen-year-old self as they crossed paths. Of course he had been far too stealthy to make an outright grab. He led with attention, then moved on to compliments and little hints of genuine grown-up admiration: *Samantha had skipped a grade—wasn't that remarkable! Samantha had won some prize, he'd heard—what a smart girl, destined to go far!* It pained her to admit that these had not been ineffective tactics. Daniel Weybridge, after all, was what passed for a sophisticate in her world. For one thing, he'd gone to the hotel school at Cornell, which was an Ivy League, and he read the newspapers from the city, not just the Utica *Observer-Dispatch*. Once, in the hotel lobby as she was waiting for her mother to finish up, the two of them had a surprisingly nuanced conversation about *The Scarlet Letter*, which Samantha was reading for eighth-grade English, and Daniel Weybridge had made a point that actually found its way into her paper. A paper for which, fittingly, she had received an A.

So when it dawned on her, as it eventually did, that there was a longer game being played here, and her mother's boss was the one playing it, Samantha was a little more surprised than she should have been. Then she took a fresh look at things herself.

By then she was a tenth grader, though a full year younger than the next youngest in her grade. Most of her classmates—*all* of the boys, if you believed them, except maybe the shyest and most backward—were busy deflowering most of the girls, and if you didn't count the trashed reputations of those two young ladies who'd already left school, nobody seemed especially exercised about it. Moments like these had a way of bringing the age difference into sharper focus, and though Samantha had been more than happy to skip that grade back in sixth she didn't especially enjoy the feeling of being *younger* than everyone else. Besides, there was nothing especially meaningful—let alone romantic—about the act in question, just as there was nothing especially obscure about what Daniel Weybridge wanted or how he was trying to get it.

Still, it had all been her decision. The stakes didn't seem all that high.

If she did nothing, Daniel Weybridge would probably continue flattering and flirting with her until the day she left home, and when that day came he'd simply shrug and turn his attention to the next daughter of the next housekeeper, or the housekeeper herself. But the more she thought about it the more she liked the idea. From a practical standpoint, she was repelled by every boy she went to school with, and Daniel Weybridge wasn't unattractive. Also, he was a grown-up and a father several times over, which meant he'd obviously know what he was doing when it came to the act itself. Also, unlike the boys in her grade who were congenitally incapable of keeping their mouths shut, it went without saying that Daniel Weybridge wasn't going to tell a soul. And finally, when she let him take her to the Fennimore Suite (not an hour after her own mother cleaned it), he made a point of telling her that he'd had a vasectomy after bouncing baby boy number three. Which sealed the deal, basically.

So maybe she really wasn't as smart as everyone had always thought she was, let alone as smart as *she'd* always thought she was. She had no idea how to go about getting rid of her problem. She didn't even know how much time she had left to figure something out. But she knew it wouldn't be enough.

CHAPTER THIRTEEN

Hurl Away

"So, you know me, I don't like to be *that pushy agent,* but . . ."

Matilda, in fact, was in every molecule of her being *that pushy agent,* which was the exact reason Jake had daydreamed, for years, about her being *his* agent. When he'd finished *Crib* after the most frenzied period of writing he'd ever experienced, it had been to Matilda Salter, and Matilda Salter alone, that he had reached out, in the most carefully written cover letter of his life:

> *Although I did have representation for* The Invention of Wonder, *and will always be proud that the novel was a "New & Noteworthy" in* The New York Times Book Review, *I'm coming back now with a very different kind of book: plot driven, suspenseful, and twisty with a strong and complex female protagonist. I would like to start fresh with an agent who understands exactly how far a book like this can go, and who will be able to handle attention from foreign markets and film interests.*

Matilda—or more likely her assistant—had responded with an invitation to send the manuscript, and things had moved with gratifying speed after that. For Jake it had all been deeply redemptive, not to say thrilling; Matilda's authors were an all-star roster of Pulitzer and National Book Award winners, permanent occupants of the better airport bookstores (and also all the other airport bookstores), literary darlings of the cognoscenti and stars of yesteryear who never needed to write another word.

"But?" he said now.

"But I had a call from Wendy. She and the gang at Macmillan are wondering if you're going to make the deadline for the new book. They don't want to pressure you. It's more important to get it right than to get it fast. But right *and* fast would be best of all."

"Yeah," Jake said miserably.

"Because, you know, honey, right now it seems like it can never happen, but it has to, at some point. Maybe only because there'll be no one left in the country who *hasn't* read *Crib*. But there's going to come a moment when all those people *will* want to read another book. We just want that book to be by you."

He nodded, as if she could see him. "I know. I'm working, don't worry."

"Oh, I'm not worried. Just inquiring. Did you see we're going back for another printing?"

"Uh . . . yeah. That's good."

"It's better than good." She paused. Jake heard her break away to say something to her assistant. Then she was back. "Okay, hon. I have to take this. Not everyone's as happy with their publisher as you are."

He thanked her and they hung up. And then, for another twenty minutes, he remained where he was on the old couch: eyes shut, dread coursing through him like a reverse meditation designed to eradicate serenity. Then he got up and went into the kitchen.

The former owner of his new apartment had done a sterile upgrade, with gray granite countertops and a gleaming steel stove suitable for someone about five levels above Jake's own cooking abilities. So far, in fact, he hadn't cooked a thing (unless you counted reheating as cooking) and his fridge contained only an assortment of takeout clamshell containers, some of them empty. His efforts to furnish the apartment had withered soon after bringing in what he already owned, and whatever intentions he'd had to address a few of the more obvious needs—a headboard for the bed, a new couch, a set of curtains for the bedroom window—had further departed in the wake of TalentedTom's arrival in his life.

Unable to remember what had brought him into his own kitchen, he poured himself a glass of water and went back to his couch. In the brief time he'd been away, Anna had texted twice.

Hi you.

Then, a few minutes later:

Are you there?

Hi! he typed back. Sorry. Was on the phone. What are you up to?

Looking at Expedia, she wrote. Flights to NYC surprisingly cheap.

Good to know. I've been thinking of going there. They say the neon lights are bright.

For a moment nothing. Then: I would love to see a Broadway show.

Jake smiled. They actually don't let you leave the city without seeing one. I'm afraid you'll have no choice.

She had some vacation days, apparently. She could take them any time.

But really, Anna wrote, how do you feel about my visiting? I want to be sure this isn't just me, hurling myself at you from the other side of the country.

Jake took a gulp of his water. How I feel is: hurl away. Please. I would love to have you here, even for a couple of days.

And you can take the time from work?

Actually, he couldn't.

Yes of course.

They arranged for her to arrive at the end of the month, and stay for a week, and after they stopped texting Jake went online and ordered a headboard and a pair of bedroom curtains. It actually wasn't difficult at all.

CHAPTER FOURTEEN

Something Out of a Novel

Anna arrived on a Friday in late November, and Jake went down to meet her cab. There were still police barriers in front of his West Village apartment building, and as she got out of the car he saw her look at them rather nervously.

"Filming," he said. "*Law and Order.* Last night."

"Well, that's a relief. I was thinking, I just got to New York and I'm already at a crime scene?" After a moment they hugged awkwardly. Then they hugged again, less awkwardly.

She had cut her hair a couple of inches, and just that small change carried with it a hint of transformation: Seattle grunge to some version of Gotham chic. She wore a trench coat over black jeans, and a gray sweater a couple of shades lighter than that silver hair, and a single misshapen pearl on a chain around her neck. After weeks of wondering how he'd feel when he saw her again, he was powerfully reassured. Anna was beautiful. And she was here.

He took her out to a Brazilian restaurant he liked, and afterward she wanted to walk: down to where the World Trade Center had been, east to

South Street Seaport. He led by vague sense of direction only; he didn't know these neighborhoods, which struck her as hilarious. In Chinatown they stopped at a dessert bar and shared something made of shaved ice with about eight toppings, including actual gold leaf. He offered to get her a hotel.

She laughed at him.

Back at the apartment he made the gesture of depositing a spare blanket and pillow on that pathetic old couch. "For me," he'd suggested, when Anna came to stand beside him. "I mean, I don't want to assume."

"You're adorable," she said, before taking him into his own bedroom, where at least there were now curtains on the window. And a good thing, too.

The next day, they didn't leave the apartment.

The day after that, they managed to get out for lunch at RedFarm, but went home immediately afterward and stayed in for the rest of that day, too.

Once or twice, he apologized for monopolizing her time in the city. Surely she'd wanted more from her visit to New York than even this intimacy and—as far as he could tell—mutual pleasure?

"This is exactly what I wanted from my visit," said Anna.

But the following morning she left him to work and went to explore, and that became the way the rest of the week took form. He did his best to get a few hours in after she'd gone, and late in the afternoon he went to meet her wherever she'd wound up: the Museum of the City of New York, Lincoln Center, Bloomingdale's. She couldn't decide which Broadway show to see, and on her final night in the city they ended up at some strange thing where everyone ran around a huge warehouse in the dark, wearing masks, and it was supposedly based on *Macbeth*.

"What did you think?" he asked her as they emerged into the Chelsea night. Her flight was early in the morning and he was already dreading the moment of her departure.

"Well, it was a long way from *Oklahoma!*"

They walked down to the newly fabulous Meatpacking District and looked at the restaurants until they found one that was quiet.

"You like it here," Jake observed after the waiter had taken their order.

"It looks good."

"No, no, I mean here. New York."

"I'm afraid I do. This place, I could fall for a place like this."

"Well," said Jake, "I'll be honest, that does not make me unhappy."

She said nothing. The waiter brought their wine.

"So, this woman you met once, for an hour, and who lives on the other side of the country, comes to visit you for a couple of days and starts making noises about how much she likes New York, and you're not even slightly freaked out?"

He shrugged. "A lot of things freak me out. But oddly, not that. I'm just getting used to the idea that you liked me enough to get on a plane."

"So you're assuming I got on a plane because I liked you and not, for example, because I got a cheap flight, and I'd always wanted to run around a warehouse in a mask, pretending I'm twenty-two and not my actual age."

"You could totally pass for twenty-two," he said after a moment.

"But why would I want to? That whole thing tonight was the emperor's new clothes."

Jake threw his head back and laughed. "Okay. You've just turned in your cool millennial card. You know that."

"I couldn't care less. I don't think I was young even when I actually was young, and that wasn't yesterday."

The waiter arrived. They had each ordered the same thing: roast chicken and vegetables. Looking at the two plates, Jake wondered if they weren't, in fact, eating both halves of the same bird.

"So why weren't you young when you actually were young?" Jake said.

"Oh, it's a long and tortured story. Something out of a novel."

"I wish you'd tell me." He looked at her. "Is it hard to talk about this?"

"No, not hard. But it's still kind of a thing that I'm doing it."

"Okay." He nodded. "I am appropriately honored."

She took a moment to begin her meal, and drink from her glass.

"So the long and short of it is, my sister and I ended up in Idaho, in the town where our mother grew up. We were both pretty young, so we didn't remember a lot about her. She committed suicide, unfortunately. She drove her car into a lake."

Jake let out a breath. "Oh, I'm so sorry. That's terrible."

"And after that our mother's sister came to take care of us. But she was very strange. She never mastered the art of taking care of herself, let alone anyone else, let alone two little kids. I think we both understood that, my sister and I did. But we handled it different ways. After we started high school I could feel the two of them moving farther and farther away from me. My sister and my aunt," she clarified. "My sister pretty much stopped going to school. I pretty much stopped going home. And my teacher, Miss Royce, when she figured out what was happening in my house, she just asked if I'd like to live with her, and I said yes."

"But . . . wasn't there any kind of intervention? I mean, social services? Police?"

"The sheriff came out a couple of times to talk to my aunt, but it never quite connected with her. I think she really wanted to be capable of parenting us, but it was just beyond her abilities." Anna paused. "I bear her absolutely no ill will, by the way. Some people can paint or sing, others can't. This was a person who just could not be in the world the same way most of us can. But I do wish . . ." She shook her head. She reached for her glass.

"What?"

"Well, I tried to get my sister to come with me, but she refused. She wanted to stay with our aunt. And then one day the two of them just left town."

Jake waited. As he did, he grew more uneasy.

"And?"

"And? Nothing. I have no idea where they are. They could be anywhere, now. They could be nowhere. They could be in this restaurant." She glanced around. "Well, they're not. But that's just how it is. I stayed, they left. I finished high school. I went to college. My teacher—I got into the habit of calling her my adoptive mother, but there was never any formal process. She died. She left me a little money, which was nice. But my sister, I have no idea."

"Did you ever try to find her?" Jake asked.

Anna shook her head. "No. I think our aunt had been living a pretty marginal life before she came to take care of us. Or try to take care of us. I think, if they're still together, they're not going to be paying rent or using an ATM, let alone on Facebook. But I'm on Facebook and also Instagram, mainly for that reason. If they want to find me, I'm a few clicks away from any public computer in any library in the country. If they reach out to me I'll get an alert through my email. I try not to think about it, ever, but even so . . . every single time I turn on my computer or my phone, some part of me is wondering: Is today the day? You can't imagine what that's like, waiting for some message that's going to totally upend your life."

In fact, Jake absolutely could imagine it. But he didn't say so.

"Did it . . . I mean, did all of this make you feel depressed? As a teenager?"

She seemed not to take the question all that seriously. "I suppose. Most teenagers get depressed, don't they? I don't think I was all that introspective as a kid. And frankly I also wasn't very ambitious back then, so it's not like I felt I was being kept from something I really wanted. And then one morning, the fall of my senior year, I picked up an application off a bench outside the guidance counselor's office at my school, for the University of Washington. It had these pine trees on the cover and I just thought . . . you know, that looks so nice. It looked like home. So I filled it out right there in the office, on their computer. Three weeks later I got my letter."

The waiter returned and took their plates. They both declined dessert, but asked for more wine.

"You know," Jake said, "if you think about it, you're amazingly well-adjusted."

"Oh, right." She rolled her eyes. "I hid away on an island for the better part of a decade. I got to my mid-thirties without ever having a serious boyfriend. For the past three years I've devoted myself to making a complete imbecile sound semi-cogent and semi-informed on the air. Does that sound amazingly well-adjusted to you?"

He smiled at her. "Given what you've gone through? I think you're some kind of Wonder Woman."

"Wonder Woman was a fiction. I think I'd prefer to be an ordinary real person."

She could never be ordinary, he thought. The sheer fact of her, this lovely, gray-haired woman out of the forests of the Northwest yet seamlessly present, here, in a thrumming restaurant in the city's buzziest neighborhood, was simply norm-defying: a thunderbolt out of the blue. But what stunned him most, he realized, was the fact that he was so entirely at peace about all of it. For as long as Jake could remember he'd been torturing himself about the books he was writing, and then the ones he wasn't writing, and the people surging past him in line, and the deep and terrible fear that he wasn't good enough—or good at all—at the only thing he'd ever wanted to be good at, not to mention the fact that all around him people his own age were meeting and pairing off and pledging their allegiance to one another and even creating entirely new baby people together, while he'd barely found a woman he liked enough to date since breaking up with the poet, Alice Logan. Now, all of that was done: suddenly, peacefully, done.

"First of all," said Jake, "making your boss sound smarter than he is—that's what most people's jobs are. And Whidbey Island seems to me like a pretty nice place to spend the better part of a decade. And as far as not having a serious boyfriend, obviously, you were waiting for me."

She hadn't been looking at him through this. She'd been looking down into her own hands and the glass they held. Now, though, she looked up, and after a moment, she smiled. "Maybe I was," she said. "Maybe I thought, when I read your novel, *Now this is a brain I could stand to get to know.* Maybe when I went to your event in Seattle and I saw you, I thought, *That's a person I wouldn't be miserable looking at across the breakfast table.*"

"Breakfast table!" Jake grinned.

"And maybe when I got in touch with your publicist I wasn't just thinking how we should be trying to get some real authors on the show. Maybe I was thinking, *You know, it wouldn't actually be horrible if I could get to meet Jake Bonner.*"

"Well now. So it comes out."

Even in the restaurant's inadequate light he could see she was embarrassed.

"Look, it's fine. I'm glad you did. I'm incredibly glad."

Anna nodded, but she wasn't looking him in the eye.

"And you're positive this isn't freaking you out at all. I acted unprofessionally because I had a crush on a famous author."

He shrugged. "I once contrived to sit next to Peter Carey on the subway, because I had this fantasy that I could strike up a conversation with Australia's greatest living novelist, and we'd start having weekly Sunday brunches together where we'd discuss the state of fiction, and then he'd give my novel-in-progress to his agent . . . you get the idea."

"Well, did you?"

Jake took a sip of his wine. "Did I what?"

"Sit next to him."

He nodded. "Yeah. But I couldn't bring myself to say a word. And he got off like two stops later, anyway. No conversation, no brunch, no introduction to his agent. Just another fan on the subway. That could have been us, if you'd been as much of a wuss as I am. But you actually reached out for something you wanted. Just like you picked up that application, off the bench, and filled it out. I admire that."

Anna said nothing. She seemed overwhelmed.

"Like your old professor said, nobody else gets to own your life, right?"

She laughed. "Nobody else gets to *live* your life."

"It sounds like that pabulum we used to serve up in the MFA program. *Only you can tell your singular story with your unique voice.*"

"And that's not true?"

"That is absolutely not true. Anyway, if you're living your life, more power to you. I can't think of anyone you owe a thing to. Your adoptive mom is gone. Your sister and aunt took themselves out of the equation, for now at least. You deserve every bit of happiness that's coming to you."

She reached across the table and took his hand. "I completely agree," she said.

CRIB

BY JACOB FINCH BONNER

Macmillan, New York, 2017, pages 36–38

Her decision was: she wanted an abortion. It should have been straightforward, given the fact that her parents seemed to want an addition to their family about as little as she did. But there was an unfortunate complication, namely that her mother and father were Christians, and not the Jesus-is-love kind of Christians but the Hell-has-a-special-room-waiting-for-you kind. Also, the laws of the state of New York gave them veto power over Samantha (who was very much not a Christian of either kind, despite her hundreds of Sunday mornings in the pews of the Fellowship Tabernacle of Norwich) and over the blastocyst inches south of her navel. Did they regard said blastocyst as a beloved grandchild, or at least a beloved child of God? Samantha suspected not. She suspected, to the contrary, that the point here was to teach her some kind of "lesson" about the wages of her sin, something along the lines of *In pain you shall bring forth children*. It would all have been so much simpler if they'd just agreed to drive her to the clinic in Ithaca.

It hadn't been part of the plan for her to drop out of school as well, but the pregnancy made that decision on its own. Samantha, it turned out, was not one of those girls who could carry on, attend the prom, throw the javelin into the ninth month, and generally power through every single quiz, test, assignment, and term paper, with only the occasional hall pass for the purpose of upchucking in the girls' bathroom. No, she got diagnosed in month four with upwardly trending blood pressure, was ordered to bed for the sake of her baby's health, and forced to summarily forfeit her position as a tenth grader without a single complaint from either parent. And not one of her teachers lifted a finger to help her finish out the year, either.

For the five brutal months that remained, she gestated uncomfortably—mainly horizontally in her childhood bed, an old cannonball four-poster that had been her mother's father's, or her father's mother's—and grudgingly accepted the food that her mother brought up to her room. She read whatever books were in the house—first her own books, then her mother's from the Christian bookstore outside Oneonta—but already Samantha was noting a disruption in the hardware of her brain: sentences folding in on themselves, meaning draining away by the midpoint of a paragraph, as if even that part of her body had been scrambled by the unasked-for tenant. Both of her parents had given up on trying to ferret out the name of the impregnator; maybe they'd decided Samantha didn't know. (How many boys did they think she'd slept with? All the boys, probably.) Her father wasn't talking to her anymore, though it took Samantha some time to figure that out, given that he'd never been all that much of a talker. Her mother was still talking—or, more accurately, screaming—on a daily basis. Samantha wondered how she had the energy.

But at least there was going to be an end point to all of it, because this thing, this ordeal, was going to be *finite*. As in: it was going to *end*. And why?

She did not want to be a sixteen-year-old mother any more than she'd wanted to be a fifteen-year-old pregnant person, and here, at least, she dared to believe that her parents felt exactly the same. Therefore, in the fullness of time, the baby would be given up for adoption, and then she, the gestational host, would be returning to high school, albeit in the company of those dull classmates she'd powered past back in sixth grade: a year further from her goal of going to college and getting away from Earlville, but at least back on track.

Ah, the naivety of youth. Or had she dared to believe her parents might one day recognize that a sentient human, with her own plans and priorities and aspirations, had lived alongside them, lo these fifteen years? She dwelt in the possibilities and even took the step of reaching out to one of those "abortion counselors" (not really an "abortion counselor," as she well knew) who advertised in the back of the *Observer-Dispatch*: "A loving Christian home for your baby!" But her mother wouldn't even look at the pamphlet they sent her.

The wages of her sin, it turned out, had a shelf life of forever.

Wait a minute! she yelled at them. *I don't want this baby and you don't want this baby. Let's let somebody who does want it have it. What's the problem with that?*

The problem, apparently, was that God wanted it this way. He'd tested her, she'd failed, and thus, this was what was supposed to happen.

It was maddening, infuriating. Worse: illogical.

But she was fifteen. So that's what was going to happen.

CHAPTER FIFTEEN

Why Would She Change Her Mind?

The Twitter account had been mercifully dormant since its inception, but suddenly, in mid-December, the tweets began—not with a bang but with a whimper into the void:

> @JacobFinchBonner is a not the author of #Crib.

There was no engagement at all, Jake was relieved to see, probably because there was no one to engage with. In its six weeks on the site, the Twitter user known as @TalentedTom was still depicted as an egg with no biography and from an undeclared location. He had managed to attract only two followers, both likely bots from points far east, but the lack of an audience did not seem to deter him at all. For the next few weeks there was a steady drip, drip of caustic little declarations:

> @JacobFinchBonner is a thief.
>
> @JacobFinchBonner is a plagiarist.

Anna went back to Seattle to settle some things. When she returned, Jake drove her out to Long Island for the traditional Bonner Hanukkah with his father's siblings and their children. He had never before brought a guest to this event, and there was a certain amount of derisory attention from his cousins, but the plank-roasted salmon Anna contributed to the meal was met with stunned gratitude.

Technically, she still hadn't entirely taken leave of her prior life—the apartment in West Seattle had been sublet and her furniture moved to a storage facility—but she straightaway found a job at a podcasting studio in Midtown and another as a producer on a Sirius show covering the tech industry. In spite of the fact that she'd grown up in a small Idaho town, it took her no time at all to ramp up to the speed with which every other New Yorker raced down the streets, and within days of her return to the city she seemed to become yet another overworked Gothamite, perpetually rushing and with a baseline level of ambient stress that would probably have alarmed anyone outside the five boroughs. But she was happy. Seriously happy, expressively happy. She began every day by wrapping herself around him and kissing his neck. She learned what he liked to eat and seamlessly took over the task of feeding them both (a great relief, as Jake never had learned to properly feed himself). She dove into the cultural life of the city and brought Jake along with her, and soon it was a rare night they were home and not at a play or a concert, or poking around Flushing in search of some dumpling stall she'd read about.

> @JacobFinchBonner's publisher had better get ready to issue a refund for every copy of #Crib.

> Somebody needs to tell @Oprah she has another fake author on her hands.

Anna wanted a cat. She had wanted a cat for years, apparently. They went to the pound and adopted a nonchalant fellow, all black but for a single white foot, who did a quick circuit of the apartment, staked out a chair Jake had once liked to read in, and settled in for the long haul. (He was to be known as Whidbey, after the island.) She wanted to see a Broadway show—a real one, this time. He got them *Hamilton* tickets through a client of Matilda's who was connected, and a Roundabout subscription. She wanted to go on food tours of the Lower East Side, guided history walks in Tribeca, gospel brunches in Harlem, all of those things native (or at least "established") New Yorkers tended to turn up their noses at, preferring to maintain a smug ignorance about their city. She started to accompany him, as her own work allowed, when he gave readings or talks—Boston, Montclair, Vassar College—and once they stayed on in Florida for a couple of days, following his appearance at the Miami Book Fair.

He began to notice a basic difference between them, which was that she perceived the approach of a stranger with open curiosity and he with dread (this predated his becoming a "famous writer"—an oxymoron if there ever was one, or so he was in the habit of saying to interviewers as a means of conveying modesty—and had been true even when he'd carried a ring of personal failure around himself like a radioactive Hula-Hoop.) New people began to enter their lives, and for the first time in years Jake was having conversations with people who were not writers or in publishing, or even avid readers of fiction, and those conversations went so far beyond whose book had been bought by whom and for how much, whose second novel was a sales disappointment, which editor was out after overspending on an overrated novelist, and which bloggers had taken which sides in an accusation of "unwanted overtures" at a summer writer's conference. There was, it turned out, a stunning variety of stuff to discuss beyond the writing world: politics, things to eat, interesting people and what they'd done in the world, and the golden ages of comedy, television, food trucks, and activism that were currently underway, all around him, and which he'd been only peripherally aware of till now.

He noticed, as his own writer friends began to meet her for a second or third time, that they greeted her with warmth, sometimes reaching for her with a kiss or a hug even before they turned to him. Anna remembered their names, their partners' names, their pets' names (and species), their jobs and their complaints about their jobs, and she asked about everything, even as Jake looked on, smiling tightly, wondering how she'd managed to find out so much about them in so short a time.

Because she'd asked, it only belatedly occurred to him.

With his mother and father they established a monthly brunch in the city, following an Adam Platt review to a dim sum restaurant nestled beneath the Manhattan Bridge which then became their regular destination. He was seeing more of his parents now, with Anna, than he had when he'd been single and theoretically unencumbered by another person's schedule and commitments. As the winter months passed, he watched her forge a deep familiarity with the two of them, his mother's work at the high school, his father's travails with a partner in his firm, the sad saga of the neighbors two houses down on the other side of the street, whose teenage twins were both in freefall and taking the rest of the family down with them. Anna wanted to go yard sale shopping with Jake's mother (an activity he himself had taken pains to avoid since he was a child) when the weather got warmer, and she shared his father's long-held penchant for Emmylou Harris (before his very eyes the two of them looked up Harris's tour schedule and made plans to see her that summer at the Nassau Coliseum). In Anna's presence his parents talked more about themselves, their health, and even their feelings about Jake's success, than they ever had when he'd been alone with them, which unsettled him even as he understood that this was good, a good thing for them all. He had always accepted the bald fact that they loved him, but it was more of a default position than an expression of organic preference. He was their child, *ergo,* and later, when he gave them such unmistakable reasons to be proud, that position was understandably substantiated. But Anna, who was not their child, and who was not a bestselling author of worldwide stature, they liked—no, *loved*—for herself.

One Sunday at the end of January, after their regular dim sum feast, his father pulled him aside on Mott Street and asked what his intentions were.

"Isn't it the girl's father who's supposed to ask that?"

"Well, maybe I'm asking on behalf of Anna's father."

"Oh. That's funny. Well, what should they be?"

His father shook his head. "Are you serious? This girl is fantastic. She's beautiful and kind and she's crazy about you. If I was her dad I'd give you a kick in the pants."

"You mean, grab her before she changes her mind."

"Well, no," his father said. "More like, what are you waiting for? Why would she change her mind?"

Jake couldn't say why, not out loud, obviously not to his father, but he was thinking about it every single day as @TalentedTom continued to hurl contempt into the void. Jake spent each morning toggling through his Google alerts and torturing himself with new word combinations to cast over the internet: "Evan+Parker+writer," "Evan+Parker+Bonner," "*Crib*+Bonner+thief," "Parker+Bonner+plagiarize." He was like an obsessive-compulsive at the mercy of his cleaning rituals, or unable to leave his apartment until he had checked the stove exactly twenty-one times, and it took longer and longer each day to feel safe enough, and then calm enough, to work on the new novel.

Who thinks it's okay for @JacobFinchBonner to steal another writer's book?

Why is @MacmillanBooks still selling #Crib, a novel its author lifted from another writer?

Why would she change her mind?

Because of this. Obviously.

Since that day in Seattle and especially since Anna had crossed the country to join him in New York, Jake had been bracing himself for the day his girlfriend finally mentioned the Twitter posts, perhaps with an entirely understandable demand to know why he hadn't already told her about them. Anna was no Luddite, obviously—she worked in media!—but having established her Facebook and Instagram outposts as a way for her missing sister and aunt to reach her, those two accounts had pretty much ossified from lack of use. The Facebook profile listed about twenty friends, a link to Anna's University of Washington class page, and a pinned endorsement for Rick Larson's 2016 congressional run. The Instagram account's first and only post dated to 2015 and featured—ah, the cliché of it—a latte art pine tree. One of her jobs at the podcast studio was to manage its own Instagram account, posting photographs of the various hosts and guests using the facility, but she apparently had no wish to chase personal likes, shares, retweets, or followers, and she certainly wasn't monitoring the peaks and valleys of *his* online reputation. Anna, it was obvious, preferred the real world, and the real-life face-to-face interactions that took place in it: eating good food, drinking good wine, sweating on a yoga mat in a room crowded with physical bodies.

Still, there was always the uncomfortable possibility that someone, knowing she lived with the author of *Crib,* might mention an accusation or an attack they'd seen floating by on their own feed, or politely ask how Jake was holding up given, you know, *that thing that was happening*. Every day might be a day the infection of @TalentedTom crossed the membrane into his actual life and his actual relationship. Every night might be a night she suddenly said: "Oh hey, somebody sent me this weird tweet about you." So far it hadn't happened. When Anna came home from work, or met him for dinner after yoga, or spent the day with him wandering the city, their talk was about anything and everything but the most consequential thing in Jake's life. Apart from her, of course.

Each morning after she left for work he sat paralyzed at his desk clicking back and forth from Facebook to Twitter to Instagram, Googling himself every hour or so to see if anything had broken through, taking the temperature of his own alarm to see whether he was afraid, or merely afraid of being afraid. Each chime announcing a new email in his in-box made him jump, as did each beep of his Twitter alert and the bell Instagram rang when someone tagged him.

> I know I'm the last person on the planet to read #Crib @JacobFinchBonner, but I wanna thank everyone for NOT TELLING ME WHAT HAPPENS COS I WAS LIKE WHAAAAAA????!

> Recommended by Sammy's mom: #Pachenko (sp?), #TheOrphanTrain, #Crib. Which do I read first?

> Finished crib by @jacobfinchbonner. It wuz eh. Next: #thegoldfinch (man its loooooong)

He thought more than once of hiring a professional (or maybe just somebody's teenage kid) to try to figure out who owned the Twitter account, or TalentedTom@gmail.com, or at least what general part of the world these messages were coming from, but the idea of bringing another person into his personal hell felt impossible. He thought of filing some kind of complaint with Twitter, but Twitter had allowed a president to suggest female senators were giving him blowjobs in exchange for his support—did he really think the platform would lift a finger to help *him*? At the end of the day he couldn't bring himself to do anything at all: direct, indirect, or even just evasive. Instead, he retreated again and again into a baseless idea that if he continued to ignore this ordeal it would one day, somehow, cease to be real, and when that came to pass he would seamlessly return to a version of his life in which no one—not his parents, or his agent, or his publishers, or his thousands upon thousands of readers, or Anna—had any reason to suspect what he'd done. Each morning he woke into some utterly irrational notion that it might all just . . . stop, but then a new speck of darkness would emerge from his computer screen and he would find himself crouching before some terrible approaching wave, waiting to drown.

CHAPTER SIXTEEN

Only the Most Successful Writers

Then, in February, Jake noticed that the Twitter bio included a new link to Facebook. With a now familiar surge of dread, he clicked on the link:

> Name: Tom Talent
>
> Works at: The Restoration of Justice in Fiction
>
> Studied at: Ripley College
>
> Lives In: Anytown, USA
>
> From: Rutland, VT
>
> Friends: 0

His maiden post was short, definitely not sweet, and thoroughly to the point:

> Blindsided by that big twist in Crib? Here's another one: Jacob Finch Bonner stole his novel from another writer.

And for some reason Jake would never understand, *this* was the post that began, at last, to metastasize.

At first, the responses were muted, dismissive, even scolding:

WTF?

Dude, I thought it was overrated, but you shouldn't accuse somebody like that.

Wow, jealous much, loser?

But then, a couple of days later, Jake's Twitter alert picked up a repost on the account of a minor book blogger, who added a question of her own:

Anybody know what this is about?

Eighteen people responded. None of them did. And for a couple of days he was able to maintain a desperate hope that this, too, would pass. Then, the following Monday, his agent called to ask if he was free later in the week for a meeting with the team at Macmillan, and there was something in her voice that told him this would not be about the second round of the paperback tour or even the new novel, which had now been scheduled for the following autumn. "What's up?" he said, already knowing the answer.

Matilda had a very distinctive way of delivering terrible news as if it were an interesting insight that had just occurred to her. She said: "Oh, you know what? Wendy mentioned that reader services got a weirdo message from somebody who says you're not the author of *Crib.* Which means you've really made it now. Only the most successful writers get these wackos."

Jake couldn't make a sound. He looked at the phone; it was in front of him, on the coffee table, with the speaker on. Finally, he managed a strangled: "What?"

"Oh, don't worry about it. Everybody who accomplishes anything gets this. Stephen King? J. K. Rowling? Even Ian McEwan! Some crazy guy once accused Joyce Carol Oates of flying a zeppelin over his house so she could photograph what he was writing on his computer."

"That's insane." He took a breath. "But . . . what did the message say?"

"Oh, something really specific like your story doesn't belong to you. They just wanted to bring Legal in to have a little chat about it. Get us all on the same page."

Jake nodded again. "Okay, great."

"Ten tomorrow okay with you?"

"Okay."

It took every fiber of his will not to immediately replicate his self-quarantine of the previous fall: unplugged phone, fetal position, cupcakes, Jameson. But this time he knew he'd shortly have to present himself in some quasi-responsible condition, and that impeded freefall, or at least irreversible freefall. When he met Matilda in the lobby of his venerable publisher the following morning he still felt impaired: woozy and malodorous, in spite of the fact that he'd forced himself into the shower only an hour earlier. The two of them went up in the elevator together to the fourteenth floor, and Jake, as he followed his editor's assistant down the corridor, couldn't help thinking about his previous visits to these offices: for a celebration in the aftermath of the auction, for the intense (but still thrilling!) editorial sessions, for the mind-blowing first meeting with the PR and marketing teams, at which he'd first understood that *Crib* was going to be given every speck of the magic publishing fairy dust his earlier books had been denied. Later visits here had been for the observation of other astonishing benchmarks: the first hundred thousand sold, the first week on the *New York Times* bestseller list, the Oprah selection. All good. Sometimes only reassuringly good, other times life-changingly good, but always good. Until today.

Today was not good.

In one of the conference rooms they sat down with Jake's editor and publicist, and with the in-house attorney, a man named Alessandro who announced that he had just come from the gym, something Jake absurdly took to be a hopeful sign. Alessandro was completely bald and the overhead fluorescents made the top of his head shine. Unless—Jake peered—was that sweat? It wasn't sweat. Jake was the only one sweating.

"So, honey," Matilda began, "like I told you, and I mean this, it's not uncommon at all to be accused of something nasty by a troll. You know, even Stephen King's been accused of plagiarism."

And J. K. Rowling. And Joyce Carol Oates. He knew.

"And you'll notice this guy's anonymous."

"I haven't noticed," Jake lied, "because I've been trying not to think about it."

"Well, that's good," said Wendy, his editor. "We want you thinking about the new book, not this ridiculousness."

"But we've been talking about it," said Matilda. "Wendy and I have, and the team, and we thought it might be time to bring in Mr. Guarise—"

"Alessandro," said the attorney. "Please."

"To go through it with us. See if there are any steps we should be taking."

Alessandro was handing around a spreadsheet, and Jake, to his utter horror, saw that it was a very comprehensive display of TalentedTom's online activities thus far: every tweet and Facebook post neatly dated and appallingly reproduced, displayed in order of their appearance.

"What am I looking at?" said Matilda, staring at the page.

"I had one of my paralegals do a bit of digging on this guy. He's been active, at least in a small way, since November."

"Were you aware of any of this?" Wendy asked.

Jake felt a wave of illness. He was, it was clear, about to tell his first outright untruth of the meeting. It was unavoidable and it was necessary, but it was also excruciating.

"No idea."

"Well, that's just as well."

The assistant stuck her head into the room and asked if anyone needed anything. Matilda asked for a water. Jake didn't think he could get even that down his throat without spilling it everywhere.

"So listen," said Wendy. "And I know you'll forgive me for asking this, but it's kind of a baseline thing and we just need to hear you say it. As far as this bullshit goes, and I understand that what he's actually saying is completely vague and nonspecific, but do you have any idea what this joker's talking about?"

Jake looked around at them. His mouth had gone about as dry as sandpaper. He wished he'd asked for the water.

"Uh, no. I mean, like you said, it's . . . what, I'm a thief? Of what?"

"Well, exactly," said Matilda.

"He does use the word 'plagiarist' in some posts," said Alessandro helpfully.

"Yeah, love that," Jake said bitterly.

"But *Crib* isn't plagiarized," Matilda said.

"No!" Jake nearly shouted. "I wrote every word of *Crib* myself. On a dying laptop in Cobleskill, New York. Winter, spring, and summer of 2016."

"Good. And not that it will ever come to this, but I assume you have drafts, notes, and the like?"

"I do," said Jake, but he was shaking as he said it.

"I'm struck by the fact that he refers to himself as 'TalentedTom,'" said Wendy. "Should we infer he's a writer himself?"

"A *talented* one," said Matilda, with extravagant sarcasm.

"When I read that," said the publicist, whose name was Roland, "I just automatically thought, you know: Ripley."

Jake, caught unawares, felt the heat rush to his face. The attorney said: "Who's that?"

"Tom Ripley. *The Talented Mr. Ripley*. You know that book?"

"I saw the movie," Alessandro said, and Jake, slowly, let out a breath. Apparently no one in the room seemed to associate "Ripley" with a third-rate MFA program where he'd taught for a couple of years.

"I think it's kind of creepy, actually," Roland went on. "Like, even as he's calling you a plagiarist he's saying: *I'm capable of a lot worse than that.*"

"Well, but it's only sometimes he says plagiarist," Wendy said. "The other times it's just the story he accuses you of stealing. 'The story doesn't belong to you.' What does that even mean?"

"People don't realize you can't copyright a plot," Alessandro said finally. "You can't even copyright a title, and that would be a lot easier to make an argument about."

"If you could copyright a plot there wouldn't be any novels at all," said Wendy. "Imagine just one person owning the rights to *Boy meets girl, boy loses girl, boy gets girl.* Or *Hero raised in obscurity discovers he's incredibly important to an epic struggle for power.* I mean, it's absurd!"

"Well, this, to be fair, is a very distinctive plot. I think you said yourself, Wendy, that you'd never come across this before, not only in submissions but in your own experience as a reader."

Wendy nodded. "That's true."

"What about you, Jake?"

Another dizzying breath, another lie.

"No. Never came across it in anything I've read."

"And I think you'd remember!" Matilda said. "If a manuscript with this plot had come into my office at any time I'd have responded the way I did when Jake sent us his manuscript. But even if I weren't the agent this writer chose to send it to, any agent would have been excited about a book with this plot. Eventually, I'd have heard about it just like the rest of us, which can only mean no such book exists."

"Maybe unwritten," Jake heard himself say.

The others looked at him.

"What do you mean?" Alessandro said.

"Well, I suppose it's possible some writer had the same idea for a novel, but never actually wrote it."

"Cry me a river!" Matilda threw up her hands. "We're going to give credit to everyone out there who *has an idea* for a novel and *just hasn't gotten around to writing it down*? Do you know how many people come up to me and say they have a great plot for a novel?"

"I might," Wendy said, sighing.

"And you know what I say to them? I say, 'Fantastic! Once you've written it, send it to my office.' And guess how many of them ever have?"

I'm going with zero, Jake thought.

"Not one! In almost twenty years as an agent! So let's say there's somebody out there who came up with the same plot. Just say! Only he didn't get around to actually writing his own damn novel and now he's annoyed because another person, a real writer, did! And probably a lot better than he ever could have. So, tough. Next time maybe do the work."

"Matilda." Wendy sighed again. (Despite their current frustration, the two were old friends.) "I completely agree. That's why we're here, to protect Jake."

"But, we can't stop people from saying crap on the internet," Jake said bravely. "There wouldn't be an internet if we did. Shouldn't we just ignore it?"

The lawyer shrugged. "We've ignored it so far, and the dude doesn't seem to be stopping. Maybe not ignoring it will work better."

"Well, what would not ignoring it look like?" Jake said. It came out sounding a little harsh, as if he was angry. Well of course he was angry! "I mean, we don't want to poke the bear, right?"

"If it is a bear. Frankly, a lot of the time, these guys are more of a deer in the headlights than a bear. You shine a bit of a light on them and they run away. Some underachiever might have keyboard courage but if he states or implies a provably false statement of fact, not just an opinion, that's defamation. They don't want to get their names published, and they definitely don't want to be sued. We don't hear from them again."

Jake experienced a faint pulse of hope.

"How would you do it?"

"We'd write something official-sounding in the comments. *Defamation, invasion of privacy, portrayal in a false light*—all viable bases for a lawsuit. At the same time we contact the host websites and the ISPs and ask them to remove the postings voluntarily."

"And they'll do that?" Jake said eagerly.

Alessandro shook his head. "Usually they don't, no. The Communications Decency Act of 1996 says they can't be held liable for defamation made by third parties. They're considered a vector for other people's free speech, technically, so they're in the clear. But they all have content standards and none of them *want* to go broke standing up for some anonymous loser who probably isn't paying a dime for their services, so sometimes we get lucky and it stops there. We like to get the host on our side if we can, because we'll still want to clean up the metadata, even if we get the posts taken down. Right now if you Google 'Jacob Finch Bonner' plus the word 'thief,' this comes right up at the top of the results. If you Google Jake's name and 'plagiarism,' same thing. Search engine optimization techniques can mitigate some of that, but it's much easier if we have the host helping out."

"But wait," said Roland, the publicist. "How can you even suggest that you're going to sue him if you don't know who he is?"

"We file a lawsuit against 'John Doe.' That gets us subpoena power. We can also serve on the ISPs to try to get the guy's registrant information, or even better, his IP address. If it's a shared computer, like a library, we'll be out of luck, but it can still be useful information. If this is coming from bumfuck nowhere maybe it turns out Jake knows somebody who lives in bumfuck nowhere. Maybe you stole his girlfriend in college or something."

Jake tried to nod. He had never stolen anyone's girlfriend in his life.

"And if it's a work computer, that's the best news of all, because then we can amend the complaint not just to add the person's name but also the name of his employer, and that's quite the powerful lever right there. He's brave enough when nobody knows it's him, but if he thinks we're going to sue his employers, you better believe he's going to shut up and go away."

"I certainly would!" said Roland cheerily.

"Well, that's . . . encouraging," Matilda said. "Because it isn't fair that Jake should have to be dealing with this. Any of us, but Jake especially. And I know it's been worrying him. He hasn't said so, but I know."

For a moment Jake thought he might cry. He shook his head quickly, as if disagreeing, but he didn't think they were fooled.

"Oh no!" said Wendy. "Jake, we're on this!"

"Right," said the attorney. "I'm going to do my thing. That sound you're about to hear is a deer in the headlights, running away through the woods."

"Okay," Jake said with a blatantly false heartiness.

"Honey," his agent said, "like I said. It's pathetic, but it's a point of honor. Anyone who accomplishes anything in this life has someone out there dying to tear him down. You've done absolutely nothing wrong. You are not to think of this as your problem."

But he had. And it was. And that was the ongoing hell of it.

CRIB

BY JACOB FINCH BONNER

Macmillan, New York, 2017, pages 43–44

Samantha's father drove her as far as the front door of the hospital. Her mother walked her into the lobby but declined to go farther. It was all a regular ABC After-School Special, except for the absurd amount of physical pain she was in. She'd been hoping for some drugs, but there was a distinctly punitive aspect to the way the nurses, in particular, seemed to handle her labor. In the end, she got nothing until somebody told her it was too late, at which point she got more nothing. To make matters worse—and worse was hardly what she needed—the mother of one of her classmates was in labor at the same time, which meant that the boy, a wrestler with raging acne, was on site, in and out of his mother's room, walking her down the corridor, and sneaking fascinated looks in Samantha's direction every time he passed her open doorway.

It was a long and interesting day, punctuated by indignities and agony and the very new and fascinating attentions of the hospital social workers, who seemed especially interested in the question of how she'd be filling out the Baby's Father line on the forms.

"Can I say Bill Clinton?" she asked between contractions.

"Not if it isn't true," said the woman, who didn't even smile. She wasn't from Earlville. She looked like she came from money. Cooperstown, maybe.

"And you plan to remain in the family home after your child is born."

It was a statement. Could it be a question?

"Do I have to? I mean, could I leave?"

The woman put her clipboard down. "Can I ask why you would want to leave the family home?"

"It's just that, my parents don't support my goals."

"And what are your goals?"

To hand this baby off to someone else and finish high school. But she never got that out, because the next contraction hit her like a boulder, then something started beeping on the monitor and two nurses came in and after that she couldn't remember much. When the pain stopped she was just waking up, it was the middle of the night outside, and next to her bed was something that looked like a portable aquarium, inside of which a red and wrinkled creature was squalling. That was her daughter, Maria, apparently.

CHAPTER SEVENTEEN

An Unfortunate Side Effect of Success

About a week after their meeting, the attorneys representing Jake's publisher inserted the following notice in the comments section after several of TalentedTom's known appearances:

> To the person posting here and elsewhere as TalentedTom:
> I am an attorney representing the interests of Macmillan Publishing and its author, Jacob Finch Bonner. Your malicious spreading of inaccurate information and unfounded suggestion of bad actions on the part of the author are unwanted and unwelcome. Under the laws of the State of New York it is unlawful to make deliberate statements with intent to harm a person's reputation without factual evidence. This serves as a pre-suit demand that you immediately cease and desist all verbal attacks on all social media platforms, websites, and via all forms of communication. Failure to do so will result in a lawsuit against you, this social media platform or website, and any related or involved responsible party. Representatives of

> this social media platform have been contacted separately.
>
> Sincerely, Alessandro F. Guarise, Esq.

For a few days there was blessed silence, and the dreaded daily trawl of his Google alert for Jacob+Finch+Bonner produced nothing but reader reviews, gossip about casting for the Spielberg film, and an actual Page Six "sighting" of himself at a PEN fundraiser, shaking hands with an exiled journalist from Uzbekistan.

Then, in the space of a Thursday morning, it all went to shit: TalentedTom produced a communiqué of his own, this one sent—again, via email—to Macmillan's Reader Services but also posted on Twitter, Facebook, and even a brand-new Instagram account, accompanied by lots of helpful tags to attract the attention of book bloggers, industry watchdogs, and the specific reporters at *The New York Times* and *The Wall Street Journal* who covered publishing:

> I regret to inform his many readers that Jacob Finch Bonner, the "author" of the novel *Crib,* is not the rightful owner of the story he wrote. Bonner should not be rewarded for his theft. He is a disgrace and deserving of exposure and censure.

So much for the deer in the headlights theory.

And so the day unfolded. It was a terrible day.

Within moments the contact form on his author website was forwarding comment requests from half a dozen book bloggers, an interview query from *The Rumpus,* and a nasty if illogical dispatch from somebody named Joe: I knew your book was crap. Now I know why. *The Millions* tweeted something about him by midafternoon and *Page-Turner* was hot on its heels.

Matilda, for one, remained sanguine, or so she was at pains to convey. This was all an unfortunate side effect of success, she said again, and the world—the world of writers in particular—was full of bitter people who believed they were owed something or other, by someone or other. The logic of this being something like:

If you could write a sentence you deserved to consider yourself a writer.

If you had an "idea" for a "novel" you deserved to consider yourself a novelist.

If you actually completed a manuscript you deserved to have someone publish it.

If someone published it you deserved to be sent on a twenty-city book tour and have your book featured in full-page ads in The New York Times Book Review.

And if, at any point on this ladder of entitlement, one of the aforementioned things you deserved failed to materialize, the blame for that must rest at whatever point you'd been unfairly obstructed:

Your daily life—for not giving you an opportunity to write.

The "professional" or already "established" writers—who'd gotten there quicker because of unspecified advantages.

The agents and publishers—who could only protect and burnish the reputations of their existing authors by keeping new authors out.

The entire book industrial complex—which (following some evil algorithm of profit) doubled down on a few name-brand authors and effectively silenced everyone else.

"In short," Matilda said—and not being a natural soother, it came out sounding strained and wrong—"please, do not worry about this. Also, you're going to get a ton of sympathy from your peers, and people whose opinion you actually care about. Just wait."

Jake waited. She was right, of course.

There was a keep-your-chin-up! email from Wendy, and another from his contact at Steven Spielberg's West Coast office, and still others from some of the writers he had once hung out with in New York (the ones who'd made it into the famous MFA program before he had). He heard from Bruce O'Reilly in Maine (Man, what is this moronic trash?) and from a number of his former coaching clients. He heard from Alice

Logan at Hopkins, who helpfully listed a number of plagiarism scandals from the land of poetry and mentioned that she and her new husband were expecting. He heard from his parents, who were offended on his behalf, and several of his MFA classmates, one of whom countered with his own stalker: She decided my second novel was a codebook about our relationship. Which didn't exist, incidentally. Don't worry, they go away.

At around four that afternoon he heard from Martin Purcell in Vermont.

Someone posted it on our Ripley Facebook group, he wrote in an email. Do you have any idea who's saying this stuff?

I was thinking, maybe, you? Jake thought. But naturally he said no such thing.

CRIB

BY JACOB FINCH BONNER

Macmillan, New York, 2017, pages 71–73

Almost exactly two years later, Samantha's father collapsed in the parking lot of the central maintenance office at Colgate University and was dead before the ambulance arrived. The biggest change in Samantha's life, following this event, was an abrupt decline in financial security and the fact that her mother started obsessing over some woman her father had been sleeping with, apparently for years. (Why she'd waited until her husband was dead to reveal all this made no sense, at least not to Samantha. It was too late to do anything about it now, wasn't it?) On the other hand, Samantha got her late father's car, a Subaru. That was a big help.

Her daughter, Maria, by then, was doing all of the normal things, like walking and talking, and one or two things Samantha considered not normal, like saying the names of letters everywhere she went and pretending not to hear Samantha when Samantha was speaking. She had been, from her first days of life, a malcontent, a blusterer, a pusher-away of other people (mainly Samantha, but also her two grandparents and the pediatrician). In due course she began kindergarten as a surly child in a corner with books, declining to parallel play (let alone cooperative play), interrupting the teacher with commentary when it was story time, refusing to eat anything but jelly and cream cheese on the heel of the supermarket loaf.

By then, all of Samantha's former tenth-grade classmates had passed out of the crepe-paper-decorated gymnasium holding their rolled-up diplomas, and they'd scattered—a few to college, others to work, the rest to the wind. If she ran into one of them in the supermarket or at the Fourth of July parade along Route 20 she felt such a surge of fury that it rushed upward into her mouth and burned her tongue, and she had to grit her teeth together when she made polite conversation. A year after those classmates moved on, her original classmates—the ones she'd leapfrogged past as a sixth grader—also graduated, and all that anger seemed to go with them. What was left after that was a kind of low-grade disappointment, and as the years continued to pass she lost even the power to remember what it was she was disappointed about. Her own mother was home less and less; Dan Weybridge—in the goodness of his heart or perhaps some festering sense of paternal responsibility—had upped her hours at the *Family-owned-for-three-generations!* College Inn, and she'd also joined a group at her church that traveled to women's health clinics to harass the patients and staff. Samantha spent most of her time in the sole company of her daughter, and the care of an infant, then a toddler, then a young child expanded to fill every corner and moment of her days. She tended Maria like an automaton: feeding, bathing, dressing and undressing, losing ground with every passing day.

CHAPTER EIGHTEEN

Another Day's Lies

There were days when he could manage an hour or two of work on the new novel, but many more when he could not. Generally, after Anna left the apartment in the morning, Jake remained on the new kilim-covered couch Anna had chosen to replace its ratty predecessor, bouncing back and forth between his phone (Twitter, Instagram) and his laptop (Google, Facebook), checking and rechecking for new posts and tracking the malevolent ricochets of those posts he'd already seen, trapped and tortured and utterly incapable of finding his way out.

When the Macmillan group reconvened a couple of weeks later, this time via conference call, there was a certain amount of chagrin at TalentedTom's response to the cease and desist, and a general dearth of other ideas to try. On the other hand, Roland the publicist reported that the book websites and bloggers seemed to have let the story pass, mainly because there wasn't much for them to write without any details at all, and also, frankly, because the anonymous poster did sound like just the kind of person who comes out of the woodwork when someone writes a massively bestselling book. (Jake's circumstances were also helped by a gloriously well-timed war between two novel-writing exes in Williamsburg, whose books—her first, his third—had been published within weeks of each other, and together formed a mutually punitive indictment of their failed marriage, albeit with different villains.)

"Of course I wish we'd had a better outcome," said the attorney, "but there's always the possibility that this was his last hurrah. He knows he's being watched now. He didn't have to be all that careful before. Maybe he'll decide it's just not worth it."

"I'm sure that's the case," said Wendy. To Jake's ears she seemed to be straining for optimism. "And anyway, there's about to be a brand-new book by Jacob Finch Bonner. What's this dickwad going to do then? Accuse Jake of stealing every book he writes? The best thing for all of this nonsense is to get the new novel into production as soon as possible."

Everyone agreed with that, and no one more so than Jake, who hadn't been able to write a word since what he had privately thought of as the regret-to-inform message had materialized online. But after he got off the phone he pulled himself together. These people were in his corner. Even if they'd known *Crib*'s comprehensive origin story, they'd probably still be in his corner! After all, people who worked with writers were fully aware of the myriad and frequently bizarre ways in which a work of fiction can take root in an author's imagination: fragments of overheard conversations, repurposed bits of mythology, Craigslist confessions, rumors at the high school reunion. Maybe the punters out there believed novels followed a visit from the muse—perhaps these same people thought babies followed a visit from the stork—but so what? Writers, editors, people who thought about it for more than a nanosecond understood how books truly begin, and at the end of the day, those were the only people he really cared about. *Basta!* It was time to turn down the noise and get to the end of his own draft.

And this, somewhat to his own astonishment, he actually managed to do.

Less than a month later he hit Send on a good first draft of his new novel.

A week after that, with requests for only minor revisions, Wendy formally accepted it.

The new book concerned a prosecutor who had once, at a vulnerable moment early in his career, accepted a bribe to sabotage one of his own cases, a seemingly insignificant matter involving a traffic stop and an open glass of rosé being enjoyed in the back seat. That small decision, however, returns to assail the character in his later success and complacency, and brings unanticipated harm to himself and his family. The novel lacked the thunderbolt of *Crib*'s plot twist, but it did have a number of course corrections that had kept Wendy and her team at Macmillan guessing, and while Jake knew this work could not bring a repeat of the phenomenon *Crib* had been (it was telling that no one from Wendy on down suggested it would), the book still looked like a viable follow-up. Wendy was happy with it. Matilda was happy with Wendy's happiness. Both of them were happy with Jake.

Jake was not happy with himself, obviously, but this had been true of his life, always, not just during the long years of professional failure but during the past two years of dizzying success, in which he had merely traded one form of dread and self-castigation for another. Each morning he woke to Anna's warm and tactile presence, and then, almost instantly, to that other presence: spectral and unwelcome, reminding him that today there might be a new message, entirely capable of destroying everything in his world. Then, all through the hours that followed, he waited for the terrible thing to happen, the one that would force him to explain himself to Anna, to Matilda, to Wendy, to sit in the James Frey–designated spot on Oprah Winfrey's couch, to "hold for Steven Spielberg, please," to rescind his Writers' Advisory Board position at PEN, to hang his head while he walked down the street, desperate not to be recognized. Each night he sank into the exhaustion of subterfuge: another day's lies coiling around him, pulling him into sleeplessness.

"I wonder," Anna said to him, one night in May, "if you're, you know, all right."

"What? Of course I am."

It was a worrying note to be striking on that particular evening, the designated observation of the six-month anniversary of Anna's arrival in New York. They were back at the Brazilian restaurant he'd taken her to that first night, and had just been brought their caipirinhas.

"Well, you're preoccupied, obviously. I have this feeling, when I get home at night, that you're making an effort."

"Making an effort isn't a bad thing, necessarily," Jake said. He was going for a light tone.

"I mean, to be happy to see me."

He felt a small surge of alarm.

"Oh. But that's wrong. I'm always happy to see you. Just, you know, in the weeds a bit. Wendy asked for some revisions, I think I told you." This was not untrue, of course, but the revisions were minor, and wouldn't take more than a couple of weeks.

"Maybe I can help."

He looked at her. She seemed serious.

"I walk a lonely road," he said, still trying to make a joke of this. "I mean, not just me. All of us writers."

"If all of you writers are walking the same lonely road it can't be all that lonely."

Now it was impossible not to hear the rebuke. Anna had never been that person, banging on the door, demanding access to his thoughts and worries. From the moment they'd met, in fact, she had quietly offered so many of the things he'd already known were missing—companionship, affection, a better class of furniture and a much improved diet—without ever once asking him that fatal and soul-crushing question: "What are you thinking?" Now, however, even Anna seemed to be reaching the limits of her goodwill.

Or perhaps, at long last, she had entered his name into a search engine during some idle moment at work or gone out for a post-yoga coffee with some acquaintance who'd said: *Hey, don't you live with Jacob Finch Bonner? What a drag, what they're doing to him.*

So far, it still hadn't happened, but—*when* it finally happened—because it had to happen at some point—would she accept some version of Matilda's reassurances (*Yep, that's me: accused plagiarist! Guess I've really made it now.*) or some pained excuse about sparing her the trauma of it?

He was thinking: no, she would not. And then she would truly see who he was, not just a person who'd been accused of an awful thing, but a person who had hidden the accusation from her. For the entire length of their relationship. And that would be that: off she would go, this loving and beautiful woman, back to the farthest end of the continent from where he was, and she would stay there.

So he'd continued to not tell her, and to justify not telling her:

How could she possibly understand? It wasn't as if *she* was a writer.

"You're right," Jake told her now. "I should try not to be so much of an *artiste*. Just, right now, I'm feeling a little bit—"

"Yes. You said. In the weeds."

"It means—"

"I know what it means."

The waiter arrived, bringing Jake's fraldinha and Anna's mussels. When he departed, she said, "My point is, whatever's making you feel so *in the weeds,* would you consider sharing it with me?"

Jake frowned. The answer, of course, was: *No fucking way*. But there were several excellent reasons not to say this.

He lifted his glass. He was hoping to get back onto a more anniversarial track. "I'd like to thank you."

"For what?" she asked, a little suspiciously.

"You know. For dropping everything and moving to New York. For being so brave."

"Well," she said, "I had a pretty good feeling, from the start."

"Checking me out at Seattle Arts and Lectures," he teased. "Deviously arranging for me to come to your radio station."

"Do you wish I hadn't?"

"No! I just can't get over the idea that I warranted so much effort."

"Well," Anna smiled, "you did. What's more, you do. Even if you're *walking a lonely road.*"

"I know I can be a bit of a downer sometimes."

"This is not about you being a downer. It's about you being down. I can take care of my own moods. But I've been a little worried about yours."

For a very uncomfortable moment, he wondered if he was about to cry. As usual, she saved him.

"Honey, it's not my intention to pry. It's clear to me that something's wrong. All I'm saying is, can I help? Or if I can't help, can I at least share?"

"No, nothing's wrong," said Jake, and he picked up his fork and knife, as if this proved his point. "It's so sweet of you to be concerned. But really, my life is great."

Anna shook her head. She wasn't even pretending to want to eat. "Your life should be great. You're healthy. You have a nice family. You're secure, financially. And look, you're successful at the only thing you ever wanted to do! Think of the writers who haven't accomplished what you've accomplished."

He did. He thought about them all the time, and not in a good way.

"What's the point of all of this, if you're not happy?" she asked.

"But I am," he insisted.

She shook her head. He had a sudden, terrible thought that she was saying something important here. Something along the lines of: *I came all this way for someone I thought was a vital, creative, appreciative person, only to find this morose creature undercutting his own happiness at every turn. So I'm going back where I came from.* His heart was pounding. What if she really was going back? Here they were together, and he was a fool, failing to appreciate what he so obviously had: success, health, Anna.

"I mean, I'm sorry if it seems I don't appreciate . . . all of the wonderful things."

"And people."

"Yes." He nodded fervently. "Because I'd hate to . . ."

"What?" she said, eyeing him.

"I'd hate to . . . not articulate how grateful I am . . ."

She shook her silvery head. "*Grateful,*" she said with disdain.

"My life," Jake said, stumbling into the apparently foreign thicket of the English language. "It's . . . so much better with you in it."

"Oh? Well, I don't doubt that, from a practical standpoint. But I have to admit, I'd been hoping for something more. I mean," said Anna, who wasn't looking at him anymore. "I feel like I knew my own feelings right away. I'll admit, leaving Seattle was probably a crazy thing to do, but we've lived together for six months now. Maybe not everyone knows how they feel as quickly as I did, but I think it's really been enough time now. And I mean, if you still don't know what you want to happen here, maybe that's its own answer. This is what *I'm* in the weeds about, if you want to know the truth."

He stared at her, and a sick feeling surged through him. Eight months since their meeting, six of them spent living together as a couple, exploring the city, adopting a cat, meeting his family and his friends and broadening their shared circle . . . what was the matter with him? Was he so distracted by some malevolent piece of shit on the internet that he was about to miss the truly life-altering and entirely real person on the other side of the table? This dinner was not, as he'd simply assumed, a rote acknowledgment of their six-month anniversary, it was the end of some private trial period for Anna. And Jake was blowing it. Or already had blown it. Or surely would blow it if he didn't . . . what?

He asked her to marry him.

It took mere seconds for her to begin grinning, mere seconds more for him to grin back, a minute at most before the idea of it, of getting married to Anna Williams of Idaho, Seattle, Whidbey Island, Seattle again, and now New York, had lost all of its unfamiliarity and become an exciting, cheerful, and above all settled thing. And then they were holding hands beside their still steaming plates.

"Wow," said Anna.

"Wow," Jake agreed. "I don't have a ring."

"Well, that's okay. I mean, can we get a ring?"

"Absolutely."

An hour later, having dispatched several additional caipirinhas and never once returning to their previous topic of conversation, they left the restaurant an inebriated and very much engaged couple.

CHAPTER NINETEEN

The Only Place Left to Go

Anna wasn't interested in anything elaborate, and neither of them saw any point in waiting. They went to the diamond district and she chose something called an "estate" ring (which meant "secondhand" with a nicer name, though it did look very pretty on her finger), and less than a week after that they were at city hall, waiting on the hard benches with all of the other couples. After a bespectacled official named Rayna pronounced them married, they walked a few blocks to Chinatown for what would serve as their wedding party. (On Jake's side: his parents and a couple of cousins, and two or three of his Wesleyan and MFA friends. On Anna's: a colleague from the podcast studio and a couple of the women she'd met at yoga.) They occupied two round tables in the back of a Mott Street restaurant, each with a lazy Susan of dishes in the middle. Jake and Anna brought champagne.

The following week, Matilda took them out to the new Union Square Cafe to celebrate, and Jake arrived a few minutes late to find his agent and his new wife with their heads together, gossiping over pink-salt-rimmed margaritas as if they'd known each other for years. "Oh my god," he heard one of them say as he sat beside Anna in the booth. He wasn't even sure which one had spoken.

"What?"

"Jake!" said his agent with unprecedented reprove, "you didn't tell me your wife worked for Randy Johnson."

"Uh . . . no," he confirmed. "Why?"

"Randy Johnson! Soundtrack of my adolescence. You know I grew up in Bellevue!"

Did he know that? He didn't, actually.

"I met him once," Matilda went on. "I went on his show with a friend of mine, because we were organizing a fun run for some worthy cause. Actually the worthy cause was probably getting-the-two-of-us-into-Ivy-League-schools, but never mind about that. My dad drove us to the station. I don't think it was the one he's at now."

"Probably KAZK," said Anna.

"Yeah, maybe. Anyway, he hit on the both of us, one after the other. On the air! We were sixteen!"

"Well-known lech," Anna observed.

"My dad was right there in the studio!" She held up her beautifully manicured hands in shock. She had buttery blond hair, expensively tended, and looked every inch the busy, accomplished, and well-compensated Manhattan woman she was. Beside her, Anna, with her silver braid, unpainted nails, and casual work sweater, seemed notably younger and immeasurably less sophisticated.

"He wouldn't do it today, probably," Anna was saying. "He'd wait till the dad was in the bathroom."

"Like, how has this guy not been Me Too'd out of his misery yet?"

"Well, I think it's come up. I know it has, actually. Even while I was there, there was some issue with an intern. But she denied it and he kind of slithered through. And anyway, he's an institution. Sorry, Jake. You have to forgive us, cackling away."

"I just met your wife," said Matilda, "and I want to cackle away with her in perpetuity."

"That's so kind," said Anna. "And I've always been told you're a no-nonsense kind of person."

"Oh, I am!" Matilda said, as Jake asked the waiter for whatever they were having. "But only in the office. That's my secret. They'd call me the Jackal, but the nickname's already taken. It's not that I love to fight, per se; I just love to fight for my clients. Because I love my clients. And in this case, I'm happy to say, I also love their brand-new spouses." She lifted her glass to the two of them. "I am so delighted, Anna. I don't know where you came from, but I'm glad you're here."

The two of them clinked. Jake lifted his water to join them.

"She comes from Idaho," he said helpfully. "A small town—"

"Yeah, very boring," said Anna, touching his leg under the table. "I wish I'd grown up in Seattle, like you. The minute I got there, for college, I was just so . . . *Yes*. All that tech stuff coming in, and the energy with it."

"And the *food*."

"And the *coffee*."

"Not to mention the music, if you were into that," Matilda said. "Which I wasn't. I could never rock a flannel shirt. But there was real excitement around it."

"And the water. And the ferries. And the sunsets over the harbor."

The two of them looked at each other, evidently sharing a single rapturous moment.

"Tell me about you, Anna," Jake's agent said, and for most of the evening they talked about her years on Whidbey, and then at the radio station, where she'd made it her mission to get *some* cultural content—literature, performing arts, *ideas*—into Randy Johnson's malodorous studio. They talked about the books Anna liked to read and the wines she preferred, and what she had already accomplished in her first months in New York. Matilda, Jake was not at all surprised to discover, followed at least two of the podcasts Anna was helping to produce, and he watched his wife take out her phone to record the names of several others she should be listening to, as well as the contact information for another of Matilda's clients who'd been making noises about a podcast of his own, and who was going to need a very smart, very strong-willed producer to help him.

"I'll get in touch with him tomorrow," Anna confirmed. "I've been reading his books since college. This is a thrill."

"He'd be unbelievably lucky to get you. And you won't put up with his mansplaining."

Anna grinned. "Thanks to Randy Johnson, king of mansplainers, I will not."

It was not unpleasant, listening to the two of them, but it was also novel. This dinner was the first time since he'd met Matilda, three years earlier, that the sole or at least disproportionately dominant topic of their conversation wasn't Jacob Finch Bonner. Only when it was time for dessert did Matilda appear to remember he was there, and she marked this recognition by asking when revisions on the new novel would be done.

"Soon," said Jake, immediately wishing they could go back to talking about Seattle.

"He's working his tail off," Anna said. "I can tell, every day when I get home. He's so stressed out."

"Well, given everything, I'm not surprised," said Matilda.

Anna turned to him with a quizzical expression.

"Second novels," he said shortly. "I mean, fourth novels, technically, but since no one ever heard of me before *Crib,* it's sort of my second act. It's terrifying."

"No, no," Matilda said, wordlessly accepting her coffee from the waiter. "Don't think about that. If I could only get my clients to stop worrying about their careers they'd write twice as many books and be a lot happier in general. You wouldn't believe how much therapy there is in these relationships," she said, directing this to Anna as if Jake—the subject of the theoretical therapy—were not right there at the table with them. "I'm not licensed! I took Intro Psych at Princeton, and I kid you not, that was the extent of my training. But the fragile egos I'm apparently responsible for! I mean, not your husband, but some of them . . . if they send me something to read and I don't get back to them for a few days because it's five hundred pages long or it's the weekend or I happen to have other clients who are in the middle of auctions or winning the National Book Award or leaving their spouses and running off with their research assistants, God forbid! They're on the phone to me with a knife at the wrist. Of course," she said, perhaps hearing herself, "I adore my clients. Every one of them, even the tough ones, but some people make things so hard for themselves. *Why?*"

Anna nodded sagely. "I know how tough it must have been in the beginning, for Jake. Before you were involved and *Crib* became such a success. It takes courage to keep going. I'm so proud of him."

"Thanks, honey," said Jake. He felt as if he was interrupting them.

"I'm proud of him too. Especially these last months."

Again, Anna turned to him with a confused look.

"Oh, it's all fine," he heard himself say. "It'll pass."

"I told you so," Matilda said.

"I'll get the book done. And then I'll write another book."

"And another!" she declared.

"Because that's what writers do, right?"

"That's what you do. And thank god for it!"

He noticed, when they left the restaurant, that she gave Anna an even longer hug than the one she gave him, but he was so relieved that he'd managed to block TalentedTom from invading their dinner that it was impossible to see the evening as anything but a win. His agent, it was obvious, really liked his new wife, and in this she had a lot of company.

In practical terms, Jake's post-marriage life didn't change all that much. Anna had opted for a modified modification, officially becoming Anna Williams-Bonner after filling out the required twenty or thirty forms and waiting on various lines at various agencies to acquire a new driver's license and passport. They merged bank accounts and credit cards and health insurance policies and saw an attorney about their wills. Anna dispatched the last of Jake's collegiate and post-collegiate furnishings—a reclining chair of faux leather, a framed Phish poster, a shag rug from Bed Bath & Beyond, circa 2002—to their just rewards, and repainted the living room. They went for an abbreviated honeymoon to New Orleans, where they gorged themselves on oysters and listened to jazz (which Anna liked) and blues (which Jake liked) and zydeco (which neither of them liked) at night.

On the night they returned to the city, Anna went to deliver a box of pralines to a neighbor who'd fed the cat while they were gone, and Jake let himself into the apartment, dropping an armload of mail onto the kitchen counter. His eye found it right away: an unremarkable envelope slipping out onto the granite countertop between Anna's copy of *Real Simple* and his own *Poets & Writers,* which, nonetheless, gave him the deepest chill of his life.

Front and center, his address. More accurately, *their* address.

And in the upper left-hand corner, the name *Talented Tom.*

He looked at it for a long, terrible moment.

Then he snatched it up and rushed with it into the bathroom, turning on the water in the sink and locking the door behind him. He slit open the envelope and extracted the single sheet of paper inside with shaking hands.

You know what you did. I know what you did. Are you ready for everyone to know what you did? I hope so, because I'm getting ready to tell the world. Have fun with your career after that.

So this, he thought, listening to the din of his own breath over the running water, was what worse felt like. This person had come through the screen into the actual, tactile world, and now Jake was holding in his hands an object TalentedTom, too, had held. There was a new and sharp horror in that, as if the paper itself held all of the malevolence, all of the outrage Jake did not deserve. The cumulative weight of it took his breath away and rendered him incapable of movement, and he stayed where he was for so long that Anna came to the bathroom door and asked if he was feeling all right.

He was not feeling all right.

Eventually, he crammed the piece of paper into a pocket of his Dopp kit, took off his clothes, and got into the shower. He was trying to think it through with whatever of his cognitive abilities remained at his disposal, but this proved impossible even after half an hour under the hottest water he could stand. Nor was it possible in the days that followed, as he added the furtive collection of the mail to his already obsessive monitoring of the internet. He simply could not think of how to go forward, and that, ironically, was what made him realize the only place left to go was back.

Ripley was what he knew. Ripley was all he could be sure of. Something relevant to his present crisis had taken place at Ripley, that was obvious, and it was understandable; the heightened camaraderie of the MFA program—even (perhaps especially?) the low-residency MFA program!—acted powerfully upon people who couldn't be "out" as writers in their ordinary, daily lives, perhaps not even to their own friends and families. Gathering on an otherwise empty college campus they were, perhaps for the first time, suddenly enfolded by their tribe and able to talk *story! plot! character!* with people they'd only just met and would know for only a brief, intense period. Evan Parker might have declined to share his infallible plot with the other students in the much touted "safety" of Jake's formal workshop, but it was entirely possible that somebody in the program had managed to connect with him, maybe during drinks at the Ripley Inn, maybe lingering after a meal in the cafeteria. Or maybe afterward, at Evan Parker's house or the other person's house, or over email, with pages of actual manuscript sent back and forth for "critique."

Whoever TalentedTom was, his obvious (if faulty!) grasp of what had transpired between Jake and his former student meant that he, too, was connected to that community, or at least had crossed paths with someone who was. And yet, Jake had allowed his own investigation to lapse with Martin Purcell of Burlington, Vermont. Now this asshole had contacted him at home, not through some social media platform, not even through his own website or publisher, but at his actual, physical place of residence. Which he shared *with his wife*. This was painfully, powerfully close. This signaled an unprecedented intensification of @TalentedTom's campaign. This was unacceptable.

Defense, never the best strategy, was obviously no longer an option, not after this. He had to return to what he knew for sure—Ripley—and start again, from there.

He hadn't bothered to open the large envelope containing Martin Purcell's manuscript pages when it arrived back in the fall. Since then it had been gathering dust in a box under his bed, mixed in among other manuscripts (sent by actual friends, looking for his "thoughts") and advance galleys (sent by publishers, looking for blurbs). Now Jake pulled the box out and went digging through it. When he found Purcell's mailer he slit open the end and extracted the cover letter:

Dear Jake (if I may),

I am so incredibly grateful to you for agreeing to look at these stories! Thank you so much! I'd be delighted to discuss if you ever have time. No comment too small . . . or too big! I've been thinking of this as a novel made up of short stories, but maybe that is because the idea of writing a "novel" is so huge and terrifying. I don't know how you novelists do it!

Anyway, feel free to email or give me a call when you're finished, and thanks again.

Martin Purcell
MPurcell@SBurlHS.org

There had to be sixty pages in there, Jake thought. He supposed he would actually have to read them. He returned to the living room, sat down on the kilim-covered couch, and opened his laptop. The cat, Whidbey, followed him, uncoiled along Jake's left thigh, and began to purr.

Hi Martin! I've been reading your stuff. Wow—excellent work. Lots to discuss.

Within a couple of minutes, Purcell wrote back:

Fantastic! Just say when!

It was late afternoon and the sun had swung around Greenwich Avenue on its way west. He was supposed to leave here soon, to meet Anna at a Japanese place they liked, near her studio.

He wrote:

I'm actually heading to Vermont in a couple of days. Why don't we meet there? Maybe easier to go over the pages in person.

You're kidding! What are you in Vermont for?

To find out more from you, duh. (Jake didn't write.)

A reading. But I was thinking of staying for a day or two. Need to get some work done. And I miss Vermont!

He so did not miss Vermont.

Where's the reading? I'll come!

Ugh, he would, wouldn't he? Where was the fictional reading?

It's actually a private event, in someone's house. In Dorset.

Dorset was one of the swankier towns in the state. Just the kind of place somebody might import a famous writer for a private event.

Oh. That's too bad.

But why don't we meet in Rutland? That is, if it's not too far for you to travel.

He knew it wouldn't be. Even without the prospect of a free private manuscript consultation with a bestselling author, Jake had long observed that Vermonters seemed willing to drive all over their state at the drop of a hat.

Not at all. Straight down 7.

They arranged to meet on Thursday evening, at the Birdseye Diner.

This was so good of him, wrote Martin, and Jake said no, it wasn't, and that was no lie, not even an exaggeration. Martin Purcell was his best way into the place that had somehow produced TalentedTom: end of story.

Also, it was time to take a closer look at the town that had produced Evan Parker. Long past time, actually.

CRIB

BY JACOB FINCH BONNER

Macmillan, New York, 2017, page 98

Samantha's mother didn't trust doctors, so she figured one of them would try to persuade her the growing lump in her right breast was cancer. By the time Samantha saw the lump herself it was actually protruding over her mother's bra strap and things had gone, of course, too far. Maria, ten by then and in fifth grade, tried to persuade her grandmother to accept the scorched earth radiation-plus-chemo the oncologist at Community Memorial in Hamilton was suggesting, but Samantha's mother found the chemo unpleasant, and after the second cycle she announced that she'd take her chances with God. God gave her another four months, and Samantha hoped she was satisfied.

A week after the funeral she moved into her parents' old bedroom, the nicest one, and put Maria into the room she herself was vacating, the room with the cannon ball bed in which she had dreamed of escape and sulked through pregnancy, all the way at the other end of the hall. That pretty much set the tone for their remaining years together. Samantha had a part-time job by then, processing bills for a branch of the Bassett Healthcare Network, and after a training course on a company computer she set up in a little room off the kitchen, she was able to work from home. Maria, since the age of six, had been getting herself up in the morning, and from the time she was eight she was feeding herself cereal and packing her own lunches. By nine she was pulling together her own dinners, maintaining the shopping list, and reminding Samantha to pay her taxes. At eleven her teachers called Samantha in for a conference because they wanted to skip Maria ahead a grade. She told them absolutely not. She wouldn't give any of those people the satisfaction.

CHAPTER TWENTY

Nobody Comes to Rutland

Opting for double duty from a single falsehood, he told Anna that he was going to Vermont for a few days to do a private event and finish the revisions Wendy wanted. Naturally enough, she wanted to go with him.

"I'd love to see Vermont!" she said. "I've never been to New England."

For a moment he actually considered letting her come, but of course that was a terrible idea.

"I think if I hole up somewhere I can kind of power through what I need to do. If you're there with me, I'm going to want to spend time with you. And I just . . . I want to do that *after* I get something to Wendy. So I can enjoy it, and not feel I should be doing something else."

She nodded. She seemed to understand. He hoped she understood.

Jake drove up through western Connecticut on Route 7, stopping for lunch in Manchester and arriving at his inn in Rutland around five. There, in his rock-hard four-poster, he finally acquainted himself with Martin Purcell's stories, which were flaccid and pointless, populated by forgettable characters. Purcell had a particular interest in young people as they faltered between adolescence and adulthood—not surprising, perhaps, given his work as a high school teacher—but he seemed incapable of looking beyond the superficial. One character had an injury that prevented him from finishing a promising track season. Another failed a test, putting her college scholarship in jeopardy. A seemingly devoted young couple—devoted for teenagers, at least—became pregnant and the boy, instantly, abandoned his girlfriend. (Jake wondered at Purcell's claim that this was, or was meant to be, a "novel in stories"—the same conceit he himself had used with his second book, *Reverberations.* Jake hadn't fooled anyone then, and Purcell wasn't fooling anyone now.) In the end he came up with a few points to make and a fairly obvious suggestion of how to move forward—focus on the young couple, let the characters in the other stories move into the background—and then he went to meet Martin Purcell at the diner.

In Vermont, people with money lived in places like Woodstock, Manchester, Charlotte, Dorset, and Middlebury, not in Rutland, and while Rutland was much larger than most other Vermont towns it felt like a semi-depressed drive-through today with many of its great old houses repurposed for bail bondsmen, abortion "counselors," and welfare agencies, and interspersed with strip malls and bowling alleys and the bus station. Jake's inn was less than half a mile from the Birdseye Diner, but he drove the three minutes. As soon as he got inside the door, a man stood up in a booth halfway down the length of the room and waved. Jake waved back.

"Wasn't sure you'd remember what I looked like," said Martin Purcell.

"Oh, I recognize you," Jake lied, sliding into the booth. "Though, you know, as I was driving here I thought, I should have tried to find a photo online, just to be sure I didn't sit down with somebody else."

"Most pictures of me online I'm standing behind a bunch of robotics nerds. I coach the club at my school. State champs, six out of the last ten years."

Jake tried to rustle up some enthusiasm to go along with his congratulations.

"Really nice of you to drive down," he said.

"Hey, really nice of you to look over my stuff!" Purcell said. He was greatly excited. "I'm still in shock. I've been talking to my wife about it. I don't think she believed me when I said you'd agreed to do that for me."

"Oh, it's no trouble. I miss teaching." This, too, was a lie.

The Birdseye was a classic specimen of a diner, with aqua-and-black-checkered tiles and a shining stainless bar and stools. Jake ordered a burger and a chocolate shake. Purcell wanted the chicken soup.

"You know, I was surprised you wanted to meet in Rutland, though. Nobody comes to Rutland. Everybody comes through Rutland."

"Except the people who live here, I guess."

"Yeah. Whoever the genius town planner was, who decided one of the state's busiest routes ought to run down the main street, he should've been tarred and feathered." Purcell shrugged. "Maybe it seemed like a good idea at the time, I don't know."

"Well, you're a history teacher, aren't you? You probably see things from more of a backward-looking perspective."

The guy frowned. "Did I tell you I was a history teacher? Most people, because they know I write stories, assume I teach English. But I'll tell you a dark secret. I don't love reading fiction. Other people's fiction."

That's no secret to me, thought Jake.

"No? You prefer to read history?"

"I prefer to read history and write fiction."

"You must have found that challenging at Ripley. Reading your classmates' work."

Their waitress brought Jake's milkshake in a full glass and a half-full steel tumbler. It tasted amazing and sank straight to the pit of his stomach.

"Oh, not really. I think when you go into a situation like that you adapt. If I'm going to be asking people in my workshop to give my work a generous and close reading, I need to do the same for them."

Jake decided this moment was as good as any. "Sadly, my own student didn't feel that way. My late student."

Purcell, to Jake's dismay, sighed at this. "I wondered how long it would take us to get around to Evan Parker."

Jake retreated instantly, but not very persuasively.

"Well, I remember you mentioned he was from this area. Rutland, right?"

"That's right," said Purcell.

"I guess he's been on my mind today. He had some kind of a business here, I think? A bar of some kind?"

"Tavern," said Purcell.

The waitress returned and set down their plates with a flourish. His burger looked mammoth, with fries piled up so high they spilled onto the table when the plate landed. Purcell's soup, despite the fact that it was billed as an appetizer, was also in a meal-sized bowl.

"They certainly know how to eat up here," Jake observed when she'd gone.

"Have to survive the winters," said Purcell, taking up his spoon.

For a moment, conversation took a back seat.

"It's nice that you two kept up with each other. After Ripley, I mean. It's pretty isolated."

"Well, Vermont isn't exactly the Yukon," Purcell said, with a definite edge to his tone.

"No, I mean . . . for us as writers. We're so alone in what we do. When you get a taste of that fellowship, it's something you want to hold on to."

Purcell nodded eagerly. "That was just what I was hoping to find at Ripley. Maybe even more than the teachers, just that connection to other people doing what I wanted to do. So yeah, I absolutely kept up with a few of the others, Evan included. Him and I sent each other stuff for a couple of months, until his passing."

Inwardly, Jake winced at this, though whether it was due to the thought of that "stuff" passing back and forth between the two writers or to the "him and I" wasn't immediately clear.

"We all need a reader. Every writer does."

"Oh, I know. It's why I'm so appreciative—"

But Jake didn't want to go there. At least, not before he absolutely had to.

"So you sent him the same stories you sent me? And he sent you his work, too? I always wondered what happened to that novel he was working on."

It was a risk, of course. He'd been pretty sure that if Purcell had actually read Evan Parker's work in progress he'd have mentioned its commonality with *Crib* by now. But after all, this was what he'd come so far to find out.

"Well, I sent him mine, for sure. He had a couple of my stories when he passed, that he was going to send back edits on, but he kept his own stuff pretty close to the chest. I only ever saw a couple of pages. A woman who lived in an old house with her daughter and worked on a psychic hotline? That's what I remember. You probably saw way more of that novel than I did."

Jake nodded. "Very reticent in the workshop itself, when it came to his project. Those same pages you mentioned, that was all he ever turned in. It's certainly all I ever saw," he said pointedly.

Purcell was digging into the bottom of his bowl for the chicken.

"D'you think he had other friends in the program he might have been talking to?"

The teacher looked up. He held Jake's gaze for a bit too long. "Do you mean, was he showing his work to anyone else?"

"Oh no, not specifically. I just thought, you know, it's a shame he got so little out of the program. Because he'd have been helped by a good reader, and if he didn't want my help, maybe he managed to connect with one of the other teachers. Bruce O'Reilly?"

"Ha! Every blade of grass has its own story!"

"Or the other fiction teacher. Frank Ricardo. He was new that year."

"Oh, Ricardo. Evan thought that guy was pathetic. No way he went to either of those two."

"Well, maybe one of the other students, then."

"Look, no offense to you, because obviously I'm not arguing with your success, so if bonding with fellow writers helped you out, that's great, and I'm all for it myself or I wouldn't have wanted to go to Ripley and I wouldn't have asked you to read my stuff. But Evan was never into the community of writers aspect. He was a great guy to go to a concert with, or out for a meal. But the touchy-feely things about, you know, *writing*? That stuff in the catalog about our unique voices and our stories only we could tell? That was so not him."

"Okay." Jake nodded. He was realizing, with a certain extreme discomfort, that he and Evan Parker had shared something else, above and beyond the plot of *Crib*.

"And all the stuff about the *craft of writing*, and the *process of writing*, and all that? Never talked about it. I'm telling you, Evan didn't share, not pages and not feelings. Like the song says: He was a rock. He was an island."

It was a massive relief to hear, but of course Jake couldn't say that. What he said, instead, was: "Kind of sad."

The teacher shrugged. "He didn't strike me as sad. It's just how he was."

"But . . . didn't you say his whole family was gone? His parents and his sister? And he was such a young guy. That's awful."

"Sure. The parents died a long time ago, and then the sister, I'm not sure when that happened. It's tragic."

"Yes," Jake agreed.

"And that niece, the one mentioned in the obituary, I don't think she even showed up at the memorial service. I didn't meet anyone there who said they were related. The only ones who got up and spoke were his employees and his customers. And me."

"That's a shame," said Jake, pushing the uneaten half of his burger away.

"Well, they couldn't have been close. He never even mentioned her to me. And the dead sister, man, that one he hated."

Jake looked at him. "Hate's a pretty strong word."

"He said she'd do anything. I don't think he meant it in a good way."

"Oh? What way did he mean it?"

But now the guy was looking at him with frank suspicion. It was one thing to spend a bit of time on a mutual acquaintance, maybe especially a mutual acquaintance who had died fairly recently and fairly close by. But this? Could it possibly be that Jake Bonner, *The New York Times* bestselling novelist, had not come to Rutland for the sole purpose of discussing a complete stranger's short stories? Because what other reason could there be?

"I have no idea," Purcell said finally.

"Oh. Sure. Hey, sorry about all the questions. He's just been on my mind today, like I said."

"Right."

And Jake thought he'd better leave it there.

"So anyway, I want to talk about your stories. They're very strong, and I have a couple of ideas about how to move them forward. I mean, if it's all right for me to share them with you."

Purcell, naturally, seemed delighted with this change of direction. Jake spent the next seventy-five minutes paying the piper. He also made a point of picking up the check.

CHAPTER TWENTY-ONE

Boo-hoo, So Sad

After they said good-bye in the parking lot he watched Martin Purcell get in his car and head north, back toward Burlington, then he waited in his own car for a few minutes, just to be on the safe side.

The Parker Tavern was just off Route 4, midway between Rutland and West Rutland, its neon PARKER TAVERN FOOD AND LIQUOR visible from far down the street. As Jake pulled into the lot, he saw the other sign he remembered from the *Rutland Herald* story, that hand-painted *Happy Hour 3–6*. The lot was very full and it took him a few minutes to find a spot.

Jake wasn't much of a tavern guy, but he had a basic idea of how to behave under the circumstances. He went inside and took a seat at the bar and asked for a Coors, then he took out his phone and scrolled a bit, so as not to seem overly eager. He'd chosen a stool without anyone on either side, but it didn't take long for a guy to move in beside him. He nodded at Jake.

"Hey."

"Hey."

"You want anything to eat?" the bartender asked the next time he came by.

"No, thanks. Maybe another Coors, though."

"You got it."

A group of four women entered, all in their thirties, he guessed. The guy on Jake's left had swiveled away from him, and was definitely keeping an eye on the women at their table. A different woman took the seat to his right. He heard her order. A moment later, he heard her curse.

"Sorry."

Jake turned. She was around his own age, and big.

"Beg your pardon?"

"I said sorry. 'Cause I cursed."

"Oh. That's okay." It was more than okay. It relieved him of having to start the conversation. "Why'd you curse?"

The woman held up her phone. The photo on the screen showed two cherubic girls, cheeks together, both grinning, but the acid green bar of a text message cut off the tops of their heads. *Fuck you*, it said.

"Adorable," he said, pretending not to have seen.

"Well, they were, back when the picture was taken. Now they're in high school. I guess I ought to be grateful about that, anyway. Their older brother wouldn't go back after tenth grade. He's over in Troy doing god knows what."

Jake had no idea how to respond to that, but he wasn't about to decline the clear overture of such an unrestrained neighbor.

Her drink arrived, though Jake hadn't heard her actually order. It was something overtly tropical, with a slice of pineapple and a little paper umbrella.

"Thanks, doll," the woman said to the bartender. Then she put away half of it in a single long swallow. Jake didn't imagine it was doing her any good. Thus fortified, she turned back to Jake and introduced herself. "I'm Sally."

"Jake. What kind of drink is that?"

"Oh, something they put together for me, special. It's my brother-in-law's place."

Score, thought Jake. He'd done nothing to deserve it, but he'd take it.

"Your brother-in-law named Parker?"

The woman looked at him as if he had just insulted her. She had long and suspiciously bright yellow hair, so thin her scalp showed through in patches.

"Parker was the name of the guy who had it before. He died, though."

"Oh, that's too bad."

She shrugged. "Not my favorite person. Grew up here. We both did."

Jake detoured to ask Sally a few of the questions she plainly wanted him to ask. He learned that Sally had moved to Rutland as a kid, from New Hampshire. Two sisters, one dead. She was raising her late sister's kids, she told Jake.

"That must be hard."

"Nah. Good kids. But fucked up. Thanks to their mother." She lifted her glass, half in salute, half as a signal to the bartender.

"So you grew up with the guy who owned this place before?"

"Evan Parker. Couple years ahead of me in school. Dated my sister."

Jake was careful not to react. "Really? Small world."

"Small town. Also, he dated pretty much everyone. If 'date' is really the word. I'm not sure he isn't the father of my nephew if you want to know the truth. Not that it matters."

"Well, that's . . ."

"That was his spot, behind the bar." She held up her already half-drained glass and tipped it toward the far end of the room. "Knew everybody who came in."

"Well, the owner of a bar has to be social. Part of the job, listening to people's problems."

She grinned at him, but it was far from a happy grin. "Evan Parker? Listen to anyone's problems? Evan Parker didn't give a shit about anyone else's problems."

"Is that right?"

"Is that right," Sally mocked him. She was slurring, ever so slightly, he noticed. It occurred to him that the tropical beverage wasn't her first drink of the evening. "Yeah, that's right. Why do you care, anyway?"

"Oh. Well, I just had dinner with an old friend. We're both writers. And my friend said the guy who used to own this bar was a writer, too. He was writing a novel."

Sally threw back her head and laughed. She was so loud that a couple of conversations around them stopped, and people turned to look.

"Like that asshole could ever write a novel," she finally said, shaking her head, declining further amusement.

"You seem surprised."

"Come on, the guy probably never even *read* a novel. Didn't go to college. Wait, maybe community college." She leaned forward on the bar and looked down to the end. "Hey Jerry," she yelled. "Did Parker go to college?"

A burly man with a dark beard looked up from his own conversation. "Evan Parker? Rutland Community, I think," he shouted.

"That your brother-in-law?"

Sally nodded.

"Well, maybe he took a writing class or something and decided to give it a try. Anybody can be a writer, you know."

"Sure. I'm writing *Moby-Dick,* myself. What about you?"

He laughed. "I'm definitely not writing *Moby-Dick.*"

Now she was slurring even more, he noted. "Dick" had been rendered as "deek," and "myself" as "my shelf." After a moment, he said: "If he was writing a novel, I wonder what it was about."

"Sneaking into girls' bedrooms at night, probably." Her eyes were half closed.

He decided to try something else before he lost her entirely.

"You must have known his whole family if you grew up together."

She nodded glumly. "Yep. The parents died. We were in high school."

"Both died?" Jake asked, as if he didn't already know.

"Together. In the house. Wait." She leaned forward on the bar again. "Hey Jerry?" she yelled.

Down at the end, the brother-in-law looked up.

"Evan Parker's parents. They died, right?"

Jake, who could have done without all this shouting of Parker's name, was relieved to see the brother-in-law lift up his hand. A moment later he'd ended his conversation and made his way to where his inebriated sister-in-law was seated.

"Jerry Hastings." He extended his hand to Jake.

"I'm Jake," said Jake.

"You asking about Evan?"

"No, not really. Just about where the Parker came from. In the name."

"Oh. Old family around here. They used to own the quarry in West Rutland. Hundred and fifty years to get from a mansion to a needle in the arm. That's Vermont, I guess."

"What do you mean?" said Jake, who knew exactly what he meant.

Jerry shook his head. "Don't mean to be cavalier. He was in recovery for a long time, but obviously he picked up again. Lot of people were surprised. I mean, some addicts, every day you think, *Wonder if today's the day.* Others, they're getting up and going to work, taking care of business, so it seems more like out of nowhere. But this place wasn't doing all that great, I happen to know. And he told some people he was trying to sell his house, get some money into the business." He shrugged.

"He heard Parker was writing a novel when he died," Sally informed her brother-in-law.

"That so? Fictional novel?"

Sadly not, thought Jake. If only Evan Parker's novel *had* been fictional, but unfortunately it was quite real.

"I wonder what it was about?" Jake said aloud.

"Why do you care?" Sally said. She had turned some corner into belligerence. "You didn't even know the guy."

He lifted up his mug. "You're absolutely right."

"What were you asking about the parents?" Jerry said. "They died."

"I know they died," Sally said with luxuriant sarcasm. "Wasn't it like a gas leak at the house or something?"

"Not a gas leak. Carbon monoxide. From the furnace." Over Sally's head he was giving the bartender a discreet hand gesture, which meant—if Jake was interpreting it correctly—*no more for this one.* "You know the house I'm talking about?" he asked Jake.

"How's he supposed to know?" Sally rolled her eyes. "You ever seen this guy before tonight?"

"I'm not from here," Jake confirmed.

"Right. Well, big house in West Rutland. Like, a hundred years old. Right near the quarry on Marble Street."

"Across from the Agway," said Sally, obviously forgetting the point she, herself, had just made.

"Okay," said Jake.

"We were still in high school. Wait, maybe Evan was out already, but the sister was your class, wasn't she?"

Sally nodded. "*Bitch,*" she said distinctly.

Jake tried hard to stifle his natural reaction.

But Jerry was laughing. "You did not like that girl."

"She was a piece of work."

"So, wait," said Jake, "the parents died in their home but the daughter didn't?"

"*Bitch,*" said Sally again.

This time Jake couldn't help staring at her. Were they not discussing a young person whose parents had both died *while she was in high school*? And *in their own home*? Which would also have been *her own home*?

"Like I said." Her brother-in-law grinned at Jake. "She did not like that girl."

"Nobody liked her," Sally said. She sounded glum now. Maybe it had gotten through to her that she'd been cut off at the bar.

"She died too," Jerry told Jake. "Parker's sister. A few years ago."

"Burned up," said Sally.

He wasn't sure he'd heard that accurately. He asked her to repeat it.

"I said, *she burned up*."

"Oh," Jake said. "Wow."

"What I heard."

"That's horrible."

And it was, it obviously was, but even so, Jake couldn't muster more than baseline human empathy for these ancillary members of Evan Parker's family, not just because he didn't truly care about any of these people, but because none of the events under discussion—a sister's premature and apparently grisly death, a carbon monoxide poisoning in an old house, decades ago, even, at the end of the day, Evan Parker's own opiate overdose—had any real bearing on his own very current, very pressing concerns. And also, none of this was exactly new information. *Predeceased by both parents and a sister* had been right there in Evan Parker's online obituary, which he'd read years ago at his own desk in Cobleskill, New York, before a single word of *Crib* had been written.

Actually, he was more than ready to leave the Parker Tavern. He was exhausted, a tiny bit drunk, and his situation had not been helped—nor his life in any way improved—by anything Jerry or Sally had told him. Besides, the two of them now had their heads together and seemed to be discussing some private matter, animatedly and with clear mutual antipathy. Jake tried to reach back to the last topic they'd shared—Evan Parker's sister, *a piece of work*—just so he could say something vaguely on topic before he left, but it all felt very distant and utterly irrelevant. Slowly got to his feet and extracted his wallet, then he put a twenty on the counter.

"Well, it's sad," he said to the back of Sally's head. "Isn't it? The whole family's gone."

"Except for the sister's kid," he heard her say.

"What?"

"You said, *boo hoo, so sad, the whole family's gone.*"

He doubted he'd used these exact words, but it didn't seem an important point at the moment.

"The *kid,*" Sally said with great exasperation. "But she was like, *out of there*. She left home the minute she could. Who could blame her, with a mother like that? I don't think she even waited to graduate from high school. *Don't let the door hit ya!*"

And then, as if to echo this dismissal, Sally turned away. He saw now that her brother-in-law had departed, and that she had made a new friend on the next bar stool over. *Wait,* he said, but actually he couldn't have said that out loud because neither of them appeared to notice. So he had to say it again: "Wait."

Sally turned back to look at him. She seemed to require a moment to get her bearings, or possibly to remember who he was. "Wait what?" she said, with real hostility.

Wait. Evan Parker's only living relative. That was what.

"Where does his niece live?" Jake managed to say.

She pinned him with a look of extravagant contempt. "How the fuck would I know?" she said. And that really was the end of their conversation.

CRIB

BY JACOB FINCH BONNER

Macmillan, New York, 2017, pages 146–47

The conventional wisdom was that they were alike, mother and daughter: both smart, both feisty, both highly intent on not spending their lives in Earlville, New York, and incidentally so physically similar—narrow and tall, with thin dark hair and a definite tendency to slouch—that Samantha struggled to see Dan Weybridge anywhere at all in the girl. But watching Maria grow up—and Samantha did watch, that was pretty much all she did—a few key differences gradually came into focus. Maria, in marked contrast to her mother's fervid planning for departure, seemed to waft toward this goal without much obvious effort, and even less in the way of apparent concern. She lacked even Samantha's small inclination to placate (let alone capitulate to) others, declined to grub for favors of any kind, and could not have cared less that there were adults in her life (notably those in her school life) who wanted to encourage her and ease her way forward. Where Samantha had been diligent with schoolwork and careful not to mess up (one significant exception there!), Maria turned in homework when she felt like it, departed from assignments if they failed to interest her, and disparaged her teachers when she thought they'd misunderstood (translation: were too stupid to understand) the material.

Also, Maria was a lesbian, which meant that whatever else might happen, she was hardly going to drop the ball just short of the goalpost, the way her mother had.

Her classmates included the children of Colgate professors and the children of Colgate grads who'd settled in the area (mostly organic farming or making art) alongside the children of the county's oldest families (dairy farmers, county employees, plain old upstate hermits), but they broke down along another divide: those determined to make high school the best time of their lives and those who expected to move on to far more interesting experiences. Maria, it was obvious to all, was just passing through. She drifted between cliques, unconcerned by a party she hadn't heard about or some rift in the social fabric of her class, even if she was one of the parties involved. Twice she shed her entire friend group, leaving people mystified and wounded. (About these social acts Samantha was completely unaware, until somebody's mother called her to complain.) And once she stopped speaking to a girl who'd been coming around to the house for years, a rupture so obvious that even Samantha knew about it without being told. Maria, when asked, simply said: "I just can't anymore, with a person like that."

When she was thirteen she taught herself to drive in the new Subaru (a replacement for her grandfather's, which had finally given up the ghost), and in fact drove herself to the DMV office in Norwich to pick up her learner's permit. When she was fifteen she made out with a senior named Lara in the lighting booth during a rehearsal for *Legally Blonde*. It was a relief and a thrill. And when Lara graduated a few months later and immediately moved to Florida, Maria spent most of that summer moping. Or at least until she met Gab at the bookstore in Hamilton. She didn't mope after that.

CHAPTER TWENTY-TWO

Hospitality

Late the next morning he drove west on Route 4 with the Taconic Range ahead and the Green Mountains in his rearview mirror, intent on finding the house where Evan Parker's family had lived. Without an exact address he wasn't sure how difficult it was going to be, but once he turned off at the West Rutland exit he discovered that the town didn't have much of a *there* there; certainly less of a there than most New England towns with their classic squares and village greens. Jake easily found Marble Street just beyond the old brick town hall, and he drove past automotive shops and supermarkets and the old quarry itself, which was now an arts center. A mile later he spotted the Agway, and slowed down. The house, just past it on the right, turned out to be impossible to miss. He pulled over and leaned forward in his seat to take it in.

It was a massive three-story Italianate with a marble base, set back from the road and frankly stunning: large, clean, freshly painted yellow, and surrounded by intentional plantings, an encouraging offset to some of the architectural decay he'd seen over the weekend. Whoever lived there now had carefully trimmed the hedges, and Jake could see the outline of a formal garden just behind the building. He was attempting to align the relative splendor of what he was seeing with Evan Parker's reported money woes when a green Volvo slowed beside him and turned in to the driveway. Jake grabbed for the key and turned it in the ignition, but already the driver had climbed out and was giving him an unequivocally friendly wave. She was a woman about his own age with a long and very red braid down her back. Despite the baggy coat she wore, it was obvious that she was rail thin. She was calling something. He rolled down his window.

"I'm sorry?" he said.

Now she was walking toward his car, and the New Yorker in Jake cringed: Who took this kind of a chance with a total stranger parked outside your home? Evidently, a Vermonter did. She came closer. Jake began grasping for some explanation of why he was here, but he couldn't think of anything, which was probably why he ended up with a version of the truth.

"I'm so sorry. I think I knew somebody who once lived here."

"Oh yeah? Had to be a Parker."

"Yes. He was. Evan Parker."

"Sure." The woman nodded. "You know, he passed away."

"I heard. Anyway, sorry to bother you. I was just driving through town and I thought, you know, I'd pay my respects."

"We didn't know him," the woman said. "Sorry for your loss."

The irony of that, of being offered condolences for Evan Parker, nearly made him confess right there. But he produced the required noises. "Thanks. I was his teacher, actually."

"Oh yeah?" she said again. "In the high school?"

"No, no. It was a writing program. Up at Ripley? In the Northeast Kingdom."

"Ayuh," she said, like a true Vermonter.

"My name's Jake. Your house is gorgeous."

At this, she grinned. She had distinctly gray teeth, he noticed. Cigarettes or tetracycline.

"I'm trying to get my partner to repaint the trim. I don't like that green. I think we need to go darker."

It took him a moment to understand that she actually wanted him to weigh in on this issue. "You could go darker," he said finally. It seemed to be the right answer.

"I know! My partner, she hired the painter one weekend I was out of town. She pulled a fast one on me." The woman grinned at this. She wasn't holding much of a grudge, in other words. "My name's Betty. You like to see the inside?"

"What? Really?"

"Why not? You're not an ax murderer, are you?"

The blood rushed to Jake's head. For the briefest moment he wondered if he was.

"No. I'm a writer. That's what I taught up at Ripley."

"Yeah? Have you published anything?"

He turned off the car and slowly stepped out. "A couple of books, yeah. I wrote a book called *Crib*?"

Her eyes widened. "Seriously? I got that out of the library. I haven't read it yet, but I'm going to."

He held out his hand and she shook it. "That's great. I hope you like it."

"Oh my god, my sister's gonna lose her shit. She said I had to read it. She said I wouldn't see the twist coming. 'Cause I'm the person who leans over in the movie and tells you, five minutes in, what's gonna happen. It's like a curse." She laughed.

"That *is* a curse," Jake agreed. "Hey, it's really nice of you to invite me in. I mean, I'd love to see it. Are you sure?"

"Sure! I wish I didn't just have a library copy! If I had my own copy you could sign it."

"That's okay. I'll send you a signed copy when I get home."

She looked at him as if he'd promised her a Shakespeare First Folio.

He followed her up the tidy driveway and through the large wooden front door. Betty, as she opened the door, prepared the way by calling: "Sylvie? I've got a guest."

He could hear a radio going off somewhere in the back of the house. Betty reached down to scoop up an enormous gray cat and turned back to Jake. "Give me a sec," she said, and went down the hall. He was trying to take it all in, greedily recording details. There was a wide wooden staircase ascending from a very grand central hallway that had been painted a fairly stomach-churning pink. To his right, a large parlor visible through an open door, and to his left, an even more formal living room through an open archway. The dimensions and the details—dentil crown molding, high baseboards—were a highly intentional display of wealth, but Betty and Sylvia had pretty much bludgeoned any trace of grandeur to death with folksy signs: ALL YOU NEED IS LOVE . . . AND A CAT! and CRAZY CAT LADY lined the wall up the stairs, and visible above the parlor mantelpiece was LOVE IS LOVE. There was also a cacophony of too-bright area rugs, all but obliterating the wooden floorboards, and everywhere Jake looked, too much of everything: tables covered with knickknacks and vases of flowers too healthy and bright to be real, and so many chairs pulled into a circle it looked as if a group was expected, or had recently left. He tried to imagine his former student here: descending this staircase, following Betty's steps into the kitchen he assumed was at the end of the hall. He couldn't do it. The women had placed a kitsch-encrusted barrier between whatever had been here before and what was here now.

Betty returned, without the cat but with a stout dark woman in a batik headscarf. "Sylvia, my partner," she said.

"Oh my god," said Sylvia. "I can't believe this. A famous author."

"Famous author is an oxymoron," said Jake. It was his go-to assertion of personal modesty.

"Oh my god," said Sylvia again.

"Your house is just beautiful. Inside and out. How long have you been here?"

"Just a couple of years," said Betty. "It was so run-down when we moved in, you wouldn't believe it. We had to replace every damn thing."

"Some of them twice," said Sylvia. "Come on back, have some coffee."

The kitchen had its own complement of signage: SYLVIA'S KITCHEN (SEASONED WITH LOVE) over the stove, HAPPINESS IS HOMEMADE above the table, which was itself covered with a bright blue cat-festooned glazed cloth. "Do you like hazelnut? It's all we drink."

Jake, who loathed all flavored coffees, attested that he did.

"Sylvie, where's that library book?"

"I haven't seen it," said Sylvia. "Cream?"

"Yes. Thanks."

She brought him the mug. It was white with a black line drawing of a cat on it, and the words "Feline Good."

"There's donuts," said Betty. "That's where I was coming from. You know Jones' Donuts in town?"

"Well, no," he said. "I don't know the town at all. I was really just driving through. I wasn't expecting all this Vermont hospitality!"

"I have to admit," said Sylvia, who came bearing a plate of oversized glazed donuts, "I sneaked a look at Google on my phone. You're obviously who you said you are. If not I'd be out back calling the troopers. In case you thought we're all hospitality and no common sense."

"Oh." Jake nodded. "Good." He was relieved he hadn't lied, out in the car. He was relieved that his recent proclivity for lying hadn't fully replaced a default instinct to tell the truth.

"I can't believe this place used to be run-down. You could never tell that, now!"

"I know, right? But trust me, the whole first year we were spackling and painting, peeling off old wallpaper. There hadn't been any serious upkeep in years. Which shouldn't have surprised us. People actually died in this house because of bad maintenance."

"No maintenance," Betty said. She had returned, bringing her own coffee.

"What do you mean? Like a fire?"

"No. Carbon monoxide leak. From the oil furnace."

"Really!"

The enormous gray cat had trailed Betty into the kitchen. Now he leapt into her lap and settled himself down.

"Does that weird you out?" She looked at Jake. "House this old, it stands to reason people have died in it. Home births, home deaths. Just how things were done back then."

"Doesn't weird me out." He tried a sip of his coffee. It was vile.

"I don't like to say this," said Betty, "but your old student died here, too. Upstairs in one of the bedrooms."

Jake nodded solemnly.

"Hey, so I have to ask," said Betty, "what was it like, meeting Oprah?"

He told them about Oprah. They were big Oprah fans.

"Are they gonna make a movie out of your book?"

He talked about that, too. Only then could he try to bring the conversation back to Evan Parker, though even as he did he wasn't sure it was worth the effort. These two might live in the Parker house, but so what? It wasn't as if they'd ever met him.

"So my old student grew up here," he finally said.

"That family was in this house from the time it was built. They owned the quarry. You probably passed the quarry, driving here."

"I think I did." He nodded. "Must have been a wealthy family."

"Back then, sure," said Betty. "But not for a long time. We got a little grant from the state to help with the restoration. We just had to agree to put it on the Christmas house tour when we were finished."

Jake looked around. There was nothing he'd seen since coming inside that merited the word "restoration."

"That sounds fun!"

Sylvia made an unhappy noise.

Betty said, "Sure, a hundred strangers stomping through your rooms, trailing snow. But we took the money, so we kept up our side of the bargain. Lot of people around West Rutland were dying to see the inside of this house, and that was nothing to do with the work we'd done. People knew this house their whole lives. And the family."

Sylvia said, "That family had the worst luck."

There it was again, that phrase, only by now it didn't strike Jake as all that surprising. By now he had the relevant information: all four of them had died, Evan Parker and his sister and their parents, three of the four of them under this very roof. He supposed they were collectively deserving of the term "worst luck."

"I didn't know he'd died, till recently," said Jake. "Actually, I still don't know how."

"Overdose," Sylvia said.

"Oh no. I didn't know he had that problem."

"Nobody did. Or at least that he still had the problem."

"I shouldn't say this," said Betty, "but my sister was in a certain anonymous group with Evan Parker. It met in the basement of the Lutheran church in Rutland. And he was a longtime member of that group, if you take my meaning." She paused. "Lot of very shocked people."

"He was in trouble with his business, we heard," said Sylvia with a shrug. "That kind of pressure, it's probably not surprising he picked up again. And owning a bar when you're sober, that couldn't have been fun."

"People do it, though," Betty said. "He managed it for years. Then I guess he stopped managing."

"Ayuh."

No one said anything for a moment.

"So you bought the house from Evan's estate?"

"Not exactly. He had no will, but his sister, the one who'd died earlier, she had a kid. Her kid was the heir. Not the sentimental type, that one."

"Oh no?" Jake said.

"She must've waited all of a week after her uncle died to put it on the market. The shape the place was in." Sylvia shook her head. "If it hadn't been for this one, nobody'd have come near it. Fortunately for her, Betty always loved this place."

"I used to think it was haunted, when I was a little kid," Betty confirmed.

"We made her an offer she couldn't refuse." Sylvia got up to lift another cat off the kitchen counter. "Or I guess we did. We never met her in person. Just dealt with the attorney."

"That was no cakewalk," said Betty. "He was supposed to get all the crap down in the basement cleared out."

"And the attic. And half the rooms had stuff in them. I don't know how many times we wrote to that joker, Gaylord."

"Gaylord, *Esquire,*" Betty rolled her eyes.

"That guy," said Sylvia, grinning. "He put that Esquire on everything. Like, we get it. You went to law school. Insecure much?"

"Finally we told him we were having it all sent to the dump if she didn't come and take it away. No answer! So that's what we did."

"Wait, so you just threw everything out?"

He had allowed himself to imagine, for one tantalizing moment, that there was a box of Evan Parker's manuscript pages, still somewhere beneath this roof. But that was quickly dashed.

"We kept the old bed. Beautiful four-poster. Probably couldn't have gotten it out if we wanted to."

"Which we didn't!" Betty said with satisfaction.

"And there were a couple of nice rugs we sent out to get cleaned. Probably for the first time in a century. The rest, we got in a hauler and sent the bill to Mr. Gaylord, *Esquire*. I bet you'll be shocked to learn it never got paid."

"I mean, if my family had a house for a hundred and fifty years I'd be going through every inch of it. Even if she didn't care about, y'know, the 'antiques,' you'd think she'd want her own things. Everything you grew up with? Just throw it all away, sight unseen?"

"Wait," said Jake. "The niece grew up here too? In this house?"

He was trying to understand the order of events, but it all seemed to resist him, somehow. Evan's parents had lived and died here, and then his sister had lived here and raised her own daughter here, and then, after his sister died and his niece departed—*out of there*, as Sally the barfly had put it—Evan had moved back in? It might be slightly confusing, but he supposed none of it was greatly surprising. At the end of the day, this house gave Jake a visual backdrop for Evan Parker's irrelevant childhood, and, he supposed, for the final years of his life. But it didn't explain anything else.

He thanked them. He had them write down their address for the signed book. "Should I send one for your sister, too?"

"Are you shitting me? Yes!"

They were behind him when he walked back down the hall, toward the front door. He stopped to put his coat back on. Then he looked up.

Around the inside of the front door was a clarion call from the old house's distant past: a frieze of faded paint depicting a chain of pineapples. Pineapples. It caught him and let him go, then it caught him again, and held. Five above the door frame. Ten at least on either side, descending almost to the floor. They had been preserved in a strip of negative space, around which the rest of the wall had been repainted that Pepto-Bismol pink.

"Oh my god," he said out loud.

"I know." Sylvia was shaking her head. "So tacky. Betty wouldn't let me paint over them. We had the biggest fight."

"It's a stencil," said Betty. "I saw the same thing once at Sturbridge

Village, just like this. Pineapples all around the door and up around the tops of the walls. It goes back to when the house was built, I'm positive."

"We compromised. I had to leave a strip unpainted. It looks crazy."

It did look crazy. It was also one of the only things left under this roof that might have deserved the word "restoration." Had it been, in any sense, restored.

Sylvia said: "I'm going to touch it up, eventually. I mean, look at the colors. So faded! If we have to keep it at least I can overpaint them. Honestly, every time I look at my door I think, why would anybody put pineapples on their walls? This is Vermont, not Hawaii! Why not an apple or a blackberry? They actually grow here!"

"It means hospitality," Jake heard himself say. He had not been able to look away from them, the faded chain of them, because he was reeling. All of those disparate pieces spun around him, refusing to land.

"What?"

"Hospitality. It's a symbol. I don't know why."

He had read it somewhere. He knew exactly where.

For a long moment, none of them said a thing. What was there to say? And why hadn't it occurred to him, way back in his office in Richard Peng Hall, that Parker's first attempt at a novel would probably describe the people he'd known best, in the house they'd once shared? It was the biggest cliché of all that a writer's first book was autobiographical: *my childhood, my family, my horrible school experience.* His own *The Invention of Wonder* was autobiographical, of course it was, and yet Jake had denied Evan Parker even this token courtesy in the fellowship of writers. Why?

The mistake, a product of his own arrogance, had cost him months.

This had never been about an appropriation, real or imaginary, between two writers. This had been a far more intimate theft: not Jake's at all but one Evan Parker himself had committed. What Parker had stolen was something he must have seen up close and very personal: the mother and the daughter and what had happened between them, right here, in this house.

Of course she was angry. Not for one minute had she wanted her story to be told, not by her close relation and certainly not by a total stranger. That much, at long last, he finally understood.

CRIB

BY JACOB FINCH BONNER

Macmillan, New York, 2017, pages 178–80

Gab had parents: a mom who "struggled" and a dad who came and went. She had a sister with CF and a brother whose autism was so bad he sometimes had to be tied to his bed. She had, in other words, a home life so desperate and sad that even Maria's domestic circumstances must have seemed like something out of a family sitcom. She was a year behind Maria, allergic to nuts and obliged to carry an EpiPen everywhere, dull as dishwater, and headed exactly nowhere.

Maria, at least, was marginally nicer to be around once Gab became a fixture. Samantha credited herself for being not a prude, not a religious freak like her own parents, and not a controlling asshole in general, so she tended to see the advent of her daughter's relationship as having a positive impact on these final years. It had all passed so swiftly that sometimes, when she was first waking up in the morning, in her parents' old bed, in her childhood home, she actually thought of herself as the person counting down the days to departure, and then she would encounter Maria and Gab at the kitchen table eating leftover pepperoni pizzas from the night before, and remember she was a nearly thirty-two-year-old mom about to say a permanent sayonara to the only child she was likely to have. Here and gone as if none of it had ever happened, and she was catapulting backward, ten years, thirteen years, sixteen years to this same kitchen table with her mother and her father and her own lost hopes, and the classroom where she had once vomited on her problem set, and the very clean room in the College Inn where Daniel Weybridge had promised her he couldn't get her pregnant, not even if he wanted to.

One morning in the spring of what should have been Maria's junior year, she got a call from Mr. Fortis, of all people, letting her know that she had to come in and sign some release so her daughter could graduate early. This was mystifying, but she went that afternoon, finding the old math teacher—he had been made assistant principal years before—more bent, more gray, and so addled that he failed to acknowledge her as a person he had ever met before, let alone a former student, let alone a gifted former student he'd failed to support when she'd been forced to drop out of school. And it was from this man she had to learn her daughter had gotten herself a scholarship to Ohio State.

Ohio State. Samantha herself had never been to Ohio. She'd never been out of New York.

"You must be so proud," said Fortis, the old fool.

"Sure," she said.

She signed the paper and returned home, where she went straight to Maria's room, formerly her own room, and found the papers in a neat file marked OSU in the bottom drawer of her daughter's old oak desk, formerly her own old oak desk. One was a formal acceptance to the Honors Program in Arts and Sciences and another was a notification of something called a National Buckeye Scholarship and something else called a Maximus Scholarship. Samantha sat there for a long time at the foot of Maria's neatly made bed, the same cannonball four-poster she herself had slept in as a child, and dreamed of escape in, and been imprisoned in while incubating that baby she hadn't wanted to carry, or give birth to, or raise. She had done all of those things without any outward complaint, simply because people in temporary power over her life had told her she had to.

Those people—her own parents—were long gone, but here Samantha still was, even as the object of all of this sacrifice was herself preparing to fuck off forever, without a backward glance.

Naturally, she had not been unaware of this exit, in itself; Maria was hardly going to mess up her chance the same way Samantha herself had, or any other way. From her earliest years, when she'd toddled about reading letters out loud, she was headed for college if not even farther, and some life—it went without saying—beyond Earlville and probably upstate New York itself. But there was something about that final year Samantha had been expecting, in her life as a mother, perhaps holding inside it some slim possibility of reversal, even redemption, which now was suddenly not there. Or possibly it was the way Maria had managed to get back at her for that skipped sixth grade she hadn't given permission for. This time, under her old calculus teacher's oblivious eye, she had signed that release, too cowed and too ashamed not to give in. It was June now. Maria, she supposed, would be gone by August, if not before.

She did not confront her daughter. She waited to see if Maria would at least invite her to the graduation ceremony, but in fact Maria had no interest in walking across that crepe-paper-decorated basketball court, and on the day in question she was off with Gab in Hamilton, possibly at the bookstore or even cluelessly hanging out on the porch of the College Inn. (The inn was now *Family run for four generations!*, Dan Weybridge having died of pancreatic cancer.) The only thing she said when she got home that night was that she had ended things with her girlfriend, and it was for the best.

The summer, a hot one, began. Maria saw no one. Samantha stayed in her office with the fan on, doing the same medical billing job she'd been doing since Maria was small, the job that had paid for her daughter's food and clothing and doctors' appointments. June passed, and July, and still Maria said not one word about the fact that she was about to depart, but Samantha did begin to see some incremental motion. Clothing was being bagged and taken to the donation box in town. Books were being boxed and dropped off at the Earlville Library. Old papers, tests from middle school, crayon drawings from all the way back to early childhood were being sorted and then wedged into the wastepaper basket under Maria's desk. It was a complete rout.

"You don't like that anymore?" Samantha said once, pointing to a green T-shirt.

"No. That's why I'm getting rid of it."

"Well, I might keep it, if you don't want it."

They were, after all, the same size.

"Suit yourself."

It was early August.

She wasn't planning it. Truly, she wasn't planning anything.

CHAPTER TWENTY-THREE

Sole Survivor

Afterward he needed to think. He drove back into town and parked outside a Walgreens for nearly an hour, head bent, hands gripping his own knees, trying to peel away the many layers of what he'd assumed he knew about @TalentedTom, and then to form some sense of what he needed most to know right now. There was much, and he was starting from a radically different place, and it was so hard not to want to hold on to his earlier assumptions about vengeful novelists and loyal MFA classmates. He had to be humble now, Jake decided, if he was going to stop this person—this, he now recalibrated, *woman*—before she caused him irreparable injury.

On his phone he hastily typed a list of what he didn't know, more or less in descending order of priority:

Who is she?
Where is she?
What does she want?

Then he stared at that for another twenty minutes, overwhelmed by the breadth of his own ignorance.

By two he was at the Rutland Free Library, trying to learn as much about Evan Parker's family as he could cram into one afternoon. The Parkers had deep roots in Rutland. They'd arrived in the 1850s with the railroad, but only twenty years later the family patriarch, Josiah Parker, owned a marble quarry on the same West Rutland street—Marble Street—where he would also build Betty and Sylvia's Italianate mansion. The house, obviously, had been a showplace for Josiah Parker's wealth at the time of its construction, but Rutland's fortunes, alongside those of the Parker family itself, had mirrored the area's general decline, and the gradual extinction of Vermont's marble industry. On the 1990 property tax rolls its value was listed as $112,000, at which time its owners were Nathaniel Parker and Jane Thatcher Parker.

Evan's parents. Or, more to the point, the parents of Evan and his late sister.

A bitch and *a piece of work,* according to his bar friend Sally (who, to be fair, could have passed for both, herself).

He said she'd do anything, according to Martin Purcell.

I heard she burned up.

There was no internet tribute page for this particular member of the Parker family, which might have spoken to her dearth of friends, or possibly just to Evan Parker's specific lack of brotherly love (since he'd presumably handled matters after his sister's passing). Her name, apparently, was Dianna, which was pathetically close to Diandra, the name he had given her in his "fictional" novel. And her death notice, on the same *Rutland Herald* obituary page that would host Evan Parker's own a mere three years later, was basic in the extreme:

> Parker, Dianna (32), died August 30th, 2012. Lifelong resident of West Rutland. Attended West Rutland HS. Predeceased by parents. Survived by a brother and a daughter.

No mention of what, in particular, had caused her death, not even one of the usual banalities ("sudden," "unexpected," "after a long illness") let alone anything personal ("beloved") or blandly regretful ("tragic"). No mention of the place where the death had taken place, or where the deceased person was to be buried. No listing of a memorial service, not even Evan Parker's own "burial private" or "memorial to be announced later." This woman had been a daughter, sister, and above all mother, and she had certainly died young after a life that was by any measure constrained and devoid of experiences. Dianna Parker hadn't even graduated from high school, not if Jake was correctly interpreting the use of the word "attended," and if she'd never left West Rutland, Vermont, he really did have to feel sorry for her. This was the most barren sendoff imaginable after not much of a life and—if she really had "burned up"—an indisputably horrible death.

Attempting to find birth records for Dianna and, more importantly, for her still nameless daughter, presented Jake with his first serious roadblock, since the state of Vermont's public records wanted a formal application, and he wasn't sure he was entitled to access, so he purchased a membership to Ancestry.com on the spot and found the rest in a matter of minutes.

Dianna Parker (1980–2012)

Rose Parker (1996–)

Rose Parker. He stared at the name. Rose Parker was the granddaughter of Nathaniel and Ruth, the daughter of Dianna, the niece of Evan. Apparently the sole survivor of her family.

He went straight to one of the search websites and started looking for her, but while there were nearly thirty Rose Parkers currently in the databases, none of them, to his extreme frustration, had the right birth year apart from one with an old address in Athens, Georgia, and the only Vermonter named Rose Parker was an octogenarian. He asked a librarian about yearbooks from West Rutland High School and was excited when she pointed to a corner of the reference section, but the collection yielded little of value. Dianna, having merely "attended" high school, had no graduation portrait in the 1997 or 1998 yearbook, and after Jake looked carefully through the years before that when she might have been pictured in clubs or teams or held class offices he had to conclude that she'd been remarkably uninvolved at West Rutland High; there was only her name on a dean's list of scholars and a single citation for a prizewinning essay on Vermont during the Revolutionary War to show she'd made any mark at all on the school. Rose Parker presented an even more frustrating absence. Born in 1996, she'd left home without graduating from high school—Sally had told him that—so it made sense that there was no Rose Parker among the graduating seniors of 2012. In fact he found only a single image of Rose Parker from what must have been her tenth-grade year: a spindly girl in short bangs and large round glasses, holding a field hockey stick in a team photo. It was small and not completely in focus, but he took out his phone and snapped a picture anyway. It might be all he'd ever find.

After that, he turned to the sale of the house on Marble Street, from Evan Parker's heir to its first owners not to be named Parker. As the women had said, Rose wasn't present for the transaction itself, and was apparently indifferent to the fate of a century and a half's worth of family possessions, not to mention her own childhood belongings. But the attorney, William Gaylord, Esquire, was right here in Rutland, and if he didn't know where Rose Parker was today he had to have known where she was at the time of the sale. That was something.

Jake gathered his notes and walked out of the Rutland Free Library and through heavy rain to his car. It was just past three in the afternoon.

The offices of William Gaylord, Esq., occupied one of those former homes on North Main Street that had once housed the wealthiest citizens of Rutland. It had gray shingles and a Queen Anne turret, and sat just south of a traffic light between a forlorn dance studio and a chartered accountancy. Jake parked beside the single car in the lot behind the building and walked around to the front porch. There, a sign beside the door read LEGAL SERVICES. He could see a woman working inside.

He hadn't given much thought to how he might justify his interest in a three-year-old real estate transaction to which he had no obvious connection, but he decided he'd have better luck knocking on the door than trying to explain his business over the phone. With Martin Purcell he had pretended to be a teacher in some small degree of mourning for his former student, and with Sally-the-barfly he'd been a clueless stranger out for a drink. With Betty and Sylvia he'd been nearly himself, a "famous writer" paying his respects to the home of a late acquaintance. None of this had been particularly easy for him. Unlike the devious fifteen-year-old girl in Saki's most famous story, romance at short notice was not his specialty; he was far more than adept at constructing untruths on the page, when he had all the time in the world to get the fabrication right. True, he'd been able to walk away from each of these previous encounters with information he hadn't had before, and that had been worth the personal discomfort, but here he couldn't simply flounder through the conversation, hoping to learn something relevant. Here he actually knew what he was trying to find out, and it was hardly something he could come straight out and ask for.

He assembled his most pleasant smile and went inside.

The woman looked up. She was dark, southeast Asian—Indian or Bangladeshi, Jake thought—and wearing an acrylic blue sweater that managed to be loose at the top and tight as a cummerbund around her thick middle. She smiled, too, when she saw Jake enter, but her smile wasn't as pleasant as his.

"I apologize for not calling first," he said. "But I'm wondering if Mr. Gaylord is available for a few minutes?"

The woman was giving Jake a very thorough appraisal. He was glad he hadn't gone full Vermont for this visit. He was wearing his last clean shirt and over it a black wool sweater Anna had given him for Christmas.

"May I ask what this is about?"

"Certainly. I'm interested in purchasing some real estate."

"Residential or commercial?" she said, still plainly suspicious.

He hadn't been expecting this. He might have lingered a moment too long. "Well, both, ultimately. But the priority is commercial. I'm thinking of moving my business to the area. I've been over at the library, and I asked one of the librarians to recommend an attorney who specializes in real estate."

This, apparently, was what passed for flattery in Rutland, because it had an unmistakable effect. "Yes, Mr. Gaylord has an excellent reputation," she informed Jake. "Would you like to take a seat? I can ask if he's available to see you."

Jake sat in the nook opposite her desk. There was a love seat facing the front window and an old trunk with a potted fern and a stack of *Vermont Life* issues, the most recent of which seemed to be from the year 2017. He could hear her somewhere behind him, talking to a man. He tried to remember what he'd just said about why he was here. *Commercial real estate, moving a business to the area.* Unfortunately he wasn't entirely sure how to get from there to where he needed to go.

"Hello there."

Jake looked up. The man standing over him was sturdy and tall, with abundant (but thankfully clean) nostril hair. He was neatly dressed in black pants, a white button-down shirt, and a tie that would have been at home on Wall Street.

"Oh, hi. My name's Jacob Bonner."

"Like the author?"

Still a surprise. Always would be, he suspected. Now what should he say about the business he was supposedly moving to the Rutland area?

"Yes, actually."

"Well, not often a famous writer walks into my office. My wife read your book."

Five monosyllabic words, speaking volumes.

"I appreciate that. I'm sorry to come in without an appointment. I was asking at the library, and they recommended—"

"Yes, so my wife said. Would you like to come in?"

He stepped out of the nook and past the apparent Mrs. Gaylord, following William Gaylord, Esq., back to his office.

Various local citations and memberships framed on the wall. A degree from the Vermont School of Law. Behind Gaylord, on the mantelpiece of a blocked-up fireplace, a few dusty framed pictures of himself and the woman with the less than pleasant smile.

"What brings you to Rutland?" Gaylord said. His chair creaked as he settled into it.

"I came up to do some work on a new book, and see a former student. I used to teach in northern Vermont. Until a couple of years ago."

"Oh, yes? Where was that?"

"At Ripley College."

He raised an eyebrow. "That place still in business?"

"Well, it was a low-residency program when I was there. Now I think it's online only. I'm not sure what's happened to the actual campus."

"That's a shame. Drove through Ripley not so many years ago. Pretty place."

"Yes. I enjoyed teaching there."

"And now," said Gaylord, taking charge of the segue himself, "you're thinking of moving your business—as a writer—to Rutland?"

"Well . . . not exactly. I can write anywhere, of course, but my wife . . . she works for a podcasting studio in the city. We've been thinking about moving out of New York, letting her set up a studio of her own. I told her I'd look around while I was here. It seemed to make sense. Rutland is such a crossroads for the state."

Gaylord grinned, showing crowded teeth. "It is that. Can't say that's always a good thing for the town. But yes, we're pretty much on the way from anywhere in Vermont to anywhere else. Not a bad place at all to put a business. Podcasting is quite the thing, isn't it?"

Jake nodded.

"So you'd want something zoned commercial, I imagine?"

He let himself be led. At least fifteen minutes on the multiple "downtowns" of Rutland, the various state incentive schemes and earmarked loans for new businesses, the waivers sometimes available for companies aiming to employ more than five people. He had to keep nodding and making notes and pretending to be interested, all the while wondering how he could get them both to the house on Marble Street in West Rutland.

"I'm curious, though," said William Gaylord. "I mean, I'm from this area, and I'm committed to the future here, but most folks, coming up from New York or Boston, they're thinking Middlebury or Burlington."

"Yeah, sure." Jake nodded. "But I came here a bunch of times, as a kid. I think my parents had some friends in the area. In West Rutland?"

"Okay." Gaylord nodded.

"And I remember visiting in the summers. I remember this donut shop. Wait . . ." He pretended to search for the name.

"Jones'?"

"Jones'! Yes! The best glazed donuts."

"A personal favorite of mine," Gaylord said, actually patting his gut.

"And this one swimming hole . . ."

There had better be a swimming hole. In a Vermont town? It seemed like a safe bet.

"Plenty of them. Which one?"

"Oh, I don't know. I was probably seven or eight. I don't even remember the name of my parents' friends. You know what it's like when you're little, what you remember. For me it was the donuts and the swimming hole. Oh, and there was also this one house in West Rutland, right down from the quarry. My mother called it the marble house, because it was on Marble Street and it had a marble base. We knew when we passed it we were almost to our friends' house."

Gaylord nodded. "I think I know the house you mean. Actually I handled the sale of that house."

Careful, thought Jake.

"It was sold?" he asked. Even to himself he sounded like a disappointed child. "Well, I guess that stands to reason. I have to tell you, I had this whole pipe dream going when I drove up here yesterday. We'd move to Rutland and I'd buy that old house I used to love when I was a kid."

"Sold a couple of years ago. But it was a mess, you wouldn't have wanted it. The buyers had to put in everything new. Heat, wiring, septic. And they paid way too much. Not my place to talk them out of it, though. I was acting for the seller."

"Well, you'd have to expect to put some money into an old house like that. I remember how run-down it looked," said Jake, recalling Betty's childhood assessment of the place. "Of course, to a kid it doesn't say 'run-down.' It says 'haunted.' I was a big *Goosebumps* reader, those summers. I was definitely into that haunted house in West Rutland."

"Haunted." Gaylord shook his head. "Well, I don't know about that. A lot of plain old New England bad luck in that family, maybe. But I don't know about any actual ghosts. Anyway, we can find you another old Vermont haunted house in the area, no shortage of them."

He had Jake write down a few of the agents he worked with, then he spent a few minutes rhapsodizing about a Victorian up toward Pittsford that had been on the market for nearly a decade. It sounded delightful.

"But does it have a wraparound porch like that West Rutland house?"

Gaylord shrugged. "Don't remember, tell you the truth. Is that a deal breaker? You can always add a porch."

"I'm sure you're right."

He was running out of ideas and on his last nerve. He also had pages of notes, by now, on commercial properties in Rutland, Vermont, that he couldn't have cared less about, and he was the proud possessor of a folder of state policies and programs and completely unneeded brochures about home buying, and also a useless list of Realtors with the William Gaylord, Esq., seal of approval, as well as printouts of listings for old houses in and around Rutland. Outside it was getting dark and still raining, and he was facing a long drive back to the city. And he still knew nothing more than when he'd come in.

"So," said Jake, making a show of gathering up the papers and recapping his pen, "I suppose there's no way of buying back that house from the new owners? I wouldn't say no to updated septic and electricity, actually."

Gaylord looked at him. "You've really got a thing for that place, don't you? But I'd say no. Not after all the work those people have put in. If you'd come along three years ago I had a very motivated seller, I can tell you. Well, technically *I* didn't have her. I was the in-state counsel for the sale, but I never dealt with her directly. She had representation down in Georgia."

"Georgia?" Jake asked.

"She was going to college down there. I think she just wanted to start over somewhere, make a clean break. She didn't come back for the closing, not even to clean out the house. With everything that went wrong in that family, I can't say I blame her."

"Sure," said Jake, who blamed her enough for the both of them.

CHAPTER TWENTY-FOUR

The Breakdown Lane

As he was passing Albany the phone vibrated on the seat behind him. Anna. He pulled off onto the shoulder to take the call. From the moment she spoke he knew there was something wrong.

"Jake. Are you all right?"

"Me? Of course. Yes. I'm all right. What is it?"

"I got a horrible letter. Why didn't you tell me this was happening?"

He closed his eyes. He could only imagine.

"A letter from whom?" he asked, as if he didn't know.

"Some jackhole named Tom!" Her voice was shrill. He couldn't tell if she was afraid or angry. Probably both. "He says you're a crook and I'm supposed to ask you about somebody named Evan Parker who's apparently the real author of *Crib*. I mean, what the fuck? I went online and . . . Jake, oh my god, why didn't you tell me this has been going on? I found posts from back in the fall on Twitter. And Facebook! And there was something on a book blog, talking about it. Why the hell haven't you told me about this?"

He felt the panic, pressing hard against his chest, liquifying his arms and legs. Here it was: the thing he'd spent all this time trying desperately to prevent, unfolding in the breakdown lane. He couldn't believe it still surprised him that another wall into his private life had been breached. Or that he hadn't prevented it from happening.

"I should have told you. I'm sorry. I just . . . I couldn't stand thinking about how upset you'd be. You are."

"But what is he talking about? And who is this Evan Parker person?"

"I'll tell you, I promise," he said. "I'm pulled over on the side of the New York State Thruway, but I'm on my way home."

"But how did he get our address? Has he ever contacted you before? I mean directly, like this?"

It appalled him, the weight of what he'd hidden from her.

"Yes. Through my website. There's also been contact with Macmillan. We had a meeting about it. And . . ." He especially hated to admit this part. "I got a letter, too."

For a long moment, he heard nothing. Then she started screaming. "Are you kidding me? You knew he had our address? And you never told me about any of this? For months?"

"It wasn't so much a decision. It just got away from me. I feel awful about it. I wish I'd said something when it started."

"Or any moment since."

"Yes."

For a long moment, silence filled up the distance between them, and Jake looked forlornly at the cars rushing past.

"What time will you get home?"

By eight, he told her. "Do you want to go out?"

Anna didn't want to go out. She wanted to cook.

"And we'll talk about it then," she said, as if he thought she might somehow forget.

After they hung up he sat there for a few more minutes, feeling horrible. He was trying to remember his own first decision not to tell her about TalentedTom, and to his surprise it went back—all the way back to the very day he and Anna had first met at the radio station. Over eight months of this, innuendo and threats and hashtags to spread the poison as far as it could go, and nothing had made it stop! It would have been one thing if he'd managed to handle the problem, but he hadn't, and in fact, it had gotten bigger, like a nautilus circling farther and farther, ensnaring people he cared about: Matilda, Wendy, now, worst of all, Anna. She was right. His worst mistake had been not to tell her. He saw that now.

No. His worst mistake had been to take Evan Parker's plot in the first place.

Did it even matter anymore that *Crib* was his—every word of it? That the book's success was inextricably entwined with his own skill in presenting the story Evan Parker had told him that night in Richard Peng Hall? It had been an exceptional story, of course it had, but could Parker himself really have done justice to it? Yes, he'd had some moderate talent at making sentences, that much Jake had recognized back at Ripley. But creating narrative tension? Understanding what made a story track and grab and hold? Forging characters a reader felt inclined to care about and invest their time in? Jake hadn't seen enough of Evan's work to judge whether his former student was capable of doing that, but Parker had been the one telling the story that night, and that came with certain rights of possession; Jake had been the one it was told to, and that came with certain moral responsibilities.

At least while the teller was . . . alive.

Was Jake really supposed to throw a plot like that into some other writer's grave? Any novelist would understand what he'd done. Any novelist would have done exactly the same!

And thus reacquainted with his righteousness on the matter, he started his car again and headed south to the city.

There was a spinach soup Anna liked to cook, so intensely green it made you feel healthier just looking at it, and she had that waiting for him when he arrived home, along with a bottle of wine and a loaf of bread from Citarella. She was sitting in the living room with the disassembled Sunday *Times,* and he noticed, as he accepted her stiff hug, that she had the book section unfurled on the coffee table, open to the bestsellers page. He knew from Macmillan's weekly dispatch that he was currently at number four on the paperback fiction list, something that would have thrilled and astonished him at any moment in his life except for the past month, when it represented an actual descent. But such were not his most pressing concerns this evening.

"You want to wash up? Are you hungry?"

He hadn't eaten since that donut, many hours earlier in West Rutland.

"I'm definitely ready for that soup. Even more, though, for some wine."

"Go put your stuff down. I'll pour you a glass."

In the bedroom he found the envelope she'd received, left for him on the bed. It was identical to his own with that single name, Talented Tom, as a return address and their own address—with her name, this time—front and center. He picked it up and slipped the page out, numb with horror as he read its single sentence:

> *Ask your plagiarist husband to tell you about Evan Parker, the real author of* Crib.

He had to fight the urge to crumple it up on the spot.

Jake went to put his dirty clothes in the hamper and return his toothbrush to its usual place. He tried, by some fearful instinct, to avoid seeing himself in the mirror, but inevitably he caught his own gaze, and there it plainly was: the impact of these last months, deeply and unmistakably etched into dark circles around his eyes. Pale skin. Lank hair. And above all an expression of intractable dread. But there was no quick fix for it now, and no way out but through. He went back to the living room, and his wife.

Anna had brought from Seattle a set of well-used knives, a "Dutch oven," an old wooden cutting board she'd had since college, and even a mason jar half full of something that looked like desiccated tapioca pudding, which turned out to be sourdough starter. With these she had been producing a continuum of actual food for months: balanced meals, confections, casseroles and soups and even condiments that now filled the freezer and the refrigerator shelves. She had also dispatched Jake's existing dishes (and silverware, and glasses) to the Goodwill on Fourteenth Street, replacing them with new sets from Pottery Barn. She was setting down sturdy ceramic bowls of the green soup as he took his seat.

"Thank you," he said. "This is beautiful."

"Soup for the raveled sleeve of care."

"I believe that's sleep," he said. "And soup for the soul."

"Well, this is for both. I figured we were going to be needing a lot of it, so I made a double batch and froze it."

"I love your pioneer instincts." He smiled, taking his first sip.

"Island instincts. Not that we didn't have supermarkets on Whidbey. But people always seemed to want to prepare for being cut off."

She tore the end off the bread and handed it to him. Then she watched him begin.

"So, how does this work? Do I have to ask you questions or are you just going to tell me what the fuck is going on?"

In that instant, and despite the long day without food, he lost his appetite.

"I'm going to tell you," he said.

And he tried.

"I had a student named Evan Parker. Back when I taught at Ripley. And he had this great idea for a novel. A plot that was . . . well, striking. Memorable. Involving a mother and her daughter."

"Oh no," Anna said quietly. It landed on him like a blow, but he made himself go on.

"It surprised me, because he had no real feeling for fiction that I could see. Not much of a reader, which is always an indicator. And the few pages of his work I saw, well, he could write, but it wasn't anyone's idea of a great book in progress. Maybe his own, but no one else's. Certainly not mine. But still—he did have this great story."

Jake stopped. It already wasn't going well.

"So . . . did you take it, Jake? Is that what you're telling me?"

He felt sick, suddenly. He put down his spoon. "Of course not. I didn't do anything, except maybe feel a little sorry for myself. A little pissed at the universe that this guy had come up with such a great idea straight out of the gate. He was a nightmare as a student. Treated everyone else in the workshop as if they were wasting his time, and not a shred of respect for me as a teacher, of course. Sometimes I wonder, would I have done it if he hadn't been such a jerk."

"Well, I wouldn't lead with any of that if you're ever asked," said Anna with heavy sarcasm.

He nodded. Of course, she was right.

"I think we might have spoken once, outside of class. In a conference. That's when he took me through this plot. But never anything personal. I didn't even know basic stuff like that he was from Vermont or what he did for a living."

"He was from . . . Vermont," Anna said slowly.

"Yeah."

"Where you coincidentally just were. Giving a reading and working on your revisions." She set down her glass.

Jake sighed. "Yes. I mean no, it wasn't a coincidence. And I wasn't working on my revisions. Or giving a reading, for that matter. I was meeting one of his friends from the Ripley program, in Rutland. His hometown."

"You went to Rutland?" She seemed horrified.

"Well, yes. I've been kind of hiding away from this. I finally felt I needed to deal with it directly. See if there was anything I could figure out, by being there. Maybe by talking to some people."

"What people?"

"Well, the Ripley friend, for one. And I went to Parker's place."

"His house?" she said with alarm.

"No," Jake said. "Well, yes, that too. But I meant the bar he owned. Tavern," he corrected himself.

After a moment she said: "Fine. What happened after you were his teacher and talked to him one time outside of your workshop."

He nodded. "Well, basically, I forgot all about him, or almost forgot. Every year or so I'd think, *Hey, that book still hasn't come out.* And maybe he found out it was a lot harder to write a book than he'd thought it was going to be."

"So finally you decided, *He's never going to write it, so I'm going to write it.* And now Evan Parker's threatening to expose you for stealing his idea."

Jake shook his head. "No. That's not what happened. And whoever's threatening me, it's not him. Evan Parker is dead."

Anna stared at him. "He's dead."

"Yeah. And actually a long time ago. Like, within a couple of months of that Ripley workshop. He never did write his book. Or at least, he never finished it."

For a moment she said nothing. Then: "How did he die?"

"Overdose. Awful, but absolutely nothing to do with his story, or me. And when I heard about it . . . I really wrestled with this, of course. But I couldn't just let it go. The plot. You see?"

Anna took a sip of her wine. Slowly, she nodded. "Okay. Keep going."

"I will, but I need you to understand something. In my world, the migration of a story is something we recognize, and we respect. Works of art can overlap, or they can sort of chime with one another. Right now, with some of the anxieties we have around appropriation, it's become downright combustible, but I've always thought there was a kind of beauty to it, the way narratives get told and retold. It's how stories survive through the ages. You can follow an idea from one author's work to another, and to me that's something I find powerful and exciting."

"Well, that sounds very artistic and magical and all that," Anna said, with a definite edge to her voice, "but you'll forgive me if what you writers think of as some kind of spiritual exchange looks like plagiarism to the rest of us."

"How can it be plagiarism?" Jake said. "I never saw more than a couple of pages of what Parker was writing, and I absolutely avoided every detail I could remember. This isn't plagiarism, not remotely."

"All right," she conceded. "So maybe plagiarism isn't the right word. Maybe theft of story gets closer."

That hurt terribly.

"Like how Jane Smiley stole *A Thousand Acres* from Shakespeare or Charles Frazier stole *Cold Mountain* from Homer?"

"Shakespeare and Homer were dead."

"So was this guy. And unlike Shakespeare and Homer, Evan Parker never actually wrote something another person could steal from."

"As far as you're aware."

Jake looked down into his rapidly cooling soup. Only a few spoonfuls had made their way into his mouth, and that seemed like a long time ago. She'd managed to put her finger on his worst fear.

"As far as I'm aware."

"Okay," Anna said. "So Evan Parker isn't the person who wrote to me. Who did it, then? Do you know?"

"I thought I knew. I thought it had to be someone who'd been with us at Ripley. I mean, if he told me about his book, why wouldn't he have told somebody else in the program? That's what the students were there for, to share their work."

"And be taught how to become better writers."

Jake shrugged. "Sure. If that's even possible."

"Says the former teacher of creative writing."

He looked at her. She was clearly still angry at him. Which he deserved.

"I thought I could make it go away. I thought I could spare you this."

"Why? Because it was going to be too much for me, this pathetic internet troll? If some loser out there decides to go after you because you've actually accomplished something in your life, that's his issue, not yours. Please do not hide this kind of thing from me. I'm on your side."

"You're right," he said, but his voice really was cracking now. "I'm sorry."

Anna got to her feet. She took her own nearly full bowl of soup to the kitchen sink. Jake watched her back as she rinsed it and put it into the dishwasher. She brought the wine bottle back to the table and poured more for each of them.

"Honey," Anna said, "I hope you know, I don't care in the least about this creep. Like, zero compassion for somebody who does what he's done, no matter how justified he thinks he is. I care about you. And from what I can see you've really been harmed by this. You must be devastated."

Well, that's absolutely true, he wanted to say, but all he could manage was: "Yeah."

They sat together in silence for a few moments. He wondered if it made her feel better or worse to know how right she'd been, all these weeks, about how bad he was feeling. But Anna wasn't a vindictive person. Just now, she might be frustrated at the extent of his secrecy and his withholding, but already empathy was getting the upper hand. What he needed to do, though, was tell her everything.

He took a sip of his wine and tried again.

"So, like I said, I thought it was someone from Ripley, but I was wrong."

"Okay," Anna said warily. "So who?"

"Let me ask you something. Why do you think *Crib* got the response it did? I'm not looking for praise, I'm saying . . . lots of novels are published every year. Plenty of them are tightly plotted, full of surprises, well written. Why did this one blow up?"

"Well," she said with a shrug, "the story . . ."

"Yes. The story. And why was this story so shocking?" He didn't wait for her answer. "Because how could that ever happen in real life, to a real mother and daughter? It's crazy! Fiction invites us into outrageous scenarios. That's one of the things we ask it to do. Right? So we don't have to think of them as real?"

Anna shrugged. "I suppose."

"Okay. So what if this *was* real? What if there's a real mother and daughter out there, and what happens in *Crib* actually happened to them?"

He watched the color drain from her face. "But that's horrible," she said.

"Agreed. But think about it. If it's real—real mother, real daughter—the last thing that woman wants is to read about what happened, let alone in a novel that's being published all over the world. They'd obviously want to know who this author is, right?"

She nodded.

"And it's right there on the back flap that I was associated with an MFA program at Ripley College. Where I would have crossed paths with the late Evan Parker. Where I could have heard his story."

"Well, but even if that's true, why be angry at you and not at Parker, for telling you in the first place? Why not be angry at whoever told Evan Parker the story to begin with?"

Jake shook his head. "I don't think anyone told Parker. I think Parker was close to it. So close he saw it happen, firsthand. And when he realized what he'd seen, maybe he decided it was too good a story to waste. Because he was a writer, and writers understand how ridiculously rare a story like that is." Jake shook his head. He was feeling, for the very first time, some actual respect for Evan Parker, his fellow writer. And his fellow victim.

"I don't think this was ever about plagiarism," Jake said. "Or theft of story, or whatever else you decide to call it. It's never been a literary issue at all."

"I don't know what that means."

"It means, okay, even if I did take something that wasn't technically mine, Evan Parker took it first, and the person he took it from was furious about it. But then he died. So: end of story."

"Obviously not," Anna observed.

"Right. Because then, a couple of years later, along comes *Crib,* and unlike Parker's attempt it's actually a finished book, and somebody's actually published it. Now the story's out there in black and white, in all its glory, and two million total strangers have read it—in hardcover, paperback, mass market, audio, large-print editions! Now it's translated into thirty languages and Oprah's putting a sticker on the cover and it's coming soon to a theater near you, and every time this person gets on the subway somebody's got a copy open, right in their face." He paused. "You know, I actually understand how they must feel."

"This is really scaring me."

I've been scared for months, he didn't say.

Then she sat up. "Wait," Anna said. "You know who he is, don't you? I can see that you do. Who is he?"

Jake was shaking his head. "She," he said.

"Wait," she said. "What?" She had a lock of her gray hair coiled between her fingers, and she was twisting it.

"She. It's a woman."

"How can you know that?" she said.

He hesitated before answering her. It seemed insane, now that he was about to actually say it out loud.

"At Evan's tavern last night, the woman sitting next to me knew Parker. She loathed him. Said he was a complete asshole."

"Okay. But it sounds like you already knew that."

"Yes. And then she reminded me about something else. Parker had a younger sister. Dianna. I knew about her, but I never gave her any thought, because she's also dead. She died even before her brother."

Anna seemed relieved. She even attempted a smile. "But then it isn't her. Obviously."

"Nothing about this is obvious. Dianna had a daughter. *Crib* is about what happened to her. Do you understand?"

She stared at him for the longest time, and at last, she nodded. And then, for what it was worth, there were two of them who knew.

CRIB

BY JACOB FINCH BONNER

Macmillan, New York, 2017, pages 212–13

For weeks, they didn't speak, and even after a lifetime of not speaking something about this felt different: harder, colder, relentlessly toxic. When they passed in the corridor or on the stairs or in the kitchen their eyes slid past each other, and Samantha felt, at certain moments, the actual physical vibration of what was accumulating inside her. She had no intention, still, just a growing idea of something approaching that would not be averted, even with effort, so what point could there be in trying to avert it? It was so much easier to just give up, and after that she felt nothing at all.

On the night Maria left home forever, she knocked on the door of her mother's office and asked if she could borrow the Subaru.

"What for?"

"I'm moving out," said Maria. "I'm leaving for college."

Samantha tried not to react.

"What about senior year?"

Her daughter, maddeningly, shrugged. "Senior year is bullshit. I applied early. I'm going to Ohio State. I got a scholarship for out-of-state students."

"Oh? When were you going to mention all this?"

Again, that shrug. "Now, I guess. I thought maybe I could drive my stuff out there, then I'll bring the car back. Then I'll take a bus or something."

"Wow. Great plan. I guess you've given this a lot of thought."

"Well, it's not as if you're going to take me to college."

"No?" Samantha said. "Well, how can I if you haven't even told me it's happening?"

She turned, and Samantha could hear her stalking back along the corridor to her room. She got up and followed.

"Why is that, by the way? Why did I have to hear from my high school math teacher that my daughter is graduating early? Why do I have to look through your desk to find out my daughter's going to college out of state?"

"I thought so," Maria said, her voice maddeningly calm. "Couldn't keep your paws off my stuff, could you?"

"No, I guess not. Same as if I'd thought you were doing drugs. Proper parental oversight."

"Oh, that's hilarious. *Now* you're suddenly interested in proper parental oversight?"

"I've *always*—"

"Right. Cared. Please, Mom, we've got, like, a couple more days to get through together. Let's not blow it now."

She got up from the bed and stepped in front of her mother, on her way, perhaps, along the hall to the bathroom, where Samantha had once confirmed her predicament with a pregnancy test from the Hamilton ThriftDrug, or down to the kitchen where Samantha had once tried to persuade her own mother that it made no sense—*no sense!*—to have or at any rate to keep this baby she had never wanted, never for one moment wanted, not then, not since, not now, and as that body passed before her she saw, shockingly, herself: slender and straight, with thin brown hair and that family way of slouching, both as she was now and as she had been in that long-ago moment, only wanting, hoping, and waiting for the day she could leave like Maria was about to leave. And without understanding what she was doing or knowing she was going to do it she reached out for her daughter's wrist and yanked it hard, swinging the body attached to it powerfully back along an invisible arc, and as she did she had an idea of herself, swinging a little girl up into the air and smiling into her smile as the two of them spun around and around. It was something a mother might have done with her daughter, and a daughter with her mother, in a film or a television commercial for dresses or Florida beaches or weed killer to make the backyard pretty for an innocent child to play in, only Samantha couldn't remember ever having done this herself, whether she'd been the spinning mother or the spun little girl, around and around in a perfect arc.

Maria's head swung into one of that old bed's wooden cannonballs, and the crack was so deep and so loud it silenced the world.

She fell like something light, barely making a sound, only there she was: half on and half off an old braided rug that had once, when Samantha herself was young, been in the hallway outside her parents' bedroom door. She waited for her daughter to get up, but the waiting ran along a parallel track to something else, which was the absolute and weirdly calm understanding that she was already gone.

Off. Fled. Escaped, after all.

Samantha must have sat there for a minute or an hour, or the better part of that night, watching the crumpled thing that had once, long ago, been Maria, her daughter. And what a waste *that* had been. What an exercise in pointlessness, bringing a human being into the world, only to find oneself more alone than before, more thwarted, more disappointed, more perplexed about what anything meant. This child who had never once reached for her or expressed love, who had never shown the smallest appreciation for what her mother had done, what she'd given up—not willingly, sure, but resignedly, responsibly—and now it had come to this. What for?

She thought, at one point in the deepest part of the night, *I could be in shock*. But it didn't stick. That thought dropped behind her, and also lay still.

Samantha was, as it happened, wearing Maria's discarded green T-shirt that night. It was soft, and it hung on her pretty much exactly as it had on her daughter: same narrow shoulders, same flat chest. She rubbed the cotton between her fingers until they hurt. There was another shirt of her daughter's she had always liked, a black, long-sleeved T-shirt that looked slouchy and comfortable and had a hood. She thought of herself wearing it and wondered if anyone would see her and ask: *Isn't that Maria's shirt?* What would she say? *Oh, Maria gave it to me when she left for college*. But Maria wasn't going to college now. Surely everyone would know that. But who would tell them?

I'm not telling them, Samantha realized. She wasn't telling anybody.

It was all so obvious after that. She finished packing up her daughter's belongings, and some of her own. She closed up the house and put everything into the car and drove west, as far west as she had ever traveled before, and then farther. At Jamestown she turned south and at last left New York state, and by late that afternoon she was deep in the Allegheny National Forest, taking at each turn the road that looked less traveled. In a town called Cherry Grove she saw a sign for a rental cabin, so remote the owner told her not to bother if she didn't have a four-wheel drive.

"I have a Subaru," she told him. She paid cash for a week.

The following day was spent looking for the best place, and that night she dug the hole with a shovel she'd brought from Earlville. The next night she brought her daughter's body and left it there, deep in the soil and covered with rocks and brush, after which she took a shower and tidied the cabin and left the key on the front porch, as she'd been instructed. Then she got back in her old car and put that, too, behind her.

PART FOUR

CHAPTER TWENTY-FIVE

Athens, Georgia

"I need to go to Georgia," he told Anna, a day after his return from Rutland. They were walking from their apartment up to Chelsea Market, and immediately they began to argue.

"Jake, this is crazy. Going around talking to people in bars and sneaking into people's houses and offices!"

"I didn't sneak."

"You didn't tell the truth."

No. But it had been worth it. He had learned, inside of twenty-four hours, more than he'd been able to figure out in months. Now he understood what he'd actually been dealing with, or at least what he'd been avoiding dealing with, all that time.

"There has to be another way," she said.

"Sure. I could go back on *Oprah* like my spirit animal, James Frey, and hang my head and whine about my 'process,' and everyone will totally understand, and it won't destroy everything I've accomplished or get the movie canceled, not to mention the new book, or make me a pariah for the rest of my life. Or I could ask Matilda or Wendy to set up some kind of public breast beating, and make Evan Parker into a tragically lost Great American Novelist, and give him credit for a book he didn't write. Or maybe just let this bitch have complete control over my life, and the power to blow up my career and my reputation and my livelihood."

"I'm not suggesting any of that," Anna said.

"I can see how to find her now, or at least where to start looking. It's the wrong moment to ask me to stop."

"It's the right moment. Because you're going to get hurt."

"I'm going to get hurt if I do nothing, Anna. She doesn't want to be exposed any more than I do. She wants to be in control, and so far she has been. But the more I find out about her, the more I can redress the balance. Frankly it's the only thing I have in my corner."

"But why is it still 'I'? I got my own nasty letter from her, remember? And even if that wasn't the case, we should be dealing with this together. We're married! We're a partnership!"

"I know," Jake agreed miserably.

Maybe he hadn't fully understood the impact of his own evasions on Anna, or even the damage he'd caused to his brand-new marriage, not until he'd been forced into this confession. Six months of hiding the existence of TalentedTom (not to mention the existence of Evan Parker himself) had worn away at him—that part he understood—but now he saw the risk he'd taken with her, and the worst part was that he probably *still* wouldn't have told her about any of it, not if he hadn't been forced to do so. It was a terrible indictment of what remained of his character, and she had every reason to be furious at him, but even as he acknowledged this he hoped the previous night's confessions would ultimately serve to make things better. Maybe letting Anna into his personal circle of the Inferno, even against his will, would bind them closer together. He had to hope so. He was desperate to get to the end of it, and when he did, he vowed to start clean—with Anna and with everything else.

"I need to go to Georgia," Jake said again.

He had told her, already, about the Rutland attorney, William Gaylord, Esquire, who'd acted in conjunction with the seller's out-of-state representation. He had told her about the Rose Parker who was the right age, and had once lived in Athens, Georgia. Now he told her what he had learned by spending five dollars on a twenty-four-hour pass to the online Vermont Town Clerks Portal: the name and address of that out-of-state attorney, an Arthur Pickens, Esquire. Also of Athens, Georgia.

"So?" said Anna.

"You know what else is in Athens, Georgia? An enormous university."

"Well, okay, but that's hardly a smoking gun. More like a big coincidence."

"Okay, if it's a coincidence, then I'll find that out. And then I can just resign myself to letting this woman destroy our lives. But first, I want to know if she's still there, or if not, then I want to know where she went when she left."

Anna shook her head. They had reached the Ninth Avenue entrance to Chelsea Market, and people were streaming out. "But why can't you just call this guy? Why do you actually need to fly down there?"

"I think I'll have a better chance of getting in to see him if I just turn up. That seemed to work in Vermont. You can come with me, you know."

But she couldn't. She needed to go back to Seattle to finish dealing with her stuff in storage and take care of some final business with KBIK. Already she'd put that off a couple of times, and now her boss at the podcast studio had asked Anna not to travel later in June (when he was getting married and going to China on a honeymoon) or July (when he'd be attending a podcasting conference in Orlando). Anna had been planning her trip for next week, and Jake couldn't persuade her to change her plans, so he gave up trying, and there remained a palpable tension between them. He booked his flight to Atlanta for the following Monday, and then he spent the intervening days finishing his revisions for Wendy. He sent off the manuscript late on Sunday night and when he turned his phone on after the plane landed in Atlanta the following afternoon, there was an email letting him know the book had been put into production. So that particular weight, at least, fell away.

Atlanta was a city he had passed through a couple of times on his book tours but never really visited. He picked up a car at the airport and headed northeast to Athens, passing through Decatur, where many months earlier, as *Crib* first surged into the national consciousness, he'd attended a book festival and experienced his first "entrance applause." He remembered that day—only two years ago—and the strange, disembodied feeling of being known by someone (in this case, by many someones) he himself did not know, and the sense of wonder that he had actually written a book strangers had paid money to buy, and spent time to read, and liked enough to have filed into the DeKalb County Courthouse just to see him and hear him say, presumably, something of interest. How far from that heady moment to this, Jake thought, passing the exit signs for Decatur on 285. He wondered if he would be permitted to feel pride in his new book when it came out, or whether he'd ever be able to write anything else after this ordeal, even if he did, somehow, manage to bring it to a peaceful conclusion. And if he didn't, if this woman succeeded in bringing him to his knees, shaming him before his peers and his readers and everyone else who'd placed their own professional reputation in support of his, Jake wondered how he could continue to hold up his head in the world, not just as a writer but as a person.

All the more reason to get the answers he'd come for.

By the time he reached Athens it was too late to do anything but eat, so he checked into his hotel and went out for barbeque, marking up a map of the locations he needed to visit as he sat waiting for his ribs and beer. He was surrounded by blond young women dressed in red UGA shirts. They had musical, inebriated voices and were celebrating some plainly nonacademic triumph together, and he thought how unlike these admittedly pretty young people his own wife was, and how fortunate he felt to be married to Anna, even if Anna was plainly distressed about the choices he'd been making and upset with him in general. He thought of how, each morning after his wife left for work, he found a nest of her long gray hairs coiled in the drain of the shower, the extraction of which gave him a powerful, if admittedly odd, satisfaction. He thought of how their home was warm, colorful, and comfortable—not one facet of which was a thing he'd been able to achieve on his own—and how the refrigerator and freezer were full of her delicious food: homemade soups and stews and even bread. He thought of the cat, Whidbey, and the particular satisfaction of cohabiting with an animal (his first actual pet since a woefully short-lived hamster when he was a boy), and the ways in which the animal occasionally deigned to express gratitude for his extremely pleasant life. He thought of the gradual addition of new and agreeable people to their life as a couple—some from the world of writers (whom he could enjoy as people now that he had no reason to envy them) and some from the new media spheres Anna was beginning to move in. All of it underscored the powerful sense that he had embarked upon the best period of his life.

Now, sipping his beer and eating his barbecued ribs as the sorority girls yelped at the next table, he marveled at the chance of it all: that late addition to his crammed book tour, which Otis (he actually had to try to remember the name of his tour liaison!) had accepted on his behalf, the irritating, borderline insulting on-air interview, the utterly spontaneous invitation to have coffee, and above all the unanticipated bravery of someone willing to upend her life and join his, leaving so much behind. And here he was, less than a year later, married to this wise and lovely woman, with a new life and a new novel that carried not the slightest taint of compromise in its conception, looking ahead to every variety of fulfillment.

If only he could put Evan Parker and his appalling family behind him.

CHAPTER TWENTY-SIX

Poor Rose

In the morning he walked to the UGA campus and found his way to the registrar's office, where he requested the records of a student named Rose Parker, hometown: West Rutland, Vermont. He had a story prepared—estranged niece, dying grandparent—but nobody asked him for anything, including identification. On the other hand, he was only offered the information allowed under something called the Buckley Amendment, and if that seemed sparse compared to all of the questions Jake had it also represented a bouquet of wonderfully concrete facts. First, that Rose Parker had enrolled at the University of Georgia at Athens in September of 2012 without a declared major. Second, that she'd requested and received a waiver for the requirement that freshmen live in an on-campus dormitory (in a welcome bonus, the off-campus address provided to the university matched the one from his previous internet search). Third, that only one year later, in the fall of 2013, there was no longer a Rose Parker among the 37,000 enrolled students at the university. Needless to say, the registrar had no forwarding address or current contact information of any kind, and if Rose's academic records had ever been sent to another institution of higher education in support of a transfer application, that information did not fall within the parameters of what he was permitted to know.

He walked out into the June morning and took a seat on one of the wooden benches in front of the Holmes-Hunter Academic Building. It was both marvelous and somehow disturbing to imagine this person walking along the collegiate pathways, perhaps sitting on this very bench in front of the distinctly plantation-esque building he'd just exited. Could she still be here in Athens? It was certainly possible, but Jake suspected she was long gone to some other town in some other state, doing who knew what else as she kept up an obsessive campaign against him and his work.

Jake found the offices of Arthur Pickens, Esquire, on College Avenue and took an outdoor table at a café a few storefronts up the street to gather his thoughts. He was looking over some of the distinctly unsavory information about Pickens gathered over the days since his visit to that other Esquire in Rutland, Vermont, when he saw an obviously irate father ushering his college-aged son, clad in the now familiar UGA red attire, into the attorney's office. The pair stayed inside for a long time, and when they finally emerged, Jake got up from his table and entered by the same door, finding himself at the foot of a steep staircase. On the second floor, the office's glass door was unlocked, and inside, a florid-faced man was seated at a massive mahogany desk. Behind him: shelves of law books, so pristine they looked as if they'd never been opened. That wasn't inconsistent with what he'd learned about Arthur Pickens, Esquire.

The man was frowning. Jake, also, was frowning. Then he remembered that he had the first line.

"Mr. Pickens?"

"I am. And you are?"

"Jacob Bonner."

Jake crossed the room with his hand extended. He was going for southern genteel, the Yankee approximation. "Sorry not to call first. If you're busy I'd be happy to come back."

Pickens, however, remained seated. He did not extend his own hand. He seemed to be giving Jake more disapproval than even an unexpected walk-in deserved.

"I don't believe that will be necessary, Mr. Bonner. I won't be able to help you, even if you come back another time."

The two of them stared at each other. Jake let his hand drop. Finally, he managed: "I'm sorry?"

"I'm sorry you're sorry. But attorney-client privilege makes it impossible for me to answer your questions."

"Are you saying you already know what I've come to talk to you about?"

"I am not at liberty to answer that," Pickens said.

"And, just to be clear, you also know which of your clients my questions pertain to."

"Again, I won't be answering."

Jake, for all of his anticipation, and despite, in particular, the hour he'd just spent waiting at the café up the street, had not considered this particular scenario. As a result, he was floored.

"So I respectfully invite you to leave, Mr. Bonner," Pickens added. He also got to his feet.

There were, apparently, very long legs underneath that big desk, and they unfolded as the attorney rose. At his considerable height he looked every inch the flower of southern manhood, from that athletic frame to the red face and swept-back hair, a mite too uniformly brown to be entirely natural. He stood, leaning forward, arms braced on his desk, wearing an oddly not-unfriendly smile but clearly expecting Jake to go without further comment.

Instead, Jake crossed the room and took one of the chairs on the other side of the desk.

"I've decided to hire an attorney," he said. "I'm being harassed and threatened, and I would like to file suit for defamation."

Pickens frowned. Perhaps what he'd been told hadn't included the parts about harassment, threats, and defamation.

"I have reason to believe the harassment originated here in Athens, and I need a local attorney to act on my behalf."

"I'd be happy to refer you to somebody else. I know some excellent attorneys here in Athens."

"But *you're* an excellent attorney, Mr. Pickens. I mean, you certainly appear to be, if you don't look too closely."

"What's that supposed to mean?" Pickens said sharply.

"Well, you obviously know who I am. I assume that means you also know I'm a writer. Writers research. And of course I've researched you."

Pickens nodded. "Happy to hear it. My online ratings are excellent."

"Absolutely correct!" Jake said. "Duke University undergrad. Vanderbilt Law. Really good stuff. I mean, there was that cheating thing at Duke, but it was your whole frat. Doesn't seem fair to single you out. And then you did have that one incident with your client's daughter. And your own DUIs, of course. But who doesn't have DUIs, right? Also, I'm sure the Clarke County cops were out to get a successful defense attorney like you. Still, that was a close shave with the Georgia bar."

Pickens sat down. He was so livid, his face had slid into an even deeper shade of red.

"Anyway, I think most people just stop with Facebook or Yelp when they're looking for a lawyer. You're probably okay."

"Now who's harassing and threatening?" he said. "I've already asked you to leave."

"Is Rose Parker the person who said I might be coming to see you?"

He did not respond.

"Do you know where she is now?"

"Mr. Bonner, I've asked you to leave, several times. Now I'm going to phone the police. Then you, too, can have a criminal complaint filed against you here in Clarke County."

Jake sighed. He got to his feet. "Well, I'm sure you know what you're doing. I'm just worried that when they come talk to you about the Vermont crimes, all that old stuff about you is going to come out. But I guess you've made your peace with that."

"I know nothing about any Vermont crimes. I have never set foot in Vermont. I have never been north of the Mason-Dixon Line."

He said this with such pride he actually sneered. What a pathetic loser.

"Well"—Jake shrugged—"that's fine, though when those Yankee investigators arrive I don't think you'll get rid of them just by asking them to leave. My guess is you'll need to hire representation of your own. Maybe one of those excellent attorneys you were about to refer me to. Maybe whoever handled your DUIs or that business with the teenager. And I'll probably be naming you in my own lawsuit. You know, when I sue your client for damages. So maybe, if they represent you for that, too, they'll give you a break on the price."

Mr. Arthur Pickens looked as if he might blow apart.

"You want to waste your money on a frivolous lawsuit, you go right ahead. As I said, attorney-client privilege prevents me from providing any information about my client. Please leave."

"Oh, you've provided plenty of information," Jake said. "You confirmed that you're still in communication with your client, Rose Parker. I had no way of knowing that when I walked in a few minutes ago, so I appreciate it."

"If you don't leave immediately I will call the police."

"Fine," said Jake, languidly getting to his feet. "If it doesn't cross an *ethical line,* I hope you'll tell your client that if she doesn't knock it off with the emails and the letters and the posts I'm going to the Vermont cops with everything I've learned. And that includes a couple of things that have been bothering me about Evan Parker's death."

"I have no idea who that is," said Pickens, barely keeping it together.

"Naturally. But if your client murdered him, and if you were involved, I can promise you're going north of the Mason-Dixon Line, because that's where they keep the Yankee courthouses. And the Yankee prisons."

Arthur Pickens, Esquire, looked as if he had lost the power of speech.

"Well, bye then. It's been a pleasure."

Jake left, rage and adrenaline coursing through him. Of the astonishing things he'd just said to a complete stranger in his place of business, approximately 100 percent had been unplanned, though he'd certainly had all the relevant facts at his disposal for days. Pickens's moral failings, along with those of his fraternity brothers, had been delineated in no fewer than four articles in the Duke student paper, complete with the names and classes of all involved. The sticky situation with his client's nineteen-year-old daughter (legal, but gross) had played out over Facebook, courtesy of the girl and her mother, and the DUIs had come right up in a basic internet search. (They really ought to have been expunged, somehow, Jake thought. Maybe he wasn't all that good an attorney.)

He hadn't planned to speak of Evan Parker's death at all, let alone as anything but an accidentally self-administered overdose, and as for the legal jeopardy Pickens might face as a result of crimes his client had theoretically committed in Vermont, he knew he was on shaky ground. Personally, Jake had no idea what would happen if he walked into the local Rutland police station with his concerns about a five-year-old drug overdose, but he had to assume that it wouldn't be taken all that seriously, and it was highly unlikely that the state of Vermont would send investigators to West Rutland, let alone to Athens, Georgia. He strongly suspected, moreover, that Arthur Pickens had little to fear from an official investigation, and his client not much more, but it had been satisfying beyond belief to utter the words "Yankee prison" in that office, and the fury he'd felt back there only seemed to be coalescing with every step he took.

He was actually stunned by what had just happened between himself and Pickens, and sort of grateful that he hadn't had the chance to consider and temper his response before he'd reacted. It wasn't as if he'd been especially optimistic when he'd entered the lawyer's office, but he hadn't expected to be blocked before he could even get his first question out. He thought he'd feel the guy out, maybe suggest that he was interested in hiring an attorney, and when asked for details about his complaint he would describe TalentedTom's activities and work his way around to revealing the name Rose Parker. Then, if Pickens declined to give him a means of contacting his client, he would leave, perhaps with some form of the message he'd managed to deliver, albeit not at quite so high a pitch. For months, he now realized, ever since that day in the car to the Seattle airport where he'd read the first of those terrifying dispatches, he'd been in a defensive posture, bracing for the next communication while hoping, against all logic, that it would never come. That had taken a lot out of him and now, for the first time, he was feeling the sheer rage he'd managed to accrue over that same period, the deep resentment against this person who felt it her business and her right to harry and persecute him, just because he'd found a story and crafted it into a fine and compelling narrative, precisely as writers had always done! There had been something about that guy, though, with his red face and his dyed hair and his shelf of law books and his preemptive stonewall. Something that grabbed Jake by the throat and made him speak in a language he might have learned from TalentedTom herself. No, these people were not going to fuck with him any longer. Or if they did, he was going to fuck with them right back.

By now he had turned onto West Hancock Street and was drawing closer to the address he'd first discovered at the Rutland Free Library. Only a little over a week had passed since he'd naturally dismissed that Rose Parker of Athens, Georgia, as irrelevant to the unfolding saga of Evan Parker and his avenging angel. Now the address, an apartment complex called Athena Gardens on Dearing Street, was his best remaining hope of finding a connection to wherever she was now, not that he was naïve enough to expect a forwarding address or any connection at all to a current resident. In a university town like Athens, the passage of six years meant a complete turnover of the undergraduates in the town's many apartment complexes, but he supposed it might still be possible to find someone who recalled this particular person: a description, a memory, anything that might bring him closer to finding her.

Athena Gardens was a bare-bones version of the luxe options he'd already seen around town, housing complexes fronted by country club pavilions and showing glimpses of pools and tennis courts through their iron gates. This one, on the other hand, looked like a redbrick rehabilitation facility, or a small office complex occupied by gently failing businesses. There was a sign out front advertising Athena Gardens's amenities (pest control and garbage removal included in the monthly rent, cleaning for a nominal fee) and layouts for the one-, two-, and three-bedroom options. Jake had little doubt which type of apartment Rose Parker might have chosen in the fall of 2012 after going out of her way to avoid having an on-campus roommate. She'd have lived alone here at Athena Gardens. She'd have kept to herself as her old life detatched and fell away.

There was a management office just inside the main entrance, and he found a woman behind a desk, working at her computer. She had a stiff pageboy haircut that only served to accentuate her very full face, and a default expression that said: *I don't like you, but I'm being paid to pretend I do.* She gave Jake a thoroughly disingenuous smile when he entered. Still, it was a far warmer greeting than the one he'd had from Arthur Pickens, Esquire.

"Hi. Hope I'm not interrupting."

She looked to be about Jake's own age. Possibly older. "Not at all," she said. "What can I do for you?"

"Just looking at a few options for my daughter. She's going to be a sophomore in the fall. Can't wait to get out of the dorms."

The woman laughed. "I hear that a lot." She stood up. "I'm Bailey," she said, reaching out her hand.

"Hi. Jacob." They shook. "I said I'd take a look at a few places while she was in class. I'll need to bring her back if I see anything that gets dad approval. I asked my cousin for some advice. His daughter lived here a few years back."

"Here at Athena Gardens?"

"Yes. He said it was safe. Safety is what I care about, really."

"Of course! You're her dad!" said Bailey, coming around the desk. "We get plenty of dads. They don't care how many stationary bikes are in the workout room. They want to know their girls are secure."

"Absolutely right." Jake nodded. "Don't want to know what color the carpet is. I want to know, do the doors lock, is there a guard, that kind of thing."

"Not that we don't have a very nice workout room. And a very pretty pool."

Jake, who had seen the pool as he came down the street, begged to differ.

"Also I don't want anything too close to Washington Street. So many bars."

"Oh, I know." The woman rolled her eyes. "A hundred in downtown Athens, did you know that? It's wild on a Saturday night. Actually, it's wild most nights. So. Would you like to see a few apartments?"

She had a dire two-bedroom that still bore the stained carpets of its recently departed occupants (very thirsty people, if the bottle collection atop the kitchen cabinets was any indication). She had a one-bedroom that smelled of cinnamon potpourri. She had another one-bedroom that actually had a tenant. Jake was pretty sure Bailey wasn't supposed to be showing it to anyone.

"You said your daughter wants a one-bedroom?"

"Yes. She's had an awful roommate this year. From out of state."

"Ah," said Bailey. Apparently, no more needed to be said.

"How long has this place been here?" he asked, and she told him nearly twenty years, though he knew this already, from his research. He also knew that Black neighborhoods all over Athens had been bulldozed so that apartment complexes just like this one (most of them much nicer than this one) could be occupied by mainly white students. But he was here for more specific history.

"And what about you? How long have you been working here?"

"Just a couple of years. Before that I was managing one of the other sites. We have four in our company, all in Athens."

"Nice," said Jake. "Like I said, my cousin's daughter lived here. She had a good experience, I think. Her name was Rose Parker. You probably don't remember her."

"Rose Parker?" Bailey considered. "No, doesn't sound familiar. Carole might remember. Carole's the in-house cleaner. It's an extra charge," she clarified.

"Wow. Cleaning for a bunch of college students. That's got to be a tough job."

"Carole loves her job," said Bailey, a bit defensively. "She's like the den mother."

"Oh, of course."

He didn't know what to say. He let her show him another one-bedroom, and the sad little exercise room, and the pool, where a couple of kids were just getting settled onto cheap loungers. When she invited him to return to the office for a brochure and a copy of the code of conduct he realized he was about to leave Athena Gardens without what he'd come for, which was anything at all. Bailey was trying to set up an appointment for him and his imaginary daughter for tomorrow, but by tomorrow he'd be home in Greenwich Village with not much to show a very worried Anna.

"Listen," said Jake. "I owe you an apology."

She was instantly wary. And who could blame her?

"Oh?" They hadn't reached the office yet. They were on one of the walkways between the pool and the complex's main building, where the office was located.

"My daughter, she's already found a place she likes."

"I see," said Bailey, who looked as if she'd expected something worse.

"I wanted to look at this place because—that cousin I mentioned? He asked me to."

Bailey frowned. "Whose daughter lived here."

"Yes, 2012 to 2013. He hasn't heard from her in a couple of years. He's very concerned. He asked me to come. He knows it's a long shot, but, you know, since I was here in town, anyway. Just on the chance that she kept in touch with someone here . . ."

"I see," said Bailey again. "Do they know," she hesitated, "is she still . . ."

"She's active on"—he provided sarcastic air quotes—"*social media.* They know she's living somewhere in the Midwest. But she doesn't respond to any kind of overture. They thought, if I managed to find someone she stayed in touch with, you know, they could get a message through. Personally, I didn't think it sounded all that promising, but . . . if it was my daughter . . ."

"Yes. How sad."

For a moment she said nothing, and Jake thought either his story or his acting must have fallen short of the mark, but then Bailey spoke. "Like I said, I was at one of our other properties till last year myself. And as for our tenants, they're about eighty percent enrolled UGA students, mostly undergrad, so if they'd been here when your cousin's daughter was here, they're already long gone. A couple of grad students stay longer, but I don't think we have any now that were here in 2013."

"That woman you mentioned before, the cleaner?"

"Yeah." Bailey nodded. She took out her phone and sent a text. "She's here today. I haven't seen her, but she started at one. I'm asking her to meet us out front."

He thanked her, perhaps a bit too warmly, and they walked together to the reception area outside her office. When they reached it, a solid woman in a faded red Bulldawg sweatshirt was already there.

"Carole, hi," said Bailey. "This is Mr. . . ."

"Jacob," said Jake.

"Carole Feeney," said Carole, obviously worried.

"Nothing's wrong," Bailey said. "This man is just trying to find a girl who lived here awhile back."

"My cousin's daughter," Jake confirmed. "They haven't been able to reach her. They're worried."

"Oh my yes," said Carole, every inch the den mother she'd been billed as.

"Before my time," said Bailey. "But I was saying, you might remember?"

"Could we . . ." Jake looked around. It hadn't escaped him that Bailey wasn't offering her own office for this interview. Now that Jake wasn't a prospect she clearly didn't want to give over the space, or perhaps she no longer cared to be in an enclosed room with him. But there were a couple of chairs in a dreary little lounge next door. On their tour, Bailey had called it the common room. He pointed in that direction now. "Do you have a few minutes?"

"Sure, sure," said Carole. She was pale with a forest of dark moles along both collarbones. Jake was finding it hard not to look at them.

"Well, good luck," Bailey said. "Keep us in mind if your daughter's place doesn't work out."

"Thank you so much," Jake said. "I will."

He wouldn't. Even she knew that.

In the lounge, he took one of the old armchairs, which was as uncomfortable as it looked, and Carole Feeney took another one. She seemed already to be in mourning for this unnamed girl from "awhile back" whose family couldn't reach her, and afraid to find out who it was.

"So, like I said, my cousin's daughter lived here, her freshman year. That was 2012 to 2013."

"Freshman year? Usually they're in the dorms up on campus."

"So I understand. She got some kind of a waiver."

Her eyes widened. "Wait, is it Rose? Are you talking about Rose?"

Jake seemed to lose his breath. He hadn't expected it to be so fast. Now he wasn't sure what to say.

"Yeah. Rose Parker."

"In 2012, you said? That sounds about right. She's missing? Poor Rose!"

Poor Rose. Jake managed to nod.

"Oh my word. That's so sad. Her mother died, you know."

Jake nodded. He was still not sure. "Yes. It was very tragic. Is there anything you remember about Rose that might help her dad find her?"

Carole folded her hands in her lap. They were big hands, and unsurprisingly rough.

"Well, she was mature, of course. Didn't have a lot in common with most of the other students. Didn't go out to the bars. Didn't go to the games, I don't think. Didn't Rush. I wasn't cleaning for her, so I wasn't in her place except now and then. I think she came from up north."

"Vermont," Jake confirmed.

"That so."

He waited for her to continue.

"Most of these girls, they got their beds covered with stuffed animals, like they're six years old. Every inch of the wall has posters. Throw pillows all over the place. A mini fridge in every room so they don't have to walk more than a few steps to get a can of pop. Some of these apartments, you can barely turn around in for all the things they bring. Rose kept hers pretty plain, and she was a tidy person. Like I said, mature."

"Did she ever speak about anyone else in her family?"

Carole shook her head. "Don't remember that, no. She never mentioned a father. Your cousin?"

"They weren't together, the parents. Not for most of Rose's life," Jake said, thinking quickly. "That's probably why."

The woman nodded. She had two thin braids of highly distressed orange hair. "I only ever heard her talk about her mother. But of course, that horrible thing with her mom had just happened, right before she got here. Probably that was the only thing on her mind." She shook her head. "So horrible."

"You're talking about . . . the fire, right?" said Jake. "Was it a car crash?"

That's what he'd been imagining, he realized, ever since the Parker Tavern, and Sally's indelible *she burned up*. Obviously it hadn't been at the house; Sylvia or Betty would have said so, folding that into the carbon monoxide poisoning and the overdose, just another dreadful thing that had taken place in an old family home where people were born and died. Since that night at the Parker Tavern with Sally he'd imagined it pretty consistently as *car hits ditch, car flips, car somersaults downhill, car bursts into flame,* and he could see a hundred film and television variations on that sequence, perhaps with the addition of a tragic/lucky passenger who'd managed to get out in time, screaming and crying and staring down at the conflagration from the road above.

"Oh no," said Carole Feeney. "Poor thing was in a tent. Rose just barely got out in time, had to watch it happen. Nothing at all she could do."

"In a tent? They were . . . what, camping?"

It was the kind of astonishing detail a cousin of an ex-husband of a fatal accident victim probably ought to have known. But he hadn't known it.

"Driving down here to Athens, from up north. I guess, you said, Vermont." She fixed him with a look. "Not everybody has the money to stay in a hotel, you know. She told me, once, if she hadn't gone so far away from home to go to school, her mother would still be okay, not in some plot in north Georgia."

Jake was staring at her. "Wait," he said. "Wait, this happened in Georgia?"

"Rose had to bury her mama in a cemetery up there, in the town near where it happened. Can you imagine?"

He couldn't. Well, he could, but then again, the problem wasn't imagining it, the problem was making sense of it.

"Why wouldn't she bring her home, to be buried in Vermont? The whole family is buried in Vermont!"

"You know what? I didn't ask her that," Carole said, with abundant sarcasm. "You think that's a question to ask somebody who just lost her mother? She didn't have anybody back there where she came from. It was just her and her mama, she told me. No sisters or brothers. And like I said, I never heard a single thing about your *cousin,*" Carole said meaningfully. "Maybe it made sense to her, to just take care of it up there. But if you find her, you can definitely ask her."

The interview, such as it was, appeared to be deteriorating. Jake frantically tried to think of what he still needed to know.

"She left the university after her freshman year. Do you have any idea where she went?"

Carole shook her head. "Didn't know she was going till they told me to clean up her place, after the fact. I wasn't really surprised she decided to go somewhere else to study. This is a party school. She was no party girl."

He nodded, as if he, too, was aware of this.

"And there's no one else who lived here then, who she might have kept in touch with?"

Carole considered. "No. Like I said, I don't think she had much in common with the other students. Even those couple of years, it makes a big difference at that age."

"Wait," said Jake. "How old was she, would you say, when she was living here?"

"I never asked." She stood up. "Sorry I can't help you. I hate to think of her as missing."

"Wait," he said again. He was reaching into a back pocket for his phone. "Just . . . can I show you a picture?" He was looking for the blurry girl on the field hockey team: short bangs, large round glasses. Because that was all he had, the only proof of the Rose Parker who'd powered through high school in three years and left home at the start of what would otherwise have been her senior year, and who should have arrived here in Georgia as a motherless sixteen-year-old. "I just want to make sure," he told Carol Feeney, holding it out to show her.

The woman leaned closer, and immediately he saw the concern fall away from her. She straightened up.

"That's not Rose." Carole Feeney shook her head. "You're talking about somebody else. Well, that's a relief. The girl's been through enough."

"But . . . this is her. This is Rose Parker."

She indulged him by looking at it again, but this time for no longer than a second.

"No it isn't," she said.

CRIB

BY JACOB FINCH BONNER

Macmillan, New York, 2017, pages 245–46

She made a point of returning a couple of times that first year, and when she ran into people she knew in Earlville or Hamilton, people she'd been around her entire life, she let them know how Maria was doing at Ohio State.

"She's going to major in history," she told the teller at her bank as she arranged a transfer of funds to her daughter's account in Columbus.

"She's thinking of transferring," she told old Fortis himself, when she saw him getting out of his car at the Price Chopper. "Wants to see more of the country."

"Well, who can blame her?" he said.

"She seems really happy out there," she told Gab, who turned up at the house one day.

"I just happened to be passing by. I saw your car?" Gab said, as if it was a question. "I never see your car anymore, when I pass by."

"I have a boyfriend just outside Albany," Samantha said. "I'm spending a lot of time out there with him."

"Oh."

Gab, it turned out, had been emailing Maria since August, texting her, calling her until she got a message that the number was no longer functional.

"She was hoping you'd get the message," Samantha told her. "I'm sorry to be the one telling you this, but Maria has a serious girlfriend now. It's someone in her philosophy class. A very brilliant young woman."

"Oh," the girl said again. She left a painful five minutes later, so that was the end of that. Or should have been.

"I'm thinking of moving out to Ohio, to live with my daughter there," she told the woman in the local ReMax office. "I'm wondering how much you think my house is worth."

It was worth a lot less than she wanted for it, but she sold it anyway that spring, and Samantha drove the Subaru west again, though this time with a U-Haul van attached and without a detour to Pennsylvania.

CHAPTER TWENTY-SEVEN

Foxfire

Even before he called her, he knew she'd be upset. Her own flight to Seattle was coming up soon and Jake had been scheduled to return the following morning after two days of a trip she hadn't wanted him to make in the first place; instead he was changing his plans, extending his rental car, and, worst of all, driving north to a place he'd never even heard of before today, in a part of Georgia he'd never had any reason to visit. Until now.

"Oh Jake, no," Anna said, when he told her.

He was back in his room at the hotel, eating a burger he'd picked up on his walk back from the library.

"Listen, I just assumed she died in Vermont. I had no idea the accident happened in Georgia."

"Well, so what?" Anna said. "Why does it matter where it happened? I mean, for fuck's sake, Jacob, what is it you think you're going to find out?"

"I don't know," he said, honestly enough. "I just want to do whatever I can to get her to stop extorting me."

"But she hasn't done that," Anna said. "Extortion implies a demand. She hasn't asked you for a penny. She hasn't even asked you to come clean."

He had to let that sit there for a moment. It was an intensely painful moment.

"Come clean?" he finally said.

"I'm sorry. You know what I mean."

But he didn't. That, it occurred to him, was becoming a bit of a problem.

"You don't find it interesting that she apparently dropped the body by the side of the road and went along on her way? There's a hundred and fifty years' worth of Parkers in a cemetery in Vermont!"

"Well, no," said Anna, "it just doesn't seem all that strange to me. Under those circumstances? She's on her way from Vermont to Georgia, she's probably got her whole life in the back of the car, and this happens? Maybe she already knew she wouldn't be going home. Maybe she wasn't sentimental in general. Maybe a lot of things! So she thinks, okay, my life is forward, not back. I'll just find a nice place around here for her to be buried, and I'll keep going."

"What about family members? What about friends? Maybe they had an opinion."

"Maybe they didn't have friends. Maybe Evan Parker wasn't a part of their lives. Maybe none of this stuff matters. Would you please just come home?"

But he couldn't. It had taken him all of thirty seconds and the search terms "Dianna Parker+tent+Georgia" to find this brief and highly problematic story from *The Clayton Tribune* of Rabun Gap:

By News Staff on August 27, 2012

Rabun County

A 32-year-old woman perished in the early hours of Sunday, August 26th at approximately 2 A.M. in a tent fire at the Foxfire

> Campground in the Chattahoochee-Oconee National Forest. Dianna Parker, of West Rutland, Vermont, had been camping with her sister, Rose Parker, 26, who escaped the blaze and was eventually able to raise the alarm. Paramedics from Rabun County EMS and members of Georgia State Patrol Troop C responded but destruction of the campsite was complete by the time they reached the campgrounds.

He sent her the link now, along with the question: *Don't you see the issue here?*

She didn't. He didn't blame her.

"Rose Parker was 16. Not 26."

"So there's a typo. One digit. Human error."

"*Sister*?" he said. "Not daughter?"

"It's a mistake. Look, Jake, I grew up in a small town. These local papers, they're not *The New York Times*."

"It's not a mistake. It's a lie. Look," he said, "don't you find it interesting that nobody seems to get sick in this family? Everyone dies suddenly in some kind of unexpected event. Carbon monoxide poisoning. Drug overdose. A tent fire, for God's sake! That's a lot to accept."

"Well, people do die, Jake, in all those ways. There weren't always carbon monoxide detectors—even with them people still get poisoned, sometimes. They also overdose. There's an opiate crisis in this country, as you might be aware. And in Seattle we had tent fires in the homeless encampments all the time."

She was right, he told her, but he was still going to take another day to drive up there. Maybe he'd find someone to talk to, who'd been at the accident site, or who'd maybe even spoken with the survivor at the time. And he could visit the campsite where the fire had happened.

"But why?" she said, with great exasperation. "Some campsite in the woods? What do you think you're going to learn from that?"

He didn't honestly know.

"Also I want to see where she's buried."

But that he could defend even less.

In the morning he drove north across the Piedmont Plateau and into the Blue Ridge Mountains, lovely enough to prod aside, temporarily, his ongoing preoccupations. What he would say when he got to Rabun Gap, and whom he would say it to, were unanswered questions, but he couldn't stop himself from feeling there was some final insight waiting for him ahead, something that justified not only the long drive (which was very much not in the direction of the Atlanta airport) and the expense of the extra day and rescheduled flight, but most of all the obvious disapproval of his wife. Something he couldn't learn anywhere else. Something that would confirm for him, finally, who this person was, and why she'd come after him, and how he could get her to stop.

He had found the campground easily on Google Maps, but finding it in actuality was considerably more difficult since his phone's GPS seemed to falter the moment he entered the mountains. He had to resort to the decidedly analog method of stopping at a general store in Clayton to ask directions, and this required an obscure exchange of information before the information could be forthcoming.

"Gotcher license?" said the man behind the counter, when Jake explained what he was looking for.

"Beg your pardon?"

"We can sell you one, if you don't."

License for what? he wanted to ask, but it didn't seem like a great way to establish a rapport.

"Oh, well, that's good."

The man grinned. His sideburns were so long they rounded the corner along his jaw, but didn't meet at the chin. The chin had a dimple, à la Kirk Douglas. Maybe that was why.

"Not here to fish, I'm guessing."

"Oh. No. Just trying to find the campground."

Foxfire's draw, as the man happily (and at length) explained to him, was trout fishing. Jilly Creek, just south of the waterfall, was a popular spot.

"How far from here, would you say?"

"I'd *say* twenty minutes. East on Warwoman Road for eleven miles. Left on the forest service road. Then it's about two miles along."

"How many campsites are there?" said Jake.

"How many do you need?" The man laughed.

"Actually," said Jake, "I don't need any. I'm just interested in something that happened there, a couple of years ago. Maybe you remember."

The guy stopped smiling. "Maybe I do. Maybe I have a pretty good idea what you're talking about."

His name was Mike. He was a north Georgia lifer and, by an undeserved stroke of luck, a volunteer fireman. Two years earlier, his company had been called to the Foxfire Campground on a crowded summer afternoon to break up a fight between two women, one of whom had suffered a broken wrist. Five years before that, a woman had burned to death in a tent in the middle of the night. Apart from those two incidents, the only notable occurrences of the past several decades had involved the failure to release undersized trout.

"I can't see why you'd have an interest in those two crazy girls from Pine Mountain," he said. "Not that I have any idea why you'd be interested in the woman who died. Except she wasn't from here and obviously neither are you."

"I'm from New York," said Jake, confirming the man's worst suspicions.

"And so was she?"

"Vermont."

"Well." He shrugged, as if his point had been proved.

"I knew her brother," Jake said, after a moment.

This had the advantage of being, at least, true.

"Ah. Well, awful thing. Terrible to see. The sister was hysterical."

Jake, who didn't trust himself to answer, merely nodded. *Sister.*

"So you were there that night," said Jake.

"No. But I was there the next morning. Nothing for the EMTs to do, so they waited for us to do the removal."

"Do you mind if I ask you about it?"

"You're already asking about it," he said. "If I minded I'd have stopped you already."

Mike owned the store along with his two brothers, one of whom was in prison, the other in the stockroom. That one emerged at around this time, and looked at Mike for an explanation.

"Wants to know about Foxfire camp," said Mike.

"Gotcher license?" the brother said. "Can sell you one, if you don't."

Jake wished he could avoid going through this again. "I've never fished, actually. I won't be starting today. I'm a writer."

"Writers don't fish?" Mike grinned.

"This one doesn't."

"What do you write? Movies?"

"Novels."

"Fictional novels?"

He sighed. "Yes. My name's Jake." He shook hands with both brothers.

"You writing a novel about that woman at Foxfire?"

It was a bit much to explain that he'd already written one.

"No. Like I said, I knew her brother."

"I'll drive you out, if you want," Mike said. His brother from the stockroom looked about as surprised as Jake himself was to hear it.

"Really? That's incredibly kind of you."

"I think Lee can hold down the fort here."

"Think I can," the brother said.

"Not that you couldn't find it on your own."

Jake had serious doubts that he could find it on his own.

They took Mike's truck, which had the detritus of at least four meals underfoot and reeked of menthols, and for eleven miles of slow country road Jake had to hear far more than he wished to know about the taxes generated by trout fishing in north Georgia, and how little of it went back into the community it came out of and not into, say, subsidies for Obamacare in other parts of the state, but all that was worth it when they turned off the road onto a track Jake absolutely would have missed if he'd attempted this on his own. And even if he hadn't, he'd still have given up long before finishing the next part of the route, along a dirt track miles deep into the woods.

"There," Mike said, cutting the engine.

There was a small parking area with a couple of picnic tables and a battered old sign with the campground's hours (twenty-four per day, of which 10 P.M. to 6 A.M. were meant to be "quiet"), reservation policy (not accepted), amenities (two chemical vault toilets, whatever they might be), and nightly fee ($10, payable at the drop box). Foxfire was open year round, maximum stay fourteen days, nearest town, as Jake now knew all too well, was Clayton, fifteen miles away. It really was the middle of nowhere.

But it was also pretty. Very pretty and very tranquil and so surrounded by forest he could only imagine what it must be like out here in the dead of night. Really the last place in the world you'd want to have a crisis of any kind, let alone of a life-threatening nature. Unless it was exactly the place you wanted to have that kind of a crisis.

"I can show you which site they had, if you want."

He walked behind Mike along the creek and then left, past two or three unoccupied campsites, each with its own fire pit and tent pitch, and farther back into the woods.

"Was anyone else staying out here that night?"

"One of the other campsites was occupied, but you see how it's set up. They're pretty spread out, along different paths. Even if the sister'd known there was someone nearby she probably wouldn't have known how to find them, especially in the dark. And I doubt they'd of been much help even if she managed it. They were a couple from Spartanburg in their seventies. Slept through the whole thing, came out in the morning to load up their car and dump their trash and found the parking lot full of EMTs and the fire marshal. No idea what was going on."

"So which way did she go to get help? The sister. Out toward the road?"

"Yep. Two miles from here to the main road, and when she got out there, no cars, obviously, at four in the morning. Took another couple of hours before somebody came along. By then she was a couple of miles closer to Pine Mountain. And it was a cold night, and she was just in flip-flops and a long T-shirt. People can be surprised by how cold it gets up in the mountains. Even in August. But I guess they'd been planning for that."

Jake frowned. "What do you mean?"

"Well, they had the heater, didn't they?"

"You mean, like, an electric heater?"

Mike, still a couple of steps ahead, turned back to give Jake a look. "Not an electric heater. A propane heater."

"And that's how the fire started?"

"Well, it's a pretty good bet!" Mike actually laughed. "Usually you're worried about CO_2 with those puppies, but you never want to set them down near anything, or put anything over them, or have them in a place somebody can knock them over. The newer ones can detect if they fall over. There's an alarm that sounds. But this one wasn't new." He shrugged. "We think that's what happened, anyway. She told the coroner she got up to use the toilet in the middle of the night. Walked down there to where we parked. Gone about ten minutes in all. Afterward, she said she might have brushed against it when she went out. Maybe it could've fallen over. She was a total mess, talking about it."

He stopped. They were in a clearing, about thirty feet long. Jake could still hear the creek but now the wind in the tall pines and hickories overhead were just as loud. Mike had his hands in his pockets. His native irreverence seemed to have departed.

"So this is it?"

"Yep. The tent was over there." He nodded at the cleared, flat place. There was a fire pit beside it, not recently used.

"It's really the back of beyond," Jake heard himself say.

"Sure. Or center of the universe, if you like to camp."

He wondered if Rose and Dianna Parker liked to camp. He realized, again, how little he knew about them, and how much of what he thought he knew had turned out to be wrong. That's what happens when you learn about people from a novel—somebody else's or your own, just the same.

"Too bad she didn't have a phone with her," Jake said.

"She had one, but it was inside the tent, and by the time she got back the whole thing was in flames. It just went up, and everything in it." He paused. "Not that it would've worked out here, anyway."

Jake looked at him. "What?"

"The phone. You found that out yourself."

Indeed he had.

"Do you have any idea why they were here?" he asked Mike. "Two women from Vermont at a campground in Georgia?"

Mike shrugged. "Nope. I never talked to her. Roy Porter did, though. He's the coroner in Rabun Gap. I just assumed they were traveling around, camping. If you knew the family you probably have a better idea than either of us." He peered at Jake. "You did say you knew the family."

"I knew the brother of the woman who died, but I never asked him about it. And he died a year after this." He gestured at the campground.

"Yeah? Bad luck in that family."

"The worst," Jake had to agree. If it was luck. "Do you think the coroner would talk to me?"

"Don't see why not. We've come a long way since *Deliverance*. We're pretty nice to outsiders now."

"You're . . . what?" Jake said.

"*Deliverance*. They shot that movie a couple miles from here."

That sent a chill through him. He couldn't help it.

"Good thing you didn't tell me before!" he said, with what he hoped would pass for a backslapping kind of tone.

"Or you wouldn't have driven out to *the back of beyond* with a total stranger and a phone that won't work."

He couldn't tell if Mike was joking.

"Hey, could I take you both out to dinner, to say thanks?"

Mike seemed to give this more consideration than it deserved. In the end, however, he agreed. "I can give Roy a call and ask him."

"That would be fantastic. Where should we go?"

It was a very New York question, needless to say, but in Clayton the range of options was not extensive. He arranged to meet the two of them at a place called the Clayton Café, and after Mike dropped him back at the store to retrieve his car, Jake found a Quality Inn and checked in for the night. He knew better than to phone or even text Anna. Instead, he lay on the bed watching an old episode of *Oprah* in which Dr. Phil advised a couple of sixteen-year-olds to grow up and take responsibility for their baby. He nearly fell asleep, lulled by the groans of audience disapproval.

The Clayton Café was a storefront on the town's main street with a striped awning and a sign that said SERVING THE COMMUNITY SINCE 1931. Inside were tables with black-checkered tablecloths and orange chairs and walls covered with local art. A woman met him at the door, carrying two plates piled with spaghetti and tomato sauce, each with a wedge of garlic bread balanced on top. Looking at them, he was reminded of the fact that he hadn't eaten since grabbing an English muffin for the road, that morning in Athens.

"I'm meeting Mike," he said, belatedly realizing he'd never asked Mike's last name. "And . . ." He had forgotten the coroner's name completely. "One other person."

She pointed at a table at the other end of the room, under a painting of a forest grove very like the one he'd visited a few hours earlier. A man was already there: elderly, African-American. "Be right over," the waitress said.

The man looked up, just at that moment. His face, as was probably appropriate to his profession, gave away nothing, not even a smile. Jake still could not remember his name. He crossed the room and held out his hand.

"Hello, I'm Jake. Are you . . . Mike's friend?"

"I am Mike's neighbor." The correction seemed highly consequential. He gave Jake's outstretched hand an appraising look. Then, apparently concluding that it met his standard of hygiene, he shook it.

"Thank you for joining me."

"Thank you for inviting me. It isn't often a complete stranger decides to buy me dinner."

"Oh, that happens to me all the time."

The joke landed about as badly as it could have. Jake took a seat.

"What's good here?"

"Pretty much everything," said the coroner. He hadn't picked up his own menu. "The burgers. Country fried steak. The casseroles are always tasty."

He pointed at something beyond Jake's shoulder. Jake turned to find the specials board. Today's casserole was chicken, broccoli, and rice. He also saw Mike enter, nod at someone seated just inside the door, and make his way across the room.

"Mike," said the coroner.

"Hi, Mike."

"Hello, Roy," said Mike. "You two getting acquainted?"

No, thought Jake.

"Yes, indeed," said Roy.

"Mike really put himself out for me today."

"So I understand," Roy said. "Not sure why he troubled himself."

The waitress came. Jake ordered what Mike was having: poppy seed chicken, mashed greens, and fried okra. Roy ordered the trout.

"Do you fish?" Jake asked him.

"I've been known to."

Mike shook his head. "He's a maniac. This man has a magic touch."

Roy shrugged, but he was up against his own considerable pride. "Well, I don't know."

"I wish I had the patience for that."

"How do you know you don't?" Mike said.

"I don't know. Not my nature, I guess."

"What is your nature, would you say?"

"I'd say, to find things out."

"Is that a nature?" the coroner said. "Or a purpose?"

"They merge," said Jake, becoming annoyed. Was this guy only here for a free dinner? He looked as if he could afford his own damn trout. "I'm very curious about the woman who died up there at the campground. Mike might have told you, I knew her brother."

"Their brother," said Roy.

"I'm sorry?"

"They were sisters. Ergo, the brother of one would have been the brother of the other. Or am I missing something?"

Jake took a breath to steady himself. "You sound as if you might share some of my questions about what happened."

"Well, you're wrong," said Roy mildly. "I have no questions. And I don't see why you should have any, either. Mike here says you're a writer. Am I being interviewed for a publication of some kind?"

He shook his head. "No. Not at all."

"A newspaper story? Something that's going to wind up in a magazine?"

"Absolutely not."

The waitress was back. She set three plastic glasses of iced tea on the table, and left.

"So I don't have to worry about looking over the shoulder of the guy sitting next to me on the plane and seeing myself in a book."

Mike grinned. He'd probably have liked nothing better, himself.

"I'd say not."

Roy Porter nodded. He had deeply set eyes and wore a blue polo shirt, buttoned up the neck, and an oversized watch on a wide leather band. He also radiated a deeply discomforting power. All that death, Jake supposed. All those terrible things people did to one another.

The waitress returned with their food, and it looked and smelled so good that Jake nearly forgot what it was they were talking about. He hadn't known exactly what it was he was ordering. He still didn't know. But he fell on it.

"Were you out at the campsite yourself?"

Roy shrugged. Unlike Jake, who was shoveling that chicken into his mouth, the coroner was delaying gratification, delicately cutting his trout.

"I was. I got there at about six in the morning, not that there was much to see. The tent went up almost completely. There was a little bedding left, and a couple pots, and the heater. And the body, of course. But the body was completely charred. I took some pictures, and had the remains taken down to the morgue."

"And could you tell anything more once you got it there?"

Roy looked up. "What, in particular, do you think I was supposed to tell? I had a body that looked like a piece of charcoal. You ever hear that thing about hoofbeats in the park?"

It sounded vaguely familiar to Jake, but he said no.

"You hear hoofbeats in the park, do you think horses or zebras?"

"I don't get it," said Mike.

"You think horses," Jake said.

"Right. Because it's going to be far more likely there's wild horses in the park than wild zebras."

"I still don't get it," said Mike. "What park has wild horses running around in it?"

He had a good point.

"So you're saying, it was pretty obvious this woman burned to death."

"I'm saying no such thing. It was obvious she had burned, absolutely.

But burned to death? That's why you go to the scene, for one thing, to see if the person moved during the fire. People who are burning alive tend to move around. People who are already dead, or at least unconscious, usually don't. And even though coroners do think horses, we're trained to check for zebras. This body had a range of PMCT, appropriate to the circumstances."

"PMCT?"

"Post-mortem computed tomography. To look for fractures, metal objects."

"You mean . . . like a knee replacement?"

Roy, who had been about to take a bite of his trout, stopped and looked at Jake in disbelief.

"I mean, like, a bullet."

"Oh. So. No fractures, then."

"No fractures. No foreign objects." He paused. "No replaced knees."

Mike was grinning. He continued to tear through his chicken.

"No bullets either. Just a lady who had burned to death in her tent, from a fire almost certainly started by a propane heater, which I personally saw was lying on its side."

"Right," said Jake. "But . . . what about identification? Did the PMCT help with that?"

"Identification," said Roy.

"Well, yes."

The coroner set down his fork. "Do you believe this young woman was mistaken about who she'd been sharing a tent with?"

Not exactly, thought Jake.

"But don't you need to prove it?" he said.

"Are we on a television show?" said Roy Porter. "Am I Jack Klugman, solving crimes? I had a set of human remains and I had someone to make the identification. That is the standard at any morgue in the country. Should I have given her a DNA test?"

Which one of them? Jake thought blandly.

"I don't know," he said.

"Well, then, let me assure you that Miss Parker was given the same protocol as any other identifying witness. She was interviewed—eventually—and signed an affidavit attesting to the identification."

"Why eventually? Weren't you able to speak with her out at the campground? Or in the morgue?"

"She was hysterical at the campground. And yes, I realize the term is out of favor today. But by then, remember, she'd seen her sister burn to death, and she'd been running around the back roads for a couple of hours in the middle of the night, in a T-shirt, trying to find help. She wasn't doing any better by the time we reached the hospital. Bringing her down to the morgue was out of the question. She wasn't sick, so she wasn't admitted, but they didn't want to let her go, either. She knew no one locally, and she'd just lost her sister. Gruesomely. Also, she believed she'd caused the accident by knocking against the heater as she went out of the tent. One of my colleagues in the emergency room made the decision to sedate her."

"And you didn't ask for any identification?"

"No. Because I was aware that her personal papers were in the tent. I believe she'd just left to use the bathroom. I don't know what it's like where you're from, but we tend to leave our IDs at home when we go out to take a leak in the middle of the night."

"So when were you able to speak with her?"

"The next morning. The GSP trooper and I took her to the cafeteria and got some food into her, and she gave us the basic details about what happened, and her sister's name and age. Home address. Social security. She didn't want anyone contacted."

"No family members? Friends back home?"

He shook his head.

"Did she say why they were here? In Clayton?"

"They were just having a trip together. They'd never been out of wherever they were from, up north—"

"Vermont," said Jake.

"That's right. She told me they'd visited a few of the battlefields, and were making their way down to Atlanta. They were going to keep going till New Orleans."

"Nothing about going to college, then?"

For the first time, the coroner looked genuinely surprised. "College?"

"It's just, I'd heard they were on their way to Athens."

"Well, I couldn't say. Just a trip, as far as I was told, then back up north. Most people coming through Rabun Gap are on their way to Atlanta, maybe stopping to fish or camp. Nothing out of the ordinary for us."

"I understand she's buried here," said Jake. "Dianna Parker is. How did that happen?"

"We have some provisions," Roy said. "The indigent, people whose next of kin we can't locate. One of the nurses took me aside and asked if we couldn't do something for this young woman. She had no other family, and also she didn't look like she had the means to ship her sister's body anywhere. So we made the offer. It was the right thing to do. A Christian gesture."

"I see." Jake nodded, but he was still numb. Mike, he noticed, had cleaned his plate. The next time the waitress passed, he asked for pie. Jake himself had given up halfway through, or at about the time Roy had used the word "charcoal" to describe the body at the Foxfire Campground.

"I'll tell you the truth, I was a little surprised she said yes. People can be very proud. But she thought it over and she accepted. One of the local funeral parlors donated the coffin. And there was a plot over at the Pickett Cemetery they made available to us. It's a pretty place."

"My grammaw's there," said Mike, apropos of nothing.

"So we had a little service, a couple days later. We ordered a headstone, just the name and the dates."

Mike's pie arrived. Jake stared at it. His thoughts were racing. He couldn't let them out.

"You all right?"

He looked up. The coroner was looking at him, though more with curiosity than obvious concern. Jake put the back of his hand to his own forehead, and it came away wet. "Sure," he managed to say.

"You know," he said, "it wouldn't kill you to tell us what this is about. You knew the family? Not sure I believe that."

"It's actually true," said Jake, but it sounded lame, even to him.

"We're used to conspiracy theorists. Coroners are. People watch TV shows, or they read mystery novels. They think every death has a devious plot behind it, or an undetectable poison, or some crazy obscure method we've never seen before."

Jake smiled weakly. He'd never been one of those people, ironically enough.

"Have I had cases I wondered about, second-guessed myself about? Sure. Did a gun 'just go off'? Did somebody just happen to slip and fall on an icy step? Plenty of things I'll never know for sure, and they stay with me. But this wasn't one of them. Let me tell you something: this is exactly what it looks like when somebody burns to death in a tent because a heater falls over. This is exactly what it looks like when somebody loses a close relation, suddenly and traumatically. And now you're here asking some pretty provocative questions about people you never met. You've obviously got something on your mind. What is it you think happened, anyway?"

For a long moment, Jake said nothing. Then he took his phone from his jacket pocket and found the photograph. He held it out to them.

"Who's this?" said Mike.

The coroner was looking closely.

"Do you know?" Jake said.

"Am I supposed to? I never saw this girl."

Oddly, what Jake felt most about that was relief.

"This is Rose Parker. By which I mean, the real Rose Parker. Who, by the way, wasn't Dianna Parker's sister. She was her daughter. She was sixteen years old, and she actually was on her way to Athens to register as a freshman at the university. But she didn't make it. She's right here in Clayton, Georgia, in your donated coffin, buried in your donated plot under your donated headstone."

"That's fucking insane," said Mike.

Then, after a long and profoundly unpleasant moment, Roy Porter began, absurdly, to grin. He grinned and grinned and then he actually laughed.

"I know what this is," he said.

"What?" said Mike.

"You ought to be ashamed of yourself."

"I don't know what you mean," said Jake.

"That book! It's that book everybody was reading last year. My wife read it, she told me the story when she finished. The mother kills the daughter, right? And takes her place?"

"Oh, you know," said Mike, "I heard about that book. My mom read it in her book club."

"What was it called?" said Roy, still staring at Jake.

"I can't remember," Mike said, and Jake, who did remember, said nothing.

"That's what this is! That's the tale you're trying to spin here, isn't it?" The coroner had gotten to his feet. He wasn't a very tall man, but he was managing a sharp downward angle over Jake. He wasn't grinning now. "You read that crazy plot in the book and you thought you'd see if you could twist what happened here to make it like that. You outta your mind?"

"Shit" was Mike's contribution. He was getting to his feet as well. "What kind of pathetic—?"

"I'm not"—Jake had to force himself to say these words—"*spinning a tale.* I'm trying to find out what happened."

"What happened is exactly what I told you," Roy Porter said. "That poor woman died in an accidental fire, and I only hope her sister's been able to put it behind her and get on with her life. I have no idea who's in this picture on your phone, and for that matter I have no idea who you are, but I think what you're implying is sick. That's Dianna Parker in the plot out there at Pickett. Her sister left town a day or so after we buried her. If she's ever been back to visit the grave, I couldn't say."

Well, I wouldn't put money on it, thought Jake, watching the two of them go.

CHAPTER TWENTY-EIGHT

The End of the Line

Afterward, he ordered a slice of that pie Mike had eaten, and a cup of coffee, and he sat for a good long while, trying to think it through, but every time he felt it come nearly into his grasp it slipped away again. Truth being stranger than fiction was, itself, a truth universally acknowledged, but if *that* was true why did we always fight so hard against it?

A mother and daughter, viciously entwined—that was everyday life in more families than not.

A mother and daughter capable of committing violent acts upon each other—thankfully more rare, but hardly unheard of.

A daughter who would murder her mother and arrange to benefit from her death—that was the stuff of sensational true crime: yes, sensational, but yes, also true.

But a mother who would take the life of her own daughter, then take it again, to live it herself? That was legend. That was the plot of a novel that could sell millions of copies and form the basis of a film by what Evan Parker had once called an "A-list director." That was a plot someone's mother would read in a book group in Clayton, Georgia, that would sell out a Seattle venue with 2,400 seats, that would get its author on the *New York Times* bestseller list *and* the cover of *Poets & Writers*. It was a plot to kill for, Jake supposed, though he himself had done no such thing; he had merely picked it up off the ground. *A sure thing,* Evan Parker had once called his story, and it absolutely had been that. But he might also have called it: *the story of what my sister did to her daughter.* He might have called it: *the story somebody might come after me for telling, because it isn't mine to tell.* He might even have called it: *the story it wasn't worth dying for.*

Jake paid the bill and left the Clayton Café. He got back in his car and found his way out to the cemetery, driving past the Rabun County Historical Society and then left on Pickett Hill Street, a narrow and overgrown road into the woods. After about half a mile, he passed a sign for the cemetery and slowed his car to a crawl. It was the last hour of light, and he felt lost in the trees. He thought of the places this unasked-for and unwanted adventure had taken him, from the tavern in Rutland, to the downmarket apartment complex in Athens, to the emptiness of this clearing in the north Georgia woods. It felt like the end of the line, which it was. Where could there be, after this? One way or the other, it came down to this plot of earth and the obliterated body underground. The track ended when he saw the headstones.

There were many graves, a hundred at least, and the first ones he came to dated from the 1800s. Picketts, Rameys, Shooks, and Wellborns, elderly men who'd fought in the world wars, children who'd lived for months or years, mothers and newborns buried together. He wondered if he'd already walked past Mike's grammaw, or the graves of other recipients of Clayton's generosity to the indigent and abandoned. The light was going fast now, leaving a deep blue above, and orange through the forest to the west. It was a peaceful place to spend eternity, that was clear.

He found it, finally, at the far edge of the clearing. The plot was marked by a simple stone, flat on the dirt and slightly reddish in color, with the name of the assigned occupant: DIANNA PARKER, 1980–2012.

Simple, remarkably understated, and yet the horror it held rooted him to the spot. "Who are you?" he said out loud, but that was purely rhetorical. Because he knew. He'd known the moment he saw those old pineapples stenciled around the door of the Parker home in West Rutland, and everyone he'd spoken with in Georgia—the outraged attorney and the cleaner who hadn't recognized Rose Parker from her high school field hockey photo, the defensive coroner who heard hoofbeats and thought horses—only underscored that knowledge. He wanted to fall to the earth and claw away at it until he reached her, that poor girl, the tool and inconvenience of her mother's life, but even if he made it through that impacted Georgia soil, all the way to her donated coffin and beyond, what would he find but handfuls of dust?

In the last of the light he took a photograph of the grave and sent it to his wife, with only the corrected name of the occupant attached. More would have to wait until he got home, for a face-to-face conversation. Then he would explain what had really happened here, how a young person on the verge of escape had wound up in a burial plot in backwoods Georgia with her mother's name on the headstone. Looking down into the dirt, as if he could possibly see the murdered girl's obliterated and entombed remains, it occurred to him that this strangest of stories warranted a full retelling, and this time no longer as fiction. In fact, maybe writing Rose Parker's real story was where this had always been heading, an unprecedented opportunity to write his book, his miraculous *Crib,* a second time, illuminating the real story even its author hadn't known existed. Matilda, when she pushed past the discomfort of it, would be intrigued, then excited. Wendy would be thrilled from the get-go: a deconstruction of the global bestseller by its own author? A phenomenon!

And even if writing it required Jake to come clean about his late student Evan Parker, he'd still be able to control the narrative as he soul-searched and pondered the deep questions about what fiction was and how it got made, on behalf of every one of his fellow novelists and short story writers! *Crib*'s second telling would be a meta-narrative, destined to vindicate every writer and resonate with every reader, and telling it would render him brave and bold as an artist. Besides, what was the point of being a famous writer if he couldn't use *his unique voice* to tell this story *only he could tell*?

In the cemetery, the last of the light died around him.

Look on my Works, ye Mighty, and despair!

Nothing beside remained.

CRIB

BY JACOB FINCH BONNER

Macmillan, New York, 2017, page 280

She'd been renting a small house on East Whittier Street in German Village, about five miles from campus, a quiet neighborhood with not too many OSU students. She still did her bill processing for Bassett Healthcare but mainly at night, keeping the days free for classes: history, philosophy, political science. It was all pleasure, even the term papers, even the exams, even the fact that she was obligated to lose herself among the 60,000 enrolled students on the Columbus campus and never become too familiar to her teachers; the deep thrill of having resurrected and met her once and forever goal, her so long buried goal, carried her through every day of her new life. Where would she be by now without that eighteen-year pause? Working as a lawyer, possibly, or a professor of some kind? A scientist or a doctor? Maybe even a writer! It didn't bear thinking about, she supposed. She was somewhere now that she had given up all hope of being.

One afternoon at the end of May she arrived home to discover that most unwelcome mouse, Gab, waiting for her on the doorstep with a sad little backpack.

"Let's go inside," Samantha said, hustling her into the sitting room. As soon as the door closed, she demanded: "What are you doing here?"

"I got Maria's address at the campus registrar," said the girl. She was small, but covered in an extra layer of flesh. "I didn't realize you were out here, too."

"I moved a few months ago," Samantha said tersely. "I sold our house."

"Yeah." She nodded. Her lank hair fell against her cheeks. "I heard that."

"I told you, she has another girlfriend now."

"No, I know. Only I'm driving to the West Coast. I want to try and live out there. I'm not sure where, yet. Probably San Francisco, but maybe LA. And I thought, I was passing by Columbus, so . . ."

She did a lot of passing by, this girl.

"So?"

"I just thought, it would be really nice to see Maria. Get some, you know . . ."

Closure? Samantha thought. She had a particular distaste for the word.

"Closure."

"Oh. Of course. Well, she's up at campus now. But she ought to be home in an hour or so. I'll pick up a pizza for the three of us. Why don't you come with me?"

So Gab did, which was just as well. Samantha certainly didn't want her poking around the house with its single bedroom, wondering where Maria slept at night. She asked Gab polite questions as they drove to Luigi's, where Samantha often ordered pizza, and learned that she—like Samantha herself—had no intention of ever returning to their hometown or maintaining ties to any living person there. Everything Gab owned, in fact, was in the Hyundai Accent she was bravely driving west, and once this last little bit of *closure* was achieved, she intended to head off, literally, into the sunset. That is, Samantha supposed, unless she made some unfortunate discovery here in Columbus that warranted a return to Earlville, New York. But really, it was all unfortunate discovery at this point. Wasn't it? "I'll just be a minute," she said as she went inside to pick up the pie.

Later, as Gab set the table for three in the small dining room, Samantha crushed a handful of peanuts between a metal spatula and the countertop, and pressed them under the oily discs of pepperoni.

Pepperoni, of course.

Because she remembered that.

Because she *had* been a good mother, and even if she hadn't, there was no one left to disagree about that now.

CHAPTER TWENTY-NINE

Such a Waste of Energy

When he arrived home, Anna wasn't there, but a pot of her green soup was on the stove and a bottle of Merlot open on the table. The sight of the two Pottery Barn place settings cheered him far more than the plain fact of them—or even the soup, or even the wine—might have warranted, but then again: he was home. That, on its own, would have been enough. But also, it had been so worth it, to know for sure.

He went into the bedroom and unpacked his bag extracting the bottle of Stillhouse Creek bourbon he'd picked up on the drive back to the Atlanta airport. Then he opened his laptop and saw, to his disbelief, that another message had been forwarded from the contact form on his website. He stared at it, and then he took a deep breath and clicked to open it.

> Here's the statement I'm getting ready to release in a day or two. Any corrections before it goes out?
>
> "In 2013, while 'teaching' at Ripley College, Jacob 'Finch' Bonner encountered a student named Evan Parker who shared with him a novel

> he was writing. Parker died unexpectedly later that year, after which Bonner produced the novel called *Crib* with no acknowledgment of its true author. We call on Macmillan Publishers to confirm its commitment to original writing by authors of integrity, and to retract this fraudulent work."

A jab at the artifice of his middle name—annoying, but it wasn't exactly a secret: Jake had told innumerable interviewers about his love for Atticus Finch and *To Kill a Mockingbird.* An indictment of his worth as a teacher—that was new, and more than mildly annoying. But the headlines here were the imminent intention to publish, and the insinuation that he had stolen every word of *Crib,* rather than its plot alone, from its unfortunate "true" author. And was it Jake's undeniable paranoia, or was there also a suggestion that he was somehow responsible for *the unexpected death* of that true author, his former student?

All things considered, he ought to be terrified by this latest missive, but even as Jake sat on the edge of his own bed and let the awfulness of the message pass over him, he wasn't afraid. That "we," for one thing, radiated weakness, like the invented comrades of the Unabomber or any other demented loner on a noble quest from his basement. More to the point, Jake now understood that his correspondent wanted to avoid exposure every bit as much as he did himself. The time had come for him to hit that Return button on their so far one-way conversation, and reveal that he knew who she was and was prepared to make her story known. And not his previous, unwitting version of that story, this time, but the actual, factual account of what she had done to her own daughter, and the fraudulent identity she was presenting to the world. And didn't that make for a pretty compelling story of its own? Like, cover of *People* magazine compelling? In fact, Jake sat for a distinctly enjoyable moment, mentally composing his very first—and with luck, his last—email to her:

Here's the statement *I'll* be releasing if you don't get out of my life and keep your mouth shut. Any corrections before it goes out?

"In 2012 a young woman named Rose Parker died violently at the hands of her own mother, who then stole her identity, appropriated her scholarship at the University of Georgia, and has been living as her daughter ever since. She is currently harassing a well-known author, but she really ought to be famous in her own right."

He could smell the soup, and all of those health-giving greens in it. The cat, Whidbey, leapt up onto his lap and looked optimistically at the tabletop, but there was nothing there for him, so he absconded to the kilim-covered couch Anna had chosen, part of her campaign to make his life better. She hadn't wanted him to go to Georgia, obviously, but when he told her everything he'd discovered she would understand why it had been the right decision, and she'd help him make the best possible use of the information he'd brought back.

He heard the door. She was home with a loaf of bread and an apology not to have been here on his return, and when he hugged her she hugged him back, and the relief he hadn't realized he was so in need of came sweeping through him.

"Look what I brought," he said, handing her the bourbon.

"Nice. I'd better not have any myself, though. You know I need to head to LaGuardia in a couple of hours."

He looked at her. "I thought it was tomorrow."

"Nope. Red-eye."

"How long will you be gone?"

She wasn't sure, but she wanted to keep it as brief as possible. "That's why I'm flying at night. I'll sleep on the plane and go right to the storage unit from the airport. I think I can get it all sorted out inside of three days, and the work stuff, too. If I have to stay another day, I will."

"I hope you won't," Jake said. "I've missed you."

"You missed me because you knew I was pissed at you for going."

He frowned. "Maybe. But I'd have missed you anyway."

She went to get the soup and brought back a single bowl.

"Aren't you having any?" Jake said.

"In a bit. I want to hear about what happened."

She put the bread she'd just gone out to buy on a cutting board, and poured wine for both of them, and he began to tell her everything he'd learned since leaving Athens: the drive north into the mountains, the chance meeting at the general store, the campsite far enough back in the woods that you could barely hear the creek. When he held out the photograph he'd taken on his phone, she stared at it.

"It doesn't look like a place where somebody burned to death."

"Well, it's been seven years."

"You said, the man who took you out there, he'd been at the scene that morning?"

"Yeah. Volunteer fireman."

"That's quite the lucky coincidence."

He shrugged. "I don't know. Small town. Something like that would involve a lot of people—EMTs, cops, firemen. People at the hospital. The coroner turned out to be this guy's neighbor."

"And the two of them just sat down with a total stranger and told you everything? It seems kind of wrong, doesn't it?"

"Does it? I guess I ought to be grateful. At the very least they kept me from poking around all the cemeteries in Rabun Gap with a flashlight."

"What does that mean?" said Anna. She refilled Jake's wineglass.

"Well, they told me where the plot was."

"The plot you sent me the photo of?"

He nodded.

"Look, I'm going to have to ask you to be more specific. I want to be exactly sure I understand everything you're saying here."

"I'm saying," said Jake, "that Rose Parker is buried in a place called Pickett Hill, just outside of Clayton, Georgia. The headstone says Dianna Parker, but it's Rose."

Anna seemed to require time to think this through. When that had been accomplished, she asked how he was enjoying the soup.

"It's delicious."

"Good. It's the other half of that batch we had before," she said. "When you got back from Vermont. The night you told me about Evan Parker."

"Soup for the raveled sleeve of care," he recalled.

"That's right." She smiled.

"I wish I hadn't waited so long to tell you about this," Jake said, bringing the heavy spoon to his lips.

"Never mind," she said. "Drink up."

He did.

"So, just because we're talking this through, what is it you think happened here, exactly?"

"What happened is that Dianna Parker, like hundreds of thousands of other parents, was delivering her kid to college in August of 2012. And maybe, like probably most of them, she had mixed feelings about that kid's departure. Rose was smart, obviously. She rammed her way through high school and into college in only three years, didn't she?"

"Did she?"

"With a scholarship, apparently."

"Genius girl," said Anna. But she didn't sound that impressed.

"Must have been pretty desperate to escape her mother."

"Her terrible mother." She rolled her eyes.

"Right," Jake said. "And probably she was very ambitious, just like her mother might have been, once, but Dianna never made it out of West Rutland. There was the pregnancy, the punitive parents, the uninvolved brother."

"Don't forget the dude who got her pregnant and then was like: leave me out of it."

"Sure. So there she is, driving her daughter farther away than either of them have ever been, from the only place they've ever lived, and she knows her daughter's never coming home. Sixteen years of putting her own life aside and taking care of this person, and now boom: it's over and she's gone."

"Without a thank-you, even."

"Okay." Jake nodded. "And maybe she's thinking: *Why wasn't this me? Why didn't I get to have this life?* So when the accident happens—"

"Define *accident*."

"Well, she told the coroner she might have knocked over a propane heater while she was leaving the tent in the middle of the night. By the time she got back from the bathroom the whole tent had gone up."

Anna nodded. "Okay. That would be an accident."

"The coroner also said she was hysterical. His word."

"Right. And hysteria can't be faked."

He frowned.

"Go on."

"So after the accident happens, she thinks: *This is terrible, but I can't bring her back*. And there's a scholarship waiting and nothing to go back to. And she thinks, *No one knows me in Georgia. I'll live off campus, take classes, figure out what I want to do with my life.* She knows she doesn't look young enough to say she's the daughter of a thirty-two-year-old woman, so maybe she says she's the victim's sister, not her daughter. But from the moment she drives out of Clayton, Georgia, she's Rose Parker, whose mother died in a tragic fire." *Burned up.*

"The way you put it, it sounds almost reasonable."

"Well, it's horrible, but it's not *un*reasonable. It's criminal, obviously, because at the very least we're talking about theft. Theft of identity. Theft of her daughter's place at a university. Theft of an actual monetary scholarship. But it's also an unanticipated opportunity for a woman who's never managed to live her own dreams, and by the way who's still young. Thirty-two is much younger than we are. Doesn't it still seem possible to make an enormous change in your life when you're thirty-two? Look at yourself! You were older than that, and you left everyone you knew and moved to the other end of the country and got married, all inside of . . . what, eight months?"

"Fine," Anna agreed. She was filling Jake's glass with the last of the Merlot. "But I have to point out that you seem to be making every excuse for her. Are you really this understanding?"

"Well, in the novel—" he began, but she interrupted him.

"Whose?" Anna said quietly. "Yours? Or Evan's?"

He was trying to remember if Evan's Ripley submission had covered this. Of course it hadn't. Evan Parker had been an amateur. How far beneath the surface could he really have gone into the inner lives of these women? Unfurling his extraordinary plot that night in Richard Peng Hall, Parker hadn't troubled himself to describe or acknowledge the complexities of Diandra (as he'd called the mother) or Ruby (as he'd called the daughter); how much better would he have done over the course of an entire novel, even assuming he'd been capable of completing one?

"In my novel. Samantha is a thwarted person, and bitterly unhappy. Those things can corrupt you every bit as much as some predisposition toward evil. I always thought of her as a person who's fallen into a hole of terrible disappointment, which over time—and as she watched her daughter prepare for her own departure—just *worked* on her, with devastating results. And then when it happened it *was* a kind of accident, or at least not something planned or prepared for. It's not like she was a—"

"Sociopath?" Anna said.

He felt genuine surprise. Of course he understood that this was the predominant view amongst his readers, but Anna had never said as much about the character.

"And that's where the dividing line is?" his wife asked. "Between something any of us might do under the circumstances and something only a truly evil person would do? Planning it?"

He shrugged. His shoulders felt impossibly heavy as he lifted them and let them fall. "It seems like a good enough place to put the dividing line."

"Okay. But only as far as your made-up character is concerned. It has no bearing on this actual woman's life. You can't have any idea what was going on in her head, or what else she might have done, before or after this *unplanned* act. I mean, who knows what else this Dianna Parker got up to? You said yourself, nobody seems to get sick in her family."

"That's true." He nodded, and his head felt fuzzy as it inclined forward. He had written an entire novel around this one terrible thing, and he still couldn't fully accept there was a real mother out there who'd been able to do it. See her child die like that and just move on? "I mean," he heard himself say, "it's incredible. Isn't it?"

Anna sighed. "There are more things in heaven and earth than are dreamt of in your philosophy, Jake. Do you want more soup?"

He did, and she went to get it, bringing him back another brimming, steaming bowl.

"It's so good."

"I know. My mother's recipe."

Jake frowned. There was something he wanted to ask about that, but he couldn't think what it was. Spinach, kale, garlic, essence of chicken; it was certainly tasty, and he could feel the warmth of it spreading inside him.

"This *plot* you sent me a picture of, it looked like a pretty place. Can I see it again?"

He reached for his phone and tried to find it for her, but that wasn't as easy as it should have been. The pictures kept shooting forward and back as he scrolled, refusing to land on the right one. "Here," he finally said.

She held the phone in her hand, and looked intently.

"The stone. It's very simple. I like it."

"Okay," said Jake.

She had picked up the single gray braid of her hair, and was twisting the end around and around her fingers in a way that was almost hypnotic. He loved so many things about the way she looked, but that silver hair, it occurred to him, he loved most of all. Thinking of it swinging loose made a kind of weighty thump inside his head. He had been traveling for days, and worried for months. Now, with so many of the pieces finally in place, he was deeply tired, and all he wanted was to crawl into bed and sleep. Maybe it wasn't a bad thing that she was leaving tonight. Maybe he needed some time to recover. Maybe they each needed a couple of days to themselves.

"So after the accident," said Anna, "our bereaved mom keeps heading south. Lemonade out of lemons, right?"

Jake nodded his heavy head.

"And when she gets to Athens she registers in Rose's name, and gets permission to live off campus for her freshman year. And that gets us up to the end of the 2012 to 2013 academic year. What happens after that?"

Jake sighed. "Well, I know she left the university. After that, I'm not sure where she went or where she's been, but it doesn't really matter. She can't want to be exposed for her real crime any more than I do for my imaginary one. So tomorrow I'll send her an email and tell her to fuck off. And I'll cc that asshole attorney to make sure she gets the message."

"But don't you want to know where she is now? And what her name is? Because obviously, she'll have changed her name. You don't even know what she looks like. Right?"

She had taken his bowl to the sink and she was washing it. She washed his spoon and the pot she'd used to heat the soup up. Then she put all of those things in the dishwasher, and started it. She came back to the table and stood over him. "Maybe we should get you lying down," she said. "You really do look beat."

He could not deny it, and he wasn't up to trying.

"It's good you got that soup into you, though. One of the only things my mother gave me, that soup."

Then he remembered what he wanted to ask her.

"You mean, Miss Royce. The teacher?"

"No, no. My real mom."

"But, she died. She drove into a lake when you were so young. Didn't she drive into a lake?"

Suddenly, Anna was laughing. Her laugh was musical: light and sweet. She laughed as if all of that—the soup, the teacher, the mom who'd driven her car into a lake in Idaho—was some of the funniest stuff she had ever heard. "You are so pathetic. What self-respecting writer doesn't know the plot of *Housekeeping*? Fingerbone, Idaho! The aunt who can't take care of herself or her nieces! I didn't even change the teacher's name, for fuck's sake! And don't think that wasn't a risk. Tempting fate to prove a point, I guess."

He wanted to ask what it was, that point, but getting his throat to breathe and talk at the same time had suddenly attained the complexity of juggling with knives, and besides, he already knew. How hard was it, really, to steal someone else's story? Anybody could do it—you didn't even have to be a *writer*.

Still, there was something about this he just couldn't work out. In fact, there were only a few things he seemed capable of understanding at all, and whatever powers of concentration he still possessed had gone to those things, like blood to the vital organs when you're stranded in a snowbank, dying of frostbite. First: that Anna was leaving for the airport soon. Second: that Anna seemed to know something he didn't. Third: that Anna was still angry at him. He didn't have the strength to ask about all three. So he asked about the last one, because he had already forgotten the first two.

"You're still angry at me, aren't you?" he said, speaking the words extremely carefully so as not to be misunderstood. And she nodded.

"Well, Jake," she said, "I'd have to say that's true. I've been angry at you for a very long time."

CHAPTER THIRTY

That Novelist's Eye for Detail

"I wasn't going to do this yet," said Anna. She had the crook of her elbow under his arm and she was lifting him, or helping him up, one of the two. He must, at some point, have become terribly light, or else the floor of the apartment had helpfully tipped to a forty-five-degree angle. She held him tightly as they passed the kilim-covered couch, and it slid up one of the walls as they went by, but magically, without actually moving. "There was no rush. And then you had to start running around like Lord Peter Wimsey. It's something I don't really get about you, this compulsion to understand everything. And all the sturm und drang! If you were going to be this troubled about what you'd done, why steal someone else's story in the first place? I mean, torturing yourself about it after the fact. Such a waste of energy, especially when I'm right here, and I'm so good at it. Don't you think so?"

He started to shake his head *no*, because he hadn't stolen, but then he understood that she was good at it, so he nodded. She probably didn't notice either one. She was helping him along the slow walk into their bedroom and he was shuffling beside her, his arm over her shoulder, her hand gripping his wrist. Jake's head was down, but he could see the cat, darting past them into the living room.

"I have some medicine for you," Anna said, "and then, I don't see any reason not to tell you my story. Because if there's one thing I know about you, Jake, it's how you appreciate a good story. My *singular story*, told in my *unique voice*. Do you see any reason?"

He didn't. Then again he didn't understand the question. He sat on the bed and she gave him the capsules, three or four at a time, and he really didn't want to but he swallowed them all, until there weren't any more. "Good job," she said, after each handful. He drank the water from the glass. That went onto the bedside table, next to the empty pill bottles. He did want to know what they were, the pills, but did it really matter?

"Well, we've got a few minutes," said Anna. "Was there anything you wanted to ask, in particular?"

There was something, thought Jake. But now he couldn't remember.

"Okay. I'll just, sort of, free-associate. You stop me if you've heard any of this already."

Yes, said Jake, though he couldn't actually hear himself say it.

"What?" said Anna. She looked up from her phone. His phone, actually. "You're mumbling," she said. Then she went on with whatever it was she was doing.

"I don't want to be that person who's always whining about her childhood, but you need to know it was always about Evan in our house. Evan and football. Evan and soccer. Evan and girls. The guy was an imbecile, but you know how it is with families. The pride of the Parkers! Scoring goals and passing his classes—*wow!* Even when he started doing drugs they thought the sun just shined out of his ass. As for me, it didn't matter how smart I was or how good my grades were or what I wanted to do in the world, I was still nothing. So there's Evan getting girls pregnant right and left and he's an angel from heaven, but when I got pregnant it was like their job to punish me, and make sure it stuck for the rest of my life. It was all: *you're dropping out of high school and keeping this baby because that's what you deserve*. Zero chance of an abortion. Zero support for giving the baby up for adoption, either. You were spot-on with all that, actually, the way you wrote it. That's absolutely what it was like for me. Which isn't a compliment, by the way."

He didn't take it as one.

"So then I have this baby I don't want and they don't want and I'm out of school, sitting at home with her all day getting yelled at by my mom and dad about the shame I've brought on the family, and one morning when they're out of the house I hear this beeping down in the cellar. The carbon monoxide alarm's going crazy, and I didn't know what that meant, but I did a little research. I just took the batteries out, and replaced them with a couple of dead ones. I didn't know if it was going to work, or how long it would take if it did, or which of us were going to go, and I did keep the window open in my room, where the baby was, too, but to be honest, I think I was okay with whatever happened."

She stopped and leaned over him. She was checking his breathing.

"You want me to go on?"

But it didn't matter what he wanted, did it?

"I tried my best. It wasn't fun, but you know, I thought, it's just the two of us here. There was no one to count on, but also no one for me to blame if it went downhill. I kind of lost my drive after the rest of my class graduated, I'll admit to that. And I got to thinking, maybe this is the way it's supposed to go, giving up my own life for this other life. I thought I could make my peace with that, and besides, I wasn't against having that thing you're supposed to have with a kid. Companionship or whatever. But that girl."

There was a ping on the phone. His phone. She picked it up.

"Oh look," said Anna. "Matilda says your publisher in France has offered half a million for the new novel. I'll get back to her in a couple of days, though I don't think your French publisher will be at the top of our list by then." She paused. "What was I saying?"

The cat had returned and leapt up onto the bed. He took one of his favorite positions, alongside Jake's right calf.

"Not once, in sixteen years, was there one sign of affection. She pushed me away, I swear, when I was trying to nurse her. She preferred not eating to being close to me, physically. She toilet trained herself so I wouldn't have that power over her. I knew she didn't plan to hang around Rutland a day longer than she had to, but I thought she'd at least do things in the normal way—graduate from high school, maybe go as far as Burlington. Not Rose. She just came downstairs one day when she was sixteen and told me she was leaving at the end of the summer. Bang. I couldn't even tell her there was no money for an out-of-state college a thousand miles away. She had a scholarship, she had a room in a dorm, she even had a stipend for living expenses from some do-gooder down there. I said I at least wanted to take her, and I could tell she didn't even want that, but when she thought about it practically she understood what it meant for her own convenience. She knew she was never coming home, so she let me drive her, and I let her pretty much fill up the car, everything she wanted, only a little room left over for my own things. But you know what? There wasn't much I wanted to take for myself. Just a few clothes and an old propane heater."

With all of his strength he turned his head to her.

"It wasn't an accident, Jake. Even with your supposedly great imagination you couldn't get your mind around that. Maybe you've got some gender blindness about motherhood, like it's impossible for a mother to do that. Fathers, sure, no one bats an eye if they kill one of their kids, but do the same thing while in possession of a uterus and *bam*: the world explodes. It's sexism, really, isn't it, if you think about it. Evan didn't have that problem, in case you're wondering. In his version I take a carving knife to my teenage daughter in the middle of the night, and bury her in the backyard. But then he actually knew me. And he knew my daughter, don't forget that. He knew what a bitch she was."

It reminded Jake of something, that word. But he couldn't think what.

Anna sighed. She still had Jake's phone. She was scrolling through photographs, deleting. Very far away, he could feel the cat, Whidbey, begin to purr against his leg.

"I let those yokels bury her," Anna said. "People always want to involve themselves when they see a tragedy. I'd been happy to take care of it myself. Have the body cremated—I mean, it was halfway there already. And sprinkle the ashes, whatever. I'm not sentimental about these things. But they offered, and all expenses paid. So I said, *I can't get over how incredibly kind you people are,* and *You've restored my faith in humanity* and *Let us pray*. And then I left for Athens."

Anna smiled down at him. "What did you really think of Athens? Can you see me living there? I mean, I was lying low, of course. I didn't get involved in any of the social stuff. It was all frats and football, and all that big hair and the good old boys, everybody living in those tacky apartment communities. I got the housing waiver by telling them my mother had just passed away, and I really wanted to be alone. I didn't even have to go into the housing office, which was lucky. I've always looked younger than my age, but I was pretty sure I couldn't pass for sixteen. Especially after this happened to my hair." She stopped to smile at him. "I did tell you it happened when my mom died, so that was kind of true. Anyway, I dyed it blond while I was in Georgia." She grinned. "Helped me to blend in. Just another bottle-blond Bulldawg."

He used every bit of his strength to turn away from her and onto his side, but he couldn't quite get there. His head, though, had moved on the pillow, giving him a blurry view of the half-empty glass and the completely empty bottles.

"Vicodin," she said helpfully. "And something called gabapentin, which I got for my restless leg syndrome. It makes the opioids work better. Did you know I have restless leg syndrome? Well, I don't really have it, I just said I did. There's no actual test for that, so all you need to do is go to your doctor and say, 'Doctor! I have a strong, irresistible urge to move my legs. Especially at night! Accompanied by uncomfortable sensations!' Then they rule out iron deficiency and neurological stuff, and voilà: you're diagnosed. I made the appointment last fall in case they wanted me to do a sleep study before giving me the prescription, but this doctor went straight to the drugs, so good for her. She also gave me some Oxycontin for the terrible pain, and she threw in the Valium when I told her there was this crazy troll accusing my boyfriend of plagiarism online, and we were both stressed out beyond belief. That was Valium in the soup, by the way." He heard her laugh. "Which definitely was not in my mother's version. I also gave you something for nausea, to make sure you don't throw up all my hard work when I'm halfway to Seattle. Anyway, it's all pretty foolproof in combination, so I'd relax if I were you." Anna sighed. "Look, I can stay a bit longer. See you through the worst of it, if you want. Do you want? Squeeze my hand if you want."

And Jake, who couldn't have said what he wanted, and had already forgotten what he was supposed to do about it, felt her squeeze his hand, and he squeezed back.

"Right," she said. "What else? Oh . . . Athens. I was loving being back in school. Education really is wasted on the young, isn't it? When I was in high school I used to look at people in my class, and my brother and his friends, and think, *This is fantastic! We get to sit here all day and learn stuff. Why are you all such assholes about it?* My brother was the biggest asshole of them all, by the way. Not once in my entire life did he ask me a question about myself, or say a single loving thing to me, and I had zero problem with never laying eyes on him again till he started trying to get in touch with me. By which I mean, in touch with Rose. And that wasn't because he was suddenly interested in her, either. It was because he wanted to sell the house. Maybe because the bar was tanking. Maybe because he was back on the drugs, I didn't know, but I guess he figured he couldn't leave my daughter out of it and not expect a lawsuit. I didn't answer any of his calls or emails, so one day that winter he just came down to Georgia. I saw him waiting in a car in front of Athena Gardens. Unfortunately, he saw me first."

Anna checked the time again.

"Anyway, I gave him the benefit of the doubt. I thought, *Okay. He's seen me. He can obviously recognize his own sister, so even a moron like my brother is going to figure out what happened here.* I hoped we were just going to leave each other alone, the same way we'd always done. And I mean, I knew he'd moved back into the house himself, so a little appreciation wouldn't have gone amiss, but of course that was never my brother's way. And one day I saw on Facebook that he'd signed up for some writing program in the Northeast Kingdom. And maybe you're thinking, *Okay, but why assume he was going to write about this one thing?* All I can say is: I knew my brother. He wasn't what you might call an imaginative guy. He was a magpie. He saw a pretty, shiny thing on the ground and he thought, *Now that's got to have some value.* So he helped himself. I'm sure you can understand, Jake, what that must have been like, having someone steal from you like that. So a couple of months later I drove back to Vermont and I waited till he left for work, and you can color me surprised because that asshole actually managed to write almost two hundred pages. *Of my story.* And don't think he was doing it for himself, either. This wasn't some inner exploration through creative writing, trying to *find his voice* or understand the pain at the center of his family of origin. I found publication contests, lists of agents, the dude even had a subscription to *Publishers Weekly*. He knew what he was doing. He had a plan to make some serious money. Off me. People today bitch if you use a culturally appropriated word or hairstyle? That bastard just helped himself to my entire life story. Now you know that isn't right, Jake, don't you? Isn't that what they say in the writing programs? *Nobody else can tell your story but you*?"

The not so distant cousin of *Nobody else gets to live your life,* he thought.

"Anyway, I went through the house and I got together everything I didn't want left behind. All the manuscript pages for his *masterpiece,* and the notes. Any pictures of me or Rose that were still lurking around. Oh, and I got my mom's cookbook with all her recipes, including the one for that soup you like. It's been out there in our kitchen for months, on the shelf over the sink, not that you ever noticed. Where's that novelist's eye for detail, Jake? You're supposed to have one, you know."

He knew.

"And I found his drugs, of course. He had a lot of drugs. So I waited for him to get home from the tavern, and when he did I said I thought it was time for us to have a civilized talk about selling the house. He needed a shitload of benzos, by the way, before I could get near him with that syringe, but that's what happens when you abuse opiates for as long as he did. I had no sympathy for him. I still don't. And the way he went, it was even more pleasant than this. And this *is* pleasant, I think. It's supposed to be.

It wasn't, but it wasn't painful, either. He felt as if he was reaching out to claw through something that had the consistency of cotton candy, but he still couldn't get to the other side of it. He might not be in pain, exactly, but there was an idea that kept hammering at him, like when you know you're supposed to be somewhere else but you have no idea where that place is or why you were going there, and also he kept thinking the same ricocheting thought, which was: *Wait, aren't you Anna?* Only that made no sense, because obviously she was, and what he didn't understand was why he'd never questioned it before, and also why he was questioning it now.

"After that I decided to leave Athens. I'm so not cut out for the south. I stayed down there long enough to pack up and find an attorney to handle the sale of the Vermont house. What did you think of Pickens, by the way? Bit of a douchebag, isn't he? He got handsy with me once and I had to threaten to contact the bar association. As you might know, he was already on thin ice with them because of assorted other transgressions, so he became very proper and attentive after that. I did call him last week to warn him a guy named Bonner might turn up, and remind him about the sacred bonds of attorney-client privilege, but I don't think he'd have talked to you, even if I hadn't. He definitely doesn't want to get on my bad side."

No, thought Jake. Jake, also, didn't want to get on her bad side. He knew that now.

"Anyway, I wanted to go west to finish my degree, but I wasn't sure where. I was thinking about San Francisco, but at the end of the day I picked Washington. Oh, and I changed my name, obviously. Anna sounds a bit like Dianna, and Williams is the third most common surname in America, did you know that? I guess I thought Smith and Johnson felt too obvious. Also I stopped coloring my hair. Seattle is full of gray-haired women, lots of them even younger than I was, so I felt super comfortable. I never lived on Whidbey, though I had a couple of fun weekends there with Randy. We did have a bit of a thing while I was interning at the station, which I'm pretty sure worked in my favor when the producer job opened up. Hey," she said. "Why don't you stop staring at those pills? You can't do anything about it, you know."

She tugged on his shoulder until he was on his back again, his eyes sometimes open, sometimes not. It was also getting harder to hear her.

"So everything's cool. I've got a house and a job and an avocado plant, and then, one afternoon, in one of Seattle's fine coffee establishments, I hear these women talking about a book they're reading, this crazy story about a mom who kills her daughter and takes her place. And I can't fucking believe it! I'm sitting there thinking, *No goddamn way!* I wasn't thinking it was connected to me, because there wasn't anyone left who could possibly have known, and besides, I took everything out of that house, and I destroyed it all after I read it. I left flash drives and pages in every trash bin on the Eisenhower interstate system. I threw his computer down a porta potty in Missouri! Like, it had to be some insane coincidence or else my fucking brother wrote his book in hell and emailed it to the publishing firm of Lucifer and Beelzebub, *lies and stolen stories our specialty*!" She actually smiled. "I went over to Elliott Bay and I asked for a book I'd heard about, about a woman who kills her daughter. And there it was. And when I looked you up and saw you'd taught at Ripley in the MFA program it was pretty obvious what happened. I mean, a plot like that doesn't come out of nowhere, does it? Well, does it?"

Jake did not respond.

"Your book had its very own table, you'll be happy to hear, right in the front of the store. Placement is so important to an author, I know. And *Crib* was number eight on the list that week, the guy at Elliott Bay told me. I didn't know what 'the list' was. Not then. I do now. I couldn't believe I had to spend my own money to read my own story. *My story,* Jake. Which wasn't my brother's to tell, and it sure as hell wasn't yours. Before I even left that store I knew I was going to get it back from you, even if it took a while to figure out how. You'd already come through Seattle, on your book tour, and that was annoying, because it meant I had to wait for you to come back, but I started working on Randy as soon as they announced the City Arts lecture. That was *my* plot, I guess you could call it," she said with extravagant sarcasm. "And I have to say, I'm pretty impressed with myself, though can you explain to me why should I have to actually marry someone who stole from me, just to get back what was already mine? *There's* a subject for a novel, isn't it? Not that I could write a *novel,* Jake. Because it's not like I'm a *writer*. Not like *you*."

He looked vaguely up at her. Already he was having trouble understanding how any of this related to him.

"Hey, wow," she said. "Your pupils. They're like little points. And you're very clammy. How are you feeling, would you say? Because what we're looking for here is depressed respiration—that's fancy medical speak for slow breathing—drowsiness, weak pulse. And something they like to call 'change in mental status,' but I'm not really clear about what that means. Besides, how am I going to get you to describe your mental status now?"

His mental status was that he wanted it all to stop. But at the same time, he was feeling that he would still scream if only he could figure out how.

"I hate to cut this short," said Anna, "but I'm going to be stressed about traffic if I stay much longer, so I'm going to head out. I just want to set your mind at ease about a couple of things before I go. First, I've left out a lot of food for the cat, and plenty of water, so don't worry about him. Second, I don't want you worrying out about how I'll manage afterward. We got all that legal stuff taken care of, and the new book's finished, so there shouldn't be any problems. Actually, I wouldn't be surprised if *Crib* went right back up to the top of the *Times* list after this, and hey, if this nice offer from France is any indication, your new book's going to do really well, too. You must be relieved. Sometimes that next book after a hit is kind of a letdown, isn't it? But however it works out, you shouldn't worry, because as your widow and your literary executor I'll do everything I can to manage your estate prudently, because that's my duty and, I think you'll also agree, my right. And finally, I've taken the liberty of writing something along the lines of a suicide note into your phone while we've been hanging out here, and I'm making it clear that no one's to feel responsible for this, and that you were in some kind of awful despair because, well, *blah, blah blah,* you were being harassed by someone online, and you have no idea who it is, but they accused you of plagiarism and that's such a devastating experience for any writer."

She held it up to show him, the phone, his phone, and he could hardly at all make out the blur of the words she'd composed. Sentences: his last, and not even chosen by him, or arranged by him, or vetted by him. It was nearly the worst thing of all.

"I'd read it to you, but I don't think you're up to making edits right now, and besides, I really need to go. I'll leave this out on the kitchen counter so you won't be bothered by any calls or texts while you're trying to rest. And I think . . ." She stopped and looked around at the now darkened room. "Yep. I think that's it. Good-bye, Jake."

She seemed to wait for him to answer, then shrugged.

"It's been very interesting. I've learned so much about writers. You're a strange kind of beast, aren't you, with your petty feuds and your fifty shades of narcissism? You act like words don't belong to everyone. You act like stories don't have real people attached to them. It's hurtful, Jake." She sighed. "But I guess I'll have a long time to get over it."

She got to her feet.

"Now, just so you know, I'm going to text you when I get to LaGuardia to tell you how much I love you. And I'm going to text you again when I land in the morning, to say I've arrived safely. I'm going to send you pictures of the storage unit I'll be cleaning out tomorrow, and maybe a few from when I meet up with my friends tomorrow night at one of our old hangouts on the waterfront. And then I'm going to start texting you to please give me a call because you haven't responded to any of my messages and I'm worried, and that'll go on for a day or two. And then I'm afraid I might have to give your mom and dad a call, but let's not think about that now. You just have a good sleep. Good-bye, sweetheart."

And she leaned over the bed, but she didn't kiss him. She was kissing the cat, Whidbey, named for the island where she'd had a couple of fun weekends with Randy, her former boss, back when she was his intern. Then she left the room and a moment later he heard the front door lock behind her.

The cat stayed where he was, at least for another couple of minutes, then he climbed up onto Jake's chest and there he remained, rising with each inhalation, falling with each exhalation, and staring into Jake's eyes for as long as there was human warmth on offer there. After that he went as far away as he could get, hiding for days under the kilim-covered couch until the neighbor who'd so enjoyed those pralines from New Orleans came at last and managed to coax him out.

EPILOGUE

The late Jacob Finch Bonner, author of the global bestseller *Crib,* was obviously not present at the S. Mark Taper Foundation Auditorium for an event marking the publication of his posthumous novel, *Lapse,* but he was represented by his widow, Anna Williams-Bonner, a former Seattle resident. Williams-Bonner, a striking woman with a long silver braid, sat in one of the two armchairs on the stage in front of a massive blow-up of the book's cover. The other chair was occupied by a local personality named Candy.

"The sad thing, for me," said Candy, with an expression of profound compassion, "is that I actually interviewed your husband, right here on this stage, about *Crib*. This was about eighteen months ago."

"Oh I know," said the widow. "I was in the audience that night. I was a fan, even before I met Jake."

"Well! That's sort of adorable. Did you meet him afterward, at the book signing?"

"No. I was too shy to line up with my book. I met Jake the next morning. I was producing Randy Johnson's show at KBIK at the time. Jake came on the show and we had coffee afterward." She smiled.

"And then you left Seattle and moved to New York. We do frown on that, you know."

"That's perfectly understandable." Anna smiled. "But I couldn't help myself. I was in love. We moved in together only a couple of months after we met. We didn't have much time together."

Candy hung her head. The tragedy of it all had overwhelmed her.

"I understand that you've agreed to make these appearances not only in support of Jake's novel but because you feel a responsibility to speak out about some of the issues your husband was dealing with."

Anna nodded. "He'd been devastated by a series of anonymous attacks. Mainly online, via Twitter and Facebook, but also in messages sent to his publisher and even a few letters actually mailed to our home. The final email actually arrived the day he took his own life. I knew he was distraught about it, and trying to understand who this person was, and what they wanted from him. I think that last message just broke his will, somehow."

"And what was he being accused of?" said Candy.

"Well, it never made much sense. The person said he'd stolen the story of *Crib,* but there were no details, really. It was an empty accusation, but in Jake's world even the accusation felt ruinous. He was devastated, and having to defend himself to his agent and the people at his publisher, and worrying about how it would impact him in the eyes of his readers if more people became aware of it, it just destroyed him. Eventually, I could see he was becoming depressed. I was worried, but you know, I thought about depression the way most people do. I looked at my husband and thought, *He has a hugely successful career, we've just gotten married, surely that's more important than this ridiculous thing, so how can he be depressed?* I'd flown back here to Seattle for a couple of days, to deal with my old storage unit and see friends, and that's when Jake took his own life. I felt so guilty because I'd left him alone, and also because he used the medication I'd been prescribed for an old condition of my own. We had dinner together at our apartment before I went to the airport, and he seemed absolutely fine. But over the next day or so he didn't respond to any of my texts, or answer his phone. I started to get worried. Finally, I called his mother to ask if she'd heard from him. That was awful, having to do that to his mother. I'm not a mother, so I can only imagine the pain of losing a child, but it was terrible to witness that."

"But you can't blame yourself," said Candy, which was of course the correct thing to say.

"I know that, but it's still hard." Anna Williams-Bonner was silent for a moment. The audience was silent with her.

"It's a very difficult journey you've been on," Candy observed. "I think the fact that you're here tonight, speaking with us about your husband, his struggles as well as his accomplishments, speaks to your own strength."

"Thank you," said the widow, sitting up very straight. Her silver braid had slipped forward over her left shoulder, and she was twisting the end around and around her fingers.

"Tell me, do you have plans of your own you can share with us? Are you moving back to Seattle, for example?"

"No." Anna Williams-Bonner smiled. "I'm sorry to say, I truly do love New York. I want to celebrate my husband's wonderful new book, and the fact that Macmillan is honoring Jake with the republication of the two novels he wrote before *Crib.* And when the film adaptation of *Crib* comes out next year I plan to celebrate that as well. But at the same time I've started to feel that maybe it's time to begin focusing on myself. I had a professor at the University of Washington who used to say: *Nobody else gets to live your life.*"

"So wise," said Candy.

"I've always thought so. And I've had some time now to really think deeply about what I want from my life, and how I want to live it. It's a little embarrassing under the circumstances, but deep down I realized that what I truly want to do is write."

"Really!" said Candy, leaning forward. "But that must be intimidating. I mean, as the widow of such a famous writer . . ."

"I don't feel that way." Anna smiled. "It's true that Jake's work was known all over the world, but he always insisted he wasn't special. He used to tell me: *Everyone has a unique voice and a story nobody else can tell. And anybody can be a writer.*"

ACKNOWLEDGMENTS

Seldom have I been so grateful for my chosen career as I was during the spring and summer months of 2020, not just for the opportunity to work at home but for the chance to escape, on a daily basis, into another reality. I am beyond thankful for my wonderful agents at WME, Suzanne Gluck and Anna DeRoy, as well as Andrea Blatt, Tracy Fisher, and Fiona Baird, and for Deb Futter, Jamie Raab, and their extraordinary team at Celadon, including Randi Kramer, Lauren Dooley, Rachel Chou, Christine Mykityshyn, Jennifer Jackson, Jaime Noven, and Anne Twomey. This book was born in Deb's office. Sorry for the mess.

My parents, under house arrest in New York City, devoured every word of this novel as it was written. My husband brought coffee in the morning and alcoholic beverages promptly at five. My sister and my kids cheered me on. My beloved friends have sustained me during the writing of this book, and I can't adequately express my appreciation to them, most especially Christina Baker Kline, Jane Green, Elise Paschen, Lisa Eckstrom, Elisa Rosen, Peggy O'Brien, Deborah Michel (and her devious daughters), Janice Kaplan, Helen Eisenbach, Joyce Carol Oates,

Sally Singer and Laurie Eustis. Also Leslie Kuenne, but that's, literally, another story.

The Plot may seem a little hard on writers, but that shouldn't surprise anyone; we're hard on ourselves. In fact, you couldn't hope to meet a more self-flagellating bunch of creatives anywhere. At the end of the day, though, we are the lucky ones. First, because we get to work with language, and language is thrilling. Second, because we love stories and we get to frolic in them. Begged, borrowed, adapted, embroidered . . . perhaps even stolen: it's all a part of a grand conversation. "Grasp that and you have the root of the matter. To understand all is to forgive all" (Evelyn Waugh, *Brideshead Revisited*).

This novel is dedicated to Laurie Eustis, with love.

JEAN HANFF KORELITZ, AUTHOR OF *THE PLOT*, ON ARTISTIC APPROPRIATION, ADAPTATIONS, AND ASKING "WHAT IF"

At the risk of sounding too meta, how did you come up with the plot of *The Plot*?

Some of my novels have arisen from (literally) decades of asking myself what-if questions. What if that insane Irish infanticide case (the Kerry Babies affair of 1984) was set in America and combined with *The Scarlet Letter*? (That was *The Sabbathday River*, 1998.) Or, what if Richard Strauss's *Der Rosenkavalier* took place in New York City in the 1990s, and everyone in it was Jewish? (That would be *The White Rose*, 2004.) Others have come out of the blue, almost fully formed, which was the case with *You Should Have Known* (2014) and with *The Plot*. This is not to say that I haven't long obsessed over the issues at the heart of *The Plot*. Like most writers I'm fascinated by plagiarism and the murkiness around creative appropriation: chefs stealing recipes from other chefs, comedians helping themselves to other comedians' jokes, academic theft, and above all creative writers appropriating work by others. I'm hardly the first novelist to write about this—there's an entire subgenre of Stephen King work on this theme—and it's not the first time I've touched on it in my own work (both *Admission* and *The Devil and Webster* feature plagiarism and plagiarists), but it's the first time I've placed it front and center in a book. I think it makes sense to write about the things that fascinate us. I love campus novels, and I wrote one (*The Devil and Webster*, 2017). I love novels about writers, and now I've written one.

While writing this book, you must have put yourself in the shoes of your main character. Do you think you'd ever steal a genius idea for a book if you knew it would never be used?

I wouldn't, but only because I'm squeamish by nature and I'd be terrified about that degree of exposure and disapproval. But, like most artists, I also understand that stories run underneath the ground of our collective experience, and we all dip into them, whether we're aware of it or not. The real question is, At what point does a collective story become the individual property of a person or an artist? Who's going to seriously accuse Jane Smiley of "appropriating" Shakespeare when she wrote *A Thousand Acres*, or Charles Frazier of stealing from Homer when he wrote *Cold Mountain*? A contender for the 2020 Pulitzer Prize for Drama was *The Inheritance* by Matthew Lopez, which openly adapts Forster's *Howards End* to contemporary New York City. This is a normal, even laudatory practice, which artists fully understand. But to help yourself to the specific plot of a recently deceased author who never completed his book? I don't know where the line is, exactly, but that might be over it.

Throughout *The Plot*, several characters posit that writing can't be taught. As a writer, do you agree or disagree?

Let's just say that I've long felt there's a limit to what can be taught. On the other hand, I have many friends who have benefited from time in MFA programs and writing seminars, and my husband teaches poetry writing at the college level, I think rather effectively. I didn't go the MFA route myself, but I did take a creative writing class in college and I learned something very important in that classroom, which was that I was allowed to *make things up*. It seems so obvious, but in my own case, I required someone to explain that to me, and I'm grateful to this day that my teacher did.

You've already published six novels, including *You Should Have Known*, which was adapted into the HBO series *The Undoing*, starring Nicole Kidman. What has been the most exciting part of seeing your novels adapted for the screen?

The most exciting thing was stepping onto the set and seeing hundreds of people running around and doing their jobs—whether that was acting, doing makeup, directing, cooking lunch, directing traffic, or any of the other countless things that get done around filming—and realizing that none of them would be there if not for something I'd made up in my pajamas. Tina Fey (who starred in *Admission*) once said that her proudest accomplishment was giving employment to so many people, and I've certainly had moments of that, but it's also worth noting that the author of the adapted work is probably the least valuable person on a film shoot. On both sets I was introduced to people who clearly had no idea there even was a novel the project had been adapted from. "Oh. There's a book? Cool."

What are you working on next?

I'll be returning to a novel I set aside in order to write *The Plot*. It's called *The Latecomer*, and it's about a family with triplets and a fourth child, born many years later from a leftover embryo. It's a big, sprawling book about siblings who wander very far from one another, but who ultimately come back—as Evelyn Waugh once wrote—with "a twitch upon the thread." Or perhaps, in this case, a yank.

DISCUSSION QUESTIONS

1. Is writing an innate talent, or can it be taught?
2. Do you think Jake would have stolen the story if he knew where it came from?
3. Does anyone have the right to tell someone else's story?
4. What constitutes plagiarism? Did Jake cross that line?
   Submitted by OMG! Bookclub (Oakville, Ontario)
5. What roles do gossip and social media play in this story?
6. Which did you enjoy more, the story within the novel or the plot itself?
   Submitted by Canadian Book Enablers (Kitchener, Ontario)
7. Who did you suspect @TalentedTom was?
8. The author includes a number of literary allusions throughout the novel; which ones did you notice?
   Submitted by Tough Old Birds (St. Louis, Missouri)
9. Consider the triple meaning of the word "plot"—a story, a grave site, a secret plan. How did the author involve each of these in the novel?
10. Discuss the conclusion. Were you surprised by the ending?

The Latecomer

ON AUDIO

READ BY AUDIE AWARD–WINNING NARRATOR

— JULIA WHELAN —

AND DON'T MISS

THE PLOT

ON AUDIO

Visit MacmillanAudio.com for audio samples and more!

Follow us on Facebook, Instagram, and Twitter.